HELLFIRE

CHRIS RYAN

HELLFIRE

CORONET

First published in Great Britain in 2015 by Coronet
An imprint of Hodder & Stoughton
An Hachette UK company

1

Copyright © Chris Ryan 2015

The right of Chris Ryan to be identified as the Author
of the Work has been asserted by him in accordance with the
Copyright, Designs and Patents Act 1988.

A CIP catalogue record for this title is available from the British Library

ISBN 978 1 444 78332 2
Trade Paperback ISBN 978 1 444 78333 9
Ebook ISBN 978 1 444 78331 5

Typeset in Bembo by Hewer Text UK Ltd, Edinburgh

Printed and bound by Clays Ltd, St Ives plc

Hodder & Stoughton policy is to use papers that are natural, renewable
and recyclable products and made from wood grown in sustainable forests.
The logging and manufacturing processes are expected to conform
to the environmental regulations of the country of origin.

Hodder & Stoughton Ltd
Carmelite House
50 Victoria Embankment
London EC4Y 0DZ

www.hodder.co.uk

GLOSSARY

1 Para	1st Battalion, Parachute Regiment (Special Forces Support Group)
AW50	anti-material sniper rifle
C-4	high-yield plastic explosive
COBRA	Cabinet Office briefing room
CP	close protection
ETA	estimated time of arrival
fan dance	the fitness and navigation phase of special forces selection
frag	fragmentation grenade
GCHQ	Government Communications Headquarters
hazmat suit	whole-body garment worn as protection against hazardous materials
head shed	military command centre
HK416	Heckler & Koch assault rifle firing 5.56x45mm NATO rounds
HK417	Heckler & Koch battle rifle firing 7.62x51mm NATO rounds
HQ	headquarters
ident	identification
L86	a variant of the SA80 assault rifle, standard issue to British armed forces
LAW	light anti-armour weapon
LZ	landing zone
MI6/SIS/the Firm	Secret Intelligence Service
MoD	Ministry of Defence
NV	night vision
PC	patrol commander

RIB	rigid-hulled inflatable boat
RPG	rocket-propelled grenade
RTA	road traffic accident
RTU	returned to unit
Rupert	military slang for an officer
RV	rendezvous
SBS	Special Boat Service
scaley	member of the Royal Corps of Signals
SF	special forces
Sig 225	SIG-Sauer P225 pistol firing 9x19mm rounds
transponder	aircraft identification device
VHF	very high frequency
white phos	white phosphorous grenade

'I know not with what weapons World War III will be fought, but World War IV will be fought with sticks and stones.'

— Albert Einstein

PROLOGUE

The Iraq–Syria border. Sunset.

It was a featureless patch of desert, but surrounded at a distance by scenes of war.

Six kilometres to the north there was an Islamic State command and control centre, reduced to rubble by American air strikes. But local command and control really took place in a small Bedouin encampment that the infidel didn't know about, and which they would never bomb, because it was a civilian target. They were weak about such matters.

Three kilometres to the west, a laser-guided Brimstone missile had blasted a crater in the sand thirty metres wide. Two hundred thousand dollars' worth of ordnance had taken out a single Land Rover, unoccupied.

Ten kilometres to the south, there was a border town that had fallen to the brutal troops of the Islamic State. It had taken the mass execution of three hundred civilians to subdue the malcontents, but now it was overrun with insurgents, completely unopposed by the terrified locals.

Here, however, the undulating sand and rough, dusty scrub under a clear sky looked just as it had done for hundreds, even thousands, of years. And a lone vehicle containing two men trundled through the twilight. For one of these men, who had a crooked nose, lank, greasy hair and wispy stubble on his chin, this was the most exciting journey of his life.

The air was hot and dry. He was sweating and dirty. But he didn't mind. Twenty-four hours ago he had been stuck in the grey drizzle of an early Peckham morning. Now he was watching a blood-red sun set over the dunes. For years he had longed to swap his old life for this.

His name was James Wilson. He hated it. It was so British. He couldn't understand why his parents, who had moved to England from Pakistan when they were seventeen – just a year older than James was now – couldn't have given him a better, Islamic, name. He was always trying to change it. On his unsuccessful YouTube music channel, where he chanted self-penned Jihadist lyrics of which he was very proud, he called himself Dubz-Manuva. And out here, on the fluid border between Iraq and Syria, he was Hassan. He much preferred that name. It sounded more noble, and he had enjoyed tearing up his British passport once he had cleared immigration at Hatay airport in southern Turkey. Out here, nobody would call him a dirty Paki bastard ever again.

Now he was looking forward to meeting with his comrades, learning how to become an ISIS fighter. He had spent many hours daydreaming about the heroic things he would do. And now those daydreams were becoming a reality.

'Did you have any trouble leaving England?' asked the lean, fierce militant who was driving him along a deserted highway.

Hassan's companion hadn't told him his name, or even where they were going. Hassan admired his confidence. Admired the way that the gangster-like border guards in military uniform had melted away with one look at his face as they crossed from Turkey into Syria and from Syria into Iraq. Admired the way his assault rifle lay carelessly on the back seat, and the handgun – he didn't know what sort – rested on the dashboard, a warning to anyone who dared to stop them.

'Piece of piss,' said Hassan. The militant frowned. He obviously didn't know that expression. 'I mean ... yeah ... it was well easy. Told my mum I had to be in college early, innit? I reckon my sister was a bit suspicious, but she's only eleven. Left the house at seven, seven thirty ... I was on the plane to Turkey by midday ... Got this girl to tell the teachers I was off sick ...'

The militant's frown grew more pronounced. 'There will be no women in our schools when the Caliphate has spread,' he said. 'They do not need to be there. It is un-Islamic.'

'Yeah,' Hassan said quietly. 'Bitches.'

About twenty metres off the road, next to a patch of low brush, he saw the shell of an old saloon car. It must have been destroyed by some kind of car bomb because jagged sheets of broken chassis were pointing outwards from its core. As they zoomed by, Hassan squinted. Was it a trick of the light, or had he seen the remains of a body slumped over the steering wheel?

'Where are we going?' he asked.

'You'll see.'

It was almost dark when they turned sharply off the highway and on to a poorly kept road. Five minutes later, Hassan could see the outline of a small desert town in the distance. Even in the half-light he could tell there had been fighting here because he could just make out, in silhouette, the slant of a toppled electricity pylon a couple of hundred metres up ahead. 'Where are we?' he asked quietly. His companion didn't answer.

On the outskirts of the town, the occasional local stood by the side of the road and gave them hard stares. Hassan realised they were a curiosity. Theirs was the only vehicle entering the town.

They passed a run-down concrete building on their left. A black flag with white Arabic lettering hung across its facade. Next to it was a mosque, outside which was a crowd of men, all bearded. There were no women on show. No children. They approached a lone acacia tree to which a few sheep had been tethered, and came to a halt in the shade of its branches. Theirs was the only vehicle around, with the exception of two old motorbikes leaning up against the side of a low stone building to their right. There were no electric lights. No kids playing in the street. Hassan felt like he had gone back in time.

'Get out.'

Hassan did as he was told. His jeans and T-shirt were crumpled and sweaty. He felt very out of place compared to his companion, who wore camouflage trousers and a black vest that showed his tough, sinewy muscles. It was strangely silent here. No music. No conversation. The men outside the mosque stared at him. Hassan stared fiercely back. 'This way,' the militant said. He strode along the road, and Hassan had to trot to keep up.

'They told me there would be other people like me here, innit?' Hassan said. 'People from the UK. Are we going to meet them now?' He was looking forward to some comradeship. He pictured himself in the desert, sitting outside a tent as the sun set, stripping down a rifle and talking with his new jihadi friends.

No response. The militant crossed the road towards another concrete building, two storeys high, whose windows had been blasted out. He didn't enter, but walked round to its left-hand side. Hassan followed. He saw there had once been a perimeter fence around the back yard, but only parts of it remained now: a few posts, the occasional fence panel, some curled and jagged lengths of razor wire. His companion turned towards the back door of the building. Hassan followed.

Then he stopped.

He blinked heavily, as though he thought his eyes might be deceiving him. But they weren't. Just fifteen metres away, resting against the back wall of the building, about four metres high and a couple of metres wide, was a wooden cross. A crucifix.

And on the crucifix was a man.

His feet were bound to the upright post with wire, and a large nail protruded from each wrist, holding the arms to the cross-beam. The face was blindfolded, and a sheet of white card covered his torso, with blood-red Arabic writing on it. The man was clearly dead. Hassan could tell because a large black bird had perched on his arm and was pecking away at the flesh, but the man didn't even twitch.

The militant turned and saw Hassan staring at this gruesome sight. 'A traitor,' he said simply. 'Accused of selling secrets to the West. We executed him three days ago.' He looked Hassan up and down. 'Some advice,' he said. 'You're about to meet someone. Do what he says. Otherwise . . .' He looked meaningfully back at the crucified man. 'Now get inside.'

The interior was a wreck. The floor was littered with broken plaster and brick. Cables hung from the ceilings. There was a faint smell of burning. The militant strode through it all, but Hassan hesitated. 'Is it . . . is it safe in here?' he asked.

The militant turned. 'You came out here to fight,' he said. 'And you expect it to be safe?' He continued to wade through the rubble until he reached a flight of steps leading downwards. Hassan felt his cheeks burning with embarrassment as he followed. He would make sure he didn't say anything like *that* again.

The stone steps led into a dark basement. It was much colder down here. He found himself in a room about ten metres by ten, with a door at the far side. It was lit by a small, smoky oil lamp in one corner. There was no rubble on the floor down here, but there were two people. One of them was tall and thin, with white skin and dark stubble. The other was sitting on a low stool. His head was wrapped in a red and white shamagh, so that it was impossible to see his face. Just his eyes, gazing out.

This man had clearly been expecting them. When he spoke to the militant who had brought him here, his voice was muffled by the cloth. They spoke in Arabic. Hassan noticed that the militant's demeanour had changed. He was respectful, almost frightened. Hassan didn't know why. The masked man didn't even seem to be carrying a gun. Hassan found his eyes drifting towards the other guy. Looking at his white skin, he wondered if he was British, and smiled at him. The smile wasn't returned.

The figure at the stool stood up. He slowly walked across the room towards Hassan, who became aware of a different smell: a pungent perfume. When the figure was half a metre away, he stopped and looked Hassan up and down. 'This is him?' His English was very clear, but with an accent. Middle Eastern. Hassan tried to place it more exactly, but couldn't.

The militant bowed his head.

'He doesn't look like much. If you've brought me a coward, I'll have you both killed.'

Hassan felt himself sweating. 'I'm not a coward,' he said.

Silence. The man's dead, dark eyes stared at Hassan from behind

his shamagh. Hassan found himself sweating even more. He realised he should have kept his mouth shut.

Very quietly, the man spoke to the white-skinned guy.

'Show him, Jahar,' he said.

Jahar nodded. He walked to the door on the opposite side of
the room, put a key in the lock and opened it. Then he gestured
at Hassan to look inside.

Hassan crossed the room and looked.

This second room was even darker – Hassan couldn't tell how
big it was. It stank of excrement. Kneeling about three metres from
the door, with his head bowed, was a man. He was white, with
shaved hair and several days of stubble. He wore bright orange
robes. He blinked in terror towards the light, but said nothing.

Hassan was aware – from the perfumed smell – of the myste-
rious figure behind him. He spun round to find him standing
very close.

'So you want to fight?' the figure whispered.

'Yeah.'

'You want to bring the law of Sharia first to Arabia, then to
Africa, then to the world? One glorious caliphate to the glory of
Allah?'

Hassan didn't even know what the man was talking about. He
just nodded.

'Every caliphate requires a Caliph,' said the man. 'And that is
what you will call me. But if you speak of me to anybody, you and
the family you have left behind can expect the same fate as the
crucified man you met on your way in. Do you understand?'

Hassan felt a knot in his stomach. But he jutted out his chin
and said, 'Yeah.'

'Good. You have probably noticed that we have a prisoner in
our midst.'

Hassan nodded.

'His name is Alan MacMillan. He calls himself an aid worker,
and he thinks that makes him important. But he is just another
infidel of no significance. Our duty is clear.'

Hassan nodded mutely.

'The lights, Jahar.'

Jahan flicked a switch on the wall of the second room. A tiny part of Hassan's brain wondered where the electricity was coming from. But by far the greater part studied the room.

It looked, in some respects, like a professional photographer's studio. Two lamps shone from the corners on to the prisoner, who was blinking in the sudden brightness. Behind him was a backdrop that showed a convincing daytime desert scene. Along one side, out of the way, was a camera on a tripod. Hassan walked into the room. He saw that the prisoner's hands and feet were tied behind his back and strapped to a post protruding from the floor behind him. There was no way he could move from his kneeling position.

The man spoke from the doorway. 'You will have the honour of dealing with him.'

At these words, the prisoner started to whimper. Jahar entered the room. Hassan saw that he was carrying a needle and syringe. He stuck the needle through the orange cloth of the prisoner's clothes and into his upper arm. Almost immediately, the prisoner's head bowed again, and he fell silent.

'Valium,' Jahar said. 'Stops them struggling. Makes it cleaner and easier.'

'Makes what easier?' No reply. 'You mean . . .' Hassan made a small slicing movement with his hand.

Jahar smirked. He moved the camera and its tripod into the doorway. Moments later he was handing Hassan a knife, about nine inches long and obviously viciously sharp, along with a black balaclava. 'Put it on,' he said. Hassan did as he was told as Jahar stood behind the camera, leaving Hassan in the room next to the drugged prisoner.

'*Show* us you are not a coward,' said the man from the other room. 'You know what to do.'

Hassan looked at the knife, then at the prisoner. He realised his hand was trembling slightly, and he tried to stop it.

'If you prefer,' the man said, his voice quiet and taunting, 'you could be given women's work. The washing of clothes and preparation of food for real fighters like Jahar. Perhaps that is all you're good for.'

Hassan straightened himself up. 'I could hurt him first,' he announced. 'Beat him up a bit. Stick something in him . . .' He put his palm flat over the hostage's face, yanked his limp head back and touched the tip of his knife to the his cheek.

'It's not necessary. Beatings do not interest anybody. Nobody watches the video of a beating. Beheadings are a different matter. You must learn the skill. You will probably start to enjoy it.'

Hassan touched the knife against the back of the hostage's neck. It broke the skin immediately, and blood started to drip down the side of his neck. Hassan's hand was trembling. He tried to steady it. He saw a little red light on the camera that told him it was recording.

The man was still talking. Hassan breathed deeply, barely listening.

'Then you will travel away from here and continue your new life as an executioner. You might even be afforded some respect like Jahar here, who has now conducted four beheadings, to the glory of Allah.'

Hassan wanted to do it quickly and cleanly. 'Where . . . where are you sending him, Caliph?' said Jahar. In a corner of his mind, Hassan knew Jarah sounded nervous, asking such a bold question of this man. But there was also a note of envy in his voice. Hassan felt pleased. He raised one hand – it was still trembling slightly – and prepared to make the first hack.

'Nigeria,' said the Caliph quietly. 'To do God's work and punish the infidel, I am sending him to Nigeria.'

PART ONE

Target Red

ONE

'Nigeria! Of all the *bell-ends* of a place, we get deployed to *fucking* Nigeria.'

Danny Black stood on the edge of a well-manicured lawn watching his Regiment colleague Tony waving a pair of barbecue tongs in the air, and listening to his constant stream of complaints. Even though they were being deployed tomorrow they were still on standby, which meant the two-pint rule applied. Both men had a Stella on the go anyway.

'Last time I was there,' Tony continued, 'mate of mine pulled this Nigerian bird down by the docks in Lagos. Got so many fucking diseases his dick nearly fell off.'

'Right,' Danny said. 'Shame.'

'Seriously, though, I'd rather do the tango along the top of the Kajaki dam than sweat my nads off in Abuja. Eh, Danny? You agree with me, right?'

Danny took a long swig from his bottle of Stella, and said nothing as Tony turned back to the barbecue and started rotating a line of sausages. The pre-deployment moan was as much a part of life in the regiment as an afternoon on the range, or being beasted up the steepest hills in the Brecon Beacons. And privately, Danny did agree with Tony. With half the regiment combing the Middle East for Islamic State militants and the other half on the ground providing forward air control for the coalition fighter pilots targeting them, their job – being packed off to West Africa to provide close protection for a British diplomat – felt like the short straw. True: there were parts of north-eastern Nigeria that were under the control of Boko Haram, a faction of murderous

11

extremists with a sickening line in beheadings, mass murder, rape, torture and abduction. But Danny and the guys wouldn't be going anywhere near Boko Haram. This was a soft job, and if it had been anybody else moaning about it, Danny would have joined in good-naturedly.

But there was something about Tony that made him keep his distance. Tony wasn't his real name. Just a joke that he'd never done anything to stop, thanks to the rumours that he was a regular Tony Soprano. Not in looks, maybe: he had thick blonde hair and tanned skin that had gone leathery from so much time working abroad. But in attitude, definitely. Danny had the sense that, with Tony – real name Craig Wiseman – as soon as you agreed with one thing he said, he'd pressure you to agree to a whole lot more.

Danny looked around. Nice gaff. A bit too nice for someone on a Regiment salary. Huge garden. Summer house at the bottom. Expensive conservatory. Danny had even noticed a jacuzzi in the bathroom when he'd gone for a slash, and he was pretty sure Tony was the only SAS soldier with one of them. Not to mention the two Beemers on the front drive. Whatever Tony used to pay for all this, he didn't earn it from his day job risking his arse for queen and country. It was no secret around HQ that he had other irons in other fires.

There was a copy of the *Mirror* lying on the table next to Tony's barbecue. Danny glanced at the front page. It was taken up by the blurry portrait of a young man whose slightly dark skin suggested he was of mixed race. A crooked nose looked like it had been broken at some point, his hair was black and greasy, and he had a light covering of wispy whiskers on his chin. Underneath the image was the caption: 'Jihadi Jim: First Picture'.

Tony noticed him looking at the newspaper. 'ISIS bastards,' he said. 'Remember the good old days, when the time to shit yourself was when someone shoved a gun in your face? Now you know you're in for a much worse time when they get their fucking iPhones out and press Record.' He sniffed. 'Hopefully one of our lot will stick a 7.62 in that fucker's head, anyway,' he said.

'Roger that,' Danny murmured. Here was something they could definitely agree on. Jihadi Jim – real name James Wilson, assumed Islamic name Hassan – was the moniker the press had given a young British man from Peckham in south London who had joined Islamic State fighters in Iraq or Syria, nobody was quite sure. A video of him beheading a British aid worker in an orange jumpsuit had gone viral. Syria held bad memories for Danny. He had no desire to go back there. But like every member of the Regiment, he'd have been happy to be the one who send Jihadi Jim packing off to paradise.

That wasn't going to happen, though. And privately, Danny had his reasons for being secretly pleased not to be in the heart of a war zone. He absent-mindedly put his hand in his pocket and pulled out his phone. He'd lost count of the number of times he'd done this over the last three days, to stare at a text message that had come through in the middle of the night. 'Not much chance of nailing him while we're driving the British High Commissioner round cocktail parties in Lagos,' he said as his thumb swiped the screen.

Tony laughed and clamped an over-friendly hand on Danny's shoulder. Danny didn't like it. They hadn't yet been told which of their unit would be in command out in Lagos. But Tony's body language was that of a guy who clearly thought he'd be in the driving seat. That was the whole reason he'd invited them to his house in the first place: to assert his authority, and let them know who was boss.

Danny stuffed his phone back in his pocket without bringing up the text, then looked meaningfully at the hand on his shoulder. Tony's friendly demeanour immediately fell away.

Before either of them could say anything, Danny's mate Spud appeared at the French doors. Spud was the spitting image of a young Phil Collins, but in recent weeks his features had been etched into a permanent scowl. Today was no different.

'Oh well,' Tony said, with a spiteful glance at Spud. 'Could be worse. Could be a bleedin' desk jockey, hey Spud?'

Danny knew Spud well enough to recognise the dangerous

look in his eyes. He turned on his heel, walked straight towards his mate and grabbed him by the elbow. 'Inside, mucker,' he said. 'Now.'

'Twat,' Spud muttered as they walked back into the conservatory. 'I'll shove those fucking tongs up his . . .'

'More beers, lads?' Tony's wife, Frances, was walking from the kitchen into the conservatory holding two bottles of Stella. Smart woman. More than a match for Tony, Danny always thought. Or maybe she just knew which side her bread was buttered. A looker, too, with her blond hair and a cleavage that was obviously making Spud forget his bad temper. She handed them the bottles, repositioned the solitaire diamond nestling at the top of her cleavage, gave them a slightly distant smile, and walked out to join Tony by the barbecue. Spud blatantly watched her hips sashaying out the door, then suddenly doubled over in a fit of hoarse coughing that lasted a full thirty seconds.

'You alright?' Danny asked, when the coughing had subsided.

'Fucking dandy,' Spud said darkly, before necking half his Stella in one hit.

In truth, Spud was lucky to be alive, and only he and Danny knew just how lucky. Their last op together had gone badly wrong. Spud had taken a round to the guts, and it was only Danny's field surgery that had saved him. In the middle of the desert he had stuck a wide-bore needle directly into his mate's lung to stop it from collapsing. Then he'd manoeuvred him across land and water to get him into the hands of the Red Cross in Eritrea, where things had turned even worse . . . The bottom line was that his abdomen had been sliced to bits, the rest of his body had been abused and broken, and it would be a while before Spud found himself on the front line again – if he ever did. It was obvious that the only reason Tony had invited him to this pre-deployment piss-up was that he didn't know exactly what had happened to Spud. Danny sensed that if there was one thing Tony hated, it was not being in the know. He'd have to get used to it, though. What had happened was entirely between Danny and Spud, and only one thing was for certain: Spud owed him one, big time.

In the meantime, though, Danny's mate had been stuck behind a desk in Hereford. Pushing paper. Babysitting the occasional spook venturing down to Hereford from the bright lights of the capital. Spud wasn't the paper-pushing type, as the top brass at Hereford had soon found out, so they'd started trying to shift the responsibility for him to someone else. For that reason, he was heading to London the following day to shadow an MI6 agent. It was obvious to Danny that he didn't relish the idea of acting as little more than muscle for the Firm, especially when his mates were on the front line. 'Like having your bollocks cut off when your pals are at an orgy,' was how Spud had described it.

Spud belched loudly. 'I should nail his missus while you're out in Bongo-bongo land,' he announced.

Danny looked around. 'You think the rumours are true?'

'About Tony?'

Danny nodded.

'No smoke without fire, mucker,' Spud said. Danny was inclined to agree. The word back at base was that Tony had a nice little sideline going, creaming off live ammo from the armoury and flogging it on to his mates in organised crime. Plenty of that round Hereford, as Danny knew well – but you didn't get a life-style like this just from shifting a few 7.62s. Danny suspected that Tony's links with the underworld didn't stop there. A man of his talents would be useful to anyone who needed some muscle. Like him or loathe him, Tony Wiseman was a very good soldier.

'Don't know how you're going to put up with the fucker,' Spud said. 'How long are you out there for?'

'Open-ended,' Danny said. 'British High Commissioner's feeling edgy. Wants a CP team. Could be a few months.'

The doorbell rang in the sound of Big Ben. Frances reappeared from the garden. Danny noticed how she brushed Spud's arm as she passed. Spud eyed her up and down as she went to get the door. His body might be all fucked up, but his considerable libido obviously wasn't.

It was Ripley at the door. He looked very similar to Danny – dark hair, dark eyes, broad shoulders. As usual, he wore a leather motorbike jacket. He was the third member of their team for the Nigerian job. As Frances fetched him a beer, he gave Danny and Spud an unenthusiastic nod. They were good mates, and that meant Ripley had a similar opinion of Tony – and of the prospect of spending weeks or months with him in West Africa. Like Spud, he gave Frances the eye as she stepped out of the conservatory. Then he turned to his two mates. 'Do us all a favour, Spud, give her a proper seeing-to while we're away. Breaks my heart to think she only gets that cunt Tony to cuddle up to at night.'

Spud grinned. 'Consider it done,' he said.

'Course, you might get one of Tony's mates knocking on your door at two in the morning with a baseball bat.'

'Bring it on,' Spud said darkly.

Ripley looked round. 'So where's our fourth member?'

'They'll be here any minute,' Danny said.

'Don't see why we can't have another Regiment guy,' Ripley said. 'What are you looking so shifty about, anyway? What do you know about the newbie?'

'Australian,' Danny said. 'On secondment. Ex-military intelligence. Nigerian specialist. At least, that's what I heard.'

'Yeah, well I hope he knows his way round an an assault rifle.' Ripley glanced outside. 'Suppose we'd better join the fucking Sopranos outside. Hope he's cooked extra, I'm Hank Marvin.' He took a swig of his beer and headed out of the conservatory. Spud followed, but Danny lingered. He pulled his phone out of his pocket again and swiped to his texts. This time he had no interruption, and the text that had been burned on his mind since it arrived filled the screen.

It was from Clara, Danny's ex. Deep down, he hadn't blamed her for walking away from him. She'd seen first-hand what it meant to be in the Regiment. She'd seen what Danny was capable of.

She'd seen him kill.

His victims had been two Polish drug dealers in Hereford. They'd kidnapped Clara and paid the price. But Danny's summary justice had been too much for her to stomach. She'd cut off all ties. Until now.

The text said: '*I'm pregnant.*'

Even on the hundredth time of looking at it, Danny's gut tightened with a kind of excitement. He'd been to see her two days ago near her parents' place in Wiltshire where she was staying until the baby arrived. Her due date was a week away. She knew it was a boy. And although she'd greeted him warily, like he was a dog who could turn at any minute, she'd told Danny that a boy needed a father. And that she needed him.

But he'd have to change, she'd said. Danny had told her that he would, and he almost believed it.

He put the phone back in his pocket and stepped outside to join the others.

There were a few spots of rain as they congregated around the barbecue. 'Get used to it, fellas,' Tony announced as he slapped a few burgers on to the grill. Danny's stomach rumbled. He didn't trust Tony, but he was looking forward to eating his food. 'Rainy season where we're going.'

'Personally I could do without it,' Frances said. Danny noticed how Tony scowled slightly at being interrupted by his wife. 'I'm running the London marathon next week,' she explained to the guys. 'I don't want to be jogging round Hereford in the rain.'

'You should try the bleedin' fan dance,' Tony said.

Frances gave him a withering look, then turned to Spud. 'Feel my thigh muscles, Spud,' she said. 'Amazing what a bit of exercise does, isn't it?'

Spud hid a smile by putting his beer to his lips as Tony shot him a poison look. 'Nah, you're okay, Frances,' he said. 'I can see you've got all the curves in all the right places.' He took a pull of his beer.

'Hey, Spud,' Tony said. His voice had a nonchalant quality that told Danny he was about to come out with something his mate wouldn't like. 'I heard your bike's up for sale. What you replacing it with – a mobility scooter?'

Spud didn't answer. For a Regiment guy, your wheels were your status symbol. But the medics had told Spud he needed to stop riding a bike and now his BMW was on the market.

The doorbell rang before Spud had a chance to answer. 'Get

that,' Tony told his wife. Frances looked like she was spoiling for an argument, but Tony gave her a look and she did as she was told. 'It'll be our fourth man,' Tony added, turning back to the barbecue. 'Don't know why the Ruperts are keeping it all so hush-hush. What is he, SBS or something?'

Danny suppressed a smile. He had one up on Tony and the others. The ops officer back at base had given him the lowdown about their fourth member, and he'd kept it quiet so he could see the look on their faces.

There was an awkward silence as the four of them stood by the barbecue watching a frowning Tony flip burgers. 'So, Danny,' Tony said after a few seconds. All his previous friendliness had disappeared and there was a dangerous edge to his voice. 'Word is you've not been getting much pussy lately, since that Clara bird dropped you. What is it, whisky dick or something?'

Danny just gave him a steady look but didn't reply. Thirty seconds later, Frances appeared again. She wasn't alone. A brunette woman, almost as tall as Danny, late twenties early thirties, stood a couple of metres behind her. Grey eyes, clear skin, no make-up – not that she needed it. She was a stunner.

'Someone to see you,' Frances said icily. Tony's frown had disappeared.

'Welcome to the party, love,' Tony said. 'What can we do for you?'

The woman looked around. 'I wouldn't say no to one of those beers,' she said. Her accent was heavily Australian.

Tony blinked stupidly at her. 'Look love, if you're selling something, we've . . .'

'She's your fourth man, you idiot,' Frances muttered.

It was too much for Spud. He snorted with laughter, and a flash of anger crossed Tony's face. 'Button it, office boy,' he snapped.

The laughter fell from Spud's eyes. Without hesitation, he muscled up to Tony and gave him an insulting jab in the chest with his forefinger. Instantly, Danny was there, pulling his mate away. Spud's face was red with anger and embarrassment, and he looked like he was about to give Tony a piece of his mind. But he suddenly doubled over coughing again. As he inhaled with a terrible wheeze, Tony turned to the woman. 'What did you say your name was, love?'

'I didn't,' said the woman. 'And if you call me love again, I'll put your fucking face in the coals.'

'Lovely barbecue,' Ripley murmured.

'This is Caitlin Wallace,' Danny announced. 'Ex Aussie army and Nigerian expert.'

'And I'm about as pleased to be here,' Caitlin interrupted, 'as you are to have a chick on the team. So spare me the dick-swinging and give me a tinnie.'

Tony's frown dissolved and a broad grin spread across his face. 'Get the woman a drink!' he announced.

Frances shot him daggers, and once again went off to fetch a beer.

'I thought the Ruperts were being a bit shifty about this one,' Tony announced. 'Never thought they were going to spring a bird on us, though. Still, it's just a babysitting job. No need to get your hands dirty, eh love?'

Spud had approached them, and even Ripley, the devoted family man, had edged closer to where Caitlin was standing. Only Danny stood a few metres apart.

'What is this?' Caitlin demanded. 'Bees round a fucking honeypot?'

'Welcome to Hereford, darling,' Tony said blandly, glancing towards the house to check his missus wasn't in earshot. 'Gets lonely when you're stuck with a bunch of hairy, sweaty blokes on the range. So, what's your background?'

'Military intelligence,' Caitlin said.

'Care to elaborate?'

'Not really.'

'Course you don't. Military intelligence are shiftier than the Ruperts, in my opinion. Don't see why you should be any different to the others.' He looked her up and down, clearly appraising her. Danny felt like he could read Tony's mind. What was her level of training? Was she up to the SF standards they'd expect of a team member? But he didn't ask these questions out loud. He just stretched out his hand. 'I'm Tony Wiseman, good to meet you.'

Caitlin didn't shake his hand, but held up one palm in greeting.

'Over here we have Alex Ripley. Don't be put off by his face, the ugly ones are always the best fighters. Fella with the cough is Spud, he won't be joining us but if you ever need a stash of paper-clips, he's your man. And it seems you already know Danny Black.' Tony's grin grew broader. 'You'll probably hear a few rumours about old Danny. Single man, last I heard. Maybe we'll have a holiday romance on our hands. Bit of a short fuse, mind. Flies off the handle now and then. Not the best combo for a man with a 9-milly in his back pocket, but there we have it.'

Danny felt his face darken, but Caitlin was clearly intrigued. She turned her back on Tony and took a few paces towards him, holding out her hand.

'Is that true?' she asked as Danny shook it.

'Which bit?'

'The bit about the short fuse.'

Danny shrugged. 'Depends who's lighting it,' he said.

'And what about the recently single bit?'

Before he could reply, Danny's mobile rang.

He answered it quickly. 'Yeah?'

'*Black, where are you?*' Danny immediately recognised Ray Hammond, ops officer back at base. His voice cracked sharply. Danny could instantly tell something was going down.

'Tony's place. What is it?'

'*Are the others with you? Ripley? Wallace?*'

'Yeah. What's the matter, boss?'

Tony looked sharply at him. He could obviously tell from Danny's voice that something was happening. He looked puzzled not to have had the call himself. 'What's going on, Black?' he demanded.

Danny zoned him out and concentrated on Hammond's voice. '*Get back here. All of you. Your op's been brought forward twenty-four hours. The shit's hit the fan. Whitehall are going ape.*'

'Why? What's happened.'

20

'Don't fucking ignore me,' Tony cut in.

'*Your man in Nigeria has just dropped off the radar. We think he's been kidnapped. You need to get your arses out there, now.*'

Danny didn't hear the line go dead. He'd already killed his phone. 'Barbie's over,' he said. 'They want us back at base.'

TWO

They moved quickly.

From Tony's house, they drove individually to base, ripping up the back streets of Hereford. The MoD policeman at the entrance to RAF Credenhill waved them through urgently, and an unmarked white Transit was already on the forecourt outside the main HQ building, its doors open. The vehicle's engine was already turning over.

The ops officer Hammond stood waiting for them by the Transit. He was a grumpy-looking bastard at the best of times, but right now he looked like a bulldog licking the piss off a thistle. 'Get your gear together!' he shouted before Danny and his unit had even left their vehicles. 'COBRA have authorised the use of a C17. It's in transit to Brize Norton now.'

None of the unit replied directly, but Danny knew what that meant. The C17 Globemaster was one of the RAF's largest assets, capable of carrying outsize military cargo. The message from Whitehall was clear: we'll give you whatever you want to sort this situation out, so you need to do whatever it takes.

Danny ran towards the Regiment building, Ripley by his side. Their bunks were next to each other, and each guy had their grab bag packed and their passports ready. They wordlessly slung them over their shoulders, then headed for the armoury.

Tony and Caitlin were already there waiting for them, clutching their own grab bags. Word of their arrival – and imminent departure – had evidently already reached the armourer. He was a squat man with broad shoulders and a grey beard, and he was laying out the unit's personal weapons on the broad wooden counter: HK416s for the guys, suppressed, each weapon's sights zeroed in for their particular user, Surefire torches and laser sights fitted to the rack. For Caitlin, a suppressed HK417. 'You know how to use one of those things?' Tony asked Caitlin. 'Those 7.62s have quite a kick.'

'Funny that,' Caitlin grinned as she slipped her assault rifle into a long black canvas weapon sleeve. 'So do I.' She looked at the armourer, who was dishing out side arms – Sig 225s, complete with holsters. 'Ammo?' she said.

The armourer looked uncomfortable talking to the woman on the team. His eyes flitted to Tony and his frown became even more pronounced. Danny remembered the gossip about Tony's sources of income. It kind of figured that the armourer wouldn't want much to do with him. So he directed a questioning glance at Danny.

'Five hundred rounds per man, armour-piercing,' Danny told him.

Danny ignored the bickering. 'Fifty rounds a piece for the side-arms,' he continued. 'Two Claymores each, four frags, two white phos.'

'Sniper rifle,' Ripley cut in.

Danny nodded. 'AW50,' he told the armourer. 'And four LAWs.'

It took no more than a minute for the armourer to get the gear together. The unit used the time to follow Caitlin's lead and wrap their assault rifles in black weapons sleeves for easy transport. When they had done, the counter was piled with boxes of ammo – 5.56s and 7.62s for the assault rifles, 9mm for the sidearms and .50 cals for the sniper rifle. Separate boxes for the grenades, four canvas bags containing the Claymores, and flight cases containing the AW50 and the LAWs. Danny signed for the equipment and the unit carried it out of the armoury and hurried back towards where the Transit van was waiting.

Minutes later they'd loaded up their gear. Danny, Tony, Ripley and Caitlin had taken seats opposite each other in the back of the Transit. Hammond was up front, next to the Regiment-attached driver from the driving pool, who was wearing jeans and a bomber jacket. Hammond's phone was glued to his ear. The van screeched its way across the forecourt and away from base. They'd been on site for less than ten minutes.

Journey time to Brize Norton: one hour thirty. As they screeched away from Hereford, Hammond looked back over his shoulder. 'Black,' he said, 'you're patrol commander.'

The atmosphere in the van immediately changed. Tony's face darkened. He looked like he was going to say something, but decided to keep quiet. Hammond faced forward and Danny felt Tony's glare on him, unswerving and unyielding, his dark suspicions about the leadership of the patrol clearly confirmed. Tony was a controlling bastard, and wouldn't be an easy man to have under him. Danny blocked the stare out. Tony didn't have to like him being PC. He just had to deal with it.

As they travelled, Hammond occasionally updated them. 'C17 wheels down in fifteen minutes.' 'You've got a support platoon from 1 Para en route to Brize, and a couple of scaleys to set up signalling.' 'The Foreign Office has set up a line of communication with the military attaché at the embassy. We'll patch you in when you're airborne.' The unit absorbed this information calmly, saying very little as they thundered down the M50. Danny found himself examining the faces of his team-mates. Ripley was a picture of calm, his expression unknowable. A good guy, Ripley. After Spud, one of Danny's closest Regiment mates. He'd helped Danny out of a hole before now, so Danny trusted him implicitly. He knew his mate would have passport-sized photos of his two kids tucked away somewhere inside his gear. Those kids meant everything to him.

Caitlin had her eyes closed and the back of her head resting against the side of the Transit van. Was there a hint of nervousness about her, behind the brash exterior? The Ruperts had bigged her up to Danny. He wasn't sure she could live up to the hype.

Tony's eyes flickered towards the female member of their crew. Danny sensed he was looking forward to a bit of close-quarter contact with Caitlin. He was a good-looking bastard, and women fell for his charm just as much as they did Spud's. It was widely known that Frances was the most cheated-on army wife in

Hereford. Danny found himself wishing Spud was there instead of Tony. But Spud's days of active service were behind him, and Tony was a good soldier. Wouldn't be where he was otherwise.

Danny focused his mind on the job. So far they had very little intel, but he knew enough to realise one thing: kidnapped in Nigeria, things weren't looking good for the British High Commissioner. It could have been almost anyone: pirates in the Niger Delta, diamond smugglers trying to diversify. And if Boko Haram militants could kidnap more than two hundred school-girls and keep them under the radar for months, what luck did one ageing white foreign-office official have?

'The High Commissioner's name is Derek Vance,' Hammond announced over his shoulder. 'Personal friend of the PM's. We're getting word through that one of his aides was kidnapped as well, a young guy called Hugh Deakin.'

'That's good to know,' Tony cut in. 'Their families can get started on the tombstones.' He laughed at his joke. Nobody else did.

The first sign that they were approaching Brize Norton was a C130 passing low overhead. Minutes later, the Transit van was screaming across the airfield. Danny looked through the wind-screen. Heavy rain had started to fall, but in the wake of the wipers he could see the huge grey structure of the C17 about thirty metres up ahead. It was surrounded by vehicles, a couple of which had blue flashing lights. Its tailgate was open, and Danny could see a black SUV driving up into the belly of the aircraft. He squinted and looked for signs of the 1 Para platoon. There was none.

The Transit skidded slightly as it came to a halt. By that time, its doors were already open. The unit started to move their gear out. 'Need a hand, love?' Tony asked Caitlin. She ignored him, grabbed her bag, personal weapon and the flight case containing the sniper rifle, and hauled it out into the driving rain. Outside the vehicle, a member of the ground staff was ushering them towards the tailgate with a glowing, handheld beacon, and shouting something unheard over the noise of the jet engines, which were already turning over. He needn't have bothered: all four members of the unit, along with their ops officer, were running towards the aircraft. 'Where are the Paras?' Danny shouted as they ran.

The ops officer didn't answer. He was already barking the same question into his phone.

As Danny ran up the tailgate, the familiar stench of aviation gas hit his nostrils. Like all military transport aircraft, the inside of the C17 was entirely devoid of comforts. The pipework and internal frame were all visible on the roof of the fuselage. At the far end of the fuselage were two portable blue toilet cubicles, which could be easily removed when loading cargo. Each seat had a dirty orange lifejacket strapped to the back, and the middle column of seats had been removed. A couple of loadies were securing the SUV to some shackles on the floor to keep it secure and immobile in flight. Danny noted that it was a Range Rover – probably supplied by the Foreign Office – artfully dented in places so that it didn't look too flash and therefore noticeable, but armoured nonetheless, with toughened glass, reinforced panels and sturdy all-terrain tyres. Despite all that, it would hopefully look unremarkable on the ground. He moved up to the front of the fuselage where two signallers – these were the scaleys Hammond had mentioned – were busily patching their way into the aircraft's radio system. They nodded a brief greeting at the members of the unit, then continued about their business.

Hammond still had his phone to his ear. 'We've got a problem!' he shouted. 'The platoon's had an RTA en route. They won't get here for another two hours.'

'Fuck's sake,' Danny breathed. He closed his eyes momentarily. Time to make a call. Did they wait for their support unit and lose precious time on the ground, or did they risk heading in-country without the security of well-prepared, well-armed backup?

It didn't take more than a moment to make the decision. For a hostage situation, time was of the essence. Every minute they delayed was an extra minute in which the High Commissioner and his aide could be wasted. 'We can't wait,' he announced. 'Let's get wheels up.'

The ops officer nodded, but suddenly Tony was in Danny's

face. 'What about that hostage rescue I did in Sierra Leone last year?' he shouted. 'If we hadn't had Para support, I'd be toast. They put in a cordon, supplied mortar support . . .'

'Yeah, well this isn't Sierra Leone,' Danny snapped back. He looked over Tony's shoulder at the ops officer. 'Wheels up,' he repeated.

Tony shook his head. 'This op's going to be a gangfuck,' he muttered. He glanced over towards Caitlin to check she was out of earshot. 'And what about the bird?' he said. 'She's just going to hold us back.'

Danny didn't say so out loud, but he quietly agreed with Tony about that. But Hammond shook his head. 'She's trained with Aussie military CT units and tactical assault groups. She's high up in Australian Special Operations Command.'

'Yeah, well I hope it's not her fucking time of the month,' Tony scowled.

'Just get on with your job, Wiseman,' Hammond said, and turned his back on them. But suddenly he turned again and gestured to Danny to join him. They moved several metres from the others.

'What is it, boss?' Danny asked.

Hammond looked like he was choosing his words carefully. 'I made a big call putting you in charge instead of Tony,' he said. 'I'm not going to lie to you. You've got a habit of going against the head shed's wishes, and they don't like it. They're watching you. Think of this as a chance to make things good. Don't fuck it up.'

Without another word, Hammond turned and disappeared back down the tailgate. Danny glanced towards Tony, who was standing five metres away, looking interested. He wandered over. 'Yeah, Black,' he said maliciously, 'don't fuck it up. What with you and Wonder Woman over there, I'm glad it's not me that's been kidnapped.'

There was a slight change in the engine's pitch as the tailgate closed up. Danny and the unit strapped themselves into the front row of hard seats along the port side of the aircraft. On the ground in front of them was a co-ax cable that the scaleys had hardwired into the aircraft comms. The cable was connected to a black box, into which four sets of headphones, each with a small boom mike, were plugged. They put the headphones on, and Danny winced momentarily as a whine of feedback pierced his eardrums. It died away, and a voice came over the cans: the refined tones of an SF flight crew captain. They always sounded the same – as calm and collected as if they were flying easyJet to Marbella. 'Afternoon gentlemen, this is Captain Ferguson, we'll have you airborne in about two minutes. Flight time Brize to Lagos a little shy of six hours. I'm patching you through to Hereford HQ immediately. It's a secure line, so you can speak plainly.'

A crackle, then a new voice. Danny didn't immediately recognise it, but that didn't matter. The important thing was what Hereford had to tell them, not who said it.

'*This is Zero Alpha, relaying through London. Your unit call sign is Bravo Nine Delta, repeat Bravo Nine Delta. Over.*'

'Roger that,' Danny replied immediately. 'Update us, over.'

'*We have a confirmed double hostage situation. The British High Commissioner Derek Vance, codename Target Red. His assistant Hugh Deakin, Target Blue. They were taken en route to an oil facility in the Niger Delta.*'

'What about their security?'

'*One driver, one member of the High Commission security staff. Both dead at the scene. The driver managed to phone in details of the kidnapping before he died of his wounds. One gunshot to the stomach. The security detail took a shot to the stomach and one to the head.*'

The aircraft had turned on to the runway and was starting to accelerate. The g-force kicked in as the engines roared.

'We don't have our Para support platoon, so the Nigerians need to get a cordon in place!' Danny shouted over the comms. 'Surround the kidnapping area, block off any escape routes.'

'*Roger that,*' replied the voice. '*We're in contact with the Nigerian military to see what assets they can supply.*'

'Great,' Tony cut in. 'I wouldn't trust the Nigerian military to get a cat out of a tree.' Privately, Danny couldn't help but agree. Maybe he'd been too hasty in ordering wheels up. He'd trust

1 Para to close off the area, but a reluctantly provided mob of untrained, unmotivated, under-equipped Nigerian squaddies was a different matter. They wouldn't give a fuck about a missing white guy.

'How long since the incident?' Danny asked.

'*Three hours twenty-seven.*'

'They could be miles away.'

'Actually,' Caitlin interrupted, 'maybe not. What was their exact location?'

'*Twenty klicks west of Port Harcourt. The Nigerians have lent us a chopper to get you out there as soon as you're on the ground, but there's poor weather conditions coming in over the Bight of Benin, so you might be delayed . . .*'

'I know the area around Port Harcourt,' Caitlin said. Her hard Australian accent cut through the noise of the engines. 'It's a maze – a network of waterways weaving in from the coast. There's a high incidence of kidnapping in the area because it's so easy for people to hide there. I'll bet they're still in the area, lying low. We need to get that cordon in immediately, then get our boots on the ground. Someone's going to know where Target Red and Target Blue are.'

'I agree,' Danny said. 'Keep us updated.'

'*Roger that.*'

The plane levelled out. The voice over the cans disappeared. For now.

17.49 hrs

The C17 had settled into its cruising altitude. The unit had clipped their hammocks to the webbing on the side of the fuselage, but nobody was getting any shut-eye just yet. The captain had come out to shake hands – he'd recognised Ripley from a previous operation – but now he'd returned to the cockpit. The loadmasters had offered them some food. So now they stood around, eating piping hot microwaved lasagnes and drinking polystyrene mugs of sweet tea. None of them knew when they'd get the chance to eat again, so it was time to refuel.

The two scaleys kept a polite distance from the Regiment unit. They were currently working on the Range Rover, fitting an under-seat radio and connecting it to a small aerial on the roof.

'Hate this shit,' Tony said through a mouthful of food. 'Specially when I left half a fucking cow on the barbie back home.'

'Don't worry,' Ripley said. 'Spud will have troughed it by now.' And he added quietly: 'Not all he'll have troughed, either.'

They'd left Spud and Frances together back at Tony's place. Tony's face darkened at the thought. 'Yeah, well, Spud looks like he's eaten a burger or two too many to me.'

Ripley immediately jutted out his chin. 'That's because every time he fucks your missus, she gives him a biscuit.'

Danny immediately stood between the two men to stop it kicking off. 'Shut up, both of you,' he said. 'None of that shit. Got it?'

Tony obviously didn't like taking an order. 'He needs to watch his fucking tongue,' he said, clearly wanting to get the last word. 'Someone might cut it out if they don't like what it says.' But then he backed down.

Danny drained his tea and looked over to the Range Rover. The scaleys had finished their work. 'Let's get the vehicle loaded up,' he said.

The team finished the rest of their food, then hauled their grab bags over to the car and placed them in the boot. It stank of diesel, thanks to the three jerrycans of fuel that were stashed in the back. Danny noticed that the vehicle was equipped with a hi-lift jack, and a winch mechanism had been fitted to the front. They unrolled their longs from the canvas weapon sleeves, and went through the careful process of loading them with rounds of 5.56s from their ammo boxes, and in Caitlin's case 7.62s. Then they laid them inside the vehicle: Danny's and Tony's along the sides of the doors, Ripley's and Caitlin's lengthwise between the two front seats. Cocked and locked, ready if and when they needed them.

Danny had a map of Nigeria spread out on his lap. He was examining it closely, committing what he could to memory. Caitlin's voice snapped him out of his concentration. She was sitting next to him. 'Bad weather in the Bight of Benin can be a shocker,' she said.

Danny nodded.

'You know the old rhyme?' Caitlin asked.

'What old rhyme?'

'Beware, beware the Bight of Benin, There's one that goes out for forty goes in.'

Danny stared at her for a moment. He found himself wanting to look at the text message from Clara yet again. But his personal phone was back in Hereford. He felt a weird sensation. Not fear exactly. More like apprehension. Ordinarily on a job you didn't think too hard about the implications of what would happen if you didn't make it back. But for Danny, things had suddenly changed. He wasn't just thinking about himself any more.

He turned his attention back to his map.

'You don't speak much, eh?' Caitlin said, her Australian accent sounding very pronounced. She grinned at him. When Danny didn't grin back, she looked momentarily narked. 'That's alright,' she said brightly. 'I like the strong silent type.'

Danny looked at her again. Her brown hair was tied back and there were little beads of sweat on her nose. Even in her military gear she was gorgeous. She knew it too. Her lips were slightly parted and her stare was full of meaning.

Before Danny could reply, Ripley had wandered up to them. Caitlin smiled, gave up her seat and wandered over to Tony. Ripley took her place. 'She's gagging for it, mucker,' he said.

Danny sniffed. 'Not my type,' he said. Which wasn't true.

'You've got a type?'

Danny looked back down at his map. 'I'm back with Clara,' he said.

Even though he wasn't looking at Ripley, he could sense his surprise. Ripley knew he and Clara had called it a day, though he didn't know why.

Danny took a deep breath. 'She's pregnant,' he said. Ripley was the first person he'd told. It felt right, somehow. Ripley lived for his own kids, and was devoted to his missus. In a weird way, Ripley had everything Danny wanted.

A pause.

'Congratulations, mate,' Ripley said. 'You'll be a great dad.' He didn't quite sound as if he meant it.

Danny looked him in the eye. 'I want you and Spud to be god-fathers,' he said.

Ripley inclined his head. 'You got it, buddy. Proud to. Let's get the job out of the way first, right?'

'Right,' Danny said.

19.32 hrs

Two hours till touchdown. The unit were all sitting, plugged into their headphones. One of the scaleys called out to them: 'Incoming transmission.' Immediately, the cans crackled into life again.

'*Bravo Nine Delta, this is Zero Alpha, do you copy?*'

'Go ahead, Zero Alpha,' Danny said.

'*Patching you through to the Deputy High Commission in Lagos.*'

'Roger that.'

A few seconds' pause. A new voice came on the line. Posh. But stressed. '*This is Christopher Manley, military attaché. We're getting some new information through from the Nigerians.*'

'Go ahead.'

'*There was one other passenger in the car when the hostages were taken. Name of Samuel Ntoga.*'

'Dead?'

'*No. He's just turned up in Port Harcourt.*'

'What's his story?'

'*He says they were held up at a road block. Random gangsters. They let him go. As he was running away he heard two gunshots. Managed to hitch a lift into town, rocked up at the local government offices.*'

'He's lying,' said Danny.

A pause.

'*The witness is a government official. We can't just accuse him of lying.*'

'Too bad, because he is. There were three gunshot wounds. The security guy was shot in the stomach and in the head, the driver just in the stomach. He's making up his story. We need to talk to this Ntoga guy. Can you get him to Lagos by the time we land?'

'*We can try.*'

'Try very hard,' Danny said, 'if you want to see your High Commissioner again.'

The line went dead. Danny pulled his cans from his head. Caitlin was staring at him intensely. 'Nigerian officials are totally corrupt,' she said. Her previous flirtatiousness had gone. 'If someone got this guy on board, they'd have made it properly worth his while. He's not going to talk.'

'That depends on how persuasive we are.'

Caitlin shook her head. 'You need the government's support. Start torturing one of their guys, they'll close ranks, I guarantee it.'

'If you've got a better idea, I'm all ears.'

The unit fell into an uneasy silence.

21.32 hrs
Wheels down.

Lagos International Airport was noisy and hot. As the tailgate opened, a blast of sultry air hit Danny. Sauna-hot, but humid with it. He could smell the sea, but with a tinge of rotting debris – no doubt blown in from the slums that surrounded this overpopulated city. It was the smell of Africa. Slightly unpleasant, slightly exciting. Different to anywhere else in the world.

Dark outside. No moon. Thick cloud cover, which explained the suffocating humidity. Danny was already wet through. He could see an Emirates 747 landing on the far side of the airfield, maybe three hundred metres away, a slipstream haze in its wake. Beyond that, sheet lightning in the distance. Ground vehicles were hurrying across the tarmac: refuelling lorries, forklifts for luggage containers. All the trappings of a busy commercial airport. But this side of the airfield was reserved for them. Nobody approached.

The loadies started unsecuring the Range Rover, but there was already a black Mercedes waiting on the tarmac. Ten metres beyond that, an unmarked saloon car with a flashing blue light on the roof. A harassed-looking man with thinning hair, brown trousers and an open-neck shirt was waiting by the Mercedes, his face sickly in the blue strobe. The unit strode down the tailgate, straight up to him. The man seemed to automatically pick Danny out as the leader, and outstretched his hand. Danny shook it.

'Chris Maloney, military attaché,' he yelled over the noise of the C17's engines, which were powering down but still loud. 'We spoke?'

Danny nodded. 'Where's Ntoga?' he shouted.

Maloney looked around the airfield, then angled his head towards the sky. 'There,' he said.

Danny followed his gaze. A hundred metres to the north-west he could see a helicopter coming in to land. It was having trouble staying stable in the choppy weather. Two open-topped trucks were heading towards it, clearly aiming for the chopper's LZ.

Danny gave Maloney a dead-eyed look. 'I need to speak to him.'

'Listen,' said Maloney. 'Ntoga's a cousin of the Nigerian Minister of Foreign Affairs. We have to go easy on him, or there'll be hell to pay. We'll get him to the Deputy High Commission, appeal to his better nature . . .'

'Forget it. Piece of shit like that hasn't got a better nature. I need to speak to him.'

Maloney shook his head. 'I'm sorry. There's a Nigerian government lawyer waiting for him at the commission. He'll be in constant attendance. Look, we can still get you on a flight to Port Harcourt in the next fifteen minutes. Leave Ntoga to us. A bit of diplomacy can work wonders sometimes.'

Danny looked over to where the chopper was coming in to land. It was a tight call. Should they waste time precious time on Ntoga, especially when this suit was being so limp-wristed, or should they get their arses out to the Niger Delta?

He decided on Ntoga. Right now, they had nothing. They needed intel.

'We'll escort him to the High Commission,' he said. 'If he's such an important guy, you want to make sure he has the best close protection, right?'

The military attaché looked deeply unsure. He glanced over his shoulder, as if he thought someone might be watching, then looked back at Danny. 'No marks,' he said quietly. 'And we'll have to drive in convoy. At this time of night, it's a twenty-minute drive to the commission, provided we're lucky with the God-awful traffic in this bloody city. If you're any longer than that, his lawyers will start to ask questions.'

Danny sniffed. 'It'll be quick,' he said.

Their Range Rover was reversing down the tailgate. Danny turned his back on the military attaché and addressed his team.

'We're escorting Ntoga,' he announced. 'We've got twenty minutes to find out what he knows. After that, he'll be lawyered up. Ripley, you and me in the back with Ntoga. Tony, front passenger. Caitlin, you take the wheel, you know Lagos.' Caitlin's face darkened: she clearly didn't appreciate being given the role of chauffeur. But she said nothing.

Danny looked over at the chopper. The rotors were still spinning, but three people were emerging from the aircraft, bowing in the downdraught. 'Let's go,' Danny instructed, 'before the Nigerians can scoop him up.'

The unit ran to their vehicle. Seconds later, they were screeching across the tarmac towards the chopper. Caitlin handled the vehicle well, pulling a ninety-degree handbrake turn just as the vehicle approached the Nigerian trio. Danny opened his door and jumped out, aware that Ripley was doing the same on the other side of the car. They were only fifteen metres from the chopper, and the roar of the rotors was deafening. 'Mr Ntoga?' Danny shouted at the three men.

One of them stepped forward. He wore a business suit, but it was scuffed and grubby. The man himself was chubby, with tightly cropped hair and beads of sweat on his forehead. He smiled, and his teeth looked improbably white against his black skin, with the exception of one gold filling. Danny didn't like that smile. It didn't suit the mood. But he didn't let that show on his face.

'British intelligence!' he shouted. 'We're here to escort you safely to the Deputy High Commission. Follow me, please.'

There was a moment of hesitation. Ntoga's two companions clearly didn't want him to leave, but Ntoga himself shrugged them off with a sharp word in an African language Danny didn't understand. Danny took Ntoga lightly by the elbow and guided him politely into the back of the car. The Nigerian clambered in without any resistance. Danny and Ripley took their places on either side of him and slammed their doors shut. Danny thought he caught a whiff of stale alcohol. Smelled like Ntoga had been decompressing with a bottle of booze.

Caitlin reversed in a sharp turning circle, then headed back towards the military attaché's Mercedes. They pulled up behind it. The attaché himself was standing next to his car. He walked up to the Range Rover and peered in through Danny's window to satisfy himself that Ntoga was there. He gave Danny himself a look full of meaning, then marched back to his own vehicle.

The convoy of three vehicles slipped away from the C17, led by the unmarked saloon car. They moved across the airfield, skirting round the runway and heading to the side of the main terminal building. Border control regulations were for other people, not for them. At a heavily armed barrier, a Nigerian soldier waved them through.

Ntoga hadn't lost his grin. He seemed unaware that his four guards were staring straight ahead, expressionless. 'This is more like it!' he announced in a marked Nigerian accent. 'I should be kidnapped more often!'

Danny turned to look at him. 'Thing is, Mr Ntoga,' he said, 'I know that you *weren't* kidnapped.'

The smile fell immediately from Ntoga's face. 'Don't you talk to me like that!' he said. 'You!' He leaned forward and rapped Tony on the shoulder. 'Open your window.'

Tony gave him a contemptuous look, then turned to face straight ahead again.

Ntoga clenched his fist. 'Do you know who I am?'

Caitlin was accelerating up a ramp onto a raised highway.

Beneath the road, a sea of tin roofs. Danny glanced at the speedometer. They were doing about fifty mph. Ntoga wouldn't try to escape the vehicle at that speed. Tony leaned forward and pressed a button on the dashboard. The central locking clicked shut.

A frown crossed Ntoga's face. 'What are you doing?' he demanded. 'Who are you? Don't you know who I am?'

'Yeah,' Danny said. He removed his Sig from its holster, cocked it, then placed the barrel against Ntoga's crotch. 'You're the guy I'm going to shoot in the bollocks if you don't tell me what the hell's going on.'

Ntoga looked down at the weapon. His face was a picture of surprise and outrage. He looked Danny in the eye, then back down at his crotch again.

Then he burst into laughter.

'You a funny guy!' he said, spitting the words out insultingly. 'You think you can take me – me! – into the British High Commission with my *hausa* hanging off? You a very funny guy!'

Danny suddenly burned with anger. With his free hand he grabbed hold of Ntoga's podgy neck, and squeezed hard. He could feel the jugular pulsing fast and hard. 'Listen to me, you piece of shit,' he hissed. 'You're going to be lucky even to make it as far as the fucking building. I'll drive you to one of the slums, put a bullet in your guts and leave you for dogs. Start talking now, or I'll . . .'

Ntoga never got to hear what Danny had in mind, because suddenly Caitlin had made a last-minute right-hand turn that jolted everyone in the car. The Nigerian official was lucky not to have taken a loose round in the bollocks. 'What the hell are you doing?' Danny barked.

'Put the gun away,' Caitlin said. 'Ntoga's right. We can't touch him.'

They sped down a slip road that turned a sharp semicircle.

'Bullshit. I can . . .'

'You asked me on the plane if I had a better idea,' Caitlin interrupted. 'I do.'

Danny looked out of the window. The other two cars in the convoy were already out of sight. Up ahead, Danny saw a sea of traffic, and he could smell the stench of exhaust fumes. Caitlin floored the accelerator, took a sharp left and sped down a dark side street.

'Where the fuck are we going?' Tony demanded. He sounded as tense as Danny felt. The last thing they needed was a wild card behind the wheel.

Caitlin didn't reply. Danny and Ripley exchanged an anxious look. They'd only been in-country ten minutes and already they were heading for an almighty fuck-up. But whatever Caitlin was up to, it had an effect on Ntoga. He wasn't laughing any more. This wasn't what he'd been expecting, and he was clearly worried. Danny decided to let the situation play out.

Caitlin negotiated the back streets of Lagos like a native. She didn't stop for pedestrians, and she cut up more vehicles than Danny could count. After a couple of minutes, she yanked the steering wheel sharp right into a busy, broad, tree-lined street. The vehicle screeched to a halt, half up on a pavement. A couple of angry-looking men in floral shirts shouted abuse at her. But then they glanced to their left and, as if they'd forgotten where they were, hurried on. Cars honked aggressively at each other all around them, and swarms of pedestrians wandered across the road as freely as if it was a pavement. From somewhere outside, Danny could hear the loud pulse of Afrobeat music. On the opposite side of the street he could see a rickety old shack selling fruit and bottled water, almost as if it was the middle of the day. And alongside them was a large, utilitarian, concrete building – four storeys high and at least a hundred metres in length. Many lights burned brightly inside. Danny had the impression that people were hurrying past it.

'You know where we are, Ntoga?' Caitlin said, without looking back.

Ntoga nodded. 'Of course.'

'Where?'

He didn't reply until Danny jabbed his handgun sharply into his ribs. 'Police headquarters,' said the Nigerian.

'Very good. Did you know that the guy who got kidnapped has a teenage daughter?'

Ntoga blinked heavily, but said nothing.

'So does the Inspector General of Police. The two girls are the same age. They're very good friends.'

Danny allowed himself a grim smile. He could see where this was going. He caught Tony's glance in the mirror. He looked reluctantly impressed. Any worries they'd shared about Caitlin's abilities were beginning to dissolve.

The atmosphere in the car had changed. Caitlin turned to look back at Ntoga. Her face looked very severe in the light of the passing headlamps.

'I knew a guy once,' Caitlin continued. 'Important guy. More important than you. Refused to pay a bribe to a pretty minor police official. He ended up in here. Next time I saw him, he couldn't walk.' She narrowed her eyes. 'Everyone in Lagos knows what's in the basement of this building, Ntoga. Those who get to see it are lucky to come out again. You and I both know that the only people in Nigeria more corrupt than the government are the police. So you've got two options. You can tell us who the hell paid you for information on the High Commissioner's whereabouts, and walk away with your money, untouched, tonight. Or we can hand you over to the Inspector General, slip him a couple of thousand naira for his trouble, and watch him get medieval on you. Don't get me wrong, I'd be more than happy to shoot your dick off myself, but why should I bother when there's a whole basement full of experts to do the job for me?'

Sweat was now pouring down Ntoga's face. He wiped it away with one hand. 'I don't know what you're talking about,' he whispered.

'No? Fine.' Caitlin dug her hand into her jacket and pulled out a old-fashioned Nokia mobile phone. She pressed a couple of buttons and a name and number came up on the screen. She held it in front of Ntoga's face. 'Know the name?' she asked.

He nodded.

'That's a direct line to the Inspector General. Did I mention that he's a friend of mine?' She pressed another button and the sound of a number being dialled filled the vehicle.

A female voice. '*Hello? Office of the Inspector General.*'

Caitlin inclined her head. 'Shall I ask to be put through?' she asked. 'Or shall I hang up?'

A pause.

'*Hello? Who is this?*'

'Hang up,' Ntoga breathed.

Caitlin killed the phone. 'Talk,' she said.

Ntoga was still sweating. 'I swear . . .' he muttered. 'I don't know . . .'

'Fuck this,' said Danny, continuing Caitlin's cue. He opened his door and grabbed Ntoga by the elbow. 'Call him now, tell him we're on our way in . . .'

'What?' Ntoga hissed. 'Wait.' Fear was dripping off him.

Danny let the door slam shut. 'I want a name. Now.'

Ntoga's eyes bulged. He swallowed hard and glanced first at Danny, then at Caitlin, then at the police building outside.

When he spoke, it was barely a whisper.

'Boko Haram,' he said.

THREE

'You'll have to do better than that,' Danny said. 'I want proper names – people, places . . .'

'That's all I know,' Ntoga said. His voice was hoarse, his skin soaked with sweat.

Danny opened the door again and started to drag him out.

'Wait!' Ntoga rasped. 'Wait!'

'You've got ten seconds to give me information I can use,' Danny said.

'I heard them talk about Chikunda,' the Nigerian breathed. 'I think maybe they take them there.'

'Where is Chikunda?' Danny demanded.

'North. Past Abuja. Very far.'

'How much did they pay you?'

Ntoga shrank back. Danny pulled out his Sig and pressed the barrel hard into the soft flesh of Ntoga's left eye. 'How much did they pay you!'

'Ffity thousand dollars,' Ntoga squealed.

Ripley gave a low whistle. 'That's a lot of dollars for bunch of Nigerian militants to cobble together,' Tony said.

'Sounds to me like they've got backing,' Danny said. He nodded at Caitlin. 'Let's get to the High Commission, turn this dirtbag over to his lawyer.'

'Yes,' Ntoga breathed. 'My lawyer . . .'

Caitlin pulled out into the busy traffic, then off into the side streets again. As she drove, heavy raindrops started to spatter on the windscreen. Within thirty seconds it had turned into a torrent that the wipers could barely clear, and which hammered so noisily on to the vehicle that it was impossible to speak.

Danny took a moment to process what he'd just learned. Boko Haram were a bunch of militant Islamists working out of northern Nigeria. They'd been responsible for kidnapping Nigerian schoolgirls and other low-risk, high-publicity targets – not to mention brutal massacres that had wiped out whole villages and thousands of people. Swiping the British High Commissioner, though, was a change of tactic. It also sounded like this particular cell had substantial funding, and that made them a hundred times more dangerous.

The journey to the British Deputy High Commission took them across two bridges, on to the islands of Lagos. They reached it ten minutes later. It was situated just off a wide, sweeping road, and was shielded by palm trees that swayed in the rain and wind. Danny noticed two photographers loitering opposite the entrance – word of the commissioner's disappearance had clearly leaked out. Instinctively, he shielded his face with one hand, and he noticed the other members of the unit doing the same.

They took a sharp left and drove straight through the open security barriers. The remaining two cars in the convoy were already parked outside the bland, brick building. As they pulled up alongside the convoy, Danny could see the military attaché standing in the rain, pulling at what remained of the hair on his head. As he saw their car approach, his expression turned from one of anxiety to one of anger.

The doors of the Range Rover swung open in unison. The unit emerged quickly, Danny holding Ntoga firmly by the arm. The military attaché opened his mouth, clearly about to give them a bollocking, but he was interrupted. Another Nigerian man, lean and older than Ntoga, with short white hair, burst out of the main entrance to the Commission. 'What are you doing with my client?' he shouted furiously. 'I demand that you release him immediately.'

'He's all yours, pal,' Danny said. He pushed Ntoga towards his lawyer. Ntoga stumbled in a puddle, then hurried to the older man with his head bowed. Together they disappeared into the Commission building.

The military attaché turned to Danny. 'What the bloody hell do you think you're ...'

'We need to talk,' Danny cut in. 'Now. Do you have a secure room?'

The attaché stared at him for a moment. Then he bowed his tired head. 'This way,' he said.

It was an ordinary meeting room on the first floor of the Commission building. Grey carpet tiles, walls that could do with a lick of paint, strip lighting, and the kind of plastic chairs you'd normally expect to find in a school hall. An air-conditioning unit rumbled noisily, but it managed to keep the humidity down a little. On one wall, a large map of Nigeria. Danny looked round for any sign of bugs or listening devices. There was no immediate sign of any, and Danny didn't have time to check the light fittings or ceiling panels. 'Are you sure we can talk freely?' he asked the attaché.

'As sure as I can be,' said Maloney.

'Get me up to date on Boko Haram.'

'They're animals.'

'They're terrorists. Goes without saying. What else?'

'Sunni fundamentalists. The name means "Western education is forbidden". They want Sharia law, subjugation of women, they kill anyone drinking or listening to music, all the usual Taliban bullshit. Those girls they kidnapped? You heard about that? The Boko Haram leader wants to sell them to his guys as wives for twelve bucks each. Says it's the Islamic way. In the last five years they've killed five thousand civilians, and displaced the best part of a million. What do you want me to tell you? They're fucking psychos.'

Danny gave him a hard stare. 'They've got your commissioner and his aide,' he said.

Maloney blanched, then pinched the bridge of his nose. 'They'll make mincemeat of them.'

'Not if we get to them first. If they wanted them dead, they'd

43

have killed them on sight. My guess is they want a ransom, or – more likely – to make a show out of them. Execute them on video, you know the drill. It gives us a little time. We think your man's being taken by Boko Haram to a village in the north called Chikunda.'

To his credit, the attaché quickly regained his composure. 'That makes some kind of sense,' he said, before gathering his thoughts for a moment. 'Traditionally, Boko Haram have been most active in the north-east, especially in the area around the Sambisa forest. But they've been heading west recently, along the Niger border. They're targeting small villages where they can wipe out the locals and set up defensive positions. Chikunda is one of them. It's a tiny place, former population of a couple of hundred people. I wouldn't have heard of it, if Boko Haram hadn't moved in about a week ago. Eyewitness reports say they burned down practically all the houses. Most of the villagers are dead or displaced. If it's not deserted, it'll just be Boko Haram fighters in the village itself.'

'We need to get there as quickly as possible.'

'I've got some good contacts in the Nigerian military. Let me make some calls. I'll see if we can scrounge a chopper and flight crew.'

'Wait,' Danny said. 'What happens when the Nigerians get a sniff of a Boko Haram stronghold?'

A shadow crossed the military attaché's face. 'Normally nothing,' he said. 'The military's a mess. Government ministers have been diverting the defence budget into their own bank accounts for years. Boko Haram are far better equipped and far better motivated. But if they do send troops in, it'll be carnage. Neither side has any concept of human rights. The government have learned not to send in under-equipped troops, so they *might* just try to bomb the target with whatever assets they can cobble together, and they won't care about civilian casualties.'

'Or about the hostages?'

The attaché thought about that for a moment, then shook his head. 'Maybe I can get on to Whitehall,' he said. 'Ask the Foreign

Office to appeal to the Nigerians to hold back for twenty-four hours.'

'We can't risk it,' Danny said. 'Boko Haram had Ntoga in their pocket and they've clearly got money to spend. They could have bought anyone in the government or military, and we don't know how deep the corruption goes. For now, this information doesn't leave this room. If Boko Haram are heading across country with the hostages, it'll be hard for them. The hostages will be slowing them down. If word reaches the kidnappers that we're on to them, the first thing they'll do is kill the hostages.'

'How long have we got?'

Danny strode over to the map of Nigeria. The attaché accompanied him. 'Where's Chikunda?'

'From memory,' the attaché said, 'about here.' He pointed to a spot in the north-western corner of Nigeria, approximately a hundred klicks south of the Niger border.

'The ambassador was kidnapped here,' Danny said, pointing to the spot west of Port Harcourt where the atrocity had taken place. 'Caitlin, what's the terrain between the two locations?'

Caitlin walked up and examined the map. 'The road infrastructure's pretty good,' she said. 'If they bypass Abuja and manage to get through any impromptu police road blocks – which they will do if they put their hands in their wallets – I'd say you're looking at fifteen hours by car, if they're travelling fast.'

'Longer if you're concealing two hostages,' Danny said. 'They'll keep them separate, so they'll be driving in convoy, which is always slower. And they'll be watching their speed if they want to stay under the radar.'

He looked out of the window, where the rain was still torrential. 'The weather's bad,' he observed. 'Whose terrain will it affect more, theirs or ours?'

'Probably theirs,' Caitlin and the attaché said in unison.

'Hostages, rain . . . I reckon they give us another ten hours. Call it twenty-four hours in all. We think the commissioner was taken at what time?'

'About 11.30 a.m.,' said the attaché.

'Which puts them in Chikunda by 11.30 tomorrow morning.' Danny checked his watch. 22.35 hrs. 'That gives us just under thirteen hours to get to there.'

Caitlin made a low hissing sound. 'Tight,' she said.

'What can I do to help?' Maloney asked.

'We need detailed mapping of the roads between here and Chikunda, plus any intelligence reports you have of the situation on the ground out there.'

'I can do that. Our people can probably get you a detailed satellite map of Chikunda itself, taken after it was occupied.'

'Good. Do it.'

'Weapons? Signalling equipment?'

'We've got what we need. But we could use some local currency. Low-denomination notes, plenty of them. It doesn't have to be a lot – it just has to *look* like a lot.'

The attaché gave an efficient nod and didn't ask questions.

'Try to keep Ntoga here as long as possible,' Danny said. 'My guess is he'll ask you for your help to leave the country. If he does, give it to him. Monitor his phone calls and escort him to the airport. The last thing we want is him warning anybody that we're on to the kidnappers. My guess is he'll want to get himself and his money as far away from Boko Haram as possible.'

'That leaves a bad taste in the mouth,' Maloney said.

'Not as bad as having Boko Haram put a round in your man's skull, and that's about the best he can hope for. This is a high-profile hostage. They'll want to milk it for all it's worth.'

'Beheading?' Maloney asked weakly.

Danny shrugged. 'Maybe. Get on to Hereford, let them know what we're doing and where we're going. They can track our movements through the GPS chips in our radio packs. They might send in reinforcements, but we can't wait for them to mobilise. Keep at the Nigerians to put in a cordon around the kidnapping area. If we're wrong about Chikunda and they're staying put in the Niger Delta, we'll need to contain them for as long as possible. And for fuck's sake do what you can to keep this out of the press. If the kidnappers get jittery they'll move things forward.' Danny turned to the rest of the unit. 'Ready?'

He received two nods in return, and one scowl. 'I think you've made the wrong call,' Tony said. 'You've only got Ntoga's word that this is where the kidnappers are heading. It's weak intel.'

'Agreed,' Danny said flatly. 'It's also the only intel we've got. Get ready to go.'

'Wait,' said the military attaché. He clutched his forehead, as if he couldn't believe he was in this situation. 'There's just four of you. You can't go up against half of Boko Haram by yourselves. They're better equipped than the army and there's about ten thousand of them. They control an area the size of Belgium, for Christ's sake.'

Danny just gave him a calm stare. 'Mapping,' he said, 'and intel on the terrain. You've got five minutes. Then we leave.'

FOUR

MI6 Headquarters, London. 00.00 hrs.

When intelligence staff gather round a table at MI6 headquarters at an hour before midnight, it's seldom good news. And if the chief of SIS himself has joined them, it's guaranteed bad.

But then, today had been the mother of bad-news days.

Sir Colin Seldon sat at the head of a long table in a featureless room overlooking the Thames. The chief had the crumpled, exhausted look of a man under pressure. Small wonder. If something passed them by that led to a serious incident, all of Whitehall would lay the blame at *his* door. So it had been with the abduction of the British High Commissioner to Nigeria twelve hours ago. The PM on the phone every twenty minutes wanting updates. Horrific conversations with the commissioner's tearful wife, assuring her that they would find her husband and keeping quiet that he thought the man was a bloody idiot to be touring round the Niger Delta without proper close protection. And constant – unsuccessful – quarrels with the Director of Special Forces to free up more than a single four-man unit to insert into Nigeria. Not that he blamed the director. The Regiment and the SBS were stretched to breaking point, and in any case, everyone quietly assumed that the abductees were dead already. No point wasting precious resources to hunt down corpses.

And now this.

He looked down the conference table. To his left sat a heavily bearded man in an electric wheelchair, his head leaning against a red padded headrest. Daniel Bixby didn't look up to much, but he was Seldon's most trusted Middle East analyst. Four of Bixby's sub-analysts completed that side of the table. At the far end sat Tessa Gorman, the Foreign Secretary, whose face was also pinched and tired. To Gorman's left sat Hugo Buckingham, an intelligence officer whose rise had, in recent months, been meteoric – much to Seldon's dismay. Buckingham was a handsome bastard, a good Arabist and a decent intelligence officer, but he was also a back-stabber and a sneak, and Seldon couldn't help but think he had his eye on the top job. Trouble was, Buckingham had political backing – the CIA seemed to love him, and he was Tessa Gorman's man. In the Firm, that was currency.

And even Seldon had to admit Buckingham had a habit of coming out of shitty situations smelling of roses.

Sitting next to Buckingham were three intelligence officers whose names Seldon couldn't remember – two male, one female. And a female clerk, taking notes that wouldn't be made public for another thirty years.

'I want to know one thing,' Seldon said, 'and so will the PM: is this a credible threat?'

'We take all threats to be credible, Sir Colin,' Bixby said mildly. He didn't – couldn't – move his head as he spoke.

The chief closed his eyes in frustration. 'For God's sake, Daniel, it's been a very long day. Give me a straight answer, would you?'

Bixby inclined his head. 'What we have is this: a single message on a single internet forum. As you know, internet forums are a very popular medium for extremists to propagate messages. The message can be downloaded to a thumb drive, given to a courier, taken halfway across the world, encrypted and then posted from any internet-enabled computer. Even if GCHQ manage to establish the IP address of the computer that posted the message, it's impossible to use that to find the location of the person who actually wrote it in the first place. To make things more difficult for us, we have thousands of people writing aggressive, extremist opinions on these forums, only a tiny fraction of whom will ever get close to providing a serious threat to our national security. So when it comes to internet forums, the challenge lies in separating the signal from the noise.'

The chief made a rolling hand gesture that said: get on with it.

'It's 20 April today,' the analyst continued. 'The London Marathon's in six days. Before major events such as this, there's always a spike in terrorist chatter. As I said, most of it's noise rather than signal, and I'd be inclined to dismiss this message as just that, if it weren't for one thing.' One of Bixby's sub-analysts handed Seldon a piece of paper. 'This is the message, verbatim.'

The chief read the message. It was brief.

26/04. 74:26-30. Ordered by the Caliph. S/N 2121311.

'You've all seen this?' the chief asked the room in general. Everyone nodded. 'And 26/04 is the date of the marathon, right?'

'Yes, Sir Colin,' Bixby said.

The chief and the Foreign Secretary exchanged a look. 'We can't cancel it,' said Gorman. 'The PM won't have it, it makes us look weak.'

'Not as weak as a re-run of the Boston Marathon bombings,' the chief muttered. 'But of course we're not going to cancel it on the back of a one-liner on some obscure internet forum.'

'I must say,' Hugo Buckingham butted in loudly, 'that it all looks rather obvious to me.' He gave the analyst a bland smile. 'I'd have though our analysts would understand that people aren't stupid. Surely a real terror suspect would encode their messages in some way?'

'I agree with Hugo,' said the Foreign Secretary. She sounded relieved that somebody had seen fit to question the validity of the threat. 'Messages like this must be two a penny in the lead-up to a major event . . .'

'I disagree, Sir Colin,' Bixby said. The Foreign Secretary gave the disabled analyst a dangerous look, but he continued regardless. 'Encoded messages are much more likely to stand out. I agree that a message like this looks like one of hundreds posted by Walter Mittys all over the world, but our opinion is that whoever posted this one could well be trying to hide in plain sight. And the reason it concerns us is this word here.' He jabbed the paper, pointing at the last word in the message: 'Caliph.'

'Go on,' the chief said.

Hugo Buckingham cleared his throat. 'If I may, sir,' he said, with the air of a man wanting to impart his knowledge. 'You understand the meaning of the word "Caliph", of course. Historically, a Caliph is the leader of a Caliphate – a sovereign state of Muslim believers, ruled according to Sharia law. It's the aim of certain extremist organisations – IS among them – to establish a modern-day Caliphate, and indeed some of their leaders have already given themselves the title of Caliph. It's window-dressing, sir. We know who all these people are. They may have very limited powers in certain parts of the Middle East, but the chances of them—'

In an uncharacteristically raised voice, Bixby interrupted. 'In the past three months, Sir Colin, we've been receiving intelligence chatter about an *unidentified* extremist figure who gives himself exactly that title. We know very little about him, and that always rings alarm bells.'

'Go on,' the chief said. 'For God's sake let him speak, Buckingham!'

'Thank you, Sir Colin.' Bixby collected his thoughts for a moment. 'I'm sorry. We haven't a lot to go on. We don't know what this S/N number represents – some kind of serial number, we presume, but we've run it through all our systems and we've come up with no positive matches. We're almost certain, though, that 74:26-29 refers to a certain passage from the Koran.' He cleared his throat and recited from memory: '*I will drive him into the Hellfire. And what will explain to you that which Hellfire is? It allows nothing to endure, and leaves nothing alone. It blackens the skins of men.*'

Silence in the room.

'Well, what the bloody hell is that supposed to mean?' the chief said finally. 'There's a type of missile called a Hellfire, isn't there? Is that what it refers to?'

'Perhaps,' said Bixby. He sounded unconvinced. He cleared his throat again. 'We know almost nothing about this self-styled

Caliph. We're pretty sure he exists, but any attempts by our assets in Syria or Iraq to find out more about him are completely stonewalled. There is a suggestion that he might be of Qatari origin, which makes some kind of sense because to stay off the grid requires large quantities of ready cash, and the Qataris are massively oil-rich. So are the Saudis, of course, and we've pretty good evidence of wealthy individuals from both states funding Islamist groups across the Arabian Peninsula and elsewhere. But a couple of independent references we have to this Caliph come from intelligence sources in Qatar. If we want to find out any more about him, I'd suggest that would be a good place to start.'

The chief nodded and fell silent for a minute. All eyes were on him. 'What assets do we have in Qatar at the moment?' he asked.

Bixby opened the manilla folder on the table in front of him and withdrew a sheaf of paper. The chief scanned it quickly: there was a picture of an Arab man in traditional headgear, and beneath it a lot of dense writing. 'Give me the edited highlights,' Seldon said.

'His name is Ahmed bin Ali al-Essa,' Bixby said. 'His SIS handle is codename Murdock. He's an oil magnate with several concessions from the Qatari government to pump oil offshore in Qatari waters. He has a massive workforce out in Qatar, as well as very close ties with the Qatari government. But he has substantive trade agreements with the UK which he very much needs to keep intact. As a result, he's open to the idea of passing intelligence on to us – we've received good stuff from him over the past five years, all high-grade, all accurate. I'd say he's a friend of the Firm, Sir Colin. Our analysis is that if he were to put out feelers among his workforce about this Caliph character, it could be beneficial.'

'Do it,' said the chief.

'It's not entirely straightforward,' Bixby said. 'Ahmed Al-Essa insists on face-to-face contact. Not surprising, really – we'd be astonished if the Qatari authorities didn't have him under electronic surveillance. But if we're going to get anything out of him, we'll need a man on the ground.'

'Or a woman,' said the Foreign Secretary.

'No,' said Bixby. 'A man. It's the way things are out there.'

'Where is Al-Essa currently situated?'

'Saudi Arabia. Riyadh. On business.'

'We don't have much time, Sir Colin,' the Foreign Secretary said briskly.

'Thank you, Foreign Secretary,' the chief said. 'If an extremist group drops a bomb on London, you'll be sure to let me know, won't you?'

Gorman visibly bristled, and the intelligence staff around the table avoided catching anyone else's eye. The chief pinched his nose again. His head ached. There was too much to take in, and he knew he didn't have a hope in hell of getting any sleep that night. Not the best state in which to be making decisions. His eyes followed the line of intelligence officers down the right-hand side of the table, and came to rest on Buckingham.

'Isn't Riyadh your old stomping ground, Buckingham?' He seemed to remember that Buckingham had once been their man in Saudi.

Buckingham looked startled. For a moment, he seemed lost for words. 'Yes, Sir Colin,' he said finally. 'Yes, it is. I spent a number of years at the embassy there.'

'I want you on the first plane to Riyadh. Make contact with our asset and see what he knows about the Caliph.' Buckingham looked distinctly unenthusiastic about the prospect. The chief didn't care. He turned to the remaining intelligence officers. 'If this Caliph is planning something in London, somebody, somewhere knows about him. I want us to comb through any and every cross-agency intelligence report that might be relevant for the past six months. If you draw a blank, start on the six months before that. Nothing slips through the net, ladies and gentlemen. And I trust it goes without saying that no word of this leaves these four walls. You don't tell your family or your friends. Any leaks will be dealt with under the Official Secrets Act. We can't afford a panic. Rest assured that the security services will act as and when it becomes necessary. Is there anything else?'

Buckingham cleared his throat.

'Yes?' the chief asked.

Buckingham looked like he was going to complain. But he just bowed his head. 'Nothing, Sir Colin,' he said. 'Nothing at all.'

'Good. Get to work, everyone. Now.'

There was a scraping of chairs, and the whirring sound of Bixby's electric wheelchair moving back, as the analysts and intelligence officers left the room. 'A word, Sir Colin,' the Foreign Secretary called above the noise.

The chief nodded, then looked towards the door where Hugo Buckingham was loitering. He raised an eyebrow at him. Buckingham looked embarrassed and left, leaving the chief and the Foreign Secretary alone.

'I apologise for snapping,' Seldon said. 'It's been a long day.'

'Forget about it. This marathon threat, is it really a thing, in your opinion?'

The chief nodded. 'Bixby's my best man. I've never known him be wrong. Something like this *will* happen, Tessa. You know that as well as me. We've foiled seven or eight plots in the final stages of planning, and that's just in the last nine months. Whether *this* is the one where those IS crazies get us, I don't know. My feeling is that our biggest threat will come from a lone-wolf jihadi, radicalised on the internet and trained up by Islamic State in Syria. But wherever the hit comes from, it *will* happen, sooner or later.'

'I'm glad you sent Buckingham. I've a lot of confidence in him.'

The chief sniffed, but didn't reply.

'You need to know that the PM is spitting feathers about this Nigerian situation,' Gorman continued. 'You have to give him some good news, and soon.'

'There's none to give. I'm sorry, Tessa, I know the guy's probably a friend of yours, but if Boko Haram have him, the chances of him turning up alive are almost zero.'

'If that happens it will look like a failure on our part,' Gorman said. 'And on yours, of course.'

The chief gave her a serious look. 'Blame can always be

reapportioned,' he said. 'The Regiment are in-country. If they fail to find the hostages, it can always be put down to incompetence on their part. Hereford never answers back in public. They can take a hit now and then.'

Gorman allowed herself a smile. 'If you say so,' she said. 'If you say so.'

FIVE

'For the record,' Tony said, 'I still think this is a shit idea. We don't even know the hostages are definitely in the backwater we're headed to. You agree with me, right, Ripley?'

There had been no let-up in the rain. As the unit climbed into the vehicle, they were dripping wet, and the interior filled with condensation as soon as Caitlin pulled away from the High Commission building. A roll of thunder cracked overhead, accompanied by a flash of lightning that lit up the stern profiles of the four soldiers in the vehicle, just for a second.

Danny had the passenger seat. He unfolded a detailed military map. Chikunda was circled with a black marker pen. He ignored Tony's comment, and was quietly relieved that Ripley had done the same. Tony was proving as difficult to manage as Danny had feared. And it was true that their intel was weak, but it was all they had. 'A1 north out of Lagos,' he said.

Caitlin nodded. 'I know it.'

'Where did you get all this local knowledge?' Ripley asked from the back.

'I was stationed in the Aussie embassy here for two years.'

'Worst two years of your life, right?'

'Not at all. I loved it.' She paused. 'I had a Nigerian husband.'

'Had?' Danny asked.

Caitlin nodded. 'The police took exception to him having a white wife. That's how I know what goes on in the basement of the police building. He never made it out.' She said it without any emotion. Danny found himself making a small mental adjustment about this woman. She must hate the police – *really*

56

hate them – but she'd been willing to use their reputation to break Ntoga. She was a good asset. Ruthless, but good.

'Do you really know the Inspector General of police?'

'We haven't been introduced.'

'So why do you have his number in your phone?'

Caitlin looked straight ahead. 'Because one of these days,' she said, 'he and I are going to have a little chat about what he did to my husband.'

'Why do I have the idea,' Ripley muttered, 'that he'll end that conversation with a face like a busted arsehole?'

No reply. The conversation died.

The Lagos traffic was nose-to-tail, the air thick with the stench of exhaust fumes and the aggressive sound of car horns. But Caitlin evidently knew the roads well, and within twenty minutes she had negotiated their way out of the busy metropolis. Through his window, Danny had caught sight of the city behind them. In the dark, the glowing high-rises looked very modern. It would be easy to forget the slums that surrounded the city, and the tumble-down shacks that housed half the population. And just beyond the illuminated buildings he could make out the coast – not that he could see much of it through the dark and the rain. Just the vague impression of lights on the ships out at sea. Lagos was a busy port, and as they headed away from the interior, it felt like they were leaving civilisation.

The road was bad as they headed north. Caitlin did what she could to avoid the many potholes that riddled the highway, but it was impossible to miss them all in the dark, and Danny felt bone-shaken after just half an hour – though he noticed that Ripley was managing to get some shut-eye in the back. The weather was terrible. It was a blessing and a curse. On the plus side it seemed to be keeping most traffic from the roads. They passed the occasional tatty old white Toyota Coaster, rusting and rickety, with drenched luggage piled high on its roof. Now and then they overtook a heavy lorry that trundled along and blinded them with spray. But not much else. With the roads so clear and the weather so bad, they passed through the built-up towns north of

Lagos without any trouble. Even better, the rain had sent the soldiers guarding the semi-regular road blocks hiding for shelter. Caitlin slowed down to pass the cement blocks placed, Iraq style, along the middle and side of the road, but they passed each one unchallenged, no doubt thanks to the weather.

On the downside, the storm limited their speed, badly. Caitlin struggled to keep a steady sixty-five mph. For two hours they travelled slowly, but without incident. The rain continued – Danny realised that the storm must be following them north. At 01.00, he decided it was time to swap drivers. 'Pull over,' he told Caitlin. Once they were on the side of the road, he looked over at Ripley. 'Take the wheel,' he said.

'I'll drive,' Tony announced, opening his side door before Ripley could even move. 'Don't want to end up in a ditch.'

A dangerous shadow fell across Ripley's face as Tony and Caitlin walked round the back of the car to swap places. 'Leave it, mucker,' Danny said quietly. Ripley remained quiet, but didn't look happy.

Behind the wheel, Tony floored the vehicle. Danny had to concede that he was a good driver. Better than Caitlin. He managed safely to keep their speed above seventy mph for the next two hours, while Caitlin caught up on her sleep. As they drove, Tony looked over his shoulder to check she wasn't awake. 'What do you think of the bird?' he asked quietly.

'She can handle herself,' Danny said. He found himself remembering the sweat on her nose and the way her lips parted when she looked at him. Then he remembered Clara.

'Yeah.' Tony sniffed. 'She's a ruthless bitch. She's a looker too. I might have a crack at her.' He glanced at Danny. 'Unless you get there first,' he said.

Danny kept his eyes on the road ahead.

By the time they reached the point where the highway crossed the River Niger, it was already 03.00 hrs. Danny estimated that they were at least seventy-five klicks further south than he wanted to be by now. But there was nothing they could do, other than keep their foot down.

'We need to refuel,' Tony said as they emerged on the northern side of a small town called Oddah. Danny nodded and Tony pulled over on to a marshy puddle to the side of the road. Danny jumped out. He saw, just ten metres from the side of the road, one of the Toyota Coasters lying upturned and long-abandoned. As he removed one of the jerrycans from the boot and carefully poured the precious fuel into the vehicle, he saw another vehicle on the other side, a saloon car perhaps, absolutely totalled. Welcome to Africa.

Once the tank was full, he walked round to the driver's side and opened Tony's door. 'Ripley's driving now,' he said. Tony looked like he was going to argue, but then glanced over at Caitlin and seemed to change his mind. He climbed out of the car and swapped places with Ripley.

The state of the road made a burst tyre almost inevitable. It happened at 04.30 hrs, a huge bang from the front left-hand side just as they were reaching the outskirts of Abuja. 'What the fuck!' Tony shouted from the back. The blow-out didn't delay them more than ten minutes, thanks to the powerful hi-lift jack, but they were all aware that another would leave them without a tyre. 'Try to keep us on the road, mucker,' Tony said from the back as Ripley started off again.

Ripley was obviously struggling to keep his cool with Tony. Danny decided to divert his attention from the arsehole in the back. 'How old are your kids again, mucker?'

Ripley shot Danny a sharp look. On an op like this, family discussion were normally off-limits – an unspoken agreement that nobody wanted to be reminded of their loved ones when they were tooled up and moving into a combat situation. But beneath his gruff exterior, Ripley was a family man who never gave up an opportunity to talk about them. Now his face lightened. 'Eleven and nine. The oldest just got his first skateboard,' he said. 'Took him to a halfpipe the other day.' He looked into the rear-view mirror. Danny did too, and saw that Tony had his eyes closed. 'Don't worry about me,' Ripley said. 'I can deal with him.'

They headed relentlessly north.

Dawn hit half an hour later. It brought with it an improvement in the weather conditions, but Danny knew it would make other aspects of the journey more difficult. Sure enough, within fifteen minutes they saw, through the grey, early morning light, men in the road a hundred metres up ahead. 'Road block,' he said tensely, and he sensed Tony and Caitlin loosening their sidearms in their holsters. Four white guys with assault rifles stashed the length of the vehicle would cause a stir, no question.

Fifty metres. There were no other vehicles at the road block. 'Six men,' Danny counted. 'Three with weapons. AK-47.' They wore army fatigues that looked grey in the half light, but he noticed that the three armed guards had painted parts of their weapons in bright, vibrant colours – one had a yellow barrel, another a red stock – like they were children's toys.

'I'd say they're regular army,' Caitlin said quietly.

'Stop about ten metres from the first guard,' Danny said.

Ripley came to a gradual halt. Danny found himself automatically calculating the distances between them and the guards: ten metres to the guy with the yellow barrel, five more metres to the two other armed guards, and another ten metres to the remaining three, who were in a little group smoking cigarettes. The red tips of their fags stood out like fireflies in the grey dawn. They all had confident, almost arrogant looks on their faces, as if their brightly coloured weapons made them untouchable. They had no idea that at a single word from Danny, the unit would have them down in less than five seconds.

But dead bodies would make people ask questions, and they couldn't afford to be slowed down by anyone trailing them. Danny looked back at Caitlin and Tony. 'We only fight if we can't buy our way through,' he instructed.

'It'll be too late by then,' Tony said, his voice taut. Danny ignored him. But he was aware of both Tony and Caitlin winding down their windows, ready to engage with their weapons if the situation required it.

'Keep the engine running,' he told Ripley. He nodded, his hands still gripping the wheel, ready to move if necessary.

Danny removed the full wallet the military attaché had supplied them with before they left, removed half the notes, then stepped outside the car. He raised his hands to show he was holding nothing but the wallet, and smiled broadly.

The guy with the yellow AK barrel stepped casually forward. He had an arrogant expression, but Danny noticed that his eyes kept flickering towards the wallet.

'Hey,' the guard called. 'White man, what you doing here?'

Danny kept walking. 'Passing through,' he called. 'Heading into Niger.'

The guard gave an unpleasant grin, as if heading into Niger was a sure way to run into trouble. 'Three men, one woman? What is it, gangbang?'

Danny just gave him a broader grin. 'Something like that,' he said. 'Hey, your job looks like thirsty work. You'd rather be having a beer than standing here talking to me, right?'

'Beer is expensive, white man.' The guard rubbed his thumb and fingers together.

Danny was a metre in front of him now. 'Maybe I could buy you one,' he said.

The guard didn't answer, but looked meaningfully at the wallet. Danny pulled out the stash of notes. 'It's all I have,' he said.

The guard gave an unimpressed sniff. But he also licked his lips, and Danny knew he was through. He handed over the notes, and the guard casually put them in his pocket. Then he turned his back on Danny and wandered over to his two mates.

'Hey!' Danny called. 'What are the roads north of here like?'

'Roads are very good,' said the guard dismissively, 'if you like to swim.' He chuckled to himself, then turned back to his mates.

Nothing on earth would have made Danny turn his back on three armed men, no matter how much he'd just bribed them. He made a gesture with his right hand. Immediately, the Range Rover pulled up beside him. Danny slipped back into the passenger seat. As Ripley drove them through the road block, he felt the hot glare of all six guards on them, and saw a flash of yellow gun barrel. But a minute later they were out of sight.

At 06.00 hrs they pulled off the main highway. The road to

Chikunda headed off at a bearing of approximately 310 degrees. As a line on the map it looked like a perfectly good road. In reality it was little more than a rough track through dense, high vegetation. As the early morning wore on, the humidity started to increase again. It felt as if the air itself was going to burst with rain again. At 06.30 hrs, it did – stronger than before. Even with the windscreen wipers going full-speed, visibility was a scant five metres. Danny watched carefully through the windscreen, scanning the road ahead for unseen danger or threats . . .

'STOP!' he shouted suddenly.

Ripley hammered the brakes. The Range Rover skidded badly. Ripley expertly drove into the skid in order to get control of the steering again, but with a lurch, Danny felt the two right-hand wheels rise for a good couple of seconds. They thumped back down on to the ground, but the vehicle still had forward momentum. They skidded down the dip in the road that Danny had only seen at the last minute. Mud and water splashed over the windscreen, completely obscuring their view as they came to a sudden, jolting stop.

The engine died. Rain hammered on the roof of the car. 'What the fuck have you done now?' Tony shouted from the back.

Danny wound down his window. One glance was enough to tell him what had happened. The dip in the road had flooded. It was like a fast-flowing river bisecting the road. They were stuck in the water, which reached at least a metre and a half up their vehicle. It was five metres from the higher ground where the road was dry, but there was no way they were getting out of here without any help.

Danny's mind immediately turned to the mechanical winch at the front of the vehicle. 'We need to winch out!' he called above the noise of the hammering rain. 'There must be a river nearby that's broken its banks – this flooding's going to get worse. Ripley, keep the wheel. You two follow me.'

They couldn't open the doors because of the depth of the water. Scrambling out of the windows was their only option. Danny brought his personal weapon with him, slung over his shoulder with the barrel slightly submerged as he crashed down into the fast-moving swamp. As his feet hit the bottom, the vehicle shifted a few inches towards him.

'We've got to hurry!' Caitlin shouted over the thunderous sound of elements. Her face and hair were already soaked. 'The current's strong enough to take the vehicle with it!' As she spoke, she stumbled in the water, and fell up to her shoulders. But Tony was right there, grabbing her with one strong arm, and getting her back on to her feet. She nodded gratefully at him, then stood firmly in the water, withstanding the current.

Danny pushed his way through the water to the front of the vehicle. There were other reasons to move fast, other than the current. If a jungle river had burst its banks, it could bring anything with it. Debris, crocs, even hippos. They needed to get out of there as quickly as possible.

The winch itself, fitted to the front of the vehicle, was submerged. Danny plunged his hands under the water and found the end of the winching cable. It had a carabiner at one end, which he tugged firmly, then started to wade across the current to the far side.

He stopped. Figures were emerging through the driving rain. Four of them, walking abreast. Distance: twenty metres.

Danny looked left and right. Tony and Caitlin were on either side. They had raised their rifles, and had crouched down slightly in the water to present less of a target.

The Range Rover shifted again. Half a foot this time. Danny estimated that they had less than a minute before the current swept it away.

The four figures had stopped. Danny waded forward. 'Keep me covered!' he shouted. 'Any sudden movements, drop them!'

He tugged the cable and moved forward. Ten tricky paces later he was emerging from the flood. Mud covered his saturated clothes, but the rain soon sluiced it away. He manoeuvred his personal weapon with one hand so that it was covering the four figures, but now he was closer he could make them out a bit better. They were all African. Two women, one man, and a child.

'Don't move!' Danny roared at them. 'Stay where you are and don't move!'

He quickly identified a sturdy tree eight metres away on the left-hand side of the road and dragged the winch cable towards it. He looped the cable round the tree, then clipped the carabiner back round the cable. He gave it a precautionary tug, then turned back and gave Ripley a thumbs-up. There was a sudden, high-pitched grinding sound above the rain as the cable went suddenly taut. The Range Rover shifted its angle in the water so it was facing the tree, then slowly started to move forward.

Tony and Caitlin flanked the vehicle, still keeping low, their weapons still aimed at the four figures. Danny kept the butt of his own weapon pressed hard into his shoulder and approached them through the rain. He reduced the distance between them to ten metres. They didn't move. They stood, bedraggled and quite motionless. Danny saw that one of the women had her arm around the man's shoulders. The man was holding his own right arm across his stomach, as though it was broken.

Only when Danny took a couple more paces forward did he see that the man's right hand was missing.

He looked back again. The vehicle was out of the ditch, but huge quantities of water were still gushing from underneath the chassis. Caitlin was untying the winch cable and Tony – hair and face dripping, clothes drenched – was striding up to the four figures, weapons still raised. 'Get out of the fucking road!' he shouted at the Africans. But as he spoke, the man's knees went and he collapsed to the floor. The woman holding him wailed, and the kid ran towards Danny, seemingly oblivious to his weapon, and tugged on his clothes.

'Help us!' she cried. 'My father need medicine! Help us!'

Danny made the decision to lower his weapon. Tony kept his engaged as Danny strode up to the collapsed man, then crouched down beside him.

'What happened?' he shouted through the rain at the woman who was still holding him.

'Boko Haram!' the woman cried. 'They come to our village.'

She pointed back up the road. 'They kill many people. We run away, but they stop us in the road. They do this.' She indicated the severed wrist.

Danny stood up. Ripley was out of the car, two metres behind him. 'We can't wait,' he said. 'And the old boy's fucked.'

Danny nodded. Ripley was right. 'Get back to the car,' he told both men. Ripley jogged back towards the vehicle, but Tony loitered. Caitlin was trying to turn the vehicle's engine over. It coughed and spluttered several times, but burst into life on the fifth go. Ripley took his place in the back, but as Danny approached the car with Tony, the kid, who had followed, started tugging on his clothes again. 'Please, mister. We need medicine. We need help.'

Danny paused for a moment. A voice in his brain told him to ignore the child. Any medical supplies they left for the wounded man would be wasted: with an injury like that, out here, he was going to die, if not of blood loss then of infection. But then the kid tugged at him again with her desperate little hands. 'Please mister,' she begged.

He thought of Clara. She would help the kid, no question.

He wiped the streaming water from his face, then ran round to the back of the Range Rover and opened the boot. From inside his pack he pulled a small medical kit and withdrew some sterile bandaging.

Tony joined him. 'What the hell are you doing?' he said. 'We might need that.' He tried to grab the medical equipment, but Danny snatched it away. 'A few fucking bandages isn't going to do anything for him,' Tony said. 'He's a goner.'

'It'll make the family feel like they're helping.'

He walked round to the front of the car, knelt down and handed the sterile bandaging to the kid. 'That's all I have,' he lied. From the corner of his eye he could see Caitlin watching him from inside the car, her lips parted again.

The child gave Danny a wide-eyed stare of gratitude. Danny looked over his shoulder towards the mother, who was standing a couple of metres away. 'Have you seen any other white men on the road?' he asked. And when she looked at him a bit perplexed, he pointed at the skin on his hand. 'White skin, like mine?'

She glanced left and right, then nodded nervously.

Danny stood up. 'With Boko Haram?' he asked. 'The white men were with Boko Haram?'

She nodded again, then held up two fingers. 'Two men,' she said. She held up her hands, wrists touching. 'Tied,' she said.

Danny felt a surge of relief. He exchanged a look with Tony, then walked round the kid to get closer to the woman. 'When?' he said. 'How long ago?'

The woman thought for a moment, then held up three fingers. 'Three hour,' she said.

'Shit,' Danny hissed. A quick calculation put the hostages in Chikunda at 09.00 – earlier than Danny had previously estimated. Danny and Tony immediately turned back to the car, but suddenly the woman grabbed Danny's arm. 'Don't go that way,' she said. Her bloodshot eyes were wide open with warning. 'There are bad things that way . . .'

He shook her off, followed Tony back to the vehicle and climbed in. 'Go,' he told Caitlin. She moved off. The African family stood by the side of the road and solemnly watched them leave. The woman was muttering to herself. As they passed, she stared directly into Danny's eyes and shook her head. He saw her mouth the words 'bad things'.

'You shouldn't have given away our fucking supplies,' Tony muttered from the back.

Danny didn't feel a moment's regret. 'Floor it,' he told Caitlin. 'Two tied-up white guys were on this road three hours ago. I reckon they'll make it to Chikunda by 09.00.' He glanced at Tony in the rear-view mirror. There was no hint of an apology in his face. He almost looked pissed off that Danny had been right.

'At least we know they're still alive,' Caitlin said.

Danny shook his head. 'Wrong. We know they were alive three hours ago. If they were planning to execute the hostages in Chikunda, there's a good chance they won't fuck around. We might be too late.'

'Bad news for you if we are, *boss*,' Tony muttered.

Danny ignored the comment, but he couldn't help remembering what Hammond had said about this being his last chance.

'We need to get out of our civvies,' Ripley said. 'We're getting too far into the interior. These clothes are no good if we need to camouflage ourselves.'

Danny nodded. 'When we can,' he said. 'But we're entering enemy territory now. When the rain stops, we're vulnerable. The kid said that Boko Haram militants stopped them in the road and did that to her father. We can expect another road block up ahead.'

'And if those bastards have got a taste for cutting things off,' Ripley said, 'we want to get to them before they go to work on the hostages . . .'

Not even Tony had an argument with that.

Eyes forward. Senses on high alert. They started to eat up the miles once again.

SIX

As they continued north, the terrain on either side of the rough road became more jungle-like. Ripley was right: they were going to need their Crye Precision camouflage gear. At 08.00, they took advantage of a break in the rain to change. Danny was the first to strip quickly out of his wet civvies, shielded by the Range Rover, while the other three formed a defensive semicircle, their weapons engaged. He fitted his kevlar helmet, along with his boom mike and earpiece. There was no hiding the fact that they were soldiers now.

Once he was changed, he swapped positions with Ripley, keeping stag on the road to the north while his mate changed clothes. He could only see about twenty metres ahead before the road curved out of sight. The sun was burning through the clouds and the whole area seemed to hiss as the water evaporated from the verdant terrain.

As he scanned the area, something caught his eye. He had to squint to persuade himself that his eyes weren't playing tricks. They weren't. Nailed to a roadside tree, just ten metres away, was a human hand, palm outwards, fingers pointing up. 'Looks like we found where our road block was,' he said, pointing at it.

'Fucking animals,' Ripley said.

'They might still be here,' Tony said, his voice suddenly tense.

'I don't think so. That's a warning. Somebody doesn't want people heading north.'

Tony was the next to change – quicker than Danny and Ripley had been – and finally Caitlin. As she changed, Danny's eyes flickered towards the vehicle's side mirror. He caught sight of her grey base layer, tightly enclosing the curve of her breasts. She suddenly caught his glance in the mirror, and smiled. Danny looked away. He noticed Tony watching him. The men's eyes met. 'She was married to a black dude, fella,' Tony murmured. 'Won't be interested in what *you're* packing.'

Danny let it pass.

Time check: 08.10. Fifty minutes till the revised ETA of Target Red and Target Blue in Chikunda. Danny reckoned the unit was still four hours out. No time to waste. They dumped their wet civvies in a pile by the side of the road.

'I'll take the wheel,' he told Caitlin. She nodded.

At 09.00 they passed through a rough village. Broad swathes of brutal deforestation marked the outskirts. The interior was a shit sandwich without the bread. Breeze-block buildings on either side of the road had fallen into disrepair, and the only vehicles they saw had rusty side panels and missing tyres. It was strangely deserted, too. No kids or pedestrians. Always a bad sign. Just a few curious locals peering from doorways, but not bold enough to step out into the street. On the right-hand side, Danny saw a woman sitting at the threshold of her poor-looking residence. Both eyes were covered with dirty cotton swabs, slightly bloodstained. Even though she couldn't see, her gaze followed the sound of the Range Rover as it passed.

Danny kept his foot on the pedal. Every second that passed was borrowed time. Their vehicle splashed through puddles and sprayed dirt across the road as it cut through the village. As they left the last building behind, he looked in the rear-view mirror. Perhaps thirty metres behind them, a solitary figure stood in the middle of the road. Danny thought he could make out the shape of a rifle slung across his chest, and he seemed to be holding something to his ear. A phone, maybe.

Eyes back on the road.

At 10.00 hrs they stopped to refuel. By now, the heat and the humidity were immense. Danny felt wetter than he had been after his impromptu swim. The Range Rover was caked in mud and dust, and so were its occupants. Over the next hour, the jungle terrain thinned out a little, but it was still forested on either side as the Range Rover mounted the brow of a hill.

To the north-west, perhaps two kilometres in the distance, a plume of black smoke rose from the centre of a small settlement. Once they'd passed the brow of a hill and no longer made an obvious target, Danny allowed himself to hit the brakes. It was worth sacrificing a minute's travelling time to get some decent reconnaissance. He jumped out of the car and retrieved a spotting scope from his pack. He focused in on the settlement. He couldn't make out much – a single road leading away to the east, and three guys on motorbikes heading out that way.

'Boko Haram?' Ripley asked.

Danny couldn't tell for sure, but it seemed likely.

'I reckon we're forty-five minutes out of Chikunda,' Caitlin said. 'If it's a Boko Haram stronghold, we're going to hit resistance sooner or later.'

'Which will hold us up,' Ripley said tersely.

'We can only play what's in front of us,' Danny said. But Ripley was right. Every minute they delayed was a minute in which the kidnappers could execute their targets.

As the road continued, the vegetation on either side grew higher. Easy to hide in, but it meant that their vision ahead was compromised every time there was a bend in the road. Ten minutes after they'd started up again, the road curved and they were suddenly faced with another road block. Four men. Like the Nigerian soldiers at the previous block, they wore camouflage gear. But even from fifty metres away, Danny could tell that these were not soldiers. Their heads were wrapped in black and white shamaghs, and they wore bandoliers of ammo around their torsos like medals of honour. The universal uniform of the guerrilla fighter. Four motorbikes lay on their side next to the road. Three of the men carried assault rifles. A fourth was clutching an RPG launcher, though it wasn't aimed at the Range Rover, yet.

Danny slowed to a crawl. 'Tell me you're not going to try to pay your way through this one,' Tony said.

Not a chance. These weren't corrupt, lazy soldiers on the take.

These were militants with heavy weapons, just looking for a chance to use them. At least, that was Danny's instinct. They needed to get through as quickly as possible. But if these men raised the alarm, they would be behind enemy lines with the potential for thousands of Boko Haram militants tracking them down. Which meant they really only had one option.

He said a single word: 'Contact.'

Tony, Ripley and Caitlin removed their side arms from their holsters, checked they all had one up the spout, and laid them carefully in their laps.

The Range Rover edged forward. Danny half wondered if these were the same people who had cut off the hand of the villager they'd met. Probably not – the Nigerian family could never have travelled that distance on foot. But he didn't doubt that these militants were cut from the same cloth. They deserved what was coming to them.

Distance to the road block: twenty metres. One of the militants stepped forward. He held up one hand to make a stop sign. In the other he held his rifle, inexpertly, but aiming in their general direction. He'd never be able to fire accurately like that, but a spray burst could be as dangerous as a well-aimed one. Danny hit the brake.

He wound down his window. The others did the same.

The militant had an arrogant swagger as he walked towards the car. Danny saw that he was wearing a necklace threaded with the teeth of wild animals. When he was ten metres away, Danny could see his bloodshot eyes through the gap in his shamagh.

He gripped his handgun firmly.

'Ripley,' he breathed, 'take the RPG. Caitlin, go left. Tony, right.'

No arguments.

The militant drew up alongside the car. He rapped one hand on the top of the vehicle wing, then bent over to look through the open window. Danny caught the musty smell of his shamagh, and the rank stench of several days' unwashed sweat.

He didn't even wait for the militant to speak. He just raised his Sig and fired a single shot into the rough cloth covering his face.

The shamagh absorbed any spatter. The militant hit the ground in a millisecond. At the same time, Caitlin, Ripley and Tony swung their doors open. Danny heard shouting from the remaining three militants: a moment of confusion that bought the unit the fraction of a second they needed to do their work.

Three rounds was all it took. The guy with the RPG was raising it to his shoulder as the unit discharged their weapons practically in unison. The three remaining militants collapsed in a silent heap, and the grenade launcher crashed uselessly to the ground.

Danny had to shove his door hard to open it, because it was lodged in by the body of the guy he'd shot. Once he was out, he discharged a second round into the corpse's head, just to be sure. Tony and Ripley had grabbed their rifles and were panning round the area, checking for threats.

Caitlin and Danny ran up to the remaining three corpses and delivered three more safety shots. The bodies juddered slightly as the rounds entered, but then remained still, blood pooling all around them.

A harsh crackling sound. On the side of the road, just by the four motorbikes, Danny saw a battery-powered radio pack. A voice came through, speaking a language he didn't recognise. He and Caitlin exchanged a look. 'Someone's going to come looking for these stiffs,' Caitlin said. 'Do we hide the bodies?'

'No point,' Danny said tersely. 'If someone's searching for them, they'll know they're missing whether they find the bodies or not.' He pointed to the radio. 'Sounds to me like they'll come looking any second. We need to get off this road as quickly as possible.'

They sprinted back to the Range Rover. By the time they reached it, Tony and Ripley were already in the back. 'We'll drive for another ten minutes,' he announced. 'Then we'll hide the car and continue on foot.'

'We should ditch the car right now,' Tony said. His voice was tense. 'Hide it in the roadside vegetation. Make a covert approach on foot from a distance.'

Danny considered it for a moment. Time wasn't on their side.

They needed to advance to target as quickly as possible. God knows what was happening to the hostages right now. The longer they could stay with their vehicle, the better. He estimated Chikunda was approximately twenty-five minutes away. If Boko Haram were to dispatch guys immediately from there, ten minutes would give the unit a decent buffer to get off the road.

'We drive for ten,' Danny said.

'You're going to get us fucking killed,' Tony scowled.

'Keep your mouth shut,' Ripley said.

Danny ignored the tension in the back as he turned the engine over and hit the gas. The wheels bumped heavily over the bodies in the road as he pushed the Range Rover as hard as it would go.

They passed through a couple of klicks of desolate terrain, where the trees in the forested area on either side of the road had either been cut down or burned, leaving stumps or black, charred patches of earth. Occasionally they passed single-storey buildings – one of concrete, others of mud and corrugated iron. They were all dilapidated and destroyed, all uninhabited. It was as if a tornado of destruction had whipped its way through the terrain. They saw nobody.

The sky was blue. The sun fierce. There was no longer any sign in the surrounding terrain of the rainstorm that had caused them so much trouble. On the contrary, Danny's eyes hurt from the glare as, three klicks on, the forested area on either side of the rough road returned.

'That's ten minutes,' Tony stated. 'Get off the fucking road.'

Danny pushed it for another thirty seconds.

They came to a solitary concrete structure embedded among the trees on the left-hand side, half covered with creeping vegetation. Perhaps it had once been a barn. Whatever, it was about five times the length of the Range Rover. The roof was partially collapsed, and a section of wall had buckled inwards. But it offered a hiding place for the vehicle. Danny yanked the steering wheel sharp left. They trundled heavily off-road and up to the barn. Ripley jumped out and quickly opened a set of rickety wooden doors. Danny drove inside.

There was only just enough room, because a pile of rubble had fallen into the centre of the barn, stopping them from moving any further forward. Several shards of sunlight pierced the broken roof. They illuminated nothing but dusty earth and broken blocks of concrete.

Danny killed the engine. The unit de-bussed.

'Quiet,' Ripley hissed.

The unit halted by the vehicle, stock still. There was a buzzing sound in the distance, growing louder. Twenty seconds later came the unmistakeable sound of motorbikes speeding past the barn. Fifty cc, Danny reckoned from the tinny sound of the engines. He counted five of them. As the engine noise died away, the unit edged towards the entrance of the barn – just in time to see the final motorcyclist before he disappeared over the brow of a hill, seventy-five metres away. He had a rifle slung over his back.

'That was too ... fucking ... close ...' Tony said. He turned to Danny. 'You've got a death wish, pal. No wonder your mate Spud came back looking like Stephen fucking Hawking.'

Something snapped in Danny's head. He felt himself ready to burst with anger, to go for Tony, put him down. But then he remembered something his unit companion had said back in Hereford. *You've probably heard a few rumours about old Danny ... Bit of a short fuse, mind. Flies off the handle now and then. Not the best combo for a man with a 9-milly in his back pocket, but there we have it ...*

He got a hold of his temper and went to grab his pack from the boot of the car.

'What now?' Ripley asked.

Danny withdrew the black-and-white satellite map of Chikunda that the military attaché had supplied back in Lagos and laid it open on the bonnet of the Range Rover. The attaché had been as good as his word: a legend at the bottom of the map told them it had only been taken three days ago. And it showed, very clearly, the signs of war.

Chikunda was a small place, less than a kilometre end to end, surrounded by forest. A single main road ran through its centre.

To the north-west, the terrain was much darker – almost black. He circled it with his forefinger. 'There's been a fire here,' he said. 'Or lots of fires. You can still see the smoke rising there.'

Ripley pointed out a few remnants of rectangular shapes in this north-western area. 'Buildings,' he said. 'Or what's left of them. Like your man back in Lagos said, they've burned most of the village down.'

'And killed most of the locals, no doubt,' Caitlin said.

There are bad things that way . . .

Danny turned his attention to the eastern side of the main road. Here the terrain was more intact. There was a large open area, surrounded by three rectangular buildings, each set at the vertex of a triangle and facing in towards each other. A quick look at the scale told Danny they were each about twenty-five metres long, and about half as deep. Thirty metres to the north of them, still on the eastern side of the road, was a walled-off compound containing three circular huts.

He pointed to the northernmost of the three rectangular buildings. 'Block North,' he said. Then he labelled the building nearest the road and roughly south-west of the central open ground 'Block West', and the third building, furthest from the road and closest to the vegetation on the eastern side of the village, 'Block East'. 'I think we can expect a concentration of militants at these blocks North, West and East,' Danny said. 'The enclosed space to the north, the one with the circular huts, is defensible, but there doesn't appear to be any escape route. I don't think they'd enclose themselves there. Everyone agreed?'

There was a consenting murmur.

Ripley examined the smaller-scale map, his forefinger tracing the contour lines around Chikunda. 'According to this map, there's high ground to the south-east,' he said. 'We can get a visual from there.'

Danny nodded. 'We'll approach from the eastern side of the road,' he said. He checked his watch. 10.35 hrs. If the hostages had been taken to Chikunda, he reckoned they would have been in situ for ninety minutes already. They needed to get moving.

'Order of march: Ripley, me, Caitlin, Tony,' Danny said. 'We'll follow the road line as closely as possible. Hit the ground if anyone passes.'

They each sprinted across the road separately, three of them covering whoever was running. Once they'd reached the eastern side, they picked their way about fifteen feet past the road, then headed north in patrol formation, keeping parallel to the road with a distance of about ten feet between them. The vegetation on either side of the road was fairly thick where the wooded area had been cut into and sunlight allowed to hit the ground. It was more than a metre high in places, and offered good camouflage.

They moved with full pack and weapons. The heat was intense. They'd have sweated heavily even if they hadn't been laden down and in full camo gear. There were times, back in Hereford, when every member of the Regiment bitched about being beasted up and down the Brecon Beacons. And there were times, in the field, when you were glad of your fitness. This was one of those times. None of the unit faltered as they moved quickly through the vegetation, their footfall silent, their breath slow and measured. The only noise they made was the gentle shake of vegetation as they passed through it. When, five minutes into their forced march, Ripley hissed 'Down', they all hit the ground in unison. With his face pressed hard against some tough, reedy plant, Danny heard the regular pounding of his own heart, and then the distant sound of the motorbikes returning from the south. The noise made a sharp crescendo as they buzzed quickly past, then disappeared as the motorbikes sped north, back towards Chikunda. There was no point stating it out loud: they would have found the dead bodies at the road block. They would know something was up, even if they didn't know exactly what. And they would suspect that someone was coming. The unit had definitely lost any element of surprise.

They let the sound of motorbikes die away. Then they pushed themselves to their feet again and continued to march. Danny fell in beside Caitlin. 'You okay?' he asked.

A flicker of a smile crossed her face. 'Maybe I'll let you rub down my sore bits when this is over,' she said. She looked towards

Ripley. 'Up your pace,' she called. The unit increased their speed through the vegetation. Danny found himself frowning. He couldn't work Caitlin out. Her ruthless soldiering and flirtatious nature seemed at odds with each other. She distracted him. Made him think about Clara and the baby, and not in a good way.

After five minutes, the terrain made an upward incline, sudden and sharp. The brow of this hill was thirty metres ahead. Danny pushed his body to maintain a constant speed and, five metres from the brow, hit the ground, along with the others. Keeping low, he crawled through the undergrowth to the brow of the hill, and looked beyond it.

Chikunda. Time check, 11.28.

Danny checked the position of the sun. Almost directly over-head, it wouldn't glint on the lens of his spotting scope, which he now removed from his pack. He scanned the main road passing through the village – distance from their position about five hundred metres – and counted two militants. There was no traffic in this out-of-the-way place, but there was movement. The militants were carrying what looked like sandbags and placing them in the middle of the road. Barricades. A couple more guys appeared from the north, with more sandbags. They piled them on top of the existing ones, then left the original two militants to engage their weapons over the top of their barricade. One of them had a rifle, the other a grenade launcher.

'They're expecting an attack from the south,' Ripley said.

'Fucking muppets,' Tony breathed. 'They've driven up and down the road. Can't they tell we're not there?'

For a moment, Danny didn't say anything. A strategy was forming in his brain. He directed his sight towards the three rec-tangular buildings – blocks North, West and East – on the eastern side of the village. There was activity there. Two guys standing guard at Block North, another five milling about the open area, and maybe three different militants coming in and out of blocks East and West. A single vehicle – it looked like an open-topped Land Rover – parked by the side of the road adjacent to the buildings, about fifteen metres from Block West.

'We've got movement of armed personnel around the target area we identified. A minimum of twelve hostiles, including the two on the road,' he said. He scanned north towards the three circular huts in the enclosed compound. There was a gate to the compound on the western side, by the road, but no sign of anyone in the vicinity of those three huts, nor anyone guarding them. 'I'd say the three circular huts are deserted. No evidence of armed personnel. We need to concentrate on blocks North, West and East. They're guarding something there. My money's on it being Target Red and Target Blue.'

'What if it isn't?' Tony said.

Danny lowered his scope and turned to look at Tony. 'What if it is?' he said.

He lifted the scope and kept eyes on for another thirty seconds. A man emerged from the westernmost building. 'What the fuck . . .' Danny breathed.

'What is it?' Ripley asked.

Danny focused in on the figure. From the brief glimpse he got of his features, he could see that he wasn't African. 'We've got a Chinese guy down there,' he said.

'What are the Chinks doing in the Nigerian bush?' Tony said. 'I'm guessing they're not here to open up a fucking takeaway.'

Danny didn't have an answer to that. Maybe when they got down there, he'd ask the Chinese guy what he found so interesting about this Nigerian backwater – if he was still alive.

But that wasn't their main concern. First they had to get down there and clear the village. Four of them, against a minimum of twelve armed militants.

He lowered his scope and turned to the others. 'Here's what we're going to do,' he said.

SEVEN

Five minutes later, they were on the move again. They headed east, away from the road, still in patrol formation – Ripley, Danny, Caitlin, then Tony – through the treeline, and started skirting anticlockwise around Chikunda. It took twenty minutes for them to reach the point where they were directly east of the village. From the treeline, they could see across about thirty metres of open, deforested ground, to where the three rectangular buildings – Blocks North, West and East – were located. Their line of sight was compromised by Block East, but they could hear the militants occasionally shouting at each other, though not in English.

Danny, Ripley and Tony bedded in, ten metres apart, protected by the treeline, prostrate on the ground with their weapons cocked and ready in front of them. Caitlin parted company, slipping silently away into the vegetation. Her objective: to continue skirting anticlockwise through the trees, heading towards the north of the village. The militants were expecting an attack from the south. Caitlin was going to give them something else to think about. It was a risk letting one person go alone, but that was all they needed to make the diversion, and Caitlin's 7.62s would make the most noise. The remaining three personnel could take advantage of it.

They lay in silence for a full twenty minutes, bathed in sweat from the burning midday sun. Heat haze rose from the ground between Danny and Block East, but nobody appeared in the open ground between the block and the treeline, although the occasional shout still pierced the air. He found himself wondering about the Chinese guy. Who the hell was he, and what was he

79

doing embedded with an Islamist faction like Boko Haram? It didn't make any kind of sense. He had the uneasy sensation that there was more going on here than met the eye.

His earpiece crackled. Caitlin's voice came through. '*In position*,' she said.

Tony's voice: '*Have you removed your suppressor, love?*'

'*Thanks, Grandad, I'm not stupid.*'

Danny checked his watch. 12.28 hrs. 'Stick to the schedule,' he said.

And the schedule meant that in two minutes' time, Boko Haram were going to get a surprise from the north. A loud surprise that would hopefully put the shits up them and throw them into confusion.

Danny got up to his knees, removed his pack, took out his two Claymores in their canvas bag and slung them over his shoulder. He was aware of Tony doing the same thing, ten metres to his right.

12.29 hrs. A minute to go.

The moment the second hand on Danny's watch clicked on to 12.30 hrs, there were two sharp explosions from the north in quick succession. They echoed around Chikunda, and were followed by a sudden surge of shouting from the area enclosed by the rectangular buildings. Danny heard Tony mutter: 'Good girl.'

Ten seconds later, they heard Caitlin release two bursts of fire towards the village. It sounded dramatic. Like the village was under heavy attack from the north.

And that was clearly what the militants thought.

The voices became louder, more argumentative. And confused. Very confused – which was just how the unit wanted them. Caitlin's dummy attack was doing its work. Danny listened hard. In the absence of eyes-on, he had to rely on his hearing to work out what the militants were doing. Amid all the shouting, he could tell that most of them were moving away from the buildings, westwards, towards the road. He didn't doubt that a few would have remained by Block North – especially if there were hostages there – but it sounded like the bulk of the armed personnel were mobilising to head off the attack to the north.

Danny looked towards Ripley and Tony. They were watching him closely, ready for his command. He held one hand up to say: hold steady.

Gunfire from the direction of the road: the sharp, distinctive bark of single rounds from AK-47s. Five seconds later, the whoosh of a rocket being fired from a launcher, followed by the shrapnel-crack as the rocket detonated.

'Caitlin, you okay?'

No answer over the radio. Caitlin's reply came in the form of a third burst of fire. It was hard to tell, but Danny thought it was coming from a slightly different direction from the first two. There was no denying it: Caitlin knew what she was doing. The Boko Haram fighters would think they were being attacked from more than one location.

Danny swiped his hand down, indicating to Tony that they should advance. Thankfully, now things were hotting up, Tony's professionalism had replaced his argumentative nature. Danny was reminded that beneath it all, he was bloody good soldier.

The two Regiment guys moved swiftly and silently. Ripley remained in position, covering them with his rifle. With their weapons engaged, Danny and Tony ran lightly across the open ground, shielded from the view of any remaining militants by the back of Block East. Ten metres from it, they stopped and laid one Claymore each on the ground ten metres apart. These rectangular anti-personnel mines contained 680 grams of C4 and 700 ball-bearings each. They could certainly do a job on a handful of militants. Danny extended the bipod legs on the bottom of his mine and dug them about a third of the way into the ground next to a tree stump, making sure that the side of the mine that read 'Front Towards Enemy' was pointing away from the trees – he always thought that if you had to rely on that printed instruction, you were probably in the wrong job ...

Tony set his mine next to a small patch of rough brush. The equipment was hardly invisible, but by the time Boko Haram saw them, it would hopefully be too late for them to do anything about it. Moving quickly, they inserted the blasting caps at the end of their firing wires into each Claymore, then unwound the wires back towards the treeline. Gunshot raged in the north of the village, and Danny heard two more RPGs being launched. Caitlin's voice came over his earpiece. '*Heading back to a north-easterly position.*' A good tactic. The militants could fire north all they wanted: they weren't going to find their attacker.

But they'd left the centre of the village long enough for Danny and Tony to lay their booby trap.

Within thirty seconds they were back behind the treeline, still unwinding the firing wires. They continued for five metres, then went to ground again. Danny faced out towards the village, the detonating clacker at the other end of his firing wire just inches from his hand, his rifle pointing back out towards the open ground.

'On my command, open up,' he said into his boom mike.

There was a pause. The gunfire in the centre of the village had died down. A few confused shouts from the militants drifted towards the unit's location.

'Go,' Danny said.

The guys had switched their weapons to semi-automatic. They each fired a couple of shots, which hit the back of the building wall, each one erupting in a little shower of loose stone. No heavy bursts: these were simply a beacon. A way of drawing the confused militants back towards their trap.

And from the sound of things, it was working.

The shouts in the village increased in intensity. They drew closer. Danny tried to separate different voices out of the hubbub and estimate how many guys were actively defending the village. Seven, he thought. Maybe eight. If they could take that many out with one hit, it would be a lot simpler to pick off the remainder.

It just required a bit of patience.

Forty-five seconds passed. The voices grew nearer. There was one, louder than most, that seemed to be coordinating the others. They sounded like they had reached the village centre. The loud voice barked an instruction.

Danny spoke into his mike. 'They're coming,' he said. 'Hold your fire.'

Ten seconds later, the first two militants appeared, one from either end of Block East. Despite the heat, they wore black woollen hats with khaki bandanas wrapped around the brow, and military jackets in the same colour. They were clutching their weapons nervously, and even from this distance of thirty metres, Danny's sharp eyes could see the sweat glistening on their faces. The militants were looking wild-eyed towards the forest: they wouldn't have seen the Claymore mines even if they hadn't been semi-concealed.

The militant to Danny's left fired a burst of rounds into the tree-line, but it was much too high to be of any concern to the Regiment. As the noise of the burst died away, the gunman called something over his shoulder. Over the next ten seconds, four more militants appeared from the other side of the building. They were dressed identically to the others, apart from one guy who had a red bandana round his hat. Danny marked him out as the leader, and this impression was confirmed when he barked an instruction and pointed sharply forward towards the trees.

Two more militants appeared from round the front of the building. Eight in all. Each of them had their weapons pointing towards the forest. Two bursts of fire thundered towards the guys, but again the rounds hit uselessly halfway up the trees. When there was no return of fire, the militants stepped forward a couple of metres, their gait suddenly a little bolder.

One more joined them from the front of the building.

Danny's hands left his rifle and felt for the clacker of his Claymore.

'In three,' he breathed over the radio – an instruction to Tony, but also a warning to the others to expect the blast.

'Two . . .'

Another random, useless burst of fire from the militants. As a group, they moved forward a metre.

'One . . .'

Suddenly one of the militants shouted out. Danny realised it was the leader with the red bandana. He'd seen one of the Claymores, and his eyes were following the firing wire back towards the treeline. He started screaming a frenzied instruction – whether to retreat or to fire, Danny didn't know.

And it didn't matter either way. They were all in the kill zone.

'Go,' he said, and with a sharp yank of his wrist he engaged his clacker at exactly the same time as Tony.

The sudden crack of the double explosion sent a shock through Danny's body as he immediately covered his head with his hands to shield his skull from any stray shrapnel that might back-blast from the Claymores, and pierce the protection of the trees. His position meant he didn't witness the immediate effect of the blast.

But he sure as hell heard it.

Two Claymores at point-blank range would have been enough to clear a football pitch. The screams that suddenly came from their direction immediately told Danny that the munitions had done their work effectively. He looked up. All nine guys were on the ground. Five were motionless, clearly already dead. One was sitting up – Danny recognised him as the leader with the red bandana. He was clutching his head as blood pissed out from behind his clenched hands. The remaining three were squirming on the ground, clutching legs and arms, inhuman wails echoing from their damaged throats.

The three Regiment men rose quickly from the undergrowth. Weapons engaged, they advanced. They burst through the tree-line and covered the open ground in less than ten seconds. When he was ten metres from the guy sitting up, and with his weapon still switched to semi-automatic, Danny released a single suppressed round to the wide open target of the man's chest. He hit the ground with a heavy slump, but Danny was already firing a shot at one of the remaining three militants, eight metres to his ten o'clock, while Tony and Ripley took out one more man apiece.

The Claymore had only detonated ten seconds ago. Already the battlefield was strewn with dead.

Danny ran to the cover of Block East, back pressed against the wall next to the right-hand corner. Tony went left and took up a similar position at the other end of the building, while Ripley went down on to one knee in the firing position, covering their backs. Carefully, Danny looked round the corner.

Of the three rectangular buildings surrounding the open area they had identified on the satellite map, Danny now had line of sight on Block North, in which he reckoned Targets Red and Blue were being held. The two guards were still there, but they looked terrified. Their backs were up against the wooden door in the centre of the building, and they were waving their rifles around like a couple of kids with sticks.

Distance to the targets: forty-five metres. Danny lined up his first shot – the nearest of the two guards – and squeezed the trigger of his assault rifle.

Target down.

The second guard fired a burst. It was poorly aimed, but Danny withdrew behind the protection of the building to avoid any stray rounds. Three seconds later he looked round again. The door to Block North was open ninety degrees. The guard was ineptly hiding behind it: Danny could see the barrel of his raised weapon peeping out from the leading edge of the door.

With his own rifle engaged, Danny stepped out from behind the protection of Block East. As he paced forward, he fired five shots directly into the solid wood door. The wood splintered harshly as the armour-piercing rounds penetrated it. The militant tumbled forward, the whole side of his body pierced by Danny's rounds.

Danny had full line of sight on the central area now. It was deserted. Two motorbikes were lying on their side in the dirt, and there was a circle of ash in the centre where they had clearly lit a fire the night before. Apart from that, nothing and no one. Tony emerged from the other side of Block East, carefully panning the area with his weapon. Ripley appeared fifteen metres behind Danny, his weapon also engaged.

'Ten guys down,' Danny said into his mike. 'We still have at least two hostiles remaining. Caitlin, what's your status?'

'*I've got eyes on the road heading north,*' she replied through the headset.

'Stay put. Lay down fire on any vehicle you see trying to head that way.'

'*Roger that.*'

'I'm heading into Block North,' Danny told Tony and Ripley. 'Keep me covered.'

Danny ran towards the building. The door was still half-open, the two dead and bleeding militants stopping it from opening fully or swinging shut. Danny didn't lower his weapon as he approached. Inside the building was an unknown quantity. He needed to be fully prepared for anything.

Two metres from the open door, his senses were hit by a musty smell. There was a chilling silence. If the High Commissioner and his aide were inside, they were keeping very still. Danny found himself holding his breath as he stepped over one of the dead bodies and used the door to shield himself from the entrance.

There was a good chance of enemy shooters inside the block. Danny couldn't present himself as a target in the doorway. Not without a distraction. He pulled a flashbang from his ops waist-coat. It would put the shits up the hostages, but they'd get over it. More importantly, it would give Danny the crucial seconds he needed to take out any enemy targets.

He switched on the Surefire torch fitted to his rifle's rack. Then he pulled the pin on his grenade, stretched out his arm and chucked the flashbang inside.

A two-second pause, then an ear-cracking explosion split the air.

Danny swung round, his huge form filling the door frame. The light from his torch pierced the smoke that had billowed into the dark room. Danny scanned the length of it, searching for figures, his finger resting lightly on the trigger.

There were no militants. No gunmen. No threats.

But there was something at the far end of the building, to Danny's right. A strange, shapeless mass lying on the ground. It filled him with apprehension, even though he didn't quite know what it was.

Danny stepped towards it, the beam of his torch cutting through the gloom and the curling tendrils of smoke, lighting up this unknown object at the end of the room.

When he was ten metres away, he stopped. He had suddenly realised what he was looking at.

He was sickened by what he saw.

EIGHT

It was a body, and it was in two pieces.

The legs and torso were naked, apart from a pair of soiled underpants. The head was resting, on its side, on the corpse's bare torso. The tendons of its severed neck glistened. The wooden floor around the victim oozed with fresh blood. The victim was, quite clearly, newly dead.

Danny took another five paces towards the grisly scene. He tilted his head so it was aligned with the victim's, and shone his torch directly at it. The eyes were open, the grey hair bloody and matted. But there was no mistaking the features: Danny recognised them immediately from the photograph he'd seen of the High Commissioner back in Lagos.

'I've located Target Red,' he said into the radio. 'He's dead. Beheaded.'

Tony's voice: '*Any sign of Target Blue?*'

'Negative. Target Blue still missing. The op is still a go. We need to find him.'

A moment's pause, then Tony's voice cracked like a whip. '*We've got movement! A car engine's just started up. Get out here!*'

Danny turned his back on the dead body and sprinted out of Block North. Tony and Ripley were already running east, past Block West towards the road. He could hear the high-pitched screeching of a car engine accelerating fast.

Tony and Ripley disappeared from view behind Block West. It took five seconds for Danny to catch up with them, by which time they were on their knees in the firing position, ten metres apart at the side of the road. The open-topped Land Rover that they'd seen from the high ground was already a hundred metres from their position, past the sandbag blockade, surrounded by a cloud of dust as it sped up the incline to the south of Chikunda, back in the direction from which the unit had arrived. Whoever was driving the vehicle knew what they were doing. Its trajectory veered slightly from left to right: an erratically moving target that was harder to fire on.

Ripley and Tony both discharged a couple of rounds in quick succession. Danny saw three of them ricochet off the Land Rover's chassis, but none found their intended mark in the vehicle's tyres. The Land Rover was 130 metres away now. The terrain dipped slightly, hiding the lower half of the vehicle from view.

'We'll never hit it!' Danny shouted. 'Ripley, find Caitlin. Finish your sweep of the village. Tony, follow me.'

Without waiting for a response, Danny sprinted back to the open area between the three rectangular buildings. The two discarded motorbikes were still lying there. He and Tony reached them at exactly the same time, and there was no need for them to discuss their next move.

The bikes had obviously been left in a hurry: their keys still hung from the ignition. Danny and Tony flicked their safetys on, slung their rifles across their backs then took a bike each, hauled them upwards and started the engines. In less than two seconds they were screeching back to the road, where they swerved sharply to the south, following the Land Rover.

Danny opened the throttle fully. Dust and small stones stung his face as he surged south, swerving to avoid the barricades that the Boko Haram militants had left in the road. In his side mirror he saw that Tony was just a couple of metres behind him, skilfully maintaining single file so they didn't present a broad, easy target for any shooters. The bike shook violently as Danny negotiated the road, whose shitty state was much more of a problem now they didn't have the good suspension and all-terrain tyres of the Range Rover.

The vegetation on either side of the road was a blur of green in Danny's peripheral vision. He kept his eyes forward, but the

Land Rover had disappeared from sight. All he could do was burn up the road as fast as he could.

As the road started to undulate, Danny almost came off the bike. But his balance was good as he flew over the dips in the terrain. The road continued at an upward incline for thirty metres. Danny flew over a sharp brow. The bike skidded as it hit the ground again. But now Danny slammed the brakes on. The bike spun ninety degrees as it came to a sharp halt, and Danny heard – but did not see – Tony doing the same thing behind him. He let the bike fall, then quickly knelt down into the firing position, every sense tuned in to the scene that had unfolded in front of him.

The road ahead was perfectly straight. At first it dipped. Then, after about fifty metres, the gradient turned sharply upwards, leading to the brow of yet another hill approximately 110 metres from their position. On the brow of the hill were two figures, one directly in front of the other. Danny zoomed in through the sight on his rifle, then described what he saw out loud for Tony's benefit.

'I've got eyes on the Chinese guy. He's armed with a pistol, and he has his weapon aimed at the head of a guy I don't recognise.'

By now, Tony was next to him in the firing position, also viewing the scene. 'Target Blue?' he asked.

'Almost certainly.'

'Can we drop him?'

Danny gave it a moment's thought. There was no wind, but the Chinese guy was too well shielded by his hostage to present a big enough target at this distance. 'Negative,' he said.

Five seconds passed. Standoff.

'You're the boss,' Tony breathed. Danny thought he detected a slightly malicious edge to his voice. 'What the fuck do we do now?'

Two seconds later, the decision was made for them.

The retort of gunfire echoed from the brow of the hill. Two shots. Through his sight, Danny saw the momentary muzzle flashes. Target Blue hit the floor. Pure instinct kicked in. Danny realigned his weapon just a fraction, hoping to take a shot at the Chinese militant. The retort from his own rifle filled the air, but the round flew uselessly as his target dived, then rolled back over the brow of the hill.

'Fucker shot our guy,' Tony shouted. 'Shoulder and leg. He's probably still alive.'

'Get to him!' Danny barked.

It was obviously a tactic to delay the two soldiers, but it was a good one. They'd lost Target Red, and Danny was fucked if they were going to lose Target Blue as well. The two Regiment guys jumped back on to their motorbikes. They floored it south, across the open ground, and accelerated up the sharp incline to where the hostage was lying on the ground. Fifteen metres from the brow of the hill, Danny could hear the hostage shouting in pain, even above the manic scream of the motorbikes' engines. They skidded to a second halt alongside him. Danny immediately let his bike fall again and knelt down beside the patient. He had scruffy, shoulder-length hair and a several days' worth of stubble. His face was caked in dirt. He was wearing blue jeans and a dirty check shirt, and blood was seeping dramatically all down his right sleeve, and even worse over his right trouser leg. He had a wonky nose – it looked like the Boko Haram fuckers had broken it at some point.

'We've lost the Chink!' Tony shouted, but all Danny's attention was now on the hostage.

'Hugh Deakin?' Danny shouted.

There was just a pained whimper from the hostage.

'We should fucking go after him!' Tony urged.

'Is your name Hugh Deakin?' Danny shouted. The blood loss was heavy – he needed to keep his guy talking.

The hostage nodded, his breath coming in short, shaky gasps. Danny ripped his bloodied shirt in two to reveal the gun wound. Bad. The round had entered his upper arm about three inches below the shoulder blade. Two-inch entry wound, exit wound not much smaller. The humerus would be entirely shattered. But the leg shot was even more of a worry: if the femoral artery had been severed, the blood loss would be catastrophic.

91

'Give him a morphine shot!' Danny shouted. 'I'm going to apply tourniquets.'

Tony was staring south along the road, his face full of frustration. 'I can fucking get him, Black!'

'No!' Danny shouted. 'We deal with the hostage first.' And with his hands covered in the young man's blood, Danny pulled two tourniquets from his med pack. He had to stop the blood loss, no matter what. He wrapped one a couple of inches above the leg wound, the other above the arm wound, and pulled them both very tight, blood pissing between his fingers and all over the hostage.

As he worked, a clearly reluctant Tony activated his radio. 'We have Target Blue, repeat we have Target Blue. Ripley, Caitlin, report your status, repeat, report your status . . .'

Now that the buzz of Danny and Tony's motorbikes had faded, the centre of Chikunda was ominously silent. Ripley went about the quick, efficient business of checking that Blocks North, West and East were empty. Block East contained an impressive arms cache – four grenade launchers, a rack of AK-47s and several wooden boxes of ammunition. But no militants. Block West had clearly been an accommodation block: ten thin, dirty mattresses were dotted around the floor, with tangled piles of clothes next to them. Still no militants. And Block North contained nothing but Target Red, his head resting grotesquely on his torso. The sight left a dry, bitter taste in Ripley's mouth, but he knew there was no point wasting time on a dead man. Boko Haram could still be hiding out in the village. His job was to hunt them down.

He edged carefully towards the central road, sweat trickling from his forehead into his eyes. From the protection of Block West, he looked north then south. The road seemed to shimmer into the distance with the heat haze. Through the sight on his rifle he studied the burned-out area to the north-west. The only sign of movement was a bird that flew in and rested on the partially demolished wall of what must have once been a house, approximately two hundred metres away.

Ripley's earpiece crackled. Tony's voice: '*We have Target Blue, repeat we have Target Blue. Ripley, Caitlin, report your status, repeat, report your status.*'

Caitlin: '*Keeping eyes on the route into Chikunda from the north.*'

Ripley clocked in. 'I'm going to clear that enclosed compound with the three huts.'

The radio voices fell silent.

Ripley edged north, twenty-five metres along the road, until he came alongside the wall of the enclosed compound. It was made of solid breeze blocks, and was a good five metres high. Unscalable without any extra apparatus. He followed the wall for forty metres, then stopped behind a wooden gate, three metres high, two wide, cut into the blocks. A sturdy, well-fitting door which was, weirdly, locked from the outside with a large padlock.

Ripley considered that for a moment. It didn't make much sense. If Boko Haram had established a secure compound like this, why had they been keeping their hostages in the relatively insecure confines of Block North? Maybe they had been keeping the prisoners in here originally, and had only moved them out to conduct the execution. Or maybe they were hiding something else in the compound. Another arms cache, maybe? Ripley wanted to find out.

It would be an easy lock to force. Ripley found a rock on the ground the size of a large orange. He struck it hard, several times, against the bolt that the padlock was holding. The wood behind it splintered, and the soft metal dented and warped. Ripley had it off in thirty seconds. He engaged his rifle again and carefully kicked. The door's hinges creaked as it swung open.

'Keeping eyes on the route into Chikunda from the north.'

'*I'm going to clear that enclosed compound with the three huts.*'

Caitlin was lying on her front, on a patch of raised terrain thirty metres from the road, camouflaged by a patch of low brush. The heat was like a hammer on the back of her head. The biting frustration of hearing Target Red was dead was only slightly softened by the news that Danny and Tony had located

Target Blue, albeit badly wounded. She had to suppress her desire to make someone pay for what they'd done. An itchy trigger finger wouldn't do anybody any favours. Her job was simple. Watch the road. If reinforcements came in from the north, inform her unit mates.

She got back to scanning the road with her handheld scope. Her position was directly opposite the burned-down part of the village, and she couldn't stop herself from focusing in on those ravaged, demolished houses. She found herself picturing what it must have been like for the villagers when these Boko Haram bastards arrived. She saw smoke rising from houses that had stood there for years. Kids and women screaming. Men trying to defend their families, only to be mown down by assault rifles. She focused on what remained of one of those buildings. It was just a dilapidated wall, black with smoke scars.

She drew a sharp intake of breath. Lying at the bottom of that wall was a figure. A body. And something about it wasn't right. She zoomed in a little closer. The body was lying on its back. She had to keep her hands very still to keep it within her magnified field of view, but after examining it for a few more seconds, she was certain of something: this wasn't a Nigerian casualty. This corpse's skin was white.

An uneasy feeling grew in her chest. Who the hell was this?

She double-checked her surroundings. There was no sign of anyone. She spoke into her radio. 'I'm crossing the road to the western side. I've just seen something I want to check out.'

'*Roger that,*' came Danny's reply.

Caitlin pushed herself to her feet and started jogging towards the burned-out area and the unexpected corpse.

The tourniquet was in place. Tony had injected morphine into the casualty's leg. It seemed to have helped, but only a bit. Target Blue was in a shit state. Fresh wet blood all down the wounded arm. It had dried on his right hand and coagulated under the fingertips.

'We're British Army,' Danny told the young man. 'We're going to get you out of here.' He stood up and spoke to Tony. 'Go get our vehicle,' he said. 'We need to get on the radio back to base, call in a casualty evacuation, even if it means getting the Nigerians on board. He's not going to make it otherwise.'

Tony nodded, but the frown on his face told Danny he was fuming that Danny had overruled him about going after the Chinese guy. Without another word, he turned and started jogging back along the road.

Danny crouched down again. 'Listen carefully,' he said. 'You and me, we're going to keep talking. You got that? We're going to keep on talking . . .'

Because Danny knew that if the kid allowed himself to fall asleep, chances were he'd never wake up again . . .

'*I'm crossing the road to the western side. I've just seen something I want to check out.*'

'*Roger that.*'

Ripley was only half aware of the conversation going on in his earpiece as he edged into the compound, his senses attuned for the slightest sound or movement. He didn't know why, but the extraordinary stillness of the village was unnerving him.

Inside the enclosed compound, his brain registered everything before him in a fraction of a second. The ground was unusually free of rubble or any other random junk, as if it had been cleared out on purpose. As they'd seen from the satellite imagery and from the high ground, there were three circular huts here, each of them about seven metres in diameter. They had roughly thatched conical roofs, mud walls and wooden doors. Like the compound itself, each door was locked from the outside.

No movement. No sound. The compound still seemed empty. But Ripley could smell something. Just faintly. Something rotten.

His rifle, the butt dug into his shoulder, followed his line of sight precisely as he crossed ten metres of open ground to the first hut. This time he didn't bother with a rock. He just kicked the door in with a sturdy strike of his heel.

The hut was empty, with the exception of a pile of white over-alls against the wall to Ripley's two o'clock.

He stepped outside, his rifle still following his line of sight, crossed to the second hut and kicked the door open.

In the centre of the hut was a wooden crate, with Chinese lettering imprinted on one side. The lid was lying to one side. The crate itself was empty. Ripley left the second hut, and approached the third.

Caitlin picked her way across the rubble, assault rifle engaged. This whole area still stank of burning. She moved, sickened, past the bodies of two Nigerian children, face down in the earth. She didn't know if they'd been killed by bullets or by fire, and she didn't really want to find out. She tried to put them from her mind as she focused on her objective: the white body. It was fifteen metres ahead of her, its back slumped against a wall, facing out towards the road. She now saw that the body had a gunshot wound to its chest. It was wearing a lightweight sports jacket and pale trousers, although both of them were now spattered with mud and blood. Short blond hair, fairly clean-shaven. She had the impression that he had died much more recently than those Nigerian kids.

She crossed the intervening fifteen metres nervously. Up close, she let her rifle hang by its cord and put her free hand inside his sports jacket. She didn't hold out any hope that there would be a wallet here – the Boko Haram militants would certainly have robbed him. But her fingers touched something: the same size and shape as a credit card. Caitlin withdrew it, and saw that it was an international driving licence.

She read the name on the licence.

Hugh Deakin.

Her blood turned to ice. She double-checked the photo. It matched the face of the corpse.

She immediately spoke into her boom mike. 'Danny, it's Caitlin.'

'*Go ahead.*'

'I don't know who you've got there, but it's not Target Blue.'

'*What the fuck are you talking about?*'

'I said, it's not Target Blue. I'm with Hugh Deakin now. He's dead.'

Danny looked at the bleeding man whose life he had just saved. He was lying on the ground, his pale face wracked with pain, despite the morphine shot Tony had given him. A dreadful suspicion washed over him.

His eyes traced down the length of his patient's arm and took in the blood that had dried on his hand and congealed under his nails. It wasn't fresh.

Slowly, Danny removed his side arm. He cocked it, then pressed the barrel against the wounded man's head.

'What's your name?' he said.

The young man gave him a glazed stare.

'What's your fucking name?'

The man closed his eyes. 'Fuck you, army bitch,' he whispered.

Danny withdrew the gun for a moment and carefully examined the face. Suddenly he was back at Tony's house in Hereford, standing in his garden and looking at the front page of the *Mirror*.

Jihadi Jim: First Picture.

The wispy stubble. The broken nose.

It was him.

Danny cursed himself for not having joined the dots before. Not that it mattered, because now he was in a position to carry out the one job every member of the Regiment would have lined up to do.

He put the gun up against Jihadi Jim's forehead, and prepared to pull the trigger.

'You don't want to do that, army bitch,' Jihadi Jim whispered. His body was shaking with pain, but he still managed to look and sound as offensive as anyone Danny had ever met.

'Wrong,' said Danny Black, his voice deadly quiet. 'I *really* do. I saw what you did to that guy down in the village.'

'He squeaked like a pig. Normally they get some Valium. Not this time.'

Just killing this bastard wasn't enough. Danny wanted to hurt him. He raised his hand and thumped down hard on the gun wound. Jihadi Jim's whole body shuddered, and he hissed in agony.

'Go ahead, army bitch,' he breathed. 'Kill me now, unless you want to know what's going on in that shitty little village.'

'Nothing's going on there. Everyone's dead.'

Jihadi Jim managed a nasty smile. 'Yeah,' he said. 'But what of?'

The rotten smell was worse here. Not bad enough to make Ripley gag, but a clear indication that this final hut contained more than a few old clothes or an empty box. He listened carefully at the door. Nothing. So he kicked the door open and, weapon engaged, entered.

An overpowering stench almost knocked him double. He retched, but managed to keep control of his guts as he stood in the doorway, peered into the gloomy hut and counted the bodies.

There were five, all African. Three men, two women. All naked. Painfully thin. They were sprawled across the floor, either on their back or curled up in the foetus position. They didn't move. Against the wall, to Ripley's eleven o'clock, was a small pile of excrement. The bodies had clearly been in here for some time before they died.

Ripley didn't know what had killed these people. Malnutrition? Lack of water? But he knew this: they'd died badly.

He was on the point of stepping backwards out of the hut, when he saw a sudden movement. One of the two women was lying on her back on the right-hand side of the hut. Her abdomen had suddenly arched upwards and she let out a groan. She was still alive.

The SAS man moved out of instinct. He had morphine and antibiotics in his pack. Maybe he could help her. He let his weapon fall and knelt down by the woman's side.

Only as his knees hit the ground did he realise that this was a very bad idea.

Now that he was inside the hut and closer to the bodies, he could see them much more clearly. Their brown skin was covered with disgusting black pustules. Some of them had crusted over. Others were still weeping. The faces of the dead were frozen in expressions of agony, as if they'd been suffering terrible pain at the moment of their death. The area around their nose and mouth was smeared with what looked like dried blood. And as Ripley's eyes grew a little more used to the dim light inside the hut, he saw puddles of dried vomit and smears of liquid faeces over the corpses' bodies and the rough rush matting on the floor.

'What the fuck . . .' he breathed.

He had to get out of there. Quickly.

'What do you mean, "what of"?' Danny demanded.

Another nasty smile. 'So you haven't found the guinea pigs, army bitch?' He closed his eyes.

'What guinea pigs? What are you talking about?'

Jihadi Jim winced with pain. 'In the huts . . . dead . . .'

A beat.

'Dead of what?'

Jihadi Jim opened his eyes again. '*I will drive him into the Hellfire,*' he whispered. '*And what will explain to you that which Hellfire is? It allows nothing to endure, and leaves nothing alone. It blackens the skins of men.*'

'I'm only going to ask you one more time, you piece of shit. Dead of what?'

'Plague, army bitch,' he said. 'Plague.'

It happened before Ripley could move. The woman's abdomen suddenly arched again. Her eyes opened and she tilted her head towards him, revealing a face whose brown skin was covered in horrible black patches. At the same time, a dreadful, harsh, grating sound escaped her throat. She coughed explosively. A warm spray hit Ripley directly in the face.

'*Jesus . . .*'

Ripley jumped to his feet and jumped back. The woman was still again. Ripley touched his face then looked at his fingertips. They were covered in a watery, pale red liquid.

'*Jesus . . . Jesus!*'

He staggered outside and felt himself wanting to retch again. This time he couldn't hold it in. He vomited on to the dusty ground. Then he wiped the watery blood from his face with his sleeve. It had turned sticky and sputum-like.

It was everywhere.

NINE

Ripley's voice, taut and stressed, came over the radio. '*Can you hear me?*'

Danny tried to keep his own voice level: 'Go ahead.'

'*Fucking hell, mate, I've got a pile of Nigerian stiffs here. They died of some kind of . . . I don't know, some kind of . . . infection, and one of them's coughed out their fucking guts, all over my face.*'

A pause.

'What's your current location?'

'*I'm in the compound. It was locked from the outside. I forced my way in. I thought there'd be another fucking arms cache or something . . .*'

Danny stood up. 'I'll be right there.'

Danny looked down at Jihadi Jim. It would be a second's work to nail him, but the reality was that they needed him alive. He had information, and that information had bought him some time – as the bastard had no doubt calculated it would.

Instead, Danny turned his back on him. He spoke into the radio. 'Tony, I'm leaving the kid. Hold off on that cas-evac. Pick him up when you've got the vehicle. Bring him back to the village, and for fuck's sake keep him alive.'

'*What's going on?*'

'Just do it.'

Danny jumped on his bike, fired up the engine and sped back towards Chikunda. As the road levelled out, he could see Caitlin, misty through the heat haze, running along the road from the north end of the village. Hard to judge distances, but she was about three hundred metres away from Danny, and probably only fifty from the compound. He didn't want to say over the radio

101

what Jihadi Jim had just told him – it would freak Ripley out – but he had to stop Caitlin making contact with his mate . . .

He crouched down over the handlebars and concentrated on maintaining his speed. The bike bumped heavily over the rough road. As he sped past Block West he could see that Caitlin was still fifty metres from him, but just fifteen from the entrance to the compound where Ripley was. He engaged the brakes and skidded to a noisy halt, before letting the bike fall to the ground, its engine still turning over.

'*Stop where you are!*' he shouted. '*Don't move!*'

Caitlin halted. She inclined her head, clearly confused by Danny's instruction. Danny sprinted towards her. He was ten metres from the entrance to the compound when Ripley appeared at the open gate. His eyes looked slightly wild, and his dirty face glistened with a faintly pink smudge.

'Tell me what happened,' Danny said.

'There are five bodies in a hut. They're infected with something. One of them was still just alive – she coughed over my face.' Ripley clearly recognised something in Danny's expression. 'You know what it is,' he said. 'Tell me.'

Danny took a couple of steps towards his mate. 'You're probably fine,' he said. But before he could take another step forward, Ripley had pulled his side arm and was pointing it directly at Danny.

'Keep your distance, mucker,' he said. 'And don't fucking mollycoddle me. What did they die of?'

Danny fixed Ripley with a stare. 'Plague,' he said.

Ripley closed his eyes momentarily, but he didn't lower his weapon. 'Wait there,' he said. 'If I see you enter this compound, I'm going to fucking shoot you, got it?' He stepped backwards.

'Ripley . . .'

'You're going to have a kid, Danny. Do the right thing.'

Danny froze as those words hit him. He hadn't even been thinking about that. Caitlin was looking at him strangely. 'He's right,' she said. 'You can't approach. I won't let you.'

Danny looked to his right. He could see the Range Rover approaching through the heat haze at a distance of about five hundred metres. He hoped Tony had managed to keep Jihadi Jim alive.

Ripley reappeared. He had a bundle of white material in his arms. 'I saw this in one of the huts. It's a hazmat suit. I'm going to isolate myself.'

'Mate . . .'

'Fucking listen to me, Danny,' Ripley said, and for the first time his voice wavered. 'You need to get on to Porton Down. There must be something I can take . . .'

He started to get into his hazmat suit. Legs first, then arms, then he pulled the white hood over his face. When he spoke again, his voice came over the radio set. *I'm going to tell you what was in there while I still can,' he said. 'There are three males, two females, all naked. Their hut was locked from the outside – I'm guessing they were guinea pigs of some kind. They have kind of black pustules over their bodies. They've been shitting themselves and vomiting. There's an open box in one of the huts with Chinese lettering on the side.'*

'It's weaponised,' Danny muttered so only Caitlin could hear him. 'Someone was checking their virus works.'

'Which is why they cleared the village first,' Caitlin said, her voice soft with shock. 'And why they didn't do this in Boko Haram heartland. They didn't want to risk killing their own.'

'You need some water,' Danny called out. He took his own water bottle from his waistcoat and started carrying it towards his mate.

Ripley didn't hesitate. He quickly engaged his weapon and pointed it directly at Danny. 'Throw it,' he said.

Danny paused, but then did as Ripley said. The water bottle landed with a thud at his friend's feet. From the corner of his vision, Danny could see that the Range Rover had come to a halt twenty metres from their position. 'We're going to get you a medic,' Danny said quietly. 'Antibiotics . . . antiviral . . . whatever you need. You're going to be alright.' He hoped he sounded convincing. He wasn't sure that he did.

He ran towards the Range Rover. He could see Jihadi Jim sitting in the passenger seat, his head back, staring at the roof. He strode round to the passenger door, yanked it open and pulled him out of the vehicle before Tony had even had chance to alight. He dragged him away from the Range Rover and gripped him by the throat. 'Get on the ground,' he hissed. 'If I see you move, I'll kill you, and I don't care what you know.'

He pushed the kid to the floor. Then he strode back to the Range Rover.

'What the hell's going on?' Tony demanded. 'What's wrong with Ripley? What's the deal with Target Blue? Why aren't we chasing that fucking Chinese guy?'

'We need to get on to comms with Hereford,' Danny told him curtly.

He crossed over to the vehicle, with its radio pack installed beneath the seats, and made the call.

TEN

Riyadh, Saudi Arabia. 15.00 hrs Arabic Standard Time.

Hugo Buckingham had hoped never to return to the Middle East. He had spent a lot of time here as a younger man, and had even grown fond of Riyadh with all its peculiarities. But a stint in Syria with a wild SAS soldier called Danny Black, and several brushes with death, had made him reluctant to leave the comfort of his desk in the MI6 building.

He had felt fear pressing down on his shoulders as the British Airways 747 cruised over the desert kingdom. Sitting in the comfort of his first class seat, he picked out the billowing chimneys of the oil fields, and desert settlements, insignificantly small compared to the vast sand dunes. And his mind drifted to thoughts of Danny Black. He knew the SAS man had walked the wrong side of the line out in Syria. Even better, he knew there were factions in the CIA who would be very happy for Black to meet with a terminal accident. All Buckingham had to do was say the word. Buckingham liked having that power. It made him feel good. As he flew into an unknown situation in Saudi, it was comforting to remind himself that he had a talent for oneupmanship. He could manipulate people. He was good at it. It gave him a little bit of confidence about the job ahead.

There were no diplomatic privileges at the airport. He was here under the radar, so he queued up at passport control with all the other ordinary passengers. A Saudi immigration official in full traditional robes and headdress examined his passport carefully, stamped it and politely let him into the country. Buckingham knew enough about the way things were in Riyadh to realise that the Saudi secret police – not an organisation you wanted to get on the wrong side of – would be aware of his presence within about twenty-four hours. When that happened, he knew that a black vehicle, probably a Mercedes, would sidle up to him in the street and a polite but firm official would ask him to come downtown for a little 'chat'. But Buckingham fully expected to be safely housed in the British Embassy by then. He was here for a single conversation, nothing more. As soon as the conversation was over, he'd head to the embassy and await further instructions.

Buckingham hadn't exactly forgotten how hot it was in this part of the world, but it was always a surprise to be hit by the brutal force of the Saudi climate. He winced as he stepped outside the air-conditioned terminal at Riyadh King Khalid International Airport. At least, he thought to himself, it wasn't high summer, when it was intolerable to be outside even for a few seconds. Still, he was glad to get into an air-conditioned taxi – it was covered with a thin dusting of sand – and head into central Riyadh.

Buckingham had always found Riyadh to be a city of contrasts. The spectacular, modern, high-rise buildings showed how rich the country was. But they sprouted from areas where the buildings were low and traditional, where the mosques, the hijabs and the burkas acted as constant reminders that this was a deeply conservative and religious place. The call to prayer sounded five times a day. Alcohol was banned. It was illegal for women to drive a car. Riyadh was modern and medieval at the same time.

'Al-Dirah district,' he told his cab driver in flawless Arabic. He had learned, in his time here, that it was quite usual to talk down to those whom you considered inferior. It was something Buckingham had no problem with, and he spoke with curt sharpness that came quite naturally. The driver was wearing white robes, just like the passport officials. And while he wasn't exactly unfriendly, Buckingham caught his suspicious glance in the rear-view mirror on more than one occasion. He understood why. Al-Dirah district could hold an unwelcome surprise for unsuspecting foreigners. 'Drive,' he instructed the driver. 'I haven't got all day.'

His voice was full of arrogant confidence. But it disguised the anxiety he felt. If the location of the meeting had been up to him, he would have suggested anywhere but Al-Dirah. But the word had come through to MI6 from their contact, by complicated means that Buckingham was hazy about, that he should present himself outside the entrance to the souq on the western side of Dirah Square, and wait for Ahmed bin Ali al-Essa to make contact.

They headed south through heavy traffic towards the centre, past high-rise construction sites and along broad, palm-tree-lined highways. They passed extravagant, elegant hotels and ornate mosques. As they continued through the centre, the impressive structures gave way to smaller, more ramshackle buildings. On the outskirts of Al-Dirah district, Buckingham told his cab to stop, paid his fare and continued on foot.

It was crowded in this part of town. In his slacks and open-necked shirt, Buckingham was out of place: the only person in Western clothes amid a sea of white robes and black hijabs. Nobody seemed to pay him much attention though – Westerners were not uncommon in Saudi – and he kept his head down as he continued south, past street stalls ripe with colourful fruit, strange bric-a-brac shops selling all manner of ornate ornaments, spice stalls and small supermarkets with neon signs brightly lit even though it was daytime.

Buckingham followed the crowds. He knew where they were headed, and was happy that he could peel away from them after five minutes, and cut through several side streets that took him in a broadly westerly direction towards the souq where his RV was to take place.

Three stalls lined the exterior of the souq. One sold cloth – it was piled high in neat compartments behind wooden counters – and sandals, hundreds of them hung up on the walls and from the ceiling, which filled the air with a smell of new leather. The second sold pungent dried fish from enormous bins. The third sold dates – huge baskets of them, many different varieties, some as fat as oranges. Buckingham took up position outside the date stall. He checked his watch. Almost 4 p.m., which meant he had arrived bang on time.

He glanced around, trying not to look anxious, but at the same time trying to ascertain if any of the pedestrians milling around this area were watching him. He had seen a picture of this Ahmed back in London, but it was difficult to distinguish individuals among a crowd all wearing the same garb. He took a starched handkerchief from his jacket pocket, and dabbed his sweaty forehead.

A voice in his ear. Arabic. 'Dates? You want to try them?'

Buckingham looked round sharply. A rather seedy-looking stallholder was giving him a toothless grin. Buckingham shook his head and looked away.

'Very good dates!' the stallholder insisted.

'Leave me alone,' Buckingham snapped back in Arabic.

'I give you a good price!'

Buckingham rounded on him. '*Leave me alone!*'

The stallholder looked offended, but he retreated behind his baskets of dates.

Buckingham checked his watch, silently cursing himself for making such a scene. He should have just bought some dates and remained forgettable. He wasn't cut out for this sort of work. Two minutes past four. He felt slightly sick. What if Ahmed didn't turn up? Informants like him were notoriously unreliable. Would Selby insist on him staying here in Riyadh until they made contact? Buckingham muttered a curse under his breath, and wiped the sweat from his brow with his right sleeve. He wished he was back in his London flat with a bottle of decent claret at his side.

'Mr Buckingham?'

Buckingham started. The voice – low and calm – came from over his left shoulder. He spun round. A handsome Saudi man in traditional Arab dress was standing just half a metre from him. He had dark skin, brown eyes and a very neatly trimmed goatee beard. He didn't look Buckingham in the eye, but instead made a show of surveying the scene in front of him.

'Mr Al-Essa,' Buckingham said, before adding a traditional greeting: '*As-salaam-alaykum.*'

'*Wa'alaykum salaam,*' the Saudi man replied. 'I suggest we dispense with the formalities, Mr Buckingham. Please call me Ahmed.'

Buckingham was about to say 'Hugo', but held back at the last minute. He wanted this foreigner to give him a bit of bloody respect, to show him who was boss.

'Were you followed from the airport?' Ahmed asked.

'You don't need to worry about that,' Buckingham replied with false confidence. In truth, he had absolutely no idea whether he'd been followed or not. He hadn't even been looking.

'I need to worry about a great many things,' Ahmed said. 'Meeting you is not entirely safe for me. Shall we walk?'

Buckingham jutted out his chin. He didn't like this man's tone. 'I'd rather talk,' he said.

But Ahmed had already stepped out into the crowd while putting on a pair of dark aviator shades. Buckingham had no option but to follow. 'I apologise that I cannot meet you in more comfortable surroundings,' Ahmed said. 'I find I can never know quite who is listening. At least in a crowd our conversation is private, even if our meeting is not.'

'It's not entirely convenient,' Buckingham said.

'Do you know where we are?'

Buckingham nodded. 'Just to the west of Dirah Square.'

'And do you know what the Western tourists call it?'

Buckingham hesitated. 'Of course. They call it Chop Chop Square.'

Nobody could live in Riyadh for any amount of time without knowing about Chop Chop Square. Most of the time it looked like any of a number of broad plazas in the Saudi capital. Sandwiched between the Grand Mosque and the medieval fort of Qasr al-Masmak, it was lined with benches and palm trees. On some days there would be a market there. On others, it served a very different purpose. In the centre of the square there was a single drain. The drain was not there to capture rainwater. It was there to capture blood, because Chop Chop Square was where the judicial beheadings of the kingdom of Saudi took place. In all his time in Riyadh, he had avoided this place. The idea of being present at an execution made him feel weak and nauseous.

'I refuse to go there, Mr Al-Essa. We can find somewhere much more suitable for our . . .'

'I insist,' Ahmed said, turning to look at him. Buckingham saw his own sweaty, crestfallen face in the aviator shades. 'There is something I want you to understand.'

Buckingham suppressed a shudder, and dabbed his forehead with his handkerchief again. 'Now look here, Mr . . .'

But Ahmed was already walking away. Buckingham had to follow.

Two minutes later, they turned a corner and found themselves in Chop Chop Square itself. It was busy – there must have been five hundred people there, Buckingham estimated, lining the perimeter and looking on to the centre of the plaza, where three police cars were parked, seemingly randomly, alongside a nondescript and unmarked pale blue van. There were the occasional shouts from the crowd, and a general buzz of excitement and impatience. Over the heads of the assembled people, Buckingham could just make out a woman kneeling on the ground, her hands tied behind her back, flanked by two Saudis in tan uniforms, armed with rifles. A few metres beyond her, standing by one of the police cars, was a burly looking man in a white *dishdasha* and red-checked headcloth. A scabbard hung by his belt, with the hilt of a sword protruding.

Buckingham felt his limbs go weak. 'Oh, good Lord . . .' he breathed.

As they loitered at the back of the crowd, nobody seemed to pay Ahmed and Buckingham any notice. They were all too busy looking towards the centre of the square. Buckingham felt his extremities trembling.

'Look,' he said. 'It's really not necessary to . . .'

'It is necessary,' Ahmed said.

Buckingham looked back towards the centre of the square, at the woman kneeling on the ground. He swallowed hard, but found himself horrifically drawn to the scene. 'Who is she?' he asked.

'A maid from one of the hotels,' Ahmed said. 'Accused of apostasy. It is a crime, in Saudi Arabia, to renounce your religion. Ordinarily, if the family of the accused's victim requests clemency, it will be granted. But apostasy is a victimless crime. The maid has no hope of surviving.'

Buckingham was revolted by the scene, yet he couldn't take his eyes off the man with the sword as he stepped forward towards the prisoner. There was a hush among the crowd. Even from a distance, Buckingham heard a faint hiss as the executioner slid the sword from its scabbard. The blade was about four feet long, rather narrow, and slightly curved at the end.

'If she is lucky,' Ahmed said quietly, 'the executioner will remove her head with a single swipe of his sword. He has plenty of practice, so he is skilled.'

The executioner stepped forward. He was now standing right by the prisoner. Buckingham would have expected her to be writhing and screaming, but in fact she was strangely still. She clearly knew there was no way out.

Suddenly, there was a shout from the crowd. Buckingham realised that several people had turned to look at him. One of them grabbed him by the wrist and started yanking him through the crowd towards the front. He went weak with panic. A sea of people opened up in front of them as Buckingham, terrified by this unexpected turn of events, didn't know whether to shout in protest or remain submissive. He found himself jabbering quietly and incoherently, struggling ineffectually to escape the Saudi man's grasp, but in ten seconds he was at the very front of the crowd. The man who had grabbed his wrist shouted, in Arabic: 'The infidel! Look at the infidel!'

He felt his knees go weak. What were they doing? *What the hell was going on?* A wild, irrational thought struck him: was *he* being taken to the executioner too?

No. The man holding him kept Buckingham at the front of the crowd. The condemned woman looked towards him and their eyes met. Buckingham had never seen an expression of such hopeless fear.

It wasn't to last for long.

The executioner put his right leg forward, his left leg back. He weirdly reminded Buckingham of a person stretching his calf before doing some exercise.

He gently touched the back of the prisoner's neck with the blade. Buckingham saw her body tense up with a jerk.

The executioner raised the sword high above his head. Sunlight glinted on the metal. He swung the blade back down in a single, well-practised, smooth motion. Buckingham clenched his eyes shut, but not quickly enough. He saw the blade slice effortlessly through the muscle and bone of the prisoner's neck. He heard the distant, wet thud of the blade splitting the flesh. He saw a momentary gush of blood spurt from the severed neck, as the head rolled to the ground and the body slumped to one side. There was a strange, involuntary moan from the crowd.

Buckingham felt an almost overpowering desire to vomit. He pressed his free hand to his mouth, and only just managed to keep it in. The Saudi man who had grabbed him released his wrist. Without even a word or a glance, he melted away with the rest of the crowd. But while all the other locals were leaving the centre of the square, Ahmed was walking towards Buckingham. His face looked deeply sorrowful.

'I am told her body will be put on display for three days after she has been beheaded,' Ahmed said quietly as he stared impassively towards the centre of the square.

From the corner of his eye, Buckingham saw the executioner carefully wiping his sword with a large piece of white cloth. Two soldiers were bending down to pick up the body at either end. A third had efficiently wrapped the head in another piece of cloth and was carrying it towards the pale blue van. They all appeared entirely unmoved by what had just happened. The aftermath of the execution was clearly of very little interest to the crowd, either, which was already quickly thinning out.

'Why ... why did that man grab me?' Buckingham asked

weakly. He realised that his heart was pumping, and he was slightly short of breath.

'Because you are an infidel. It is said that if the last face the condemned person sees is not a Muslim's, all hope of reaching Paradise is lost to them. That is why they pulled you to the front of the crowd: to ensure that poor woman is damned for all eternity.' He bowed his head and paused for a few seconds, allowing Buckingham to steady his breath. 'Perhaps you are wondering why I brought you here,' he continued. 'Let me explain. Whenever I am in Riyadh, I come here to remind myself of what occurs on a regular basis.' He gave Buckingham a strange, sad smile. 'I'm sure you have been told that my reasons for ...' – he glanced around, and seemed to search for words that wouldn't incriminate him – '...for helping you are broadly financial. They are not. I am a proud Muslim, but this? This is not right. I can only hope that the West's influence on Saudi, and on my own poor country of Qatar, will put an end to atrocities like this.' He turned to look at Buckingham. 'All that remains here is for a janitor to wash away the blood from the ground. I do not think it is something we need to watch, do you?'

Pale-faced and subdued, Buckingham shook his head. Ahmed turned and walked away from the square, Buckingham following. He was finding it difficult to get the measure of Ahmed. It was a given, in this line of work, that informants were likely to be peculiar people. And Buckingham supposed it made some sort of perverse sense that Ahmed would want to justify himself and what he was doing.

Ahmed led them to a small, bustling cafe five minutes from Chop Chop Square. There was no sign here that a woman had been casually executed nearby. They took a seat in the corner. Ahmed ordered coffee in small, handleless cups, and a plate of sweet cakes. Then he turned to Buckingham, his expression serious. 'So, Mr Buckingham, what is it that I can do for you?'

Buckingham sipped his coffee. He noticed that his hand was still shaking slightly, and he took a moment to steady it. He drew a deep, calming breath. 'You can tell me about the Caliph,' he said.

He immediately noticed a slight tightening around Ahmed's eyes. His informant took a sip of his own coffee, then neatly placed his cup on the table in front of him.

'You want to know what a caliph is?' Ahmed asked. He didn't catch Buckingham's eye.

'Not a caliph, old sport,' Buckingham said. His voice cracked slightly as he spoke. '*The* Caliph.'

No response.

'London is getting chatter about a Middle Eastern figure – possibly Qatari – who goes by that name. We're very keen to find him. We know you have a large, gossiping workforce. Let's face facts – there must be a substantial number of people in your employment who actively support the extremist policies of ISIS and the like. We know that you keep your ear to the ground for information such as this. Your intelligence has been very useful to us in the past. Someone in your organisation must have heard of this character. I need to find out as much about him as possible.'

Ahmed stared out across the cafe. Almost absent-mindedly he took his coffee cup and drained it. Only when he had put the empty cup back on the table again did he turn to Buckingham. 'I'm sorry,' he said. 'I have no idea what you're talking about.' He made to stand up. 'If you'll excuse me, Mr Buckingham, I have business to attend to.'

Buckingham grabbed his arm. Ahmed looked at his fist in surprise.

Buckingham blinked heavily. He was still in a state of shock, but he managed to put a bit of firmness in his voice. 'Sit down, please,' he said quietly.

His informant meekly did as he was told.

'You say you've never heard of the Caliph?' Buckingham continued. 'I'm afraid I don't believe you.'

Ahmed's face grew angry. 'Mr Buckingham, how dare you ...'

'It would be a simple matter,' Buckingham interrupted, his words falling over themselves, 'to let it be known that we've spoken.'

Ahmed fell silent. He eyed Buckingham carefully.

'Let's face facts, Ahmed,' Buckingham said. 'I can't imagine that all your business associates across the Gulf are as well disposed as you are towards British Intelligence. And it would be the simplest thing in the world for a substantial payment to land in one of your bank accounts that could easily be traced back to Whitehall. And even easier to leak the paperwork.'

A mixture of emotions crossed Ahmed's face. Irritation. Reluctance. Maybe even fear.

'You are blackmailing me?'

'I prefer to think of it as gentle persuasion.'

Ahmed bowed his head. 'You ask too much,' he said.

'I don't see why.'

'Of *course* you don't see why,' Ahmed hissed. 'That is because you know nothing of the Caliph.' He looked around the cafe, as though he was checking whether anybody else was watching them. Then he pulled a mobile phone from his pocket and dialled a number. Buckingham, fluent in Arabic, understood the instruction he gave when the call was answered: *Meet me outside the Saad Habbal cafe immediately.* Ahmed hung up and then addressed Buckingham. 'Follow me,' he said.

A black Rolls Royce with tinted windows had already pulled up outside the cafe by the time they stepped outside, one passenger door held open by an Arabic man. Ahmed held out one hand to indicate that Buckingham should climb inside. Buckingham looked around a bit nervously, but then did as his informant told him. Ahmed climbed in next to him, and the vehicle slipped away into the traffic.

There was a glass screen dividing the front of the car from the back. Buckingham took that to mean they could talk freely. Ahmed removed his sunglasses, tucked them into his robes, then looked out of his tinted side window. 'I know nothing of the Caliph except rumour and hearsay,' he said quietly. 'But what I have heard turns my stomach more than the sickening events we have just witnessed in Chop Chop Square.'

'Go on.'

'They say he is a man of great cruelty. He wishes to establish a single Islamist caliphate as it used to exist in antiquity, not only across the Middle East, but across Africa as well. Such a caliphate would be ruled under Sharia law, and sights such as the one we have just witnessed would be commonplace. You know something of how the Taliban ruled in Afghanistan, before 9/11. This caliphate would make *their* foul regime appear positively moderate. The rumour is that the Caliph is behind insurgencies across the Middle East and Africa. Islamic State, Boko Haram – few of their militants would recognise the Caliph's face, or know his real name, but their activities have his fingerprints all over them. Or so it is said.'

'How can we find out more about him?' Buckingham demanded.

'Have you not listened to a word I've said, Mr Buckingham? *Nobody* will talk to you about him.' Ahmed gave him an angry stare, then suddenly flicked a switch on his door. The glass dividing screen slid down with a hiss, but the driver kept his eyes forward as he continued to negotiate the afternoon traffic.

'Mustafa,' Ahmed said, still speaking in English. 'Tell this gentleman what you know about the Caliph.'

Buckingham happened to be watching Mustafa's face in the rear-view mirror. The driver visibly flinched at the question. He didn't reply.

'Mustafa?'

'I am sorry, sir. I do not know what you are talking about.'

Ahmed gave Buckingham a meaningful look, then turned his attention back to his driver. 'It's okay, Mustafa,' he said. 'What you say will not leave this car. I will see to it that you receive double pay for your troubles today.'

Mustafa nervously moistened his lips. 'I'm sorry sir,' he said. 'I do not know anything about any Caliph.'

An uncomfortable silence as Mustafa's gaze flickered nervously in the rear-view mirror.

'Thank you, Mustafa,' Ahmed said finally, and he raised the dividing window again. 'Mustafa has children, you see,' he told Buckingham. 'Their safety is more important to him than anything else. But he would not have been able to tell you any-thing useful. Few people have ever seen the Caliph. Fewer still know who or where he is.' He paused for a moment. 'Perhaps he doesn't really exist. Perhaps he is just a story, invented to scare people. *Say your prayers, or the Caliph will come for you.* Perhaps he is a high-ranking Qatari politician. Perhaps he is a desert wan-derer. I do not know, but I have told you everything I can.' Before Buckingham could interrupt, he held up one finger. 'Do not ask me any more,' he said. 'I will help you up to a point, but if the rumours about the Caliph are true and he finds out that I have spoken to you about him, it will not be me whom he targets. It will be those closest to me, and I will not risk their safety for any-thing. Not even for your precious British Intelligence.'

Ahmed turned to look out of the window again. 'I will be returning to Qatar in the morning,' he said, 'and I have a lot to do before then. May I offer you the use of my driver to take you somewhere. The airport? The British Embassy? I would seri-ously recommend that you do not spend any more time than is necessary in this part of the world, if you insist upon making enquiries about that type of person.' From a pocket in his robes he removed his sunglasses and put them on. 'As you've just wit-nessed,' he said, 'dark things have a habit of happening here, even when the sun is out.'

Sir Colin Seldon, Chief of MI6, had a glass of Laurent Perrier in one hand and a canapé in the other. Sometimes he felt he lived off canapés. He popped it in his mouth, took a sip of champagne, and smiled blandly at the woman in the sequinned dress who was wittering on at him. He could hardly hear what she was saying, here under the vaulted ceilings of Westminster Hall. It was packed with people chattering noisily, the men in dinner suits, even though it was only early evening, as they congregated to welcome the French president on a state visit. Their conversations almost drowned out the sound of the excellent string quartet in the far corner of the hall. He glanced at his watch. Another half hour before he could politely leave.

Over the shoulder of the woman he saw a face he recognised. Smart suit, neat black hair – an SIS intelligence officer, though Seldon was damned if he could remember his name. He was trying to catch Seldon's eye, and his face was serious.

Seldon gave the woman his most winning smile. 'I'm terribly sorry,' he said. 'Would you excuse me for just one moment?'

Without waiting for a reply, he walked over to where the intelligence officer was standing. 'News?' he breathed.

'Bixby sent me, sir.' And from the look on the officer's face, Seldon could tell it was going to be bad. He was practised at absorbing information at events such as this without allowing his expression to register what was going on. But this tested his skills. He grew increasingly nauseous as listened to the intel.

'Dead?' he repeated, when the officer paused for breath. 'Both of them?'

The intelligence officer nodded.

'How?'

'The aide was just shot, Sir Colin. The High Commissioner, I'm afraid . . .' He used his forefinger to make a slicing gesture at his throat.

Seldon removed his glasses and pinched his nose. 'Fucking animals,' he breathed. 'Boko Haram?'

'Yes, Sir Colin. And I'm afraid there's more.'

Seldon stared at the intelligence officer as he reeled off more bad news than the chief had heard in a year. Not only was a British-born jihadi on the site, it seemed to be Jihadi Jim, last seen performing executions on the Iraq–Syria border. And that wasn't the worst of it. There was the suggestion of a biological agent in the vicinity. One of the SAS team infected. The chief felt his blood chilling at this new intelligence.

'We've protocols in place?' he asked.

'Yes, Sir Colin. Porton Down are on standby. We can get them there overnight, on your say-so.'

'Do it,' Seldon said. 'Is there any sign that the beheading was videoed?'

'None,' said the intelligence officer. 'But I think we must

assume that it was. There's no real reason to do it otherwise. Could be an hour before they release it, could be a month. The median wait time is six days.'

Seldon swore under his breath. 'Keep this from the media until I've discussed it with Whitehall. Are the Nigerians aware?'

'No sir.'

'Keep it that way. They'll only mess things up even more. Now get to work.'

The intelligence officer nodded and left. Seldon scanned the room. It didn't take long for him to pick out Tessa Gorman's face. The Foreign Secretary was talking to a couple of minor dignitaries on the other side of the room. Their gazes locked, and she seemed immediately to understand that Seldon had something serious to say. She excused herself and crossed the chamber to talk to him.

'Well?'

He gave her the news. She was a lot worse at hiding her emotions than he was.

'Is the bioagent being contained?' she asked.

Seldon nodded. 'A Porton Down team are on their way. But in my opinion, if Boko Haram want to start spreading diseases round their country, that's the Nigerians' problem, not ours.'

'Agreed. I need to tell the PM about the High Commissioner immediately,' she said.

'Wait,' Seldon told her. 'It's more complicated than you think.'

Gorman raised an eyebrow, clearly indicating that she didn't appreciate being spoken to like that. But she kept quiet and allowed Seldon to continue. 'Think about it, Tessa. Someone needs to take the fall for this. We can't shift the blame to the Nigerians. It'll mean military action against Boko Haram, and nobody's got the stomach for that. Your lot aren't going to take the blame. The way I see it, we're only left with one option.'

'The army?'

Seldon nodded. 'A catastrophic failure by the Regiment. I know these people – I can promise you they'll have broken a few SOPs along the way which we can make stick. It's by far the best way. The public hold them in high regard. They can take a hit far better than we can.'

'You're thinking along the lines of Gibraltar?' Gorman asked. 'I heard it was touch and go whether those SAS men got put away for excessive force.'

'Exactly. Or even Northern Ireland – we're pulling back Regiment personnel to be questioned about jobs in the Province as we speak. They can deal with it, and it gets us out of a hole.'

The Foreign Secretary thought about that for a moment. 'Let's get the team out of Nigeria as quickly as we can,' she said. 'We can work out what to do with them when they're back in the UK. Now excuse me, the PM's over there, I need to catch him before he gets up to give his speech . . .'

'Call sign Bravo Nine Delta, this is Zero Alpha.'

The radio communication from Hereford was scratchy and indistinct. But welcome. It had been forty-five minutes since Danny had made the call. He'd explained in detail about what had happened: about the High Commissioner and his aide, about Jihadi Jim and the strange Chinese man, and of course about Ripley. The radio operator had listened in silence, then told them to stand by.

'Go ahead, Zero Alpha,' Danny said.

'A team from Porton Down is en route to your location. ETA 05.00 hrs. Covert insertion – we're keeping this quiet from the Nigerians.'

'Roger that.'

'Your instructions are to keep the patient isolated. You understand what that means?'

Danny, Tony and Caitlin exchanged a look. 'Yeah,' Danny said, 'we understand.'

'What's the status of your prisoner?'

Danny looked over at Jihadi Jim. He was lying by the side of the road shivering, his eyes rolling, his pale face sweating. 'Bad,' he said.

'Can you question him?'

'He's barely conscious.'

'*Do what you can to keep him alive until the medics get there.*'

'Are we being airlifted out?'

'*Not immediately. When the medics arrive, they'll try to treat the patient in situ. You need to stay on the ground and provide close protection while they do that.*'

'Roger that.' A pause. Danny glanced at Tony. 'We need to track the Chinese guy down.'

'*That's a negative. Your instructions are to remain where you are.*'

'We can locate him. The roads are bad, we can catch him up.'

'*Negative. Keep the patient isolated. Do not move from your position, repeat, do not move from your position.*'

Danny swallowed his frustration. 'Do Ripley's family know what's happening?'

'*Negative. London want this kept quiet for now. Any more questions?*'

Danny had none. 'Bravo Nine Delta out,' he said, and the radio went quiet.

But Danny's head was noisy. Something wasn't right. London were making a bad call. Why were they so insistent that all the unit stayed *in situ*, when some lunatic with a bioweapon was on the loose?

Time check. 17.32. Caitlin moved over to where the prisoner was lying. She knelt down beside him and started examining the wound. Tony sidled up to Danny. 'He'll try to make a run for it, you know.'

Danny glanced at the prisoner. 'He's not going anywhere.'

'I'm not talking about this fucker. I'm talking about Ripley.'

'Why would he do that? He isolated himself, didn't he?'

'He's all fucking noble now, but there'll come a point when he's not thinking straight. He won't want to just sit there and take what's coming to him. Look, Black, all I'm saying is, nobody would know if we put Ripley out of his misery before he has a chance to spread the infection. I'll do it if you don't want to. We can say he tried to escape and we . . .'

'Forget it, Tony. The medics are going to sort Ripley out.'

Tony gave a dismissive snort. 'Right,' he said.

'We've got other things to worry about, apart from Ripley,'

Danny said. It was true. He estimated that it was an hour till sunset. And just under twelve hours until the Porton Down team got here. In the meantime, they were exposed and in the open. Boko Haram militants could return at any minute.

Danny turned to what remained of his team. 'We need to get off the road,' he said.

ELEVEN

'What you have to understand, is that the secret of effective counter-terrorism intelligence work lies in answering three simple questions: who, what and how.'

Spud Glover stood by the door of a small office on the third floor of the MI6 building. It was getting late – almost seven – and he was pissed off. A petite woman with dark skin, a head scarf, fashionable thick-rimmed glasses and a smart navy trouser suit sat at a desk. She had a small pile of manilla folders in front of her. Her name was Eleanor. When they'd met for the first time that morning, she had taken Spud rather by surprise. It wasn't just that this woman who was clearly a Muslim, with her rather plain hijab, was working for the security services. It was also this: Eleanor was a looker. She floated his boat.

His first thought was one of relief that he'd kept his powder dry by not responding to the advances of Tony's missus the previous afternoon, after the others had been hauled in to base. Don't dip your pen in the company inkwell, he'd told himself. Or maybe he'd been giving himself an excuse not to reveal the network of scars and sores that now made up his abdomen. And maybe that was why he hadn't found himself flirting with Eleanor quite as outrageously as he once might have done.

As the day went on, however, she had started to irritate the hell out of him – not least because she was reading the folders at the same time as talking rather absent-mindedly to him, as if he was just an afterthought. And then, of course, there was the way she sounded like a teacher talking to an ignorant schoolboy.

'*Who* do we think might represent a threat? *What* opportunity might such a person have for carrying out such a threat? And *how* might they do it? Does that make sense, Spud? You'll tell me if I'm going too fast for you?'

'Don't you worry about it, love. I'm just about keeping up.'

'Once you've answered *those* questions, you have a more *important* question to answer: what behaviour does your subject display when they're preparing a strike? We call these behaviours "terrorist attack pre-incident indicators", or "TAPIs" for short.' She gave him a hard look when she saw he was staring into the middle distance above her head. 'Can you tell me what TAPIs stands for?' she asked.

'Aren't you supposed to be reading those files?'

Eleanor removed her glasses, laid them upside down on the files, and turned to look at him.

'Spud,' she said. 'The idea of you shadowing me is that you *learn* something about what we do here. It's going to be rather difficult for both of us if you're going to take that attitude.'

'Terrorist attack pre-incident indicators, TAPIs for short. Trust me, love, I've seen more terrorists than you've had hot dinners. The best indicator that they're going to attack is when they pull out a gun and try to shoot you. And the best counter-attack is to shoot them first. Maybe they didn't teach you that at spy school?'

'There's no such thing as spy school,' Eleanor said primly.

'Did they sit you down in a classroom and teach you this stuff?'

'Well, yes, but . . .'

'Then you've been to spy school. And it sounds to me like you never bunked off.'

She gave him a withering look. 'You're impossible,' she said. She replaced her glasses and turned back to her file. Spud continued to loiter by the door. It was true what she said. When it became clear that Spud was in no state for active service, the Ruperts and suits had given him a choice: honourable discharge with full army pension, or they'd try to find other work for him within the Regiment. That meant a desk job, pushing bits of paper from one side of a desk to another. But for Spud, paperwork was one down from scrubbing the toilets, and so some bright spark had come up with the idea of having him shadow an MI6 intelligence officer. The idea was that he would learn something about the intelligence trade, with a view to moving into that field.

At least, that was the headline. The reality, Spud knew, was that everybody at the Firm saw him as a lump of muscle, only there to provide spooks like Eleanor with backup when they were out in the field. He was a glorified bodyguard, and his first day in the new job had been about as bad as he'd expected. He'd have given anything to be out in the field, even if it was just tagging along on the Nigerian job with Danny and the others. And at times he thought his body would be up to it. But then, he'd make an unexpected movement – not much, just a sudden turn or a twist of his head – and a sharp jolt of pain would shoot down his abdomen, or he'd be overcome with a fit of coughing that wouldn't stop. A constant reminder that his last op had left him in a very bad state indeed – a state in which he was of no use to his Regiment mates.

As these thoughts repeated themselves in his mind, Spud stood in silence as Eleanor continued reading through her files. He supposed she meant well, but her habit of talking like a text book didn't half get on his wick. He'd like to put some of these spooks on the ground in a war zone, see how far their so-called expertise got them then.

He noticed that Eleanor seemed to be reading a particular file for the second time. 'Something interesting?' he asked.

'Maybe,' she murmured.

Spud knew what she was looking for. The order had come down from the head shed: there had been intelligence chatter about an extremist who called himself the Caliph. A selected batch of intelligence officers were now hunting down any reference to such a character. It was a painstaking operation. Lots of police and other intelligence reports were computerised, but plenty had been written by hand. Hence the pile of manilla folders on Eleanor's desk. And hence Spud's reluctance to help her with the donkey work. Reading wasn't his strong point.

He stepped towards the table and glanced at the file. It was neatly packed with small type, and had a black and white picture of a Middle Eastern–looking man with a trim beard. 'What is it?' he said.

'West Midlands Police report.'

'And?'

She scanned down the document again.

'*All* these files have some sort of mention of a "caliph", but they're all very non-specific. A caliph is an Islamic ruler – that's a historical fact. We can't drag people in simply for talking about history. I've got files here on university professors, TV researchers, all sorts of people. They've all made public utterances about caliphs and caliphates, and they're all entirely innocent, so far as I can tell. *This* one's a little different. West Midlands Police pulled over this cab driver, name of Kalifa al-Meghrani, in Dudley, on the outskirts of Birmingham, about five weeks ago. Nothing serious – it seems he was just operating without a licence, but they took him into custody when he started losing his temper with them. Here's the interesting bit – one of the police officers involved reported that he shouted words to the effect of "I'll set the fucking Caliph on you."' She frowned. 'It's pretty thin,' she said, half to herself.

'What's the problem?' Spud said. Finally, here was something he knew how to deal with. 'We can be up the M1 in three hours. Let's go ask this weirdo what he meant.'

He was halfway to the door when Eleanor said, 'Sit down, Spud, for goodness sake.'

'What's the problem?'

'We can't just go barging *in* on this man. There are *protocols* we have to follow.'

Spud blinked. 'You think this piece of shit might know where the bad guys are, and you're worried about protocol? Take my word for it, love – ten minutes with me and you won't be able to stop him talking. He'll be *begging* to talk.'

'This isn't the dark ages, Spud. Confessions obtained by coercion are notoriously unreliable. In any case, there is a lot we can learn without even making contact with this man.'

'For fuck's sake,' Spud said. 'Look at him. You telling me he doesn't tick all the boxes?'

Eleanor sighed. 'You're making an elementary mistake, Spud. It's the first thing we're taught. You're making decisions based on stereotypes and your own prejudices. I mean, look at me – if you saw me in the street, would you think I worked for MI6?'

She had a point.

'*Anyone* can be a terrorist, you know. Race is a particularly poor indicator. If you're only looking for one type of person, you'll miss hundreds of other groups and individuals who might be planning . . .'

'Alright, alright.' Spud waved one hand to shut her up. 'You're the one that's been to spy school. Just don't blame me when the nutter blows up a plane.'

'You see?' Eleanor said. 'You *see*? He's gone from a minicab driver to a crazy plane bomber in your head in about thirty seconds. Things are a lot more complicated than that in our world. Terrorists are rarely insane, you know? If you're going to beat them, you have to get inside their heads, try and see the world from their point of view . . .'

'You wouldn't want to get inside the heads of some of the cunts I've met.' Spud knew he sounded surly, but he couldn't help it. 'What's his address?'

'If you think I'm going to tell you *that*, you're quite mistaken.' And as Spud's frown darkened, she continued: 'Look, I'm not saying we won't *speak* to him.'

'What are you saying then?'

'That we're going to do our homework. We're going to find out everything there is on record about Kalifa al-Meghrani, and we're going to decide whether he's a likely suspect based on more than just the colour of his skin.'

'That could take ages.'

'Of *course* it won't. We'll just pull in everything we know from the police national computer and GCHQ, we'll examine his banking records and passport applications. We'll have a measure of the man within a few hours. You didn't have any *other* plans, did

127

you?' She gave him a slightly sheepish smile. 'You think you might be able to manage an all-nighter without getting too exhausted?'

Jesus, Spud thought. Was she flirting with him? He almost replied. He *almost* told her that if he could withstand a 36-hour resistance-to-interrogation training session, or dig in to a jungle ditch for a week on hard rations and nothing but a plastic bag to shit in, or endure the worst excess of the Syrian *mukhabarat*, a night in a warm London office sifting through dry old intelligence papers was unlikely to tax him unduly. But he didn't. What would be the point? Eleanor had made her decision about him, and that wasn't going to change in a hurry.

'I'll fetch us some coffee, shall I,' she said brightly, 'and then I'll order up the relevant information. Make yourself comfortable, Spud. I think you'll learn a lot tonight, about the way the world *really* works.'

She smiled at him, scraped her chair back and left the room. Spud walked over to the table and looked again at the picture on the file. Kalifa al-Meghrani looked back. Was she right, he wondered. Was Spud just assuming the worst about this guy because of the way he looked?

He didn't think so. Spud didn't care about his nationality or the colour of his skin. He didn't care if he was white, black, brown or fucking purple. Experience had taught him that it was a very good idea to mistrust everyone.

And he knew this: a man who hurled abuse like that at a copper needed a few questions asking of him, and Spud would be more than happy to be the question master.

TWELVE

21.00 hrs, African Standard Time.

Nightfall. The air was heavy again. More rain was on its way.

Danny was alone, lying on his front, on the western side of the road that ran through Chikunda. The ETA for their pick-up was 05.00 hrs. Eight hours from now. Ordinarily they would have moved away from the village and hidden elsewhere, in case more militants turned up. But Ripley couldn't be moved, and Danny sure as hell wasn't going to leave him.

He was facing the compound where his mate was holed up, and was positioned about thirty metres from the entrance, camouflaged by a patch of scrubby vegetation. His weapon was engaged, and he was surveying the entrance through the sight clipped to the top of his rifle. Caitlin had headed off to watch the road to the north. Tony was i/c the vehicle, along with the prisoner. Jihadi Jim was in a shit state. He'd lost a lot of blood and it looked like infection was setting in to the wound. He was barely conscious. He needed medical treatment before they could interrogate him any further. No point asking a question of a man who can't understand you. So Tony had taken him with him to the south of the village, where he could stay in the relative protection of the car. Tony himself had opened up the back of the vehicle, put the rear seats down and set up the .50 sniper rifle, so it was pointing out of the boot towards the road. That meant he could warn the unit of any movement into the village from that direction, and deal with it if necessary.

So far there was nothing. It seemed like everyone was avoiding this tiny, out-of-the-way village. Maybe this part of the world was always this quiet. Or maybe people were scared to come here.

A voice came over Danny's earpiece. Ripley. Or at least, a washed-out version of him. His voice was thin and weak, but strangely matter-of-fact: '*I've got shivers . . . cramp in my lower abdomen.*'

There had been no movement from Ripley's compound, at least not for the past three hours. At about 18.00 he had appeared at the open gate. Danny had watched him carefully through his viewfinder. His mate looked terrible. He had removed the hazmat hood. There were streaks where sweat had run down his dirty face. His eyes looked bloodshot. His lips were dry and cracked. As he stood there, looking out, there was a kind of desperation in his expression. Danny remembered what Tony had said. *He'll try to make a run for it, you know . . . He's all fucking noble now, but there'll come a point when he's not thinking straight. He won't want to just sit there and take what's coming to him . . .* For a moment, Danny thought Ripley was going to prove Tony right, and with a tight ball of heat in his chest he was ready to squeeze his trigger finger if that happened. But it didn't. Ripley had replaced the hood and disappeared back into the compound.

Danny hadn't seen him since. But he'd heard him. Irregular updates, dispassionately reported over his headset, like he was a doctor reporting objectively on a patient.

'*My eyes are burning . . .*'

'*My temperature's rising . . .*'

'*I can feel fluid on my chest . . .*'

Danny knew what his friend was doing: trying to give them as much information as possible for the medics when they arrived. Frustration bubbled under his skin. Somewhere, not far away, a Chinese man knew something about a weaponised strain of plague. Danny recalled learning about plague in school. The Black Death – contagious, virulent, responsible for the death of millions. Whoever it was who thought playing with this virus was a good idea needed to be stopped. But all Danny and the unit could do was hole up, hunker down and wait.

And wait.

21.45. The rain arrived, heavy and brutal. Danny was soaked in seconds, but he didn't change his position. Just after 22.00 hrs Ripley appeared again. It was hard to make him out in any detail through the darkness and the rain, but Danny could tell he had deteriorated. He collapsed to his knees in the gateway to the compound, clutched his head in his hands.

His voice came over the radio, cracked and indistinct. '*I fucking shat myself . . .*'

Danny himself felt sick. As Ripley staggered back into the compound, he felt anger burning in his stomach. He wanted to get to the vehicle, slap their prisoner into consciousness and pump him for information, to find out who was behind this. But they had their orders from Hereford. Stay in position. Keep Ripley isolated. Wait for the team from Porton Down.

05.00 hrs seemed a very long way off. Danny wondered how the team from the government's high-security military science park would get here. His money was on a military aircraft taking the team as far as an aircraft carrier somewhere in the Atlantic, then a long-range stealth chopper bringing them into Nigerian airspace. He told himself that if anyone could sort Ripley out, it was them. But they needed to get here quickly. His mate was going downhill, fast.

The rain seemed to seep into his bones as his earpiece crackled. Caitlin's voice: '*Vehicle heading in from the north.*'

Danny gave it moment's thought. 'Let it pass through,' he said. 'If it stops in the village, I'll deal with it.'

'Roger that.'

Sixty seconds later, bright headlights burned through the rain along the road to Danny's left. Distance, three hundred metres, but approaching fast. Twenty seconds later, a beat-up old saloon car sped just ten metres past Danny's covert position in a cloud of spray. Muddy water sluiced over the SAS man, but the car didn't stop. White headlamps turned to red rear lights. Danny spoke into his radio. 'All clear from my position. Let us know when it's passed to the south.'

Two minutes later, Tony's voice: '*All clear.*'

Chikunda was dark again, and the only sound was the hammering of the rain. Danny shivered. He realised his temperature must be dropping, but he couldn't move or get protection from the rain. He needed to keep eyes on the compound.

Sudden movement. Ripley's dark silhouette appeared at the compound gateway. His shoulders seemed hunched, and his head looked from left to right. He took several steps forward. He was limping.

'Shit,' Danny breathed. His trigger finger suddenly felt very heavy. Ripley was five metres out of the compound, and he was looking round, clumsily. It was clear to Danny that his mate's head wasn't in the right place. No Regiment man's movement was as leaden as that.

I'll do it if you don't want to. We can say he tried to escape . . .

Danny stood up. Rain dripped from his clothes and hair. 'Ripley!' he shouted.

Ripley stopped. There was twenty-five metres between them. Danny raised his weapon and eyed his mate through the scope. He switched on his Surefire torch.

Jesus.

Ripley had winced sharply, but was now looking directly towards the light. He'd removed his hazmat hood again. Danny could see why: there was dark staining round his mouth where he'd been coughing up blood, and maybe vomit. There were sores over his face. He was clutching his chest, as though worried his lungs might spill out. He was shivering badly, and Danny could tell he was in pain.

'There's medics on their way, mucker. They'll sort you out . . .'

As he said these words, he heard his voice falter. At the rate Ripley was going downhill, God only knew what state he'd be in by the time the Porton Down contingent arrived. And it was suddenly clear to Danny that Ripley knew this too. He spoke into the radio in a weak voice that was all but drowned out by the persistent rain.

'*Make me a promise,*' he said. He didn't wait for a reply. '*Find the fucker who did this to me, Danny . . . just find the fucker who did this.*'

Danny nodded. Then he shouted, 'You're going to beat it!' But Ripley had already turned. He was limping back to the compound. A metre from the door he suddenly bent double and Danny could hear the sound of a barking cough. It lasted for thirty seconds, before Ripley made it back through the gate.

Danny stood alone in the bleak rain of the Nigerian night. He asked himself how much longer Ripley had. It couldn't be more than a few hours. He returned to his OP, trained his weapon on the compound once more, and continued his miserable surveillance.

There was no let-up in the rain. And so, when the chopper arrived at 04.38 the following morning, it was camouflaged by the darkness and the noise. Only when it was hovering twenty metres above the main road, about fifty feet north of Danny's position, did he see or hear it: a black shadow in the sky, flying blind without any lights.

Danny got on the radio. 'The bird's coming in to land. Hold your positions until you hear from me.'

Two sets of double pressel clicks told Danny his message had been understood. Nothing from Ripley. There had been no sound from him since 22.00.

Danny rose from his lying position. His joints ached, and he had to force them into movement. He kept one eye on the compound gate as the heli touched down in the middle of the road. He'd been right. He could tell by the pointed, angular shape of the aircraft's chassis that it was a stealth Black Hawk, designed to be almost silent and to cause minimal radar splash. The rotors continued to spin as the aircraft touched down. Only when it was on the ground did the chopper's side door open – it needed to remain closed during flight for full stealth capability. From his vantage point Danny saw shadows spilling out of the aircraft. Hard to say how many – somewhere between five and ten, some of them carrying what looked like heavy flight cases. They were out of the aircraft in less than a minute. The helicopter immediately rose into the air again, banked steeply and silently, and then flew off to the west.

Danny crouched down again and examined the figures through his scope, hoping to make some kind of positive ID before he approached them. They were standing in a huddle by the side of the road. It took a moment to get his vision straight through the rain haze. There were four people in white hazmat suits, their heads and bodies completely enclosed. Accompanying them were four soldiers in desert camo gear. Danny saw the red flash of 1 Para on one of their arms, and recognised an M16 assault rifle that the Paras would certainly be carrying.

That was enough. He pushed himself up to his feet and ran towards the newcomers. No time or need for introductions. When he was fifteen metres away from them, Danny pointed towards the compound. 'He's in there,' he shouted. 'He's in a bad way. Move!'

It started to get light at 05.10 hrs. On Danny's instruction, the Para unit had already headed off to take up positions around the village to relieve Tony and Caitlin. Their orders: to stop anyone entering the village by road. The situation was highly volatile. Boko Haram militants could return at any moment. Random civilians could stray into the village. Whatever happened, they had to keep anyone and everyone away from the isolation zone. Now Caitlin was crouched down in the firing position by the external wall of the compound, ready to target anyone who tried to approach. Tony was guarding their prisoner in the Range Rover, which he'd parked up in the shadow of Block West. Danny was twenty metres from the compound entrance, keeping eyes on the Porton Down team's activities.

The lab team had been on the ground for thirty minutes. They hadn't wasted a second. Fully protected by their hazmat suits, they had entered the compound where Ripley had been isolated. From his vantage point, Danny could now see that they had erected a tent just inside the compound. He understood that it would serve as a makeshift field hospital, and also as a lab.

The rain had stopped, and as the sun rose steam hissed from the vegetation, and also from Danny's wet clothes. One of the white-suited medics appeared at the gate. He was carrying a package, which he laid on the ground, before gesturing at Danny to approach. He did so. The package was a sterile hazmat suit. Danny ripped it open and pulled the white suit – which included integrated rubber boot fittings – over his damp gear. He covered his hands with elasticated gloves. He lowered the rebreathing mask over his head and strapped the small air canister to his back. Only when he was fully protected did he move into the compound, his breath heavy and hot inside the confines of his rebreather.

Up close, he could see that the Porton Down guy had a ginger beard and glasses beneath his mask. 'Dr Mike Phillips,' he said, his voice slightly muffled by the suit. 'Is the patient a friend of yours?'

Danny nodded.

'I'm afraid it isn't good news. Come take a look.'

Danny followed him into the tent. It was rectangular, about ten metres by eight. Collapsible steel shelves containing medical equipment were lined up along the far end, with three unopened flight cases next to them. The remaining four lab guys stood round a stretcher bed in the middle of the tent. Lying on the stretcher bed was Ripley.

Or what was left of him.

The lab guys had cut open his clothes so now he was lying naked. A saline drip hung from a drip stand, the cannula inserted into his right arm. Ripley himself was unconscious. Mercifully. His hands and feet had turned black. The remainder of his body was covered in angry red lumps. Some of them were whole, others weeping a milky effluent. His lips were stained with blood, his face deathly pale. He was breathing, but with each breath there was a ghastly rasping sound, as if his lungs were protesting at having to work.

'Can you fix him?' Danny asked.

Dr Phillips shook his head. 'I don't think so. We've pumped him full of antibiotics, but he's too far gone. I need to ask you some questions. They're very important.'

Danny nodded.

'Can you tell me when the patient first came in contact with the infected bodies?'

Danny could, precisely. Ripley had radioed in his status just as Danny and Tony had made contact with Jihadi Jim. That would put it at 13.00 hrs yesterday. He relayed this information.

The lab guys exchanged a worried look. 'That means he's been infected for approximately seventeen hours, agreed?'

'Agreed,' Danny said.

Dr Phillips glanced down at his patient. 'Let's take a walk,' he said.

They left the tent. 'I don't need to tell you this is serious?' Phillips said. And when Danny didn't reply, he asked: 'How much do you know about plague?'

Danny looked towards the tent, as if to say: just what I've seen.

'Okay,' Phillips said. 'In a nutshell, what we call plague is in fact an infection called *Y. pestis*. There are three types: pneumonic, septicemic and bubonic. Bubonic plague is what people think of as Black Death – killed millions in the seventeenth century. But pneumonic is a lot more deadly.'

'Which one has Ripley got?'

Danny could see that Phillips looked uncertain through his mask. 'Both,' he said. 'And more. Look, we need to test this infection in a proper lab, but the symptoms are consistent with *Y. pestis*, with one exception. The usual incubation rate is two to three days. Ordinarily within eighteen to twenty hours, we'd be able to give the guy an antibiotic jab and he'd have a forty to sixty per cent chance of survival.'

'What are you saying?'

'It's not hard to alter the genetic structure of a bacterium,' Philips said. 'To force it to mutate, if you will, into something more virulent. I can't be certain, but I think that's what we're dealing with here. This isn't ordinary plague. It's modified. More aggressive. More deadly.'

'And weaponised?' Danny said.

'Any bio-agent can potentially be used as a weapon. If you're asking me if it's been specifically adapted for that purpose, I don't know. But I will tell you this: *Y. Pestis* is just about the oldest bio-weapon known to man. During the Second World War, the Japs

136

dropped plague-infected fleas over China. The Americans used it against the Native Americans, the Russians weaponised it in ICBMs during the Cold War. We're fully aware that rogue states *have* weaponised the bacterium. Personally I've been trying to persuade the government that the threat of an attack is very real, and it's far easier for a terrorist to release a biological agent than plant an explosive device – and potentially far deadlier. But it's amazing how they don't listen to what they don't want to hear.'

Danny felt a mass of anxiety in his gut.

'Maybe it's something else,' he said.

'Maybe. We've taken samples and we can examine them back in the UK.' He looked over at Ripley. 'But in my professional opinion, it *isn't* something else. It's modified *Y. pestis*. I'd stake my reputation on it, and between you and me, that's saying something.'

'If that virus gets released, what happens?'

'Yes, well technically it's not a virus, of course, but a b ...'

'*What happens?*'

The lab guy gave him a piercing look. 'Have you heard of Dark Winter?' he asked.

Danny shook his head.

'It was a simulation of a bio-terrorism attack, conducted about three months before 9/11. In the simulated scenario, twenty people in Oklahoma city are infected with smallpox. The study concluded that after two weeks, six thousand new infections were occurring daily, and after six weeks almost a million are dead.'

'We're talking bigger than 9/11?'

'Forget 9/11. Explosions are yesterday's news. Bombs are expensive and difficult, bioweapons are cheap and easy ...'

'I get the message. How would someone spread this particular strain of plague?'

'Any one of a number of ways. Aerosol dispersal would be effective. You could include the agent in an explosive device. A suicide cell could turn themselves into human vectors. It's a versatile weapon in the right–' He corrected himself. 'I mean the *wrong* hands.'

Danny remembered the Chinese guy, and the cool way he had shot his accomplice. He cursed himself for not having gone after the bastard, no matter what his orders had been from the head shed. He could be anywhere by now.

Now was the time to take action. The head shed wouldn't agree with what he had in mind, but they weren't here on the ground, making the calls.

Danny looked over at the tent again. 'What do we do with Ripley?' he asked.

'I estimate that he'll die within the hour. When he does, we need to burn his body and those of the other victims. It's the best way of destroying the infection. Then I understand we're to wait with you until nightfall, when the helicopter will return to pick us up. We're to bring your prisoner with us and do what we can to keep him alive until he can be questioned properly in the UK.'

Danny felt bile rising in his throat. He heard Ripley's desperate voice from the previous night. *Find the fucker who did this to me, Danny.*

Danny didn't care how good these Porton Down guys were. The chances of Jihadi Jim surviving a journey back to the UK were non-existent. What the *hell* were London playing at? The clock was ticking. Somewhere out there was a Chinese guy who knew about a weaponised strain of plague that could be deployed at any moment. There was no time to fuck around.

A second thought hit him. The ops officer's warning as they were leaving Brize Norton. *I'm not going to lie to you. You've got a habit of going against the head shed's wishes, and they don't like it. They're watching you. Think of this as a chance to make things good. Don't fuck it up.*

Danny hesitated for only a moment. 'If I need to get our prisoner conscious, can you sort it?' he asked the lab guy.

Phillips shrugged uncertainly. 'I guess,' he said. 'An adrenaline shot should do it.'

'Give me two,' Danny said.

The lab guy didn't look keen.

'You see Ripley?' Danny said. 'Two young kids. You want to

explain to *them* that you didn't do everything you could to find out how this happened?' As he spoke, he pictured Clara, heavily pregnant. The thought occurred to him that his view of the world had changed in the past few days. For him, this wasn't about the ops officer or the head shed any more.

Phillips still looked reluctant, but he couldn't withstand the hard stare Danny gave him. He walked over to the medicine shelves and retrieved two sealed, sterilised syringes, which he handed over to Danny. 'Only one shot to start with,' he said. Danny nodded. He stormed towards the exit of the compound.

'Wait,' Phillips said. Danny turned. The Porton Down guy was holding something up. A loop of green paracord with a metal disc hanging from it: Ripley's dog-tag with his army number, name and blood group etched on to it. 'It's been disinfected,' Phillips said. 'I thought you might want to keep it. Give it to his family, maybe.'

Danny accepted the dog-tag. On closer inspection, he saw there was something else hanging from the paracord. Ripley's wedding ring. They were always told to leave items like that back at base, and for good reason: if you were captured, and your enemy found your wedding ring, they could use it to torment you and get inside your head. But for a family man like Ripley, some rules were meant to be broken.

Danny clutched it firmly and turned again towards the exit.

'Leave your hazmat suit there!' Phillips shouted after him. 'We need to burn that too!'

At the exit, he stripped out of the gear, leaving it in a pile on the ground. Then he strode out towards the road, engaging his radio as he did so. 'Tony,' he spat, 'where are you? Where's the prisoner?'

He didn't have to wait for an answer. He could see the headlights of the Range Rover heading towards him from the south. He watched them approach with grim satisfaction.

To hell with Hereford and London, he told himself. It was time to get this bastard to talk.

THIRTEEN

Danny ran to the Range Rover. Tony had his back up against it, clutching his personal weapon as it was slung across his chest, carefully scanning the surrounding countryside. He looked very tired – none of them had slept for forty-eight hours – but alert nonetheless. 'What's our status?' he asked as Danny approached.

'Ripley's going to the dark side,' Danny said. 'He's got an hour, maybe less.'

There'd been no love lost between Tony and Ripley, but that didn't matter. Tony's face darkened at the news that they were about to lose one of their team.

Danny looked through the car window at Jihadi Jim. He was lying on the reclined passenger seat. His face was waxy and pale. His breathing seemed shallow. The tourniquets Danny had applied to his wounded arm and leg were saturated with congealed blood.

'The head shed wants him airlifted back to the UK for questioning,' Danny said.

'That's insane,' Tony said. 'He'll never make it.'

'Agreed. If you want my opinion, the head shed want to keep this as an African problem, like the ebola thing. But I want to know who that Chinese guy was, what he's up to and where he's going. He could be anywhere in the world by the time we get this cunt back to the UK. I say we question him now.' He held up the two shots. 'Adrenaline. These will give us a few minutes. Let's get to work on him.'

Tony shook his head. 'We can't hurt him,' he said.

'Fuck's sake, Tony, tell me you're not going soft, now of all times.'

'Just listen to me for once, Black. Look at the state he's in. If we

140

hurt him badly, he'll fucking snuff it. Then we're left with nothing.'

Danny glanced at the wounded prisoner again. Tony was obviously right. But Danny couldn't get the image of Ripley's body, rotting while he was still alive, out of his head. 'We haven't got a choice!' he spat. 'We question him now. He's not going back alive.'

'I said, *listen* to me. We *do* have a choice.' Tony was looking shifty. 'We know who this fucker is. We know who his family are and where to find them – it's in all the papers . . .'

'The Firm will never go for it.' Because the Firm, Danny thought, have got some other agenda we don't know about.

'Who said anything about the Firm?' Tony replied. 'We've got a sat phone. I know people in London who can help.'

'Who?'

'Best you don't know, sunshine,' Tony said. 'But put it this way, they owe me some favours.' He gave Danny a piercing look. 'It could be our little secret.'

Danny didn't get a chance to reply. His earpiece crackled. Caitlin. '*We've got a shooter.*'

Both men hit the ground immediately. Not a second too late. A round slammed against the chassis of the Range Rover and ricocheted on to the ground just a couple of feet from where Danny was crouched. 'Where is he?' he said into the radio, silently cursing himself for taking his eye off the ball.

'*Fifty metres on the other side of the road. I think he's got a mate. There's two of them.*'

Danny squinted in that direction. His sharp eyes picked out movement in the burned-out vegetation on the western side of the road.

'If I'm going to make the call,' Tony said, 'I need to do it now. This fucker could die on us any minute.'

'No,' Danny said, his eyes still scanning the opposite side of the road. The ops officer's words rang in his mind. Again he thought of Clara and the baby. With them back on the scene, he *definitely* didn't want to get involved with the underbelly of Tony's world. He caught more movement, approximately ten metres to the right of the original shooter.

Tony shrugged. 'Your call,' he said. Then, in a persistent, needling voice, he said: 'Fucker in the car's beginning to smell. I reckon those wounds are turning rotten. Shame about Ripley, hey? Seemed like an okay geezer. Nasty way to go.'

Danny looked back towards the compound. He heard Ripley's voice again. *Find the fucker who did this . . .*

'Caitlin,' he spoke into the radio. 'You've got eyes on both shooters?'

'*Roger that.*'

'You take the one on the right. Wait till we both have a clear shot.'

Danny set his weapon to semi-automatic. Lying flat on the ground, he focused in on the area of burned vegetation where he'd seen the movement. Half his thoughts were on the shooter. The other half were on the prisoner in the car. Tony was right. He'd never survive the questioning they needed to put him through. They needed some other kind of leverage.

An uncomfortable feeling washed over him. Who were these 'people' Tony was talking about? What side of the law did they walk, and how far did Danny want to become implicated with his activities?

The less he knew, the better.

'If you call your people,' he said, 'you do it for Ripley.'

'I'm not doing it for anyone, Black,' Tony said. 'You're the boss, remember. It's your call.'

A silence. Danny felt the anger growing in him again. He mastered it.

Find the fucker who did this . . .

Without taking his eye from his sights, he said: 'Do it.'

South London. 06.00 hrs GMT.

It was a smart detached house. A swimming pool out back. Marble columns framing the porch. And no lights on, because the household had not yet woken. In the large master bedroom, a couple were asleep beneath silk sheets. The woman had bleached blond hair and botoxed lips. The man was shorter than her, and a lot fatter. He looked and sounded pissed off that the mobile phone on his bedside table was vibrating. He swore under his breath, grabbed the phone and answered it with a distinct lack of grace.

'Who the …'

He was cut short, but the voice at the other end of the line made him sit up.

'Tony, mate, what's the fucking time? Where are you anyway? The line's awful.' He belched noisily, as if to confirm just how awful it was.

As he listened to the voice he padded naked to the door, where his kimono dressing gown was hanging on a brass hook. He perched the phone between his ear and his shoulder as he put it on.

'What?' he said as he wandered into the en suite, lifted up the toilet seat and started to piss thunderously against the porcelain. 'Yeah, I've got a couple of guys. For you, mate, anything. I'll send them round sometime this week. What is it, they owe you money or something?'

He flushed the chain and padded back out into the bedroom. His wife was still fast asleep.

'What?' he continued. 'Now?' He whistled, to demonstrate what a tall order that was. 'I dunno, mate, maybe in a couple of hours …'

He fell silent and listened to the response.

'Right,' he said quietly. There was a sudden hint of steel in his eyes. 'Immediately. But let's be clear, Tony, after this, we're quits. Understood?' He walked across the bedroom to the dressing table, where his wife's eye-lining pencil was lying at an angle. 'Where the fuck are you anyway?' he asked as he started to scrawl an unfamiliar number across the glass of her mirror. 'Bring us back a souvenir, won't you? Box of, I dunno, 7.62s always goes down nicely. Least you can do, after a favour like this …'

'Done,' Tony said.

Danny didn't move. His shooter had just stood up. Approximate distance, 70 metres. He wore the standard Boko Haram garb: camouflage gear, rifle, black woollen hat. The cross hairs of Danny's scope were in line with his chest.

Radio communication to Caitlin: 'Eyes-on.'

No reply.

Silence.

Thirty seconds passed. The militant was moving forward. Distance: 60 metres.

Caitlin: '*Eyes on.*'

Danny didn't hesitate for a second. 'Take the shot,' he said. Immediately he squeezed the trigger of his HK. The suppressed round made a dull knocking sound as it exited the barrel of his rifle. A fraction of a second later he heard a second round from Caitlin's direction. And a fraction of a second after that, the militant in his sights collapsed.

'Target down,' he said.

'*Target down,*' came Caitlin's reply.

Danny stayed where he was. 'What now?' he asked Tony.

'Now,' Tony said, 'we wait.'

07.28 hrs

The inhabitants of Eastwick Drive, Peckham had grown used to seeing strangers in their road. First it had been the police, knocking on the door of number thirteen where that nice Pakistani couple lived who were always giving sweets to the local children, and helping out at community events. After the police had gone, some of the neighbours had knocked on their door to see if everything was okay. There had been no reply.

The following day the police had turned up again, and stayed longer this time. A couple of hours later there were reporters outside the door. Even a news crew. Nobody in the street knew why, until they read about it in the papers, and after that they could talk about nothing else: how the nice couple's son, who they'd always thought was a bit of a strange one – not like their eleven-year-old daughter, who was very sweet – had travelled to Syria to fight with those terrorists. Who would want to do such a thing, they wondered. They felt so sorry for the parents, who must be worried sick.

Their concern had soon turned to annoyance when the unwanted visitors kept coming. Their address was all over the internet. Anyone who wanted to come and ogle at the house of the kid who'd gone off to fight and had ended up as Jihadi Jim, the brutal executioner, could rock up at any time of the day or night and throw stones at the parents' windows, or spray graffiti on the low wall of their front garden.

And so, the sight of two unfamiliar, broad-shouldered guys walking silently up the road was entirely unremarkable. A couple of kids, up early and playing on their bikes, gave them the eye, but nobody challenged them as they walked up to number thirteen carrying a large bouquet of flowers, and rang the doorbell.

At first there was no reply, so they rang again. A minute later there was the sound of footsteps approaching the door. A thin, slightly frail man's voice came from the other side. 'Who is it?'

'Flower delivery,' said the guy holding the bouquet.

A pause.

'Who from?' said the voice suspiciously.

'There's a card here, mate.'

Another pause. Then the sound of three separate locks being unfastened.

The door opened a couple of inches. The visitors didn't wait for more. The guy who was not holding the flowers barged inwards. The owner of the house gave an alarmed shout as he fell backwards, but by that time the two heavies were inside, the door closed behind them. They dropped the flowers carelessly on the floor and both pulled out handguns. Not that they needed them. The man of the house, who was wearing nothing but a pair of striped pyjama bottoms, had thin arms and balding hair and was skinny enough for his ribs to be showing. He staggered backwards as the men barged in. As he challenged them with a feeble 'Who are you? What do you want?', one of the intruders answered him with a sturdy boot in his ribs, then dragged him into the front room to the left of the hallway, while his companion climbed the stairs.

145

Three minutes later he returned. He had the wife with him, dressed in a floral nightdress, and the little girl in a panda onesie. Both were crying, and neither could take their eyes off the gun which the intruder who had just yanked them from their beds was waving at their heads.

'Get on the ground,' he said. 'Face down, arms out. All of you. Now.'

The terrified family did as they were told. The sound of desperate sobs filled the room, but the two intruders were unmoved.

'Make the call,' one of them said. 'Then we can get the fuck out of here.'

His companion took his phone from his pocket. He stuck it on to loudspeaker, and it beeped noisily as he dialled the number.

A thick plume of acrid smoke was rising from the isolation zone. Danny was standing in the main road. He knew what that smoke meant. He wondered if the lab team were burning just the Nigerian corpses, or if Ripley had been added to the impromptu funeral pyre. His lip curled at the thought. The whole village was strangely silent. Apart from the two stray militants, nobody had approached. It was as if they knew Chikunda was cursed.

His earpiece crackled into life. Tony's voice. '*The sat phone's ringing. Get here, now.*'

Danny turned and sprinted towards the vehicle. It took him twenty seconds to get there. By that time, Tony had opened the driver's seat and was sitting there, the sat phone to his ear. Danny opened the passenger door. 'Is it them?' he demanded of Tony.

Tony nodded. 'It's them.'

Danny didn't hesitate. He pulled out the adrenaline shots, released them from their sterile wrapping. He held the shot between his teeth as he ripped the sleeve on his prisoner's good arm. When the skin was exposed, he sharply jabbed the needle into his arm and squeezed the syringe.

The effect was immediate. Their wax-faced prisoner's eyes

opened suddenly. He took in a sharp, noisy breath and for a moment he looked as if he was going to sit up.

Danny removed the spent adrenaline shot, chucked it on the floor, and then put his Sig to the prisoner's head.

'Listen carefully,' he said.

Bang on cue, a scratchy, distant scream came over the phone. It sounded like a kid. Terrified and whimpering. Then a man's voice, strained, quiet, but also scared. '*James*,' the man said. '*It's me, it's your father. They have your sister . . .*'

The prisoner made a sharp intake of breath. His bloodshot eyes rolled. Danny had the impression that he was trying to say something, but couldn't.

Another scream. A different voice. Older. Female. '*Leave her alone!*' shouted the man at the other end of the phone. '*Don't hurt her . . .*'

The prisoner was breathing very heavily. He managed to whisper three words. 'Make . . . them . . . stop . . .'

'There's only one person that can make it stop,' Danny said. 'You. Who was the Chinese guy? Where was he going?'

Another pained, noisy intake of breath. The prisoner's eyes rolled again. No reply.

Danny grabbed the sat phone from Tony. 'Kill the father,' he shouted into it, figuring that a cunt like this would be more attached to his dad than to the girls in the family.

'No!' the prisoner breathed. 'Wait! No!'

'Wait!' Danny instructed down the phone.

Another scream from London, but then silence.

'What's the Chinese guy's name? You've got five seconds to answer.'

'Chiu,' the prisoner breathed. 'That's all I know. I called him Mr Chiu.'

'What was he doing here?'

'Tests,' the prisoner whispered. His voice was cracking badly. 'On the Nigerians . . . to show that the weapon worked, before . . .'

His eyes drooped closed.

'Before *what?*' Danny shouted.

He handed the phone to Tony and nodded. Tony spoke into the mouthpiece. 'Hurt them.'

Another scream instantly crackled down the phone. The prisoner started to shake. 'Before they use them,' he managed to say.

'How are they going to use them? I said, *how are they going to use them!*'

'Vectors,' the prisoner said. 'That's all I know ... vectors ...'

'What the fuck are vectors?'

The prisoner's eyes were closed. He shook his head, then winced suddenly with pain. 'Let my father go,' he whispered. 'Please, let him ...'

He couldn't finish his sentence. His breathing had become alarmingly shallow. Danny pressed two fingers to his jugular. The pulse was there, but weak.

He unwrapped the second adrenaline shot. One fierce jab and the liquid was pumping into the prisoner's veins. He drew another sudden intake of breath.

'What do you mean by vectors?'

'I don't know,' the prisoner croaked. 'I just heard the word. Please let him go ...'

'Where was Chiu going? He was taking you somewhere? *Where?*'

'A ship.' His voice almost wasn't there. Danny instinctively knew the bastard didn't have long.

'Which ship? Where?' His body shuddered. His breathing sounded worse than Ripley's had. 'I swear to God your old man gets a bullet in the head if you don't tell me where!'

'Bight ...' The prisoner caught his breath. 'Bight ... Benin ...'

Finally. Something concrete. But Danny wasn't done yet. 'What are the Chinese doing in the pocket of Islamist militants? Who's he working with? Who's he taking orders from?'

The prisoner shuddered again. His lips were blue.

Danny leaned in close. He could smell the prisoner's stinking, dying breath. 'This is your last fucking chance,' he said. 'Give me a name, or your family get it.'

His eyes rolled up into the top of his sockets. He seemed to sink lower in the seat of the Range Rover, and the deep, long breath that he exhaled had a dreadful air of finality about it. But as he breathed out, Danny caught one word, barely audible as the prisoner expired.

As Jihadi Jim's eyes rolled to the top of his head, Danny heard Tony talking to the hoods at the other end of the phone. 'If you can get away with it, clean up and don't get caught,' he said.

A part of Danny wanted to object. The last thing they needed was to be linked to three dead bodies in a Peckham semi, even though it would probably just look like a vigilante killing. But he said nothing as Tony gave his brutal instruction. He was still trying to make sense of Jihadi Jim's dying word.

The word was: 'Caliph . . .'

PART TWO

Hellfire

FOURTEEN

Doha, Qatar. 11.30 hrs, Arabia Standard Time.

It was, by any standards, an extravagant apartment. This pent-house flat, the crown on the top of a sparkling, mirrored skyscraper, would have comfortably housed a family of six, with a bedroom and bathroom for each of them, and a personal ele-vator that gave private access to the pool on the top of the building and the health suite in its basement. There was art on the walls – a blue-period Picasso of a crying woman took pride of place in the main reception room – and all the floors were clad with expensive marble and furnished with luminous Persian rugs. Fresh flowers, imported all the way from Holland, were delivered daily.

By any measure, it was far too big for the elderly couple who lived here alone.

Their names were Ali and Nafy Al-Essa, and they would never have thought that their old age would be lived out in such luxury. Every day they gave thanks, and since they wanted for nothing, they made sure they gave all they could to charity, in accordance with the wishes of the Prophet.

This morning they sat, as they always did, in orthopaedic leather chairs that reclined electronically. The sofas in the apart-ment were all too low for them. If they tried to sink in to them, they always told anyone who would listen, the chances were that they'd never get up again. It was probably true. There was a zimmer frame by Nafy's chair, and a single crutch by Ali's. Walking was a slow and painful process, so they did it as little as possible – a few steps from the bedroom to the chairs in the morning, then back to bed at night. The old lady wore a urinary bag, for medical reasons.

In the meantime, they spent their days surrounded by luxury, gazing out of wide windows over the impressive skyline of the capital city they were now too decrepit to enter. At their age – they were both seventy-eight – there were worse ways to spend your life. They certainly knew they enjoyed a better old age than their own parents had – weather-hardened Bedouin for whom surroundings like this would have been unimaginable. On very clear days, like today, they could see far towards the ocean horizon, and on clear nights they could see little lights twinkling out there. Those little lights were a reminder of the riches that kept them in such style. They were the burning flames atop the oil rigs owned by their son, Ahmed bin Ali al-Essa. Those rigs were the source of his great wealth, and of his parents' luxury.

They were proud of their only son. Prouder than they could say. His photograph stood on a small Chippendale table beneath the Picasso, and they always looked at it more fondly than they did the painting. It was true that they seldom saw Ahmed. He was a very busy man. Why, even now he was on business in Saudi Arabia. But he ensured that they lived a comfortable life, and he called in to see them whenever he could. In the meantime, he saw to it that their simple needs were attended to by a series of very capable carers and nurses who popped in at regular intervals throughout the day.

When they heard a pinging sound from the doors of the private elevator, they knew it was the chef, arriving to prepare their lunch. He was a Frenchman called Ducasse. It always took him about an hour and a half to prepare their three courses, and he would stay until they had finished so he could clear up. They had got to know him well – well enough for him to have his own lift pass to get into their apartment – and they looked forward to his cheerful '*Bonjour*' when he arrived each day.

There was a hissing sound as the elevator doors slid shut. But there was no '*Bonjour*'.

'Ducasse!' Ali called from his reclining chair. They always spoke in English – the only language they had in common. 'What delicious morsels do you have for us today?'

They expected Ducasse to reel off a list of exotic and expensive ingredients. But he was silent.

'Ducasse?'

Silence.

Ali pressed a button on the arm of his reclining chair. There was almost no noise as the back moved up to a right angle. With a painful wince, Ali straightened his old bones, then grabbed hold of his crutch with his left hand. With difficulty, he hauled himself to his feet. 'Why so quiet today, Ducasse?' he asked. He had a smile on his thin face as he looked round to greet the Frenchman.

The smile soon fell from his face.

Ducasse was there alright, but so were three other men. At least, Ali assumed they were men. Their faces were covered with black balaclavas that matched their black trousers and tops. One of them stood directly behind Ducasse. He was clutching the Frenchman's hair with one hand and had yanked his head back so that his neck was fully exposed. Resting against the flesh of the neck was a broad-bladed knife. Ducasse's normally jolly red face was pale and drawn.

There was a horrible moment of stillness, as if everybody in the room had frozen. Then, with just the faintest flick of his wrist, the knifeman sliced into the neck.

The cut was no more than two inches long, but it was deep. There was a sudden fountain of blood, which splattered on the marble floor a good couple of feet in front of the chef. It quickly subsided into a relentless ooze that drained down his neck and soaked grimly into his cooking whites.

Ali stepped back. He glanced, horrified, towards his wife. She was still reclining, her eyes closed. She had no idea what was happening.

Ducasse tumbled heavily, first to his knees, then flat on his face. The three masked men stepped forward. Ali couldn't speak from horror. He shook his head, and stretched his arm out towards his wife, who still didn't know what was going on behind her. He wished, more than anything, that he could make her remain oblivious to it all.

But that wasn't possible. Because as they moved towards the reclining chairs, the man who had cut Ducasse's throat, and was still carrying the bloodied knife, spoke. No English now. Arabic. 'Ali Al-Essa?' he asked.

Ali nodded as his wife's eyes pinged open. 'Who is it, Ali?' she asked. 'Isn't it Ducasse?'

He looked at his wife, and suddenly found his voice. 'Whatever you do,' he whispered, 'don't look back.'

She gave him a confused look as the knifeman repeated his question. 'Ali Al-Essa?'

Ali nodded.

'You are the father of Ahmed bin Ali al-Essa?'

Ali felt a knot of anxiety in his stomach. What could men like this possibly want his son for? He peered more closely at the knifeman, and only then did he see, on the shoulder of his black top, a badge with the insignia of the Islamic State. Like most ordinary citizens, he loathed the very thought of that organisation. But he had learned to fear them greatly.

'Ahmed isn't here,' he breathed.

'We know he's not here, you stupid old man. You'd do better to answer the questions we ask you. It will be easier that way. Are you his father?'

Ali nodded, then shrank back. The two other men had taken up position right behind Nafy's chair. She clearly knew somebody was there, and she was shaking.

'What do you want?' Ali said. 'Why did you . . .' He was about to say 'kill Ducasse', but he held back because he wanted to spare his wife the horror.

'Your son is as stupid as you,' said the knifeman.

'What do you mean? My son is very intelligent, a very rich man. If this is about money, I can assure you that he will be able to pay you anything you . . .'

The knifeman spat. 'It is nothing to do with money,' he said. 'Your son has done a very stupid thing.'

'Who is talking about Ahmed like that?' Nafy said in a small, frightened voice.

She tried to sit up, but Ali immediately said: 'Don't move!'

She shrank back down in her seat again. 'What has Ahmed done?' Ali said. 'And what does it have to do with Ducasse?'

The knifeman looked over his shoulder. 'You mean *that* infidel? He was in the wrong place at the wrong time. As for what your son has done, he has spoken to the infidels about someone he should not have mentioned.'

'What?' Ali replied. 'What are you talking about. Who?'

The knifeman stared at him for a moment. Then he suddenly turned on his heel and walked back towards Ducasse, whose almost dead body was quivering on the marble floor. He bent over and dipped the point of his knife in the dying man's bleeding wound. Then, on the wall behind him, he started drawing some Arabic symbols. He had to return to the wound four times to get enough blood to finish whatever he was writing – Ali couldn't make it out because he was standing in the way. Only when the knifeman was done did he step back to admire his work.

Ali's weak eyes squinted at the gruesome graffiti. It was a single word. It said, in Arabic: 'The Caliph'.

'Ali,' Nafy whimpered. 'I'm scared. What is happening?'

'I don't understand,' Ali said. 'Who is the Caliph? What does all this mean?'

'The Caliph,' said the knifeman, who was now walking back towards him, 'is the person your son informed on. When that happens, the Caliph demands a punishment. But not from the person who committed the crime. What kind of deterrent would that be? The Caliph demands that the punishment is exacted upon the family of his enemies.' A sickly smile appeared on his lips. 'That means you.'

This was too much for Nafy. She sat up with great difficulty and looked over her shoulder. When she saw the masked men standing behind her reclining chair, she screamed. It wasn't a long scream, nor a particularly loud one – her old lungs weren't up to it – but it was clearly enough that the intruders wanted it to stop.

So they killed her first.

They killed Nafy in the same way as Ducasse: by pulling back her head and quickly slicing the neck with the easy skill of a practised butcher. Nafy's heart was weaker than Ducasse's had been, so the initial fountain of blood that erupted from her neck was much less powerful. She made a strangled, gurgling sound and reached out to her husband. He saw that her fingertips were already stiffening, and as her thin arm flopped down, a moan of dread and despair escaped his lips. His wife. *His wife!* Who had been by his side since they were teenagers . . .

Anger followed on the heels of his despair. He wanted to fight these people. But there was nothing he could do. He was a statue, frozen in terror and helplessness. As the original knifeman stepped round his reclining chair towards him, he raised his crutch, hoping to swipe this animal round the head with it. But it was a pathetic attempt. Supported now only by his frail two legs, he stumbled and fell against the reclining chair.

He felt hands on him. The knifeman was turning him over so that he was sitting properly in the chair.

'Get off me! Get off me!'

The knifeman didn't reply. He pressed his free hand against the old man's chest, then activated the button that forced the chair to recline. Ali tried pathetically to wriggle, but it was no good. His attacker was far too strong. Just a few seconds later he was fully lying on his back, the masked man looking over him, clutching his knife: a diabolical surgeon standing over his terrified patient.

'People need to understand that the Caliph does not want to be talked about, and he does not want to be seen. Tell me, old man, what do people use to talk?'

At first Ali didn't reply. But when his attacker swiped him brutally across his face he whispered: 'Their tongue . . .'

'Good,' said the knifeman. 'And what do they use to see with?'

'Their . . . their eyes,' the old man stammered.

'Their eyes. Very good. Now then, to make a proper example of you will take some time.'

Ali tried to cry out again, but as soon as he opened his mouth,

158

the knifeman stuffed two fingers inside it and forced his jaws to open even wider. Ali retched at the feeling, and his eyes bulged as he saw the monster bring the tip of his knife into his mouth. He knew he was going for the tongue, and Ali tried to force it into the back of his throat so that the blade couldn't reach it. But the knife was longer than his mouth was deep. Ali whimpered as it cut into his upper lip, then let out a pained gasp as he felt the tip of the blade scoring along the wet muscle of his tongue. His mouth filled with warm, foaming blood. It ran down his throat and choked him, so that when the second slice came and removed the tongue in its entirety, he was making a harsh, gargling sound. The panic he felt at his sudden suffocation outdid the pain, for a few seconds. But then the agony of his wound kicked in, and he grew dizzy with it. He blew a mouthful of blood all over his clothes, clearing his blocked throat and inhaling desperately. He was about to shout out in pain when it became obvious that his attacker hadn't finished with him yet.

The masked man grabbed Ali's neck with his free hand, then allowed his knife to hover over the old man's eyes. It was as if he was deciding which one to carve out first.

Ali tried to say, 'No!' But all that came was a formless, gurgling grunt. His attacker seemed to settle on the right eye, and Ali saw the bloody tip of the blade move in close. It brushed his eyelashes, and he clamped his eye shut. A fraction of a second later he felt the incision, carefully made, circling the eye socket. He tried to move his head but couldn't, because the masked man had such a firm grip on his neck. He could do nothing but lie there, everything spinning, the pain beyond imagining, blood dripping down the side of his head.

The knife left his skin. For the briefest of agonised seconds he was relieved. He managed to open his good eye, but wished he hadn't, because it meant he had advance warning of what happened next. He saw that the knifeman was handing his blade to one of his accomplices, before extending his two forefingers like a child making a pretend gun. The forefingers moved towards his bad eye. Ali clamped the good one shut and made another futile attempt at shouting out as he felt the fingers worm their way into his eye socket and try to get purchase behind the eyeball. He felt the eyeball squirming within the socket, and then a sudden flash of excruciating light flashed within his brain as his attacker yanked the eyeball from the head.

Amid the pain and the half-shout that emerged from his damaged mouth, Ali could just feel the way the wet optic nerve flopped onto his cheek as his attacker dropped the eyeball. He vomited with pain, but the vomit caught in his throat, merged with the blood from his still-weeping tongue, and started choking him for the second time.

His skin shrieked as he felt the tip of the knife scoring around his left eye. By this time, the room was spinning more violently. The dizziness wasn't just in his head. It seemed to penetrate every part of him. It was a horrific whirlwind of nausea and pain, so intense that he couldn't even feel sorrow for his murdered wife, or the injustice of knowing he would never see his son Ahmed again.

All he wanted was for it to be over.

Within thirty seconds, it was. As his attacker wormed his fingers behind his right eyeball, the pain magnified to a peak that no human could endure. And as he pulled it from the socket, there was a second blinding flash.

And then there was nothing. No pain. No choking.

No life.

The three masked men stood back and examined their handiwork.

It wouldn't have been enough simply to kill them. A message had to be sent. Their intention had been to make the scene look horrific. There was no doubt they'd achieved that. The chef lay in a glossy pool of his own blood. The old woman, lying on her reclining chair, had a rictus grin on her face that exactly mirrored the curved wound on her throat. But the old man was the stuff of nightmares: two gaping wounds where his eyes had once been, and a bloody, mushy mess for a mouth. His fingers clutched the arms of his reclining chair, as if he'd thought that by holding on tight he might be able to save himself.

Their work was not yet done. Silently, each man dipped his fingers in the blood of one of the three corpses. Then they started writing the same Arabic word – Caliph – that one of them had already scrawled with the point of his knife. They covered the room with this blood graffiti: over the Picasso, across mirrors and marble floors. It took five minutes, by which time the room was bathed in blood.

One of them took the picture of Ahmed bin Ali al-Essa, the old couple's son, which sat underneath the Picasso. He ripped the photo out of the frame, then laid it carefully over the bloody face of his father. While he was doing this, the knifeman approached the old lady. There was one more indignity he wished to impose upon her. He ripped open the legs of the loose trousers she was wearing, to reveal the urinary bag strapped to her leg. With one quick slash of the knife, he cut it open so that its foul contents spilled all over the reclining chair, some of it dripping down on to the floor. The sight and smell of it disgusted him, and he spat at the woman, as if it was her fault that he'd been exposed to the contents.

They took photographs. They knew how easy it would be for whoever discovered this scene to clean it up and pretend it hadn't happened. But it was harder to erase a photograph. If the Caliph wanted the dead couple's son to receive proof of what had happened, they would be in a position to obey him. And they were certain of one thing: obeying the Caliph was the only way to ensure a long life.

They turned their backs on their victims and left the room. They were pleased with what they had done. And they knew the Caliph would be pleased too.

FIFTEEN

London, 08.00 GMT.

The MI6 building never sleeps. Sometimes the same is true of the people who occupy it, although Spud hadn't expected to have to pull an all-nighter on his first day shadowing a spook. Eleanor was incredibly persistent. Spud was almost impressed. As he leaned against the wall of her office and sucked down his fifth cup of coffee since midnight, she explained to him what she had learned about the cab driver in Birmingham whose name had jumped out of the files at them.

'Kalifa al-Meghrani,' she said, 'is a British citizen who has lived in the UK all his life – and so have his parents.' She held up what looked like a photocopy of a birth certificate. 'His grandparents arrived here from the area of the Persian Gulf coast that is now the United Arab Emirates. My neck of the woods, actually. Or at least my parents'. He went to school at the local comprehensive in Dudley and he had no previous criminal record up until his recent run-in with the police.' She gave Spud a little matter-of-fact smile.

'So what are you trying to say?' Spud asked. He took another gulp of coffee.

'You know what I think, Spud? I think you *want* this guy to be a terrorist. I think you judged him the moment you heard his name.'

'No,' Spud said. 'He used the word "caliph". Those ISIS nutters are always talking about the caliphate . . .'

'*Despite* the lack of anything resembling a terrorist attack pre-incident indicator,' Eleanor interrupted, 'you've got it in your head that because he's a Muslim, he has some sort of case to answer.'

'Wrong,' Spud said. 'I've got it in my head that because he yelled abuse at a police officer—'

'It's the very fact that he yelled at a police officer that makes him *incredibly* unlikely to be a suspect of any kind.'

'Why? That doesn't make any sense at all.'

Eleanor removed her glasses and inhaled deeply, as though calming herself before explaining something to a child for the umpteenth time. 'Listen carefully,' she said, putting her glasses back on. 'You were in 22 SAS, right?'

'I still am,' Spud said.

'Fine. You *are* in 22 SAS. So if I'm a terrorist, and I'm trying to judge who is a greater threat to my activities, do I put you at the top of the list, or some fresh-faced teenager in the cadet force?'

'That's a stupid question.'

'Not at all. Obviously you're the greater threat. You've undergone millions of pounds' worth of training. You're highly competent with weapons. You're extremely fit. You can observe me without me knowing I'm being observed. When the time comes you can kill me swiftly and silently, then melt into the background without anybody knowing you've been there. You don't feel the need to boast about it. In fact, you go out of your way to keep your activities covert and quiet. Am I right?'

Spud shrugged.

'Your kid in the cadet force? Chances are he mouths out about what he does every Friday night down the pub in front of his mates.'

'What's your point?'

'That terrorists are no different. The higher their skill level, the more adept they are at melting into the background, at being invisible. The dangerous ones are sane, rational and highly organised. They take very good care to stay on the right side of the law up until the point that they carry out their atrocities. They just want to get their job done quietly and efficiently, and they know they can't do that by mouthing off at police stations late at night.

It just doesn't fit the profile.' She held up the birth certificate again. 'Mr al-Meghrani doesn't fit the profile.'

Spud stared at her. Maybe she was right. Maybe Spud was so keen to get out into the field that he was overlooking the obvious.

'I still think we should have a word with him,' he murmured.

'*We're* going to do nothing of the sort, Spud. *You're* shadowing *me*, remember. You're here to observe, and nothing more. If we go to Birmingham to speak to this guy, I'll do the talking and you'll do the listening. Is that clear?'

Spud felt himself flushing. 'Whatever,' he muttered.

'Don't be so childish,' Eleanor said. 'I'm very obviously a Muslim. If I ask the right questions he will open up to me. Anyway, I've been trained to interview suspects effectively. You never know, you might actually learn something.'

'I doubt it.'

'I beg your pardon?'

'I said, I doubt it. Look, love, I've been on the front line and stared these fuckers down. I know what I'm looking for. I've *been* to terrorist training camps that you've only read about in intelligence reports.'

'Well, you won't have seen Kalifa al-Meghrani at any of them.'

'How do you know that?' Spud said. 'How can you *possibly* know that?'

She gave him a cool look. 'Because he was born in this country and he's never owned a passport. He's never even left the UK.'

Spud had no answer for that.

'It may be that Kalifa al-Meghrani is a nasty piece of work. It may be that he's been operating a minicab without a licence. But I'm afraid that neither of these make him a terrorist, or a terrorist sympathiser. And even if he name-checked the Caliph, I'm quite sure that he did so on the basis of hearsay and rumour – unless you think that one of the Firm's most wanted Middle Eastern terrorists is hiding out in Dudley.'

'It's not impossible,' Spud said. He sounded surly even to himself.

'No. Not impossible. Just very unlikely.'

'So we *should* go and talk to him.'

'I thought I'd made myself clear, Spud.'

'What do you mean?'

'*I* talk, you listen. Of course I'm going to talk to him, because I want it to be belt and braces. But if you learn one thing by shadowing me, Spud, I hope it's this: stereotypes don't help terrorist-detection. They get in the way. Is that understood?'

Spud nodded curtly.

'I'll tell you what, though,' Eleanor added. She stood up and, on her way to the door, slapped Spud on the buttocks. It felt like an outrageous act from a woman in a hijab. 'I know you're not just a pretty face, and I'm sure you're jolly good behind the wheel, so I *will* let you drive. Shall we go?'

She opened the door. At that very moment, an older man in a crumpled suit strode past the room.

'Good morning, Sir Colin,' Eleanor said brightly.

'Not now,' the man said, and he disappeared from Spud's view.

'Who's that?' Spud asked.

'That,' said Eleanor, 'is the Chief of SIS.'

Spud raised an eyebrow. 'He didn't look that pleased to see you.'

His barbed comment clearly hit its mark. Eleanor puckered her lips. 'Sir Colin is a very busy man,' she said. 'Come on, I want to cross this cab driver off my list for sure, and I want to do it today. We need to get moving.'

'Good morning, Sir Colin.'

Sir Colin Seldon glanced to his left to see a young intelligence officer, whose name he simply couldn't remember, standing in a doorway and smiling hopefully at him. Like every other intelligence officer, she obviously wanted some face time with the Chief. Behind her, a squat, broad-shouldered man whose face was set in a scowl.

'Not now,' he said. There simply wasn't the time. The Nigerian situation was developing fast. He needed to get a handle on it.

Two minutes later he was in the soundproofed confines of a secure meeting room. Along one wall was a series of five computer

165

screens. Three were blank, but the remaining two each showed a pixellated face in real time. Seldon recognised Hugo Buckingham as one of the faces, whom he knew to be on a secure line from the British Embassy in Riyadh. The second face belonged to Tessa Gorman, who was still in her dressing gown at home.

There were two others present in the room: Seldon's trusted analyst Bixby – his beard woollier than ever and his head leaning, as it always did, against the headrest of his wheelchair – and Brigadier Jeremy Lamb, Director Special Forces, who didn't look any too pleased to be summoned at eight in the morning. 'What the bloody hell's going on, Colin?' he said before the Chief could even sit down.

'Go ahead, Bixby,' Seldon told his analyst. 'Words of one syllable please.'

'To bring everyone up to speed,' Bixby said, 'we've had several communications from the Bravo Nine Delta unit. The High Commissioner to Nigeria is dead – beheaded by Boko Haram militants, despite the presence of a team from 22 Regiment—'

'Just hold it one minute,' the Brigadier interrupted. 'If anyone thinks they're going to lay this shitstorm at our door . . .'

'Please, Jeremy,' Seldon said quietly. 'Let Bixby finish.'

'The High Commissioner's aide is also dead and we've lost a member of 22 Regiment to a biohazard which we believe to be a modified strain of *Y. Pestis*.'

'Plague,' Seldon clarified.

'The situation on the ground is extremely fluid. The remaining Regiment representatives have good reason to believe that a man of Chinese extraction – we have a name of Mr Chiu, but that's almost certainly a pseudonym – is heading to a ship off the Nigerian coast to arm several vectors with the disease.'

The Foreign Secretary spoke, her voice unnaturally loud through the computer loudspeaker. '*Explain to me what a vector is, please.*'

Bixby blinked heavily, as though he expected this to be something that she should understand. 'The fear has long been, Foreign Secretary, that a terrorist cell might deliberately infect themselves with a contagious disease. We call it HumanBioWeps – human-deployed biological weapon systems.'

'Suicide bombs without the bombs,' the Brigadier muttered.

'Exactly, sir. A vector is the first link in the chain. If he or she infects, say, five people, and each of those five people infect anther five, and so on . . . I think you can see you'd have a very serious problem. And if there's more than one vector—'

'*Yes, yes, I understand. But what I don't understand is what the Chinese are doing in Nigeria?*' the Foreign Secretary interrupted.

'Investors, oil technicians, migrant workers. There's a reasonably large Chinese population in Lagos itself. Forgive me, Home Secretary, the bigger question is what the Chinese are doing in bed with Boko Haram. We only have a working theory. We know that certain elements within the Chinese government have weaponised various diseases – plague, anthrax, possibly even smallpox. The unit on the ground also seems to have established a link between the Chinese national and our friend the Caliph.'

'Who the bloody hell's the Caliph?' the Brigadier asked.

'We don't know,' said Bixby. 'We believe he's a high-profile Islamist militant with links to the Islamic State. We think he plans to make a strike on the UK. It's now looking possible that it's intended to be a biohazard strike.'

There was a moment of silence as the assembled company took that in.

'*That still doesn't explain Mr Chiu,*' Gorman said.

'If the Caliph is in a position to influence both a triumphant Boko Haram in Nigeria and Islamic State in the Middle East, Foreign Secretary, then he will be in control of vast reserves of oil. This would be very attractive to the Chinese.'

'*Attractive enough for them to facilitate a bioterrorism strike against the West?*' Gorman sounded as aghast as she looked.

'We can only analyse the information we have, Foreign Secretary.'

The Foreign Secretary had bowed her head. '*How the hell are we supposed to keep this country safe when what happens here depends on the actions of a few individuals thousands of miles beyond our borders?*'

'Welcome to my world,' Seldon said. 'Mr Buckingham, did you make contact with our Qatari asset in Saudi?'

Buckingham coughed nervously. His picture degraded slightly before he spoke. *'I did, Sir Colin.'*

'Well?'

'I filed a report immediately, Sir Colin: haven't you read it?'

Seldon clicked his fingers impatiently. 'Edited highlights.'

'I . . . I'm afraid it wasn't terribly productive. Our man knew of the Caliph by name, but was too scared to say anything more. The same went for his driver.'

'And you didn't push him?'

'It was rather difficult to persuade him that—'

'We need to get our Regiment assets back out to the Nigerian coast,' the Brigadier cut-in. 'Our only hope of stopping this situation from escalating is to stop the vectors at source.'

Seldon exchanged a look with the Foreign Secretary over the computer screen. 'Our intention was to have your people flown back to the UK tonight, Jeremy.'

'I bet it was,' said the Director Special Forces.

'I really don't know what you mean.'

'Spare me, Sir Colin. We have two excellent Regiment men in Danny Black and Tony Wiseman on the ground, and they need to be left to do their job, not dumped on from a great height. And be under no illusion that if this situation does escalate, I shall make it known that it was you who opposed the deployment of the only people in a position to make a positive identification of Mr Chiu, or whatever his name really is. Do we understand each other?'

A frosty stare between the two men. 'Perfectly,' said the Chief.

'Good.' The Brigadier stood up. 'My understanding is that there's an Australian SAS team on piracy patrol in international waters off the Nigerian coastline. They'll have the necessary equipment for a waterborne assault, if need be. I'll make arrangements for our unit to transfer there. We need all agencies to focus their attention on locating Mr Chiu's position, and direct any findings through to the ops room at Hereford.'

A nervous cough from the screen that displayed Buckingham's face. *'Brigadier, I'm sorry, the line is a little crackly. Did you say, Danny Black?'*

'Problem with that?' the Brigadier asked.

'Not at all. Just . . . just curious.'

The Brigadier gave him a dismissive nod. 'Let's get moving,' he said. 'This could blow up in our faces any second.'

He turned his back on the spooks, and left the room. As he did so, Tessa Gorman said: *'I need to update the PM.'* Her screen flickered and went black.

Seldon glanced towards Buckingham's face. 'I'll need the room, Bixby,' he said. The analyst looked slightly offended, but he reversed his electric wheelchair and wheeled himself out without complaint. The Chief shut the door behind him, and only then did he address Buckingham again. 'This Regiment man, Black,' he said. 'Do you know him?'

A shadow passed Buckingham's face. *'Oh yes, Sir Colin,'* he said, *'I know him alright.'*

'What's he like?'

'A liability, sir. Hot-headed, impetuous, thinks he's above the law – I really can't understand why the Brigadier thinks so highly of him.'

Seldon waved one hand to shut him up while he thought for a moment.

'You're ambitious, Buckingham,' he said finally. 'I can see that.'

'We all like to get on, Sir Colin.'

'A bioterrorism attack is our worst nightmare. We haven't got a hope in hell of stopping it. Heads are going to roll when it happens. Ours, to be precise.' Buckingham's face stared impassively out from the screen. 'I want you to join the Regiment unit on this Australian ship. MI6 liaison. I'll make the necessary arrangements with my Saudi counterpart immediately to get you out there. We can spin it that you're now following the same lead, the Caliph. If Black puts a foot wrong, I want to know about it. You understand why?'

There was no need to spell it out loud: that when the time came for dishing out blame, they certainly would need the scapegoat to which the Brigadier had referred.

'*I understand perfectly, Sir Colin*,' Buckingham said. '*Don't worry about Danny Black. I know how to deal with him.*'

'I bloody well hope so,' the Chief said. 'All our necks depend on it.'

He nodded at the screen, then left the room.

SIXTEEN

'*Call sign Bravo Nine Delta, this is Zero Alpha. Do you copy?*'

'This is Bravo Nine Delta. Go ahead.'

'*Your instructions are to remain in position until nightfall. A bird will be along to pick you up and transport you to an Australian Navy frigate in international waters.*'

'Do you know where Chiu went?'

'*We're working on it. Be prepared for a waterborne assault tonight. You're the only ones who can make a visual ID of this guy, so you'll need to lead the assault. Get some rest.*'

The radio fell silent. Tony snorted. 'Get some rest?' he said. 'Where do they think we are, the fucking Ritz?'

Danny checked the time. 08.37 hrs. 'We haven't slept for forty-eight hours,' Danny said. He looked around. Smoke was still rising from the isolation zone. The sun was already hot. 'We'll round up the others,' he said. 'Dig in till nightfall. Get some shut-eye.'

'What about him?' Tony looked at the dead body of Jihadi Jim lying in the passenger seat of the Range Rover.

Danny sneered, then opened the door, yanked the limp corpse out of the vehicle and threw it to the ground. 'There'll be some wild animals when we've gone,' he said. 'They could do with a decent meal.'

Tony gave an appreciative nod. It looked like for once they'd found something they could agree about.

'You sort out Caitlin and the Paras,' Danny said. 'I'll get the Porton Down guys together. We'll head a couple of hundred metres back into the vegetation. That should keep us clear of any of those Boko Haram cunts who come sniffing about.'

'Agreed,' said Tony. The two men started running away from the vehicle, back towards the centre of Chikunda.

11.30 hrs, GMT.

Spud had joined up because he wanted to see the world. He hadn't really had the arse end of Dudley, just outside Birmingham, in mind. The sun was out, and it was unseasonably warm, but even under a blue sky it was a shit hole here.

He was sitting behind the wheel of Eleanor's nondescript Renault Laguna, courtesy of the Firm's car pool, in the car park of a pub called the Hand and Flower. It was situated opposite a busy roundabout and had a big placard outside advertising two meals for a fiver. Spud could have eaten those two meals himself, but food wasn't on the agenda. They were parked up here because this position gave them a direct view of the Park Lane Minicabs office opposite the car park.

'I thought you said he'd been operating without a licence,' Spud had said as they were flooring it up the M1.

'Well remembered,' Eleanor had replied as she adjusted her hijab in the mirror of her sun visor. Spud had decided she was one of those women who couldn't help patronising you. 'After the police picked him up, he got himself one. Nice and legal, pays his taxes – which is why we know where he works.'

And that place was Park Lane Minicabs, whose office comprised a tiny glass frontage plastered with two telephone numbers in huge white lettering. There was a launderette on one side and a cafe on the other, with prices of its specials – lasagne and chips, apple crumble – painted on the front window. At this time of day, between breakfast and lunch, only the launderette seemed busy. Three saloon cars were parked up on the kerb outside, and through the window of the cab office Spud could see three or four guys hanging around, smoking cigarettes.

'So what now?' Spud asked.

Eleanor frowned. 'I guess we wait for him to arrive, and when he does we go in and ask specifically for him to take us somewhere,' she said.

Spud gave her an amused look. 'Great idea. Because that won't seem weird to him at all, two strangers picking him out by name.'

'There's no need to be sarcastic. If you've got a better idea . . .'

'Watch,' Spud interrupted her. He pointed towards the cab office. A woman was walking in with a couple of bags of heavy shopping. Thirty seconds later, she walked out again accompanied by one of the men from inside. He opened the boot of one of the saloon cars, packed away the shopping, then opened the rear passenger door to let the woman in, before pulling out into the traffic and driving off.

'Am I supposed to have just seen something?' Eleanor asked.

'They'll be on a rota,' Spud said. 'The next fare will go to the cab driver that's been waiting the longest. We need to keep surveillance on the cars parked outside. When – if – our man turns up, we wait until we know he's next in line, then we go in and ask for a cab. We don't have to mention him by name at all.'

Eleanor's eyes narrowed. She looked as if she was trying to find fault with Spud's strategy. 'Alright,' she said reluctantly. 'We'll do it your way.' She handed him a photograph. Just an ordinary-looking Middle Eastern guy with neat hair in a side parting and a brown leather jacket. 'Think you'll recognise him?'

Spud, who had spent more of his life than he cared to think about conducting detailed surveillance, nodded. 'Yeah,' he said. 'I'll recognise him. How about I put a bit of pressure on the fucker to talk once we're in the back of his vehicle?'

'You'll do nothing of the sort,' Eleanor said. 'I've already told you, *I'll* do the talking.'

'Right,' Spud said. 'So I guess you just ask him if he's best mates with a major international terrorist?'

'No,' Eleanor said with exaggerated patience. 'I ask him some carefully considered questions that will help me make an informed decision about whether he's a threat or not. Remember, I'm a Muslim. He'll trust me much more than he'll trust you.'

Spud shrugged. 'You're the boss,' he said, and he looked at the photograph again. If he was going to put in surveillance on the cab firm, he needed to commit his target's features to memory.

Daniel Bixby's wheelchair trundled across the operations room in the bowels of the MI6 building: a large space, filled with computer terminals, satellite phones and three large screens – each of them nine or ten square metres – showing real-time black and white satellite images of the Nigerian coast.

He went through the variables in his head again. The intel from the SAS team on the ground told them that Mr Chiu, or whatever his name really was, had left their location by car at approximately 13.00 hours the previous day. Unless he'd managed to get on an aircraft – and Bixby didn't think that was likely because they had a man in Nigerian air traffic control who had provided them with flight data for the past twenty-four hours – the analysts' best estimate was that it would take him twelve hours to get back to Lagos, which took them to 01.00 that morning. So Bixby had had almost his entire staff poring over satellite imagery stills from midnight to right now, searching for a needle in a haystack: a tiny passenger boat – probably no bigger than a RIB – heading out to sea to RV with a larger vessel.

He looked up at the large screens. Little dots, slightly lighter than the grey ocean, were just visible. There was no getting away from it: the waters were crowded. There had to be at least 150 vessels in the 100 square kilometres off the Lagos coast, and there was no way to be sure that their target would be on any of them. Bixby was perspiring heavily. He didn't see how they would *ever* find their man.

One of his subordinates strode up to him. 'Mr Bixby, we've been through everything. There's no sign of what we're looking for.'

Bixby swore.

'But we think the Americans might have separate imagery of the same area over the same time frame. I'd like permission to contact Langley to see if they'll share that information.'

Bixby thought for a few seconds. Strictly speaking he should clear this with the Chief. But Seldon was acting strange. Stressed. Probably the pressure. Bixby decided to make the call himself, and deal with the fallout later.

'Do it,' he said. 'Call the Americans. I want everything they've got, as quickly as they can send it.'

14.00 hrs

Eleanor's all-nighter had caught up with her. She was asleep in the passenger seat, breathing heavily, her body occasionally twitching. Spud kept his eyes on the cab firm, as he had done for the past two and a half hours. There were now only two cars parked outside: a black Peugeot estate and a metallic green Honda.

A shabby old tramp swayed past the cab firm, carrying a bottle of Thunderbird. That was the fourth time Spud had seen him. He passed every forty-five minutes. Ordinarily, a regular appearance like that would ring alarm bells. But Spud could see that the level of liquid in the bottle was decreasing each time, and the tramp's gait was increasingly erratic. Now, a young mum with a kid in a pushchair and another in the oven came in the opposite direction. She wrinkled her nose and avoided the tramp. Spud was satisfied that he was nothing but an old wino circling the block.

A third vehicle pulled up. It was an old white VW, its side panel slightly dented. Spud watched the driver climb out. As soon as he caught sight of his face, he nudged Eleanor. 'Wake up,' he said. 'Your man's here.'

Eleanor started. Her eyes pinged open and she looked around as though she didn't know where she was.

'Over there,' Spud said.

Kalifa al-Meghrani wore a shapeless tan-coloured leather jacket, and dark woollen gloves. He was clean-shaven and his black hair was neatly combed. He had some kind of shoulder bag over his left shoulder.

'There's two cab drivers ahead of him,' Spud said. 'We wait till the Peugeot and the Honda have gone, then we move in.'

It didn't take long. After three minutes a young couple entered the cab office and were ferried away by the Peugeot. A minute after that, the Honda pulled out into the traffic without a passenger – Spud assumed the driver was on his way to carry out a telephone booking.

'Go,' he said, as the vehicle pulled away. He and Eleanor alighted from their Renault and crossed the road. Seconds later they had entered the cab office. It was a cramped, dingy little place. A couple of threadbare seats along one side and an enormous, laminated map of the Birmingham area on the wall. There were only two people in there: the controller behind the desk, and al-Meghrani himself.

'Cab to the Bullring, please,' Eleanor said. Spud found himself double-taking: she had exaggerated a Middle Eastern accent that she didn't have in real life. He almost found himself smiling at her subterfuge.

The cab driver looked them up and down. Hardly a surprise: they must have looked a strange couple. But he didn't seem suspicious. 'Alright, babs, follow me,' he said in a very pronounced Birmingham accent. He nodded at his controller, then led the way to the car. Spud stood back to let Eleanor go first, then followed her out on to the pavement.

'You go round the other side,' he breathed. He wanted to make sure he was sitting directly behind their man. In the absence of a weapon, he'd have to make do with the driver's seatbelt if anything went wrong.

Once they were installed into the back seat, and al-Meghrani had dumped his shoulder bag on the front passenger seat, he started the car. 'Rocket Man' by Elton John played softly from the radio and he turned it up a fraction as he pulled out into the traffic. 'I blimmin' love this song,' he announced to his passengers, and as he accelerated along the road he started humming along.

Eleanor gave Spud a sidelong glance. A glance that said: how many terrorists do you think listen to Elton John?

Spud just kept his eyes fixed on the back of the cab driver's head.

'Have you been busy?' Eleanor asked.

'What's that, love?'

'Have you been busy?'

'Oh, yeah, crazy busy. *Don't you know it's gonna be a long, long time . . .*'

'I suppose you get some time off over Ramadan,' she said.

'Not really, babs.'

'How come?'

'Lots of cabbies take time off over Ramadan. More work for the rest of us. Got to earn a living, you know.'

Eleanor pursed her lips disapprovingly. Spud had to hand it to her: her performance was a fucking masterclass. He saw the cab driver glance at her in the rear-view mirror. 'You don't approve?' he said quietly.

Eleanor shrugged and looked out of her window. 'Either you obey the Qu'ran,' she said, 'or you don't.'

The cabbie frowned. He killed the radio, cutting off Elton in mid-song. 'You're not one of those crazy ones, are you?'

'What do you mean?' Eleanor asked.

'Some of the Muslims round here, they want to go off and fight stupid wars. Some of the other cabbies, they've got badges for that Islamic State in their cars. You one of *those* crazy ones?'

'Maybe they're not so crazy,' Eleanor said.

The cabbie looked at her over his shoulder. There was no doubt about it: his expression was one of disgust. He slammed the radio back on and turned it up much louder than it had been. Elton John had given way to One Direction, but the cabbie didn't sing along this time. He accelerated on to a busy ring road and started overtaking wherever he could. It was obvious what he wanted to tell them: *I don't like what you've just said, and I want you out of my car.*

It took fifteen uncomfortable minutes to get to the centre of Birmingham. Al-Meghrani pulled up in a cab rank outside the Bullring. 'Seventeen pounds,' he said.

Eleanor handed him twenty. 'Keep the change,' she said. But the cabbie made a big show of finding the three quid – he fumbled a little because of the woollen gloves he was wearing – and handing it back to her. Eleanor shrugged again, then stepped out of the car. Spud did the same, and the cabbie pulled out again immediately he'd slammed his door shut.

'I think that went pretty well, don't you?' Eleanor said.

Spud watched the cab disappear into the traffic.

'Coffee?' Eleanor said. They were standing outside a McDonald's, and she pointed towards it.

Spud nodded. Two minutes later they were sitting at a small table in the window, their conversation drowned by the noise of the busy restaurant.

'You're a good actress,' Spud said.

'Why, thank you.' She fluttered her eyelashes at him.

He looked at her over the brow of his polystyrene cup as he took a sip of scalding hot coffee. 'You should consider al-Meghrani a person of interest,' he said quietly.

She blinked. 'What?'

'You heard me.'

'Spud, the guy almost kicked us out of his car for mentioning the Qu'ran.'

'Did you notice his shoulder bag?'

She frowned. 'Yeah, I guess . . .'

'What did it look like?'

Eleanor screwed up her face, clearly trying to remember. 'Green?' she said tentatively.

'Khaki,' Spud said. 'Canvas material.'

'So what? It was just a bag.'

'It wasn't just a bag. It was a Claymore bag.'

She looked at him for a moment. Then, suddenly, she started to laugh. 'Oh, Spud,' she said. 'You really *did* want him to be the bad guy, didn't you?'

Spud stared her down. She stopped laughing. 'Do you know what a Claymore mine is?' he said.

'Yes,' she said patiently. 'I *know* what a Claymore is. I also know that you can probably get those bags off eBay for ten a penny.'

'Not like that one,' Spud said. 'I've carried those things halfway across the world and I know the difference between one that's been in the field and one that's come from army surplus. It was all scuffed. Well used. Frayed round the edges. I think there were even bits of sand in the canvas. Trust me, that bag didn't come off eBay.'

They exchanged a long look. Finally, Eleanor reached out and put one hand over Spud's. She squeezed it slightly. 'Look, Spud,' she said. 'I *know* this must be hard for you. I *know* you must miss your old way of life. But you have to understand that we can't afford to chase shadows. We have to make sure we see what's there, not what we *want* to be there. He's just a cabbie, going about his business. We need to do the same. We're going to head back to London, and we're going to carry on looking through files. I'm sorry if you think it's boring, but that's intelligence work.' She drained her coffee cup and stood up. 'Your army days are over, Spud. The sooner you come to terms with that, the better. Coming?'

She walked away from the table. Spud stood up quickly to follow her. He winced as a sharp pain cut through his abdomen. It was almost as if his body was telling him that the cute spook in the hijab was right. Maybe he should be listening to her after all.

Your army days are over.

He frowned. Fuck that, he thought. And fuck *this*. He wasn't going to be an MI6 lackey for the rest of his working life. He caught up with Eleanor just as she was opening the door out on to the street. He held up the car keys. 'Yours,' he said.

'What do you mean?'

'Take them. I'm through with this. You can drive yourself back to London.'

She looked at him warily as she took the keys. 'Where are you going?'

'Back to Hereford,' Spud said.

On the outskirts of Lagos, no more than a couple of miles as the crow flies from the grand residences of some of the wealthiest men in Africa, a very poor fisherman was preparing to go home.

His name was Randolph and home, for him, was a single room in a shack. The shack itself sat on rickety stilts protruding from the waters of Ajegunle, a vast slum. Randolph had heard people call Ajegunle the Jungle. A bad name, he always thought. In the jungle, things grow. Nothing could ever grow here. The streets, such as they were, were thick with debris. Plastic bottles, waste packaging, faeces, urine: everywhere. The bank leading down to the water was impossible to see, and the water itself was fetid and filthy. Its surface was slick with oil – the same oil that made a handful of Nigerian families super-wealthy, while the rest of the population, like Randolph, struggled on in poverty – and swarming with rubbish, since the inhabitants of this slum had no way of getting rid of their waste other than throwing it into the water. Nor was there any proper sanitation. The cleanest thing the inhabitants of Ajegunle could do was to urinate and defecate directly into the water. It made the water smell foul, but Randolph had lived here for so long that he didn't really notice the stench any more.

Randolph's creaky shack housed not only him, but also his twin nine-year-old children, both girls. Their mother had died in childbirth, all those years ago, and Randolph did the best he could to bring them up. They were the only joy in his life, always smiling despite the hardship of their existence. Barely enough to eat, and shunned by their peers – not because they were poor or orphaned, but for the silliest of reasons. Randolph was always perspiring: his face was constantly drenched in sweat, and the one shirt he possessed always had dark stains under the armpits. Here in the slum, nobody smelled too great, but Randolph smelled worse than most, and his precious daughters were taunted for having a stinky dad. He knew how much it upset them, even though they tried never to let it show in front of him.

The most valuable object in their lives was the small boat that he now paddled through these polluted waters. He was not alone, of course. The waters were busy. Hundreds of other boatmen were making their way home, many of them shouting at each other. There always seemed to be shouting in Ajegunle, but Randolph had learned to keep quiet and avoid confrontation. Take this evening, for example. To get into an argument would be to risk losing the one small fish he had managed to catch in twelve hours of fishing – and that only because he had found it floating dead on the oily surface of the poisonous water. There were too many fishermen here, and far too few fish. But how else

180

could he earn a living? He didn't want to join the gangs who swaggered round the slums extorting money, unopposed by the police who never ventured into the Ajegunle slum.

He paddled carefully through the crowded network of houses on stilts until he finally came to his own – no different from the others, except that his daughters had tied a pretty red ribbon to one of the stilts to cheer their father up when he got home. It always had the desired effect. Randolph smiled as he tied his boat to the same stilt, grabbed the plastic bag that held the dead fish, and climbed the ladder that led directly into the doorway of the shack.

'I'm home,' he said as he entered. It was dark in the shack – even if they were connected to the electricity supply, it would be optimistic to expect power for more than an hour a day – and it always took a few seconds for his eyes to grow used to it when he got back. 'Who's got a hug for their daddy?'

'Not me,' said a man's voice.

Randolph blinked in the darkness. He could just make out the silhouette of someone sitting in the only chair the family owned. 'Who are you?' he demanded. 'Where are my girls?'

'Safe,' said the figure. 'Actually, that's not true. They're not safe at all. But they are alive. For the moment.'

Randolph felt his perspiration getting worse. Sweat dripped into his eyes and down the nape of his neck.

'They were right,' said the figure. 'You really do smell.'

Randolph stared at the figure. Then he winced. The figure had held up a small screen – Randolph assumed this was one of the smartphones he'd heard people talking about – and the light hurt his eyes. But then he started to understand what he was looking at, and he took two horrified steps forward.

He was watching video footage, and he could just make out his daughters. They were bound, side by side, to two chairs. Both girls were gagged by a piece of rope tied round their head. Their eyes were bloodshot – wide open and terrified. Behind them stood a man in a black balaclava, wide holes for the eyes and mouth roughly cut out. In his right hand was a short, curved blade, which he held over the children's heads.

Nothing else happened. The video footage finished on a frame of the children looking straight ahead, not moving. Randolph's knees went beneath him. He collapsed to the floor of his shack, his hands clenched in front of him. 'My children,' he whispered. 'What have you done with them?'

'What we've done with them isn't the question,' said the man. He stood up, and towered over Randolph. 'The question is: what *will* we do to them, you stinking piece of filth.'

Randolph felt tears coming to his eyes, and perspiration to the rest of his body. 'I'm a poor man,' he said. 'I don't have any money.'

'You don't need money,' said the figure. He looked down on Randolph with curling disdain. Only now could Randolph properly make out his features: flared nostrils, pockmarked cheeks and a frown of pure hate. 'You just need to do exactly as you're told.'

18.45 hrs
Night fell over Chikunda.

The stubborn stench of the burned bodies in the isolation zone lingered in the air. The only sound, now that the sun had set, was the occasional squawk of a bird from the thick vegetation surrounding the village, and the very distant rumble of thunder in the heavy air. And the only movement came from scavenging birds. Long beaks, cloak-like wings. They looked to Danny like old-world vultures. Endangered in this part of the world, but unable to resist a feast. Three had landed on the dead body of a young man with his arm and leg in tourniquets, and were pecking at his flesh with a clockwork regularity. Rather more were feasting on the bodies of dead Boko Haram militants dotted around the village.

One of the scavengers stopped pecking for a moment. It cocked its head and listened for five seconds. As one, every scavenging bird in the village launched itself into the air with a noisy flap of wings.

Silence.

Another shadow appeared in the air, much larger than the birds it had displaced, and certainly sleeker. Its nose was pointed and

182

angular, its rotors a circular blur with a slight reflection of moon-light. It was a chopper, flying in over the isolation zone. The sound of its rotors was very quiet. Inaudible to any humans within fifty feet of it. It shape was sleek and angular. The ends of the rotor blades were curved downward to reduce radar splash and noise. It touched down in the middle of the road, its nose facing west.

New movement, this time from the east of the village. Eleven figures emerged from the vegetation. They were led by two men and a woman in camouflage gear, carefully gripping the rifles slung round their necks as they advanced towards the road. Behind them, four guys in dirty white hazmat suits, carrying their rebreathing helmets under their arms. Taking up the rear, four more soldiers, carrying guns and heavy flight cases of gear.

The company advanced carefully but quickly, picking their way over the bodies of the dead militants as they hurried towards the stealth chopper. Only when they were ten metres from the aircraft did the side door open. A uniformed loadie ushered them in. Once all eleven of them had embarked, he closed the door.

The chopper immediately rose from the ground. Danny Black stared out of a tiny porthole of a window, winding the paracord with Ripley's dog tag and wedding ring round his fingers. He was pleased to leave this place, even though it meant deserting the pile of ashes that was all that remained of his friend. He had the uneasy sensation that there were a hell of a lot more piles of ashes to come.

Caitlin was sitting next to him. 'So you've got a kid on the way?' Her voice was just loud enough that only Danny could hear it over the engine noise.

He nodded.

'You should have said. You had me barking up the wrong tree.'

He didn't look at her. Thoughts like the ones he was having were too much of a distraction. 'Maybe the middle of an op isn't the right time for games like that,' he said quietly.

Caitlin gave a short, dismissive, mirthless laugh. 'Where else do you think I'd find a guy who can deal with the way a girl like me lives her life?'

Danny didn't reply. He wanted the conversation to be over. But Caitlin pressed on. 'When's the baby due?' she asked.

'Any day now.'

'You don't know the due date?'

He looked down. 'In case you hadn't noticed, I've got other things on my mind.'

'So you're not so different to me.'

Danny felt silent. From the corner of his eye, he could tell that Caitlin was staring across the body of the chopper to where Tony was sitting. He remembered what Tony had said about her. *She's a ruthless bitch.* He was right. But there was much more to her than that.

'You should be careful of him,' Danny warned her quietly.

'You had your chance, Danny Black,' Caitlin breathed. She was smiling, but Danny could tell it was the kind of smile that hid something. Was she stung by his rejection? 'Anyway,' she said lightly, 'I always had Tony down as the alpha male round here.'

The chopper banked sharply so that it was heading south. Invisible and almost noiseless, it sped across the Nigerian countryside, back towards the coast.

SEVENTEEN

The journey away from Chikunda was a hell of a sight easier than the journey towards it. The stealth Black Hawk kept low, skimming thirty feet over the ground or above the treetops, depending on the prevailing terrain. It seemed unnaturally quiet within the body of the aircraft. Danny was used to the deafening growl of a regular chopper. Stealth technology made this one strangely ghost-like.

They flew in silence. Danny's eyes picked out the faces of the Porton Down team. They looked exhausted, and a bit frightened. Was that because of their unusual circumstances, or were they unnerved by what they'd found in Chikunda? Danny had a definite feeling that their work wasn't done yet. He hoped that they were up to whatever the next few hours held.

After ninety minutes' flight time, the loadie spoke up. 'We need to refuel,' he said. 'The Nigerians don't know we're in their airspace so we're gonna take a pitstop. There's a deserted football pitch on the outskirts of Lagos. Won't be anyone there at this time. The Foreign Office have arranged for the BA lads at Lagos International to bring a bowser of fuel to meet us.'

As the loadie spoke, the chopper banked to the left. From his tiny port window, Danny saw the bright glare of a vehicle's headlights down below, maybe a hundred metres from the chopper's position. They disappeared as the Black Hawk straightened up, only to reappear again as it lowered itself in to land. The loadie opened up and jumped out. The headlamps of the fuel bowser immediately made Danny squint, but he regained his vision as the tanker drew up alongside the chopper. It had a bright yellow cab,

185

but the long, cylindrical tank itself was rusting, its paint peeling off. A Nigerian guy – obviously on the Firm's payroll – jumped out of the cab, head bowed from the downdraught of the rotors that were still spinning.

Danny, Tony and Caitlin alighted from the chopper and immediately took up defensive positions around it, Danny down on one knee at the angular nose of the aircraft, the butt of his HK pressed in against his shoulder. The flat surface of this deserted football pitch was hard and dusty. No grass. Certainly no goalposts. Fifty metres ahead of him was a dilapidated grandstand, but it was clear this was a place nobody came to, especially at this time of night.

It took ten minutes to refuel. The unit got back into the Black Hawk and immediately took to the skies again.

They flew higher this time – maybe eight hundred feet – and through the window Danny saw why. There were more lights down below: as they approached the coast, the terrain was more populated. He knew they'd be avoiding flying over Lagos itself – their route would be taking them north of the city. Out of sight and earshot.

Ten minutes later, land turned to sea. Danny saw moonlight trails reflecting on a rough ocean, with the sleek shadow of the Black Hawk cruising across the wave tops.

'Five minutes out,' the loadie announced. Danny caught a glance from Tony.

'Thirty seconds out.' The Black Hawk was banking and losing height at the same time. From the window, Danny saw the bright lights of a frigate, about 120 metres in length. He could just make out the white foam of the vessel's wake and the pale glow of the LZ to aft. The frigate grew closer dramatically quickly, and before Danny knew it the Black Hawk had touched down on the landing deck. The unit were the first to alight and Danny instantly smelled the sharp tang of the sea and felt the spray stinging his dirty face. As the Black Hawk's rotors slowed down he heard a thunderous crash, and the frigate yawed dramatically. The sea was very rough.

There were two guys waiting on the landing deck. They wore Crye Precision multicam trousers with small, dark green life vests, black boots and sturdy gloves. Both had stubble and short hair that was dishevelled by the stiff wind on board. Like Danny's unit, each had a boom mike at his mouth. Danny knew at a glance that these were Australian SAS.

'Regiment?' one of them shouted in an Australian accent. He was eyeing Caitlin uncertainly.

Danny nodded.

'Welcome on board HMAS *Anzac*.'

'Briefing room?' Danny asked.

'This way.'

They ran across the deck of the frigate, wind howling in their ears, and through a heavy metal door which led to a cramped, winding steel staircase. Their footsteps rang out as they headed down below and through a network of low, narrow corridors. After thirty seconds they turned left through another door and into a decent-sized room, about fifteen metres by fifteen. Benches along the walls held several laptops plugged into comms sockets, showing a mixture of GPS coordinates, satellite imagery and naval mapping. There was a white-noise crackle from a radio unit in the corner of the room. There were another four Australian SAS guys here, dressed identically to their mates. A fifth guy – Danny took him to be an ops officer – wore multicam trousers but no life jacket. A sixth man wore dark naval uniform. He stepped forward, hand outstretched. 'Captain Enston,' he said. 'I hear you have an Aussie with you?' His eyes picked out Caitlin. 'I've set aside a separate female berth for you, Major Wallace, if you need it.'

'I don't think there'll be any time for that, Captain,' Caitlin said.

'I've told my men to leave you fellas – and lasses – alone. But you need anything – food, drink, anything – you just shout.'

Danny shook the captain's hand and nodded his thanks. He was already turning his attention to the ops officer when the captain added: 'Oh, one other thing, fellas. I've just had a communication that an MI6 liaison officer is on his way to the frigate. ETA about two hours. I'll show him down here when he arrives.'

Danny nodded, then turned to the ops officer. 'What's our status?' he demanded.

'We've just had a communication from London,' the ops officer said without introducing himself. 'They've received imagery from an American satellite. You need to look at this.'

The ops officer spread the paperwork out on a table in the centre of the room. Danny, Tony, Caitlin and the six Aussie SAS guys gathered round.

'We're after a man of Chinese appearance who we believe to be heading to a ship in this vicinity,' the ops officer announced. 'The analysts in London think that this CIA image shows us what we're looking for.' He pointed at a dot in the middle of the image. 'We think this is an RIB, possibly a Rigid Raider, heading west-south-westerly at about 07.00 this morning. We also think this corresponds to the time our target would be heading out to sea.' The ops officer rolled up that image and unrolled another. 'The next piece in the jigsaw,' he said. 'On that trajectory at that time, the RIB was heading into the vicinity of this vessel here.' He pointed to another satellite smudge on the ocean. 'That's the MV *Golden Coral*, about fifty nautical miles from the coast, which would put it within range of the RIB. It's now twenty nautical miles west of our position.'

'Registered in?' Danny asked.

'Panama. Currently transporting cargo from Ivory Coast to Singapore.'

'Any Chinese links?'

'None that London can find.'

'It's pretty fucking thin,' Tony said.

'It's all we've got,' the ops officer said with an irritated glance at Tony. 'We have a copy of the ship's manifest. It lists five crew members, which is about standard for a cargo vessel. But you need to be prepared for there being more – your Chinese national at the very least, since there's nobody of that description listed on the manifest. We've got two options: a waterborne assault or an aerial assault. I've got to tell you guys, the sea state is pretty high. I know which one I'd want to go for.'

Danny addressed the assembled company. 'Okay guys, listen up. We've reason to believe that the Chinese target is in possession of a bioweapon. We don't know if it'll be ready for him to deploy, but we suspect it will be and we'll have to assume that's the case. If we go for an aerial assault, there's a much higher chance they'll see us coming. I know it's rough out there, but my vote goes for the waterborne option. Anyone disagree?'

There were no dissenters.

'That's your call,' the ops officer said. He walked to the other side of the room, and spoke into an intercom. 'Prepare the raiders,' he said.

A crackly 'Aye sir' came back over the intercom.

'Do you need hazmat gear?' the ops officer asked.

Danny shook his head. 'Impractical,' he said. 'Anyone got a problem with that?'

No one did.

'Good. Our primary objective is to secure the ship and locate the Chinese target. We need him alive: I think he'll have intel about who's behind a bio-attack, potentially on the UK, and we need that information. But if you get any hint that he's going to *deploy* a bioweapon, drop him. Trust me, you don't want what he's dishing out.'

'What about the remaining crew?' one of the Aussies asked.

'Do what you need to do,' Danny told him. 'Once the target's secured, we'll get our Porton Down guys on board. Our secondary objective is to isolate any bioweapons there might be on that ship.' He turned to the ops officer. 'What are our timings?'

'We're on course now. Current coordinates of the target vessel: 4.27221 north, 3.26328 east. That puts us in a position to have a visual on the *Golden Coral* at approximately 22.00 hours.' He checked his watch. 'That's in about forty-five minutes. We're going to kill the frigate lights so they don't see us approaching over the horizon, and hold off when we're about a nautical mile from its position. You've got three RIBs at your disposal. The high sea state will at least reduce the chance of them seeing you approach – those cargo ships get pretty wonky in these kind of

189

conditions, so my guess is they'll have cleared the decks. But you'll need to take extra care boarding. Once you've secured the ship, we'll draw up alongside and transfer whatever personnel you need.'

'Do we have a plan of the cargo ship?' Caitlin asked.

The ops officer frowned. Danny sensed he had woman trouble. But he turned to one of the laptops and brought up some rough schematics. 'It's about seven hundred feet in length. The bridge and living quarters are directly above the engine room approximately a hundred feet from aft. The bridge structure has three levels above deck: two for living quarters, the top for navigation. Engine room down below.'

Danny pointed out three of the Aussie SAS guys. 'Team one,' he said. 'Secure the engine room.' He pointed out the remaining three. 'Team two, secure the living quarters.' He indicated Tony, Caitlin and himself. 'Team three,' he said. 'We'll secure the bridge.'

'What is this,' one of the Aussies said, 'the invasion of the Brits?'

'What's your name?' Danny said.

'Goldie.'

'Our target's most likely to be on the bridge. We're the only ones who can ID him. Got a problem with that, Goldie?'

Goldie fell silent and shook his head.

'Good man. Any other questions?'

There were none.

'They're getting ready to winch the RIBs into place now,' the ops officer said, 'and we've got three coxswains on line to transport you. We'll monitor you on VHF channel 15 so you can let us know when you've secured the ship. We need to get your personal radios synced up, sort you out with NV, then you're good to go.'

'Okay,' Danny said curtly. He checked his watch. 22.00 hrs exactly. 'I want us ready to get in the water at 22.15. Let's move.'

22.10 hrs

It was very busy on deck. The air was filled with shouts and the humming of machinery. Thirty metres from Danny's position, over on the landing deck, two engineers were folding back the rotors of the Black Hawk while a third was fitting a motorised towing vehicle, about the size of a golf cart, to its front. They were clearly preparing to tow that aircraft into the ship's dedicated hangar, where no doubt another heli was waiting, more suited to the task of ferrying the Porton Down team on to the cargo ship once it was secure. Danny expected a Sea King of some description, but so far that was still under wraps.

It was good to have the Aussie SAS involved. They had close ties with the Regiment, who would often send a couple of guys to them on a two-year attachment. The Aussies would return the favour by sending a couple of their lads to Hereford. The Australian SAS were easily as good as the Regiment, and in recent years they'd been putting rounds down in Afghanistan alongside the boys from 22. In short: they knew their stuff. If you needed soldiers to support you, you couldn't ask for better.

The Aussie SAS guys had provided all the gear they needed. Carabiner, loop line, even a digital camera in case they needed to take photos of whatever they found. He double-checked that the bright-orange rubberised portable VHF unit they'd given him to contact the frigate was securely in his ops waistcoat. Then he slung his life vest over his neck and rolled it down over his webbing. It would automatically inflate if he found himself in the water. If that happened, he'd be in for a long evening: the frigate would mark the point where he went overboard, but the mission would have to continue. It could be hours before anyone came back to find him. He had clipped a set of night-vision goggles to his helmet. Fully waterproof, they'd be crucial during the boarding process. He lowered them to check they were working properly. The world turned to a grainy green haze, and he found he could make out each individual wave in the ocean. He raised the goggles again for now, and double-checked his personal weapon.

Danny was standing in the shadow of the huge mechanical arm of the winch that would deposit the three Rigid Raiders into the ocean. The Raiders themselves were in a row, the first one ten metres to Danny's right. Each boat was just shy of seven metres in length. Small craft, but mobile and speedy – they'd get up to at least thirty knots in calm seas, which would give them the edge on a container ship like the *Golden Coral*. It shouldn't take more than a few minutes to catch up with it over the distance of a nautical mile. Three members of the frigate's Aussie navy crew were checking them over – these would be the coxswains that would be transporting them to the *Golden Coral*, and a couple of the guys from Team One were loading rolled-up caving ladders and telescopic poles into each of the RIBs.

Suddenly, a voice echoed over the ship's tannoy system. 'This is the captain. We're cutting power to all non-essential lighting systems in ten seconds. Repeat, cutting power to all non-essential lighting systems . . .'

Instinctively, Danny closed his eyes and engaged his NV. When he opened them again, the frigate had been plunged into darkness, but his goggles meant he could see everything clearly. Tony was approaching, and Danny could tell from the grin on his face that he was seething with excitement for the job ahead. 'To think we were expecting months of babysitting diplomats!' he shouted over the noise of waves booming against the hull of the frigate. 'This op's turning out better than we thought.'

'Tell that to Ripley,' Danny said.

Tony shrugged. 'Could have been any of us, mucker,' he said. He checked the time. '22.13. Let's load up.'

Within two minutes, each member of the unit was settled in their Rigid Raider – two fore, one aft, with the coxswain in a central position by the steering wheel and a screen displaying GPS and radar information. The outboard motor of each boat was hinged up, but the engines were already turning over. Danny could hardly hear them over the waves crashing against the hull of the frigate. The huge winch groaned and creaked in the darkness as it moved slowly over the top of the first Rigid Raider. The coxswain attached the grappling hook to four strong points on the hull – two fore, two aft. The winch lifted the boat, its crew and its buzzing motor ten metres off the deck, and then lowered it into the water. Danny's unit was the last to have their boat winched. As they rose into the air, he looked to the south-west. His eyes picked out the twinkling lights of a ship in the distance.

'Is that our target?' Caitlin asked.

Danny nodded. It was good to clap eyes on the thing. They'd be navigating towards it largely by eye.

There was a booming thump as the Rigid Raider's hull hit the water. Danny clutched the edge of the boat fiercely as they made impact, then he and Caitlin unclipped the front quick-release fasteners from the winch as Tony and the coxswain unclipped the rear two. The second they were free, the coxswain knocked the outboard down into the rough sea. They immediately jolted forward, and within seconds they were curving away from the frigate.

They'd barely travelled fifteen metres when Danny wondered if they'd made the wrong call, going for a waterborne rather than an airborne assault. A wave crashed over the side of the boat. Instantly soaked by the spray, Danny fell from one side of the Raider to the other. He blindly grabbed the edge of the boat and gasped for air as the wave subsided. One glance in Tony's direction showed that his unit colleague had raised his NV goggles and had a fierce glint of enjoyment in his eye as the coxswain navigated the boat at speed through the choppy water.

The Rigid Raider slammed into troughs and crested peaks – which appeared in various shades of green through the night-vision goggles – as they sped in a south-westerly direction. Danny only caught occasional glimpses of the other two boats when their positions at the crests of waves coincided. And occasionally, he saw the lights of the cargo ship, a little closer each time they came into view.

Time to target, seven minutes. Only when they were about three hundred metres out did the MV *Golden Coral* come into constant view. The coxswain altered the trajectory of the Rigid Raider so that they were curving in from aft.

Two hundred metres to target. The wake of the cargo ship was heavy and violent. The Raider juddered through it, foam and spray stinging and blinding the occupants. Danny scanned the deck, searching for lookouts. He saw none. The bad weather at least gave them that advantage.

A hundred metres to target. The vast hull of the *Golden Coral* seemed to cast a shadow over them, even at this distance. They ploughed on through the wake, which grew more treacherous the closer they got. Danny was completely deafened now, by the roar of the ocean and the boom of the cargo ship's engines. The stench of fumes overpowered the tang of sea salt, and his soaked clothes clung icily to him.

Thirty seconds later, they were alongside the vessel. The three Rigid Raiders were about ten metres apart. As the coxswain lowered his speed to match that of the *Golden Coral*, Danny grabbed the rolled-up caving ladder with soaked hands, double-checked the grappling hook at its leading end, and then picked up the telescopic pole. In his periphery vision he saw that one guy in each of the other boats was doing the same. He clipped the end of the telescopic pole to the leading edge of the caving ladder and started to extend it length by length. As the pole grew longer, the caving ladder unfurled. It was made of sturdy wire uprights, and wire rungs surrounded by narrow metal tubing that were no more than eight inches wide. Danny raised it five metres. Ten metres. Keeping the telescopic pole stable in these rough seas was a challenge. It rocked and scraped against the hull of the ship as Danny extended it to a full twenty metres, and the caving ladder flapped crazily with the movement of the vessels and the sea. His muscles burned as, his feet planted on the unstable deck of the Rigid Raider, he held the ladder up and tried to get purchase on the railings of the cargo ship with the grappling hook. It took a long twenty seconds to achieve. Danny grabbed at one of the metal-tubing rungs of the caving ladder and tugged hard to satisfy himself that it was properly attached. Then, with a nod at Tony and Caitlin, he prepared to climb it.

The cargo ship itself was rocking heavily in the waves, and the rungs of the caving ladder felt flimsy beneath his feet. Several times, Danny felt like he was in freefall, or as if the rungs had disappeared entirely. He gripped the ladder *very* firmly.

He was a third of the way up when it happened. The air seemed to boom and there was a sudden downward lurch from the *Golden Coral*. Danny was losing height. For a moment he thought he'd fallen: his body was swinging away from the hull of the ship, and water was approaching fast from below. He had a fraction of a second to reassure himself that he was still clutching the ladder when his body slammed into the ocean and he found himself completely submerged.

He had to suppress a moment of panic. If the grappling hook at the top of the ladder came loose, he was fucked. His life vest was inflating and his ears were full of the deadened grind of the ship's engines. *Hold on*, he told himself. *Just hold on . . .*

And then, just as suddenly, he was yanked back up out of the water as the cargo ship straightened up. He flew through the air and his body slammed hard against the side of the ship. All the wind was knocked from his lungs, but he forced himself to keep on climbing, his cold hands gripping the narrow tubing that formed the rungs for all they were worth, the metal digging hard into his hands.

The ship yawed a second time, and the sea rose, but now he was high enough up the ladder that he only skimmed the surface of the water. He carried on climbing, and thirty seconds later he was clambering over the railings of the cargo ship.

Danny was the first on deck, though he could see the grappling hooks of the other two ladders spaced at ten-metre intervals towards the front of the ship, and it only took a couple of seconds before he saw Goldie climb over the railings, dripping wet. The deck itself was wet and slippery, and the yawing of the vessel felt even more pronounced up here. He immediately checked up and down the bridge for hostiles – none, but he knew he wasn't more than twenty or thirty metres from the bridge, so he remained hyper-alert – then unclipped a carabiner and loop line from his ops waistcoat and used them to clip the ladder more permanently to the vessel. Then he gave two flashes of his Surefire torch over the side to indicate to Caitlin and Tony that the next of them could board.

Goldie did the same, then crouched down in the firing position, his weapon pointing forward. Danny pulled off his wet, inflated life vest then crouched down and covered aft, his eyes picking out the main features of the vessel. It was heavily laden with storage containers. They were three units high, and the closest of them was just five metres from Danny's position. The bridge tower – which Danny knew housed both the crew rooms and the engine room down below – loomed above them, the lights from inside glowing bright in the darkness. He raised his NV goggles, and took a moment to acclimatise and work out the geography of their position.

To reach the bridge tower, they would have to move along the deck twenty metres from Danny's position, then take a left where the line of storage containers ended. He tried to calculate the odds of there being any guards on deck. Minimal in a high sea state like this, but still a possibility. They would need to be very careful. At least, he thought to himself, the massive grind of the ship's engines and the crashing of the sea would entirely camouflage any gunshot, if only while they were out on deck.

He looked over his shoulder. All three teams were aboard. Danny raised one hand above his head and sharply jabbed his finger forward twice. Silently, Team One – led by Goldie – moved past him, their weapons engaged. When they reached the end of the cargo containers, one of them swung round the corner, then made a hand gesture to indicate the all-clear. Their movements were sharp and efficient. Danny could tell that the Aussies were good soldiers.

At another hand gesture from Danny, Team Two moved carefully in the same direction. Covered by Team One, they turned the corner. Ten seconds later, Goldie raised one hand. It was time for Danny's unit to move.

With the butt of his rifle still pressed hard into his shoulder, Danny led Tony and Caitlin along the deck. They swung round the corner towards the bridge tower. Team Two were in the firing position ten metres along. The entrance to the bridge tower was fifteen metres beyond them: a grey steel door with a circular porthole window near the top. As they approached, Danny saw that the inside of the window was misted with condensation. Three metres out, he turned to Tony and Caitlin.

'Cover me.'

Caitlin stepped towards the door, ready to open it. Tony positioned himself behind Danny, ready to fire if necessary as Danny crossed the threshold. Danny nodded at Caitlin and she swung the door open.

A blast of hot air from inside the ship slammed into Danny's face. No personnel. Four metres beyond the door, a spiral steel staircase, much like the one they'd used in the frigate. Danny stepped towards it. Checked up. Down. No sign of the crew. He spoke into the radio. 'Stairwell clear. Team One advance.'

It took fifteen seconds for Team One to leapfrog the others and arrive at the stairwell, by which time Tony and Caitlin were inside the bridge tower. Without waiting for any further instruction, Team One headed down the stairs towards the engine room, which it was their role to secure.

Danny felt his jugular pumping. A minute passed. Ominous creaks and groans echoed from the body of the cargo ship. It sounded as if it was going to break up any second, but Danny knew that there was movement and give in these old vessels, especially in rough seas. He kept his attention focused on the stairwell, ready to drop anyone who appeared from the top of the bridge tower.

A radio communication burst into his earpiece. '*This is Team One leader,*' said an Australian voice. '*We have the engine room secured. Three crew members down.*' And before Danny could ask the question, he added: '*No Chinese. But one of them managed to put a Mayday through to the bridge. They'll be expecting you up there.*'

Shit, Danny breathed. Then, louder, into his radio: 'Can you kill the lights on the bridge tower?'

'*Give me thirty seconds.*'

They waited. The ship creaked and groaned.

The lights died.

Danny immediately clipped down the NV goggles on his

197

helmet. The world turned hazy green. 'Team Two, go,' he instructed into his radio.

Fifteen seconds later, Team Two were moving into the bridge tower. Danny, Tony and Caitlin kept their weapons trained on the stairwell as their three Aussie colleagues, who also had their NV engaged, advanced up to the first floor. Once more, they remained in position, listening to nothing but the storm outside and the creaking of the ship.

This time it was a full two minutes before they had a communication. *'Team two leader. First floor clear. No personnel.'*

'Roger that. Team Three moving to the bridge now.'

Danny nodded at Tony and Caitlin. It was time to move up.

Tony went first, weapon and NV engaged. Eight steps before he reached a winder on the metal stairwell. He stopped and covered the next flight while Danny and Caitlin advanced. Danny grew warier with each step. Whoever was on the bridge, they knew someone was coming. There would be resistance. Probably armed.

They passed the main entrance on to the first-floor crew quarters, then continued single file up the stairs, Danny following Tony's grainy green figure, his finger resting lightly on the trigger of his HK.

They found themselves on a metal landing, a single door leading off it. Danny knew from his study of the ship's plans that this was the entrance to the bridge. He could make out rivets in the door which told him it was made of sturdy steel. If there were shooters behind it, it would act as a shield, of sorts.

Tony had taken up position by the door, lowered his gun and removed a flashbang from his ops waistcoat. He squeezed the lever, then pulled the pin. Danny and Caitlin stood three metres from the door, covering it with their assault rifles. Danny raised three fingers.

Two fingers.

One.

Go.

EIGHTEEN

Tony kicked open the door, just a couple of inches. Danny immediately heard two sounds.

The first was the ocean. Even though they were indoors, the sound of waves was loud.

The second was gunshot.

There was a burst of fire from the bridge. Danny estimated four weapons. There was a tinny sound as the rounds ricocheted off the metal door, immediately followed by a deafening crack as Tony chucked in the flashbang and stood clear as it exploded. Danny closed his eyes momentarily to stop himself being blinded by the flash, but opened them as soon as he heard the noise, and started to advance.

The grenade had killed the gunfire. Now Danny could hear nothing but panicked shouting. Tony kicked the door open.

The doorway framed a picture of chaos. In the green haze of his NV, Danny saw three figures – ten metres from his position, at the far side of the bridge, backs up against the window that surrounded it. It was clearly pitch black for them, here in the middle of the ocean with no light to see by: they were staring at different angles across the room, obviously totally disorientated by the blinding flash and deafening crack of the flashbang. They all had weapons, though – pistols – and were waving them around wildly, evidently wanting to fire but not knowing in which direction to aim.

They couldn't see the Regiment unit, but the Regiment unit could see them. From his brief glance, Danny didn't think any of them were Mr Chiu. But they could start shooting any second, so they needed to be put down in any case.

Danny and Caitlin had clear shots. Two from Danny, one from Caitlin. The targets were on the floor less than a second after the door was opened.

As soon as the three targets were down, Danny saw why the noise of the ocean was so loud. Someone had smashed the re-inforced window opposite the entrance to the bridge. Impossible to do without a sturdy tool, and sure enough Danny saw a fire axe lying on the floor just in front of it. Someone must have escaped.

He stepped over the threshold of the bridge. The needed to move fast while any further occupants were still disorientated. A metre into the room he scanned left, then right. He quickly picked out the one remaining person there: a figure crouching down to his two o'clock by a panel of instruments.

It wasn't Chiu. A single shot from Danny's HK and he was neutralised. Danny ran to the broken window and looked out. It was a drop of seven or eight metres to the deck – doable, with a lucky landing. And luck had been on the side of whoever had jumped from the bridge. The aft deck was an open space of about fifty square metres, leading up to a high railing that overlooked the water. Danny could make out shattered glass on the deck. But no sign of anyone.

He spoke immediately into his radio. 'All units, the bridge is clear. We have personnel on deck, most likely armed. We need a full sweep of the deck, from aft forward. *Go!*'

He turned to Caitlin and slung her the orange portable VHF radio. 'Stay here,' he said. 'Make contact with the ops room. Update them. Tony, with me.'

Caitlin caught the radio with one hand as Danny and Tony hurried back through the darkness of the bridge tower. Danny tried to tread as lightly as he could so that his feet didn't clatter down the metal staircase.

On the ground floor, they pushed through the heavy door and manoeuvred themselves on to the aft deck. The six Aussie SF guys were waiting for them there, evenly spaced across the open deck, weapons engaged. A quick examination of the broken glass from the bridge window revealed a puddle of blood. Someone had injured themselves jumping out. As there was no sign of enemy targets here, they needed to check all points on the vessel forward of this position. 'We sweep the top deck first,' Danny said, 'then we move down. Remember, we need Chiu alive. If you see him, hold your fire and apprehend him.'

Danny ran to the starboard side of the vessel, while Tony stayed port. Since the central part of the vessel's top deck was taken up by storage units, to sweep the ship they would need to move forward in two groups, one along the deck on either side.

They did this with quiet, clinical efficiency. Danny and his three Aussie colleagues moved four abreast, the butts of their weapons pressed sharply into their shoulders, safety switches on semi-automatic. Danny's ears roared with the noise of the ship's engines, and with the sea crashing against the hull. But he kept his focus laser-sharp on the deck in front of him, sensitive to any unexpected movement that would give him a split warning of an incoming threat.

They moved forward twenty metres. To their left, a three-metre-wide gap in the storage containers. Danny made a gesture with his left hand and one of his team headed silently down this corridor. The remaining three kept moving forward.

Tony's voice. *'There's a trail of blood on the deck. Someone came this way.'*

'Keep following it,' Danny instructed.

Another twenty metres. They were about halfway along the vessel. A second corridor to the left. Another member of the team – Goldie this time – peeled off to secure it. Danny and his remaining colleague moved forward.

Twenty metres.

Thirty.

Forty.

The ship yawed dramatically as they came to the end of the storage containers. Danny and his Aussie colleague pressed their backs up against the wall formed by the final container. Danny shuffled up to the corner of the storage container and peered round.

He took in everything in an instant.

The fore deck was more than twice the size of the aft deck. At the far end was a small crane, about twenty feet high. On either side of it were fixed steel scaffolds, each one about ten metres high. And on top of each scaffold, fixed to a ramp slanting down towards the sea, was a bright-orange closed lifeboat.

And at the foot of the crane, twenty-five metres from Danny's position, were two figures. One was on his knees. The other was behind him, holding a gun to his head. It was almost an action replay of the scene that had played out in front of Danny's eyes on the outskirts of Chikunda.

With one difference. The gunman was African. And the guy on his knees was Mr Chiu.

Neither the African militant nor Mr Chiu had seen Danny. They were screaming at each other in English – clearly their only mutual language.

'*Put gun down, idiot!*' Chiu was shouting. '*What you think you doing? My orders come from Caliph himself!*'

'*So do mine! Climb up and get into the lifeboat!*' shouted the African militant.

As he spoke, he happened to look in Danny's direction.

Their eyes met.

Danny wanted Chiu alive. He lined up the sights of his rifle with the broad target of the militant's chest.

He prepared to take the shot.

'This is *Golden Coral*, do you copy?'

Caitlin stared furiously at the orange handheld VHF radio. It emitted nothing but white noise. She cursed under her breath. Something was wrong with the comms. She couldn't make contact with the frigate.

She strode across the bridge to the ship's VHF radio unit. She assumed the *Golden Coral* would have a decent-sized antenna, and she adjusted the frequency to channel 15.

'This is *Golden Coral*, do you copy?'

A five-second pause.

'*Go ahead,* Golden Coral.'

'We have control of the bridge. Six targets down.'

'*Do you have Chiu?*'

'That's negative, over.'

'*Roger that, over.*'

The radio fell silent. As the ship lurched, so did Caitlin's stomach. She headed away from the instrument panel to look at the sea state through the broken window. Her night-vision goggles picked out the foam of a curling wave battering the rear of the ship. She suppressed a shiver, and it wasn't just because her clothes were saturated. She hadn't told the others how much she hated the water. It would have made them think less of her.

She felt something sticky under her wet boot. She looked down. Blood, seeping from the chest of one of the men they'd put down. Her eyes moved to the corpse. The dead face – African – seemed very calm.

But something wasn't right.

The dead man's head seemed somehow too small for his body. Or was it that his torso was too big? Caitlin bent down immediately and ripped open the buttons of his camouflage top.

She blinked. The entry wound was directly in the centre of the man's clavicle. But that wasn't what attracted her attention. There were four black straps surrounding his otherwise naked torso, and each strap had four pouches, about the size of cigarette packets, each one with a wire protruding. The wires met at his left armpit, where a thicker cable ran down his arm. Caitlin looked at his left hand. The dead limb was clutching a small detonating button.

Her mouth went dry. She spoke urgently into her radio. '*All teams, this is Caitlin at the bridge. Our targets are wearing suicide vests. Handheld detonators. Repeat, our targets are wearing suicide vests . . .*'

Caitlin's panicked voice burst into Danny's earpiece. '*Our targets are wearing suicide vests! Handheld detonators! Repeat, our targets are wearing suicide vests!*'

Time slowed down.

Danny's eyes flickered to the free hand of the militant who had Chiu at gunpoint. It was twitching.

He had to take him out. But not a chest shot – it could detonate a vest.

He moved his rifle to the man's head, and that fraction of second's hesitation meant he was too late.

The explosion was immense. It came from the very front of the ship where the militant was standing. There was an intense flash of bright green light in Danny's NV goggles. A shock wave knocked him several metres back along the side deck. At the same time, the noise of the explosion split the air and echoed deafeningly off the metal sides of the storage containers, drowning out – for a few seconds – even the roar of the ocean.

Winded from his fall, Danny had to force himself to his feet. His Aussie colleague had been knocked back too, but was also painfully trying to stand. 'What the *fuck*?' he shouted at Danny.

Danny lurched back along the side deck, clutching his weapon, gasping for air. Having staggered the five or six metres he'd been knocked back, he stared at the devastation of the fore deck.

There was no sign of Chiu or the militant. The explosion had clearly taken them out. But right now they had bigger problems than that. The explosion had also ripped the crane from its footings, and it now hung precariously over the edge of the ship. Both orange-covered lifeboats had clearly tumbled into the water, and only a twisted fraction of the scaffolds that held them still remained. The railings that surrounded the deck had been blown away, and a chunk of the deck itself, a good ten metres deep, was twisted and torn. A sinister stench of burning hung in the air, and Danny saw a brief flicker of flames lick up from down under the deck. He looked left. Tony was running towards him.

'What the fuck happened?' he screamed.

'Suicide vest,' Danny shouted. 'Chiu's dead.'

A sneer of anger crossed Tony's face. 'There was a smear of blood on the handle of one of the doors leading below decks. I reckon whoever was bleeding went down below, towards the engine room. I'll take a couple of guys and follow ...'

Even as he spoke, the sound of two more explosions hit them in quick succession. Danny could tell that they came from deep inside the ship's hull – the echo was low and muffled, but it went on for a full ten seconds, and seemed to make the whole vessel vibrate.

'We're going to lose the ship!' Danny shouted. He activated his radio. 'All units return to the bridge. The ship's going down, lifeboats compromised ...'

Another explosion from down below. Even deeper and more sinister. The ship yawed dramatically. 'The fuel tank's gone!' Tony shouted.

A reply in the earpiece. It sounded like Goldie. Urgent. Maybe even a bit frightened. '*There's something here you need to take a look at, mate.*'

Danny turned to Tony. 'Get to the bridge,' he said. 'Make sure Caitlin's contacted the frigate. They need to airlift us off.' A huge, mechanical groan rose up from the belly of the vessel. '*Go!*' Danny shouted.

Tony ran along the starboard deck, two of their Aussie colleagues alongside him. Danny followed, but when, after twenty metres, he came to the corridor in the storage containers that Goldie had followed, he turned into it. His stomach went as the ship took a downward lurch, and there was an ominous creak from the containers that surrounded him.

Ten metres in, there was a right-angle turn to the left. Danny followed it. Then he stopped.

He estimated that he was pretty much in the centre of the deck. Ten metres from his position, blocking the corridor, was an open storage container, end on. Goldie was standing five metres from it, shining a very bright torch in to the interior. Danny flicked up his NV goggles, then hurried up to Goldie's side.

'What is it?' he breathed.

'You tell me,' Goldie said.

Danny peered at the contents of the container. They immediately reminded him of the field lab the Porton Down guys had set up in Chikunda: modular steel shelving along the sides, a table bolted to the floor, and fitted to the table, some kind of mechanical apparatus Danny couldn't recognise. Littering the floor were cardboard boxes, about ten, half of them opened, half of them still sealed. He could just make out the lettering on some of them. *Gillette. Lynx. Right Guard.*

'What are they doing with boxes of fucking deodorant?' Goldie asked.

Danny didn't immediately reply. He was remembering something Dr Phillips from the Porton Down team had said about spreading the plague virus, while they were watching Ripley die.

Aerosol dispersal would be effective . . .

He scanned the storage container for a couple more seconds. His eyes focused on one of the open boxes. He could make out the canisters of deodorant inside. They were small. Just three inches high.

'See those?' He pointed them out to Goldie. 'Who buys miniature deodorants?'

Goldie stared at him. 'People getting on airplanes,' he said.

Danny nodded. He took his digital camera from his ops waistcoat and quickly fired off a few pictures. Then he grabbed Goldie's arm and pulled him away from the storage container.

'We need to get off this ship,' he said.

All nine members of the unit had congregated on the bridge. Goldie, who had announced himself to be a demolitions expert, was moving around the corpses of the dead militants, carefully cutting the wires of their suicide vests. There was an acrid smell and a burning sound in the air that told Danny there was a major fire down below.

Tony was shouting into the ship's radio. 'We've got a Mayday, repeat, we've got a Mayday. The *Golden Coral* is scuttled, requesting immediate pick-up.'

There was a crackly pause, then a mild Australian voice came over the radio. *'What the hell have you boys been doing?'*

'Just get us a fucking chopper!' Tony shouted down the phone.

'Winds are high. ETA, ten minutes.'

'GET IT HERE NOW!'

Even though his clothes were still damp, Danny was sweating badly. It had been approximately three minutes since the blast, and the ship was already hovering around a five-degree angle. The more water entered the hull, the quicker the ship would sink. Two of the corpses rolled down the sloping floor of the bridge. It was hard for the living to remain upright. He doubted they had more than fifteen minutes.

'We need to get on to the aft deck!' he shouted at his team mates. 'That'll be the last to go down. Let's move out there now.'

Tony led the way, and the rest of the team filed out behind him. Danny prepared to take up the rear, holding on to the edge of the instrument panel to stop himself falling. A high-pitched grinding sound was coming from the ship's engines. It didn't sound good.

Something caught his eye. It looked like a shoulder bag, and it had slid across the floor and come to rest alongside the two bodies, no more than four metres from Danny's position. He staggered across the incline of the floor to grab it. It was made of soft leather, sticky with blood and very light. As Caitlin left the bridge, Danny opened it up. There was a piece of A4 paper inside, folded together three ways and slightly crumpled.

Danny peered at the piece of paper in the darkness, and frowned. It seemed to be an airline e-ticket confirmation: British Airways, Lagos to Paris Charles de Gaulle, departing 23.55 hrs.

Danny was alone on the bridge now. Alone and staring at the e-ticket in his hand. He checked the time. 23.49 hrs.

A suicide cell could turn themselves into human vectors.

The cargo ship juddered alarmingly. Its incline in the water steepened. Danny's earpiece exploded into life. '*Where the hell are you, Danny?*' Tony demanded.

He hurled himself across the room towards the radio. 'This is *Golden Coral*, do you copy?'

Silence.

'*THIS IS* GOLDEN CORAL, *DO YOU COPY?*'

No reply. The radio was dead. But he had to try and get his message through. 'There's an aircraft leaving Lagos in the next fifteen minutes, BA to Paris. Ground that flight and isolate all passengers. Repeat, ground the flight and isolate the passengers. DO YOU COPY?'

Nothing.

Shit.

He changed the frequency to channel 16, the international calling and distress channel, and repeated his message.

Nothing.

Another loud groan from the bowels of the ship.

'Black, where the fuck are you?'

He had to get out of there. He hurled himself across the bridge once again, towards the door this time. Out on the landing, he could see the staircase descending below him at an alarming angle. He grabbed hold of the railings and half-ran, half-fell down the two flights of stairs, then pushed the heavy deck door open.

Outside, it felt like the whole deck was vibrating. Looking to his right, he saw piles of cargo containers toppling against each other as they slipped down the incline of the ship towards the sinking forward deck. He stumbled breathlessly to the side of the ship, where he could grab the deck railings fiercely, then started pulling himself up towards the aft deck. In his peripheral vision he could see the bright searchlights of an approaching chopper cutting through the darkness. Distance, half a klick. Their pick-up was arriving.

The others were clinging to the deck railings at the very rear of the ship. Waves were swelling over the side. Danny pulled his way along the railings, muscles burning under his saturated clothes. It took thirty seconds to join the others. By that time, the chopper was hovering fifty feet above the sinking ship. Looking up, Danny could see the side door open, and a rope lowering, a mess of harnesses swinging from its tail and buffeting in the wind. The chopper itself wobbled precariously – Danny could tell the flight crew were struggling to keep it steady. He looked over the side of the railings. Half the ship's hull was submerged. They had minutes before they were underwater . . .

The harnesses hovered a metre above their heads. Goldie caught them. 'Team One, go!' Danny shouted. It took no more than thirty seconds for the team to strap themselves in. Goldie raised his Surefire torch and flashed it three times in the direction of the chopper. Instantly, the three Aussie SAS guys rose from the deck, spinning in the air as the rope pulled them up towards the aircraft. The ship lurched downwards again. Danny gripped the railings more fiercely than ever. It took a full minute to get the first three guys into the chopper, which still looked very shaky as the rope descended again.

'Team Two, go!' Danny shouted. The guys strapped themselves in, and moments later were rising into the air.

'What the fuck were you doing in there?' Tony shouted at Danny. Even here, on a sinking ship, he clearly didn't like not being in the know.

'They're going to hit a plane!' Danny shouted. 'I was trying to make contact with the ops room.'

'How do you know?' Tony demanded.

Danny didn't answer. The vessel had just given its loudest groan yet. It sounded like it was breaking up. Half the bridge tower was submerged. Water lashed over the railings. He looked up. Team Two were scrambling into the chopper. Seconds later, the harnesses were descending for a third time. Tony grabbed hold of them the moment they came within his grasp. He started fitting his own harness while Danny handed one to Caitlin, before fitting his own. 'Everyone good?' he shouted.

Tony and Caitlin nodded, so Danny withdrew his own Surefire and made the sign to the loadie up above. They were immediately airborne. As they winched up to the chopper, buffeted by winds, Danny looked down at the *Golden Coral*. It was more than three-quarters submerged, and the sea all around it bubbled and foamed. He felt a grim satisfaction that if any instances of the plague infection were aboard, they were being consigned to the deep. But then he remembered the flight number, and the knot of panicked urgency that had been with him since they landed in Nigeria returned to his gut.

Halfway to the chopper, he turned his attention to his unit mates. Caitlin was tightly gripping Tony's arm. For some reason, that made the knot in Danny's stomach tighten even further. Tony clearly saw him noticing and despite everything – the roar of the ocean, the wind, the spray and the thundering beat of the chopper's struggling rotors – a smug, self-satisfied look crossed his face.

Danny forced himself to look up. Just five metres to the chopper's entrance. He could see the loadie reaching out one hand to help them in. A moment later, they were scrambling into the body of the chopper. The door slid shut. The chopper banked sharply. Danny unclipped himself at the harness.

'Get me on to the ops room!' he shouted. '*Now!*'

Danny felt the eyes of the unit on him as the confused loadie handed him a headset. He ripped off his helmet, NV gear, radio earpiece and boom mike, then fitted the headset over his ears. 'Do you copy!' he shouted.

'*Roger that, this is Alpha, go ahead.*'

Danny plunged his hand into the leather shoulder bag to get his hands on the crumpled e-ticket. 'Listen carefully!' he shouted. 'There was a makeshift lab on that ship. I think they were filling aerosol canisters with the bioweapon, and I also think one of those canisters is on flight Brave Alpha Three Three Four Eight Nine, Lagos to Paris Charles de Gaulle. You *have* to stop that flight taking off and isolate all the passengers. Do you copy?'

A crackly pause. Then: '*Roger that.*'

The line went quiet. Everyone in the chopper – they had all heard every word Danny had said – stared at him in horror.

The chopper roared through the air back towards the frigate. Danny found he was holding his breath as he waited for the radio operator to make contact again.

Thirty seconds passed.

'What the fuck's going on?' Tony demanded.

At that very moment, the radio burst into life again. '*This is Alpha.*'

'Have you grounded the flight?' Danny shouted.

A pause.

'*That's a negative. The flight is already airborne. Repeat, the flight is already airborne.*'

NINETEEN

Flight BA33489 had not yet reached its cruising altitude. But the captain had switched off the 'fasten seatbelt' sign, the air stewards were busily pouring out Bloody Marys and there was already a queue for each of the toilets. It had been a bumpy take-off and there was still a little turbulence. Flight attendant Ailsa Pritchard hardly noticed it. Ten years a British Airways air stewardess, she sometimes thought she spent more time in the air than on the ground. She'd long since stopped being nervous about the occasional bump, but she'd also learned to keep a full smile on her face, because whenever there *was* turbulence, the more nervous passengers always watched the expressions of the cabin crew to double-check that they shouldn't be panicking.

And so she smiled her way sweetly down the starboard aisle of this airbus, politely pouring drinks and trying not to let it show that she was massively looking forward to touching down in Paris, where her boyfriend would be waiting to whisk her off to their favourite little hotel in Montmartre, where they would be spending her two days off.

The passengers were a mixture of French and Nigerian, and a smattering of Brits. When the captain came over the loudspeaker to inform the cabin that they had a decent tail wind and were hoping to shave a few minutes off their flight time of six hours twenty-five minutes, he did so in French first, then English. Ailsa herself was not fully bilingual, but she certainly had enough French to deal with the drinks orders of the passengers, and to respond cheerfully to any minor requests or problems that they had.

She had been serving drinks for fifteen minutes, and was more than halfway along the aisle, when she drew up alongside a Nigerian man who looked to be in a terrible state. He had very short cropped hair, almost bald, and Ailsa could see that his entire head was sweating. He was oddly dressed in mismatched, rather grubby clothes, and she could just see his shoes, which were falling apart. He kept licking his cracked lips, and his eyes – the whites of which were a creamy yellow – kept darting left and right. He wore a denim shirt and that too was soaked, with huge dark patches under the armpits. There was a rather unpleasant smell of stale sweat about his person – Ailsa was glad he had an empty seat either side of him, or there might have been some embarrassing complaints. He was nervously clutching a leather holdall in his lap.

'*Tout va bien, monsieur?*' Ailsa asked. '*Je peux vous offrir quelque chose a boire?*'

The man looked up sharply, as if he was surprised that anyone should be talking to him. He shook his head. '*Non.*'

'Is everything okay?' she continued in French. 'Nervous flyer?'

Another sharp look.

'No,' the man said.

'You might find it more comfortable to put your bag in one of the overhead lockers, sir?'

'Leave me alone.'

Ailsa gave him the thin-lipped smile she saved for all rude passengers. 'Certainly, sir,' she said, and she started to push the drinks trolley further down the aisle. The plane gave a sudden shudder of turbulence. Ailsa was forced to grab hold of the top of one of the seats. As she did so, she saw from the corner of her eye that the Nigerian man had opened up his holdall. He had removed a small canister of Lynx deodorant, and she thought she could see a second canister in the bag.

She found herself softening towards him. Poor man, she thought. He must be rather embarrassed. He obviously has a bit of a sweat problem, after all.

The Sea King containing Danny and the rest of the unit touched down precariously on the flight deck of the frigate. Danny alighted the moment the loadie had opened the door, and was the first of them to hit the deck. The rotors were powering down, but their downdraught was still strong. He crouched slightly as he ran across the flight deck.

He heard them before he saw them: three aircraft, flying in an arrowhead formation from a south-westerly direction. He knew at a glance that they were Tornadoes. As they sped overhead, a deafening sonic boom hit his ears.

Grimly, he watched them disappear towards land. He couldn't tell for sure where they were going, but he had a pretty good idea.

Randolph's forehead was crushed into a semi-permanent frown. This was the first time he had ever been in a plane, but that wasn't why he was nervous.

It was warm in the cabin, but as he looked at the small canisters of deodorant in his hands, he felt himself shiver. His instructions made no sense. Why would anyone want him to do this?

With very sweaty hands, he removed the lid from one of his bottles of Lynx. It popped off easily.

The seat in front of him shook slightly. A head popped up above it: a Nigerian child, about the same age as his twin daughters. Her hair was tightly braided, and she had a smile that lit up her whole face. This flight was obviously an exciting adventure for her.

'Hello, mister,' she said. 'What's your name?'

Randolph just stared at her, unable to make his mouth work. The pad of his forefinger nervously stroked the indentation on the white spray cap of the canister. As he stared at the child, he couldn't help but remember the awful video of his daughters he had been shown in his shack.

The child inclined her head. 'Mister?' she said.

Randolph was not a stupid man. He knew that the canister in his hand contained something other than deodorant. Something dangerous. He just didn't know what. An explosive of some kind? Would this whole plane be blasted out of the air the moment he squeezed the cap? He imagined himself hurtling through the air, and wondered if he was more likely to die up here, or when he hit the ground. He thought of his precious daughters, and wondered if they would cry when they heard their daddy was dead.

More sweat. His seat was damp.

'Sit down properly, child,' he told the little girl, who was still watching him. Her face fell, and she disappeared back into her seat.

Randolph closed his eyes and muttered a prayer.

He sprayed the canister.

His finger had only been pressed for a second when his eyes pinged open again. There had been no explosion. Just a hiss, and that had been so quiet that the noise of the aircraft's engines and the general hubbub of the cabin had drowned it out.

But what about the smell? He looked across the aisle to check that nobody could see him behaving oddly, then bent down with the aerosol to his nose. He squeezed the cap again and sniffed deeply. There was just a faint, odourless mist.

Randolph released his finger and leaned back, relief crashing over him. He wasn't going to plunge to his death. He *was* going to see his children again.

He squeezed the cap again. This time he held it down for a full thirty seconds until the hissing became weaker and finally stopped. He put the dead canister back in his shoulder bag, then took out the second one. His face broke into an almost carefree smile as he removed the lid and started spraying its odourless contents into the gap between his seat and the seat in front. The little girl's face appeared again, and she gave him a slightly amused look. A look that said: *what are you doing?*

Randolph just winked and made a shushing sign as he emptied the canister. When it was done, he stuffed the empty can back in his shoulder bag, which he then dumped on the spare window seat next to him.

He looked down. His shirt was wet with perspiration, but now he was sweating with relief. Perhaps I'll have a drink now, he thought to himself. Something to steady my nerves. He looked up, and pressed the overhead button for calling the air hostess.

She arrived a minute later. '*Oui, monsieur?*'

'I think I would like a drink now,' he said. He knew he had been very rude to her before, so he tried to smile.

'Of course, sir, what can I get you?'

He waited another minute for her to bring his beer: an almost cold bottle of Kronenbourg, along with a plastic cup, a paper mat and a small packet of salted pretzels. She leaned over to give him the bottle and he had just opened his mouth to thank her when he sneezed explosively. Right at her. It was the sort of sneeze that makes people turn and look.

'What on earth . . .' the air stewardess said.

Randolph blinked. 'I'm very sorry,' he mumbled, massively embarrassed that his sneeze had sprayed a thin mist of saliva at the woman's face.

But the air stewardess didn't seem to be worried about the sneeze. She was staring through Randolph's tiny window. Randolph frowned again. He looked out of the window. He blinked.

He found it hard to say how close the aircraft was that flew alongside them. Only tens of metres, because he could see, quite clearly, through the side windows of the aircraft's cockpit, the pilot. He had a grey helmet and a boom mike to his mouth. As Randolph stared at him, the pilot turned his head to the left, and it was almost as if their eyes met.

A bell-like sound from within the cabin. Randolph looked up to see that the 'fasten seatbelt' sign was turned on. The air stewardess had straightened up. Randolph looked at her face. There was no doubt about it: she was frightened.

He glanced guiltily at the shoulder bag on the seat next to him, then back out of the window.

The captain's voice came over the loudspeaker. 'Ladies and gentleman, the fasten seatbelt signs are now on, so I would ask you to return to your seats.' A pause. 'Some of you may have noticed military aircraft on either side of us. I would like to take this opportunity to assure you that there is absolutely no cause for alarm.'

But anyone who heard the captain's voice would be able to tell that he was far from calm. A murmur of barely restrained panic filled the cabin, and Randolph found that he was sweating more than ever.

Danny stormed into the ops room on the frigate, Tony and Caitlin following closely. Their clothes were still dripping wet and their weapons were still slung over their shoulders. The ops room itself was buzzing with activity. Radios blaring. The ops officer and his team of Aussie naval guys urgently issuing updates. The Porton Down team standing quietly in one corner, their faces studious as the heart of the military machine pumped in front of them.

Danny strode over to the Porton Down team and handed Dr Phillips his camera. 'You need to look at what's on that.'

Without bothering to answer, Phillips took the camera and plugged it into a nearby laptop. Meanwhile, the ops officer strode up to Danny. 'I've got London on the line for you.'

'What's happening to the plane?' Danny demanded.

'Three RAF tornadoes have just caught up with it.'

'Where is it now?'

'Mauritanian airspace.'

A beat.

'Are they going to . . .'

'No decision's been made.' The ops officer pointed at a laptop on the far side of the room. 'London,' he said. 'They want to talk to you.'

Danny moved over to the laptop and sat in front of it. There was a grainy video image of a bearded man in a wheelchair, his head resting against a headrest. '*Daniel Bixby, SIS,*' he said. '*Are you Black?*'

Danny nodded.

'*I need a full debrief of what occurred on the* Golden Coral.'

Danny didn't fuck around. He gave a detailed explanation of everything that had occurred on the ship. When he got to the bit about the open storage container, Dr Phillips crouched down next to him and interrupted. 'The apparatus in there was an

216

aerosol filling machine. You use it to fill an empty aerosol can. I'm uploading the pictures to your server now.'

'*If one of those aerosols is released into the cabin of an aircraft, what happens?*' Bixby asked.

'The air recirculates through the cabin once every few minutes. The aircraft acquires a certain proportion of fresh air from outside, but it'll only take seconds for the pathogen particles to diffuse across the plane.'

'*Just tell me what that* means,' Bixby snapped.

Phillips sniffed. 'How many people on that plane?' he asked.

'*Two hundred and seventy-nine, including crew.*'

'Then you have two hundred and seventy-nine vectors infected with an extremely aggressive, modified form of *Y. pestis*. If our previous experience is anything to go by, they could become symptomatic within an hour. You *can't* let them come into contact with anyone, or you'll have an epidemic on your hands.'

Bixby stared into the screen for a moment.

'*I need to speak to the Chief,*' he said, before wheeling his chair back and disappearing from sight.

They had been circling for an hour.

The initial panic in the cabin had subsided into a tense silence. It was only occasionally broken when one of the passengers lost it with a member of the cabin crew. *What was going on*, they wanted to know. *Why weren't they being told anything?* Randolph would strain his ears to hear the cabin crew calmly trying to tell them that the captain would update them as soon as he had any information. But they didn't sound any more reassured than the alarmed passengers.

Randolph couldn't take his eyes off the military aircraft to his right. It stuck so closely and exactly to the larger plane that he almost had the sensation that they weren't even moving. When they passed through a patch of cloud, which momentarily obscured the fighter jet, it made him start, as though he was jumping out of a hypnotic trance. He realised that somebody was coughing a few rows behind him, and that they had been doing so for several minutes.

There was a sudden change in the sound of the aircraft's engines. Randolph felt a momentary sense of weightlessness, and there was a general gasp around the cabin that told him he was not the only one. For only the second time since the fighter jets had appeared, the captain's voice came over the loudspeaker. He sounded deadly serious. 'Ladies and gentlemen, you've probably noticed that we've started to lose height. It's nothing to be concerned about, but we will be performing an emergency landing in approximately ten minutes. You will need to adopt the brace position, and I would ask you to study the card in the seat in front of you very carefully . . .'

The volume of anxious chatter in the cabin increased again. Randolph pulled the laminated safety card from the pouch of the seat in front of him. The captain was still talking, but Randolph wasn't listening any more. For some reason his attention had focused in on the sound of the person coughing behind him. He felt irritation building in his own chest.

He suddenly, involuntarily, coughed.

He stared at the laminated card. A thin film of mucus covered the images of smiling figures sliding on to life rafts.

The mucus was streaked with blood.

'Where's the landing site?' Sir Colin Seldon's voice cracked with tiredness.

Bixby clicked on a map of north-west Africa, then used his forefinger to outline a blank region of desert. 'Eastern Mauritania,' he said. 'About a hundred and fifty miles west of the Mali border. It's completely deserted, sir. About a hundred miles in any direction from any human habitation. There's a possibility of Bedouin wanderers . . .'

'Can we hide a plane there?' Seldon said.

'I think so, sir. For a few days at least.'

'The aircraft's transponders were killed while it was still on its original flight path?'

'Yes, sir. And we've arranged for it to be wiped from the air traffic control radar systems. It looks like it disappeared in mid-air.

We've got cross-agency support and we've spoken to the Americans, the Australians and the French. Everyone's singing from the same hymn sheet. Until we know if there's some kind of pathogen on board, the aircraft has, to all intents and purposes, disappeared from the sky.' He coughed uncomfortably.

'What is it, Bixby?' the Chief said. 'Spit it out?'

'Are you sure this is a good idea sir? The press will be all over it, and if someone finds out we forced an emergency landing in the Mauritanian desert and lied about the aircraft's location . . .'

'Is it a *good idea*?' Seldon snapped. There was a tremor in his voice that Bixby had never heard before. 'We have nearly three hundred passengers in mid-air infected with a highly contagious, highly aggressive strain of weaponised plague. We let them land in Paris, the whole Western world goes into a mad panic. Even if we contain the infection, the terrorists win the moment we start carrying the body bags out of the plane. The genie will be out the bottle and we'll see bio attacks left, right and centre. So is this a good idea? Of *course* it's not a good idea. The rule book hasn't been written on this yet. There *are* no good ideas any more.'

Bixby had never seen him so fierce. So out of control. So pale.

'We don't even have any fucking *leads*,' the Chief muttered.

'We have one, sir,' said the analyst.

'What?'

'The Caliph, sir,' Bixby said quietly.

'Oh,' the Chief said, his voice heavy with sarcasm. 'The Caliph. The one nobody's ever seen and who nobody will ever talk about. *Great.* Let me know as soon as *he* turns himself in, won't you?'

He stood up and stormed away from the computer terminal, leaving Bixby with his head resting against the padded headrest, his face impassive.

There was a clunking sound from below the aircraft. Randolph didn't know what it was, but he heard someone in the row behind him say it was the landing gear extending.

He had moved to the window seat. Several people were crying nearby. Plenty of others were coughing. They all had a dry, hacking cough, and Randolph wanted to join in. He was *desperate* to join in, but after seeing his own blood-stained mucus, he didn't dare. He found that he was wheezing heavily as he looked out of the window. He kept thinking about his daughters, wondering if they had been released yet, and if he was ever going to see them again. The thought that he might not caused a very real pain in his chest.

He tried to occupy his mind by guessing the plane's altitude. They had been descending for some time, but all he could see was the fighter jet travelling alongside them. Suddenly, though, as he was watching, he heard a roar from the jets' engines as they peeled away. Within seconds they were out of sight.

Randolph blinked. He looked down to earth. He could see, in the moonlight, that they were only a hundred feet above the ground. They were over the desert – there were ripples in the moonlit sand below, where the ground was flat.

The captain's voice over the loudspeaker. Tense. Urgent. '*Brace! Brace! Heads down, stay down!*'

The hubbub of the passengers swelled into a terrified moan. Randolph bent forward, rested his forehead against the seat in front and laid his hands on the back of his head. The aircraft's engines became very high-pitched. The sound of crying from inside the cabin grew louder. Several people screamed.

There was a sickening jolt as the aircraft's wheels hit the sand. The aircraft bounced. Five seconds later it hit the ground again and Randolph felt a rush of g-force as the spoilers on the wings angled upwards and the aircraft dramatically lost speed. But suddenly there was another jolt. The aircraft spun forty-five degrees and the screeching of the engine was matched only by the screaming of the passengers inside. Randolph wanted to shout out, but fear silenced him. He just muttered a prayer as the fuselage wobbled and the wing tip to his right-hand side brushed against the sand.

This is it, he thought to himself. *This is the moment I die.*

But then, unexpectedly, there was silence and stillness.

There was a moment when it sounded as if the whole cabin was taking a collective breath of relief.

Then Randolph coughed again, and there was blood over the underside of the table folded into the seat in front.

It was over.

Danny had left the ops room. The place was doing his head in. He needed some air. Out on the deck, he gripped the railings and allowed a film of spray to wash over him. They'd failed. Targets Red and Blue were dead. Ripley was dead. A plane full of innocent victims were, right now, going the same way as his SAS mate. He didn't know what the head shed would be doing with that flight, but he knew there would be a cover-up of some sort. If word got out that there had been a successful bio-attack on the West, all bets were off. They'd be seeing copycat scenarios all over the world.

Danny felt for his Sig. Before, that hunk of metal slung close to his body had made him feel secure. Not any more. Guns were for a different kind of war. Danny couldn't shake the feeling that in the past few days, war had changed. He thought of what he'd left back home. Clara. The baby. What kind of world was his kid about to be born into?

He turned. Thirty metres further along the deck he saw Tony and Caitlin. They were facing each other, and standing very close – closer than ordinary colleagues. Danny felt a bit of a pang. Tony suddenly looked over in his direction – he clearly knew his Regiment colleague was looking. Danny didn't feel he wanted to see any more. He turned his back on them and walked back towards the flight deck. He was looking forward to getting back to Hereford.

He squinted. In the distance, maybe half a klick away, he saw the lights of a chopper approaching. The flight deck itself had been cleared, and one of the frigate's loadmasters stood in the centre of the deck carrying two glowing, handheld beacons. Thirty seconds later he was waving them above his head to bring the chopper safely in to land.

The side door opened. A man exited and started running almost directly towards Danny to escape the downdraught. He wore slacks, an open-necked shirt and a lightweight jacket. His tousled hair blew in the wind, but Danny recognised him immediately. Hugo Buckingham.

He felt his face go craggy. What the hell was Buckingham doing here? Just when he'd thought this shitstorm of an op couldn't get any worse, the person he loathed more than any other had just landed on the frigate. He stood very still as Buckingham ran with his head bowed towards him. He was only ten metres away when Buckingham finally looked where he was going and saw Danny standing there.

The MI6 man stopped in his tracks. He made a futile attempt to smooth down his hair, then shook the dust from the lapels of his jacket. 'Black, old sport,' he said finally.

'Buckingham.'

'Presiding over what I understand you fellows like to call a clusterfuck?'

'What are you doing here? Has the captain got some filing that needs doing?'

'Actually, *actually*, I made the decision to come straight here from Saudi. Following up a lead. Not to mention that the Firm want somebody to take *you* in hand.' He strode up to Danny, jutting out his absurdly handsome chin. 'They're baying for your blood in London, Danny. The bad news for you is that I'm the best friend you've got.' He smiled.

The last time Danny had seen Buckingham, the MI6 man had ended up wincing in the gutter after Danny had laid into him. It took every ounce of self-control to stop himself from doing the same thing now.

'Take me to the ops room,' Buckingham said. 'I require a full debrief. Get a move on, Black. I haven't got all bloody night, you know.'

Randolph stared in horror at the blood.

He was almost unaware of the commotion in the cabin. Almost, but not quite. The silence after the emergency landing had lasted no more than a few seconds before it dissolved into renewed panic. Several people were crying – including, Randolph realised, the little girl in the seat ahead. The aisles were full of people surging to the emergency exits. Randolph stood up and saw the nice air hostess standing with her back to one of the side doors while three angry customers shouted at her to get out of the way and let them open up and escape the plane.

'*Ladies and gentlemen, this is your captain speaking.*' He sounded rattled. Not nearly so suave and calm as he had when they took off. '*For your own safety, please return to your seats. The exterior temperature is below freezing and we have very little information about our surrounding terrain. The aircraft is the safest place for us to remain while we wait for . . .*'

The captain's voice dissolved into a sudden fit of coughing. The loudspeaker went dead. For a moment, the volume in the cabin reduced too. But only for a moment. The three men started yelling at the air stewardess again. Two more came to help her, standing in front of the door with their arms folded.

Randolph realised that the little girl in the seat in front was looking at him. He stared at her. A thin patch of blood had stained the area under her nostrils. And maybe Randolph was imagining it, but there was also a swelling on her left cheek.

He collapsed heavily into his seat. His body was aching. His skin was burning up. He stared at the back of his rough, calloused, fisherman's hands, and saw that there were swellings appearing there, too.

Daniel Bixby wheeled his way across the floor of the operations room deep beneath the MI6 building, his head immobile against the padded headrest. One of his assistants walked briskly alongside him. 'Flight BA33489 is on the ground. The pilots have been instructed to keep the passengers contained. The African air traffic control agency is already going nuts. It looks to them like the aircraft disappeared into thin air over Niger . . .'

If Bixby had the strength to shake his head, he would have done. Nothing good could come of this. But the decision was above his pay grade, and it was already made.

Another of his assistant analysts came striding up towards him. His eyes were alight.

'What is it?' Bixby asked.

'GCHQ have picked something up. A satellite call from the *Golden Coral*, made approximately thirty-five minutes before the ship went down. The call lasted just over ten seconds.'

'Can we listen to it?'

The analyst shook his head. 'I'm afraid not,' he said. 'But we have a rough location of the sat phone that received the call.'

'Go on.'

The analyst pointed to a large VT screen on the wall which showed a map of the world. He momentarily tapped a keyboard just below it. A dot appeared on the screen, surrounded by a wider circle. The dot itself was centred on the ocean in the middle of the Persian Gulf. The circle covered a large patch of sea, but also the northern coast of the United Arab Emirates, the eastern coast of Saudi Arabia, and almost all of Qatar.

Bixby stared at the screen for a moment.

'Get me the Chief,' he said.

Flight BA33489 had been on the ground for a full hour. The lights were off to preserve power. It was almost pitch black.

Randolph was sweating even more than usual. His limbs were weak, his chest hoarse. Two more swellings had appeared on the back of his hand, and he could feel others elsewhere on his body. They hurt, badly, but he was too scared to look at them. His head was spinning, and it was hard to keep track of what was going on. Every time he closed his eyes he saw his children as they had been in that awful video. And every time he opened them, he was presented with a scene that was almost as chilling.

To his left, on the other side of the aisle, three passengers were wheezing badly. In front of him, he heard the sound of the little girl retching. Nobody was trying to leave the plane any more, and he understood why: they felt too ill. Randolph himself was desperate to use the lavatory, but he didn't have the strength to get up. And when, two minutes later, he soiled himself, it was with a strange mixture of disgust and relief. The stench in the cabin told him he was not the first person to do this.

His head fell listlessly to the right. He stared out into the darkness and shivered. The temperature in the cabin was dropping. He wondered if he should tell someone about the deodorants, but he knew he never would. Not while he knew those monsters had his daughters.

He winced. A sharp pain cracked through his head. Lights, outside. They were descending from the sky, and great clouds of sand were billowing up and surrounding them, no more than ten metres from the tip of the aircraft's wing. There was noise. The noise of engines.

Helicopters.

A murmur in the cabin. Had help arrived?

Randolph felt dizzy as he watched three helicopters land. Their lights shone through the tiny cabin windows and cast strange, terrifying shadows inside the plane. He wanted to vomit, but managed to control himself as he watched the side doors of the helicopters open, and silhouettes spill out from inside. He didn't know how many. Fifteen or twenty, maybe. Backlit by the lights of the helicopters, their shadows extended, long and thin, in the direction of the plane, the helicopters' headlamps gleaming blindingly between them.

The figures advanced on the aeroplane. As they reached the wing tip, Randolph caught a better view of one of them. He – or she – was wearing some kind of all-in-one body suit, white, or maybe yellow. His head was completely covered by a mask, and his hands by tight rubber gloves that covered the sleeve of the suit.

Panic surged through him. And through the cabin as well. A man three seats in front of Randolph stood up and pushed his way into the aisle. He looked back. Randolph saw terror in his eyes and a swelling to the left of his nose. He was sweating almost as badly as Randolph himself. He looked wild. Like he was about to do something crazy.

Randolph stood up to watch him. The man ran along the aisle to the emergency exit door. The air stewardess feebly tried to stop him, but he pushed her away and yanked the red opening lever 90 degrees anticlockwise. The door hissed a few inches inward, then swung upward. Light flooded into the cabin, illuminating the man's face and casting a long shadow to the far side of the cabin. He shouted something in French, but it was garbled and Randolph couldn't understand what he was saying. But he knew this: the man was about to jump out of the aircraft.

He didn't get the chance.

From outside, there was the sound of gunfire. Just one round, and from the corner of his eye Randolph thought he saw a muzzle flash through the cabin window. The man at the door staggered backwards. He looked down at himself in shock, held his hand to his chest and raised it to see that his palm was coated in blood. He collapsed out of Randolph's sight.

Randolph collapsed too. There was a moment of shocked silence. It lasted no more than five seconds, before several people started to scream.

Randolph wanted to scream with them. But he couldn't. He was too busy vomiting into the seat next to him: a horrific mixture of blood, mucus and semi-digested salted pretzels.

'What's happening?' someone screamed from further along the cabin. '*What the hell's happening?*'

I know what's happening, Randolph thought. *I'm going to die. We're all going to die.*

He hoped it would happen soon.

TWENTY

05.00 AST, Doha, Qatar.

In the prominent, wealthy district of West Bay in the Qatari capital of Doha, a young man stood at the entrance of an enormous skyscraper. His name was Saad, and he had a black rucksack over his shoulder. Even though it was four in the morning, it was still very warm. Saad wore Western clothes: dark trousers, and a pale short-sleeved shirt. In a few hours' time he would have to change into his uniform – Saad was a low-ranking member of the Qatari police force. But for now, the only evidence that he was a police officer was the ID card in his back pocket. Saad was here very much under the radar. In Qatar, under the radar was a dangerous place to be.

He had been in the police force for eighteen months now. In that time he had seen a dark side to the law enforcement in his country that he had never known existed when he was a naive recruit. He had seen his superiors brush away reports of unlawful deaths among the Indian construction workers upon whose sweat the magnificent buildings in Doha were built. He had seen a Muslim man condemned to forty lashes for the illegal consumption of alcohol. When two young extremists had beaten and raped a woman for listening to Western music in public, he had seen a highly religious police commander bury the report. Saad believed in freedom for everyone. And although, like most Qataris, he knew there was a dark side to the shining buildings and ostentatious wealth of his country, he had never dreamed it was as bad as that.

Saad had taken the address of this skyscraper from the police files. The penthouse was the home of a rich oil magnate called Ahmed bin Ali al-Essa. Saad walked into the reception of the building. It was cool and air-conditioned in here. The floor was covered with shining marble, and there were magnificent indoor palm trees dotted around. He stepped up to the concierge desk – burnished wood and brass – and spoke to the man behind the counter, who was wearing full robes and headdress.

'*Salaam,*' said the young man.

'*Salaam,*' the concierge replied.

'I am here to see Ahmed bin Ali al-Essa.'

The concierge gave a barely sympathetic smile, as if many people would like to do such a thing, but few would have the honour. He was clearly about to turn Saad away when the young policeman presented his official identification. 'I am sure he will thank you for keeping this discreet,' he said.

The man gave him one of those wary looks that seemed to be reserved for policemen, then bowed his head slightly. 'If you will excuse me for a moment, I will see if he is available.'

Saad stepped back from the concierge desk so that he could make the call. A moment later, the man nodded at him and led the policeman towards an elevator at the far side of the desk. He pressed a key card to a sensor on the right-hand side, then stepped back as the doors slid open. 'This only goes to the penthouse,' the man said. Saad stepped inside, pressed the top of two buttons and within seconds was hurtling up to the top of the building.

The lift opened up into another reception area with a magnificent tank full of brightly coloured tropical fish. More marble flooring. A comfortable-looking leather sofa. A door at the far end with the logo of a helicopter, and another opposite the lift. Saad was just wondering whether he should knock on the door, when it opened. A man appeared. He wore a white robe, but no headdress. He was a handsome man, with a neat goatee beard, but his eyes were tired.

'Mr Al-Essa?'

The man nodded. 'How may I help you?'

Saad had learned that the best way to deliver bad news was

directly and without embellishment. 'Mr Al-Essa, I'm very sorry. It's about your parents. I'm afraid they're dead.'

Al-Essa blinked. 'What do you mean?' he breathed. 'When?'

'Yesterday morning.'

The older man's face darkened. 'Why am I only hearing about this now?'

'That's why I'm here, Mr Al-Essa. May I come in?'

Al-Essa bowed his head. 'Of course,' he said. He stepped into the apartment. Saad followed.

Saad had never witnessed such luxury, and in the oil-rich state of Qatar, that was saying something. The room in which he found himself was huge and ornate. Marble statues. Gold-framed art-works. An incredible vista over the bay, where the lights of skiffs and other fishing boats twinkled in the early morning darkness. Al-Essa sat down in a comfortable armchair. He looked very shaken as he indicated that Saad should sit opposite him.

'What happened?' he asked in a cracked voice.

'They were killed, sir. Murdered. I'm very sorry.' Saad allowed that shocking news to sink in before he continued. 'I'm afraid my superiors don't want you to know that. They have spent the last twenty-four hours trying to cover it up. But your parents . . .' He tried to find the right words. 'Your parents are wealthy, sir. Mine are not. A few years ago, your father helped mine out with a little money when he was struggling. Our family have not forgotten his kindness.' He bowed his head. 'It is hardly a happy way to repay the debt, but I thought you would want to know the truth.'

Al-Essa stared at the young man. 'Thank you, my friend,' he said. 'I am grateful.'

Saad opened his rucksack and pulled out an A4 envelope. He hesitated for a moment. 'Your parents died in a bad way, sir. What I have to show you is unpleasant. If you would prefer to . . .'

Al-Essa shook his head. 'Show me,' he said.

There were ten photographs of the crime scene, all extremely detailed. One showed an old woman lying in a reclining chair, her throat deeply cut. Another showed her legs, smeared with the contents of her split urinary bag. Then the photographs became more gruesome. An old man with gaping wounds for eyes and a bloody mess of a mouth. A third person – a younger, fatter man – lying in a pool of his own blood. Al-Essa stared at these pictures, clearly aghast. He was halfway through them when he said, 'Excuse me', and disappeared into an adjoining room.

Saad sat silently for two minutes. When Al-Essa returned he looked like a different man. Deeply shaken, as though he had aged years in those two minutes. He sat down again. 'Why would your superiors cover this up?' he asked finally.

The young police officer had more pictures to show him. A mirror, with a word scrawled across it. A painting, with a word scrawled across it. A patch of floor, with a word scrawled across it. In each picture the word was the same: *Caliph*.

Saad watched Al-Essa's face turn pale. He stared at the police officer. '*He* did this?'

Saad nodded.

'And your superiors are scared?'

'Some of them. But some . . .'

'Some would prefer to live in a world where this sort of thing is allowed to happen?'

Saad inclined his head. 'I would be in a great deal of trouble, Mr Al-Essa, if anybody were to find out that I came here this morning.'

'I understand,' Al-Essa said. He stood up. 'Thank you for your honesty. I would like to give you something for your trouble.'

'It's not necessary. I have a job now. My family no longer needs to live off charity.'

'May I keep these photographs?'

Saad nodded. 'I'll show myself out, Mr Al-Essa,' he said.

As the young police officer walked towards the door, he looked back over his shoulder. Al-Essa was staring out of the window over the bay. Saad caught a glimpse of his reflection. It chilled him. Al-Essa was distraught, there was no doubt about it. But there was something else in his expression that seemed to master all other emotions. Saad recognised it only too well. He had seen it in the faces of men condemned to forty lashes for small crimes, and in the eyes of a woman raped and disbelieved.

There was no doubt about it. Above everything else, Ahmed bin Ali al-Essa, one of the richest men in the world's richest country, was scared.

Spud awoke in the darkness.

He winced. There was a cracking pain in his head, worse even than the dull ache in his abdomen. The sort of pain that only comes from too much booze. And there was no doubt about it. Spud had hit the bottle hard. So hard that for a moment he couldn't quite remember where he was.

He was in a bed. A big one. Bigger than the standard double in his own grotty little flat. And there was a woman next to him. She rolled over and cosied up to him, draping one hand across his broad chest. She smelled of perfume, wine and sex.

Spud groaned inwardly as he remembered pitching up on Tony Wiseman's front door after taking the train from Birmingham to Hereford, to be greeted by his missus, Frances. How she'd invited him in and plied him with Tony's red wine. How she'd flirted with him by asking his advice about how to get fit for the marathon in three days. How she'd started crying, telling him what a shit Tony was.

How one thing had led to another . . .

He barely dared move, because that would wake her up. He glanced left. A radio alarm told him it was four in the morning. He breathed deeply to stem a surge of nausea. What the *hell* was he doing here?

Frances muttered something in her sleep. Spud didn't move. He felt like a total bastard. Tony was no mate of his, but shagging the wife of another Regiment guy was a low thing to do. It was almost as if he'd been trying to prove something to himself, but he wasn't quite sure what.

He thought back to the previous day. His trip to Birmingham with Eleanor the spook to check out the dodgy cab driver who didn't seem so dodgy after all. On the train all the way down from

Birmingham Spud had tried to get the facts straight in his head. The guy had never owned a passport. Which meant he'd never even left the country. He'd come to the conclusion that he had to face facts: the idea that he'd acquired that Claymore bag from some jihadist training camp was clutching at straws. Pretending he was on a real job, when in fact he was two steps away from the scrapheap.

Slowly, he moved Frances's hand from his chest. She muttered again, but then rolled over to face the other way. Spud eased himself out of bed and silently – groggily – pulled his clothes back on. He crept out of Frances's enormous bedroom and down the stairs – almost tripping up over the petite running shoes lying in the hallway. A minute later he was out on the pavement, bathed in the yellow light of a street lamp. It was deserted at this hour. He looked back over his shoulder at the house, knowing that Frances would be pissed off with him when she woke. But she'd get over it. And she'd keep quiet with Tony. Something told Spud she *really* wouldn't want her husband to know she'd crossed that line.

It felt good to be up and breathing cold, early morning air. It was a mile from here to his own flat, and as he purposefully paced the street he felt his hangover subside. It was a quarter to five when he walked up to his front door. His motorbike – a BMW, his most treasured possession – was parked right outside. The curtains were shut. A few junk mail leaflets protruded from the letter box. He let himself in.

It was dark and musty in his one-room pad. The sparse accommodation of a single man who barely spent any time at home. He stood alone in the darkness of the hallway. There was a key rack on the wall to his left-hand side. The keys to his car were hanging there. He stared at them.

Something was troubling him. What was it?

He closed his eyes and pictured himself sitting in the cab yesterday with Eleanor. He ran through the conversation in his head, as best he could remember it. He pictured the Claymore bag, and suspicion washed over him again. But there was something else. Something he'd seen, but hadn't pieced together. He felt his forehead wrinkling as he closed his eyes and forced his hazy mind to picture the cab driver again, just as he'd seen him. Every last detail.

The neatly combed hair. The tan-coloured jacket.

The gloves.

It had been sunny in Dudley yesterday. Why the hell had he been wearing gloves?

His eyes pinged open. He could almost hear Eleanor's patronising voice. *You think he's a terrorist because he was wearing gloves? You've got a lot to learn about intelligence, Spud . . .*

But when it came to intelligence, Spud knew one thing for sure. Sometimes, you just have to follow your gut.

He hurried into his bedroom. From a rickety old cupboard he grabbed a leather jacket and his bike helmet. He wished he had a firearm handy, but he didn't. No problem. He could always improvise a weapon if he needed to. Back in the hallway he grabbed the bike keys from the key holder. He also owned a car – an old Honda – but for some jobs a bike was better. Easier to follow someone. Easier to get up close to traffic lights on red, or to cut the wrong way down a one-way street. He strode outside and locked the door of his flat behind him. Thirty seconds later he was revving the bike's engine. A face appeared through parted curtains on a first-floor window opposite, obviously wondering what the noise was about. Spud ignored it. He pulled out and burned down the street. At this time of day, if he pushed it, he could be back in Birmingham in an hour.

Dawn broke over the eastern Atlantic, the sun's rays gleaming off the steel grey of the frigate. The waters were calmer now. An exhausted Danny stood in the corner of the ops room. Caitlin and Tony were at the other side of the room, out of earshot, talking quietly to each other. Buckingham, however, was with Danny, facing him, just a metre away.

'So let me get this right, Black,' he said quietly. 'On leaving the UK, you elected *not* to wait for a supporting platoon from the Parachute Regiment. You *blackmailed* a high-ranking member of the Nigerian government. And you *failed* to locate the British

High Commissioner and his aide before they were killed. You allowed one of your team to become infected with the *Y. pestis* virus – *very* careless . . .'

Danny stepped forward, but Buckingham looked around meaningfully. 'You need to put a lid on your temper, old sport,' he whispered. 'Especially in front of everyone.'

Danny took a deep breath, then stepped back.

'And when you had the man responsible for all this in your sights,' Buckingham continued, 'you allowed a Nigerian suicide bomber to *kill* him before we could bring him in for questioning. All in all, hardly a very auspicious couple of days' work, wouldn't you say?'

Danny didn't say anything. He knew the beginnings of a stitch-up when he heard it. But before he could speak, the ops officer had marched up to them. 'We've got London on the line.' He nodded at Buckingham and Danny. 'They want both of you.'

Danny noticed a slight tightening around Buckingham's eyes. He obviously didn't like being put on a level pegging with the SAS man. But there was nothing he could do. They crossed the ops room together and, at the ops officer's instruction, sat down at a laptop screen. Being this close to Buckingham made Danny's flesh creep, so he focused on the screen itself. The ops officer tapped the keyboard and an image appeared. A man in a crumpled suit was sitting at a desk. To his left and slightly behind him was a second man sitting in a wheelchair – Danny remembered that his name was Bixby. He had a big bushy beard and his head was resting against a cushioned side-panel.

'*Is this thing working?*' said the man in the suit.

'It is, sir,' Buckingham said. 'This is Buckingham, by the way.'

The man peered into the computer screen. '*Is that Black next to you?*'

'Yes, sir, Danny Black. I've been reading him the riot act—'

'*Bloody good work, Black,*' the man cut in. '*Colin Seldon, Chief of SIS. Bixby here will fill you in.*'

Danny could almost feel the heat of Buckingham's outrage. 'Go ahead,' he said.

The guy in the wheelchair cleared his throat. '*Flight BA33489 has made an emergency landing over the Mauritanian desert. That's classified – word's already leaking through the press that an aircraft has disappeared over African airspace, and we want to keep it that way. It's early days, but the bioweapon is on board and it's looking like a hundred per cent infection rate.*'

'*Show them the footage, Bixby,*' the Chief said.

The image on the screen changed. Suddenly they weren't looking at two spooks in a London office. At first, it wasn't quite clear *what* they were looking at. The screen was dark, but with occasional flashes of torchlight. After a few seconds, they saw a figure in a white hazmat suit and rebreather mask. He was walking towards the camera, down what looked like the aisle of an aircraft. The camera panned left. The torch beam illuminated a face: a passenger in an aisle seat. In the brief few seconds that the face was lit up, Danny saw that it was a woman with white skin. Her nose had been bleeding. Her lips were cracked. There were two painful-looking welts on either side of her face, one of them glistening with some kind of discharge. But the worst thing was the expression in her eyes: a chilling mixture of horror and fear.

'Jesus,' Danny breathed. An image of Ripley's blistered, bleeding body flashed in front of his eyes.

The camera panned back to the aisle. By the light of the torch Danny saw rows of passengers extending towards the back of the plane.

Then the screen went black again. The Chief and Bixby reappeared.

'Is there any hope for them?' Danny asked.

The Chief and Bixby exchanged a look. '*None,*' the Chief said.

'So what happens now?'

'*We're currently evaluating our options. But if word gets out about this, there'll be mass panic. The economic implications will be—*'

'Can't you just make it known you've compromised the strike?'

Bixby and Seldon glanced at each other again. '*We would if we could,*' said the Chief. '*But we haven't.*'

Danny blinked. 'What do you mean?'

'This isn't over yet,' Bixby said. 'Not by a long stretch. It's looking very likely that flight BA33489 was just a secondary strike, designed to keep our eyes off the main event. What I'm about to tell you doesn't go beyond ourselves. We've credible intelligence of a similar strike at the London Marathon. That's in approximately forty-eight hours.'

Danny stared at the screen. Then he looked over his shoulder. Tony and Caitlin were standing there, just a metre behind him and in earshot of the briefing. Tony's jugular was pulsing, but his face remained impassive. Danny couldn't help thinking that if *his* missus was about to take part in an event identified as a major terror target, he'd be a bit less calm.

Danny turned back to the screen. 'It could be a different threat. I bet there's loads of cells targeting the marathon.'

Bixby shook his head. He stretched out one hand to his own keyboard and the image on the screen changed. It was blurry, but Danny recognised the picture immediately. It was one of the shots he'd taken on the *Golden Coral* of the storage container where the aerosols had been filled. 'You see the top edge of the storage container?' Bixby said. 'There's a number there?'

Danny strained his eyes to read it. *2121311.*

'The number's identical to a serial number on the intel that warned us of an attack on April 26, in two days' time. We take that to mean there's going to be a serious attempt at a bio-attack.'

'Call it off,' Danny said.

'What do you mean?'

'The marathon. Call it off. I've seen what this bioweapon does to people. If you let it loose in London, you'll—'

'Impossible,' the Chief said. 'Number Ten will never allow it. There's an election in a month and it'll just make the government look weak.'

'And besides,' Bixby added, 'all our modelling suggests that if we call the thing off, it'll just alert the terrorists that we're on to them and encourage them to bring the strike forward.'

'They know you're on to them already,' Danny urged. 'You downed that flight from Lagos.'

'Don't be a bloody idiot, Black,' Buckingham said. 'That doesn't mean they know we've predicted the main event.'

Much as it pained Danny to admit it, Buckingham was right. But they were fresh out of leads, weren't they?

Bixby immediately answered that unspoken question. '*In the last few minutes, we've traced a call made from the* Golden Coral *to a cell phone most likely positioned off the coast of Qatar. Our working theory is that this was the militants making contact with someone on a higher rung.*'

'The Caliph,' Buckingham muttered.

Danny gave him a sharp look. He supposed he shouldn't be surprised that the MI6 man knew the name.

The Chief cut in. '*Our only hope of stopping this event is by getting our hands on this Caliph before it starts.*'

'But sir,' Buckingham said, 'we've already been down this line. Nobody will talk about him, they're too scared.'

'*Tell him, Bixby,*' the Chief said.

'*Buckingham, we've just received a communication from your man Ahmed in Doha. He has a number to call in the event he needs SIS assistance. He goes by the handle of codename Murdock. He's been told to keep his communications obscure, but this is the first time he's ever made a distress call and he's obviously very frightened. We're relaying GCHQ's recording of the conversation now.*'

There was a pause. A crackly hiss came over the laptop's speakers.

Go ahead, caller.

This is Murdock.

Please hold.

A twenty-second pause, then a new voice came on the line.

Go ahead, Murdock.

He's killed my parents. He's going to kill me. You have to help me.

The caller's voice was trembling. He sounded terrified.

Please try to keep calm, caller. Who are you referring to?

Him . . . him . . . The Cal . . .

The caller checked himself before speaking the word.

I'll . . . I'll do whatever you need. To help you catch him, I mean. Otherwise he'll . . .

Caller, please be discreet.

I have an idea how we can find him . . . I . . . Send Mr Buckingham. Send him quickly . . . I have an idea . . .

The line went dead.

'Why me?' Buckingham breathed.

'*Because he recognises you. And in his situation, he's not going to trust anyone he doesn't recognise.*'

'I don't understand his sudden change of heart,' Buckingham said.

'*Nor do we, and it makes us nervous. Maybe he really is just very frightened.*'

'Have you been able to confirm that his parents have been killed?' Danny interrupted.

'*Not directly, but we've put out some feelers and the Qatari authorities have clamped shut. That's normally a good indication that something untoward has happened. They're keeping it quiet for some reason.*'

Danny could sense Buckingham tensing up. 'Sir, surely you don't actually intend to send me?'

'*That's exactly what I intend to do, Buckingham.*'

'But sir, what if the Caliph has *got* to him? What if it's all a trap?'

'*That's why Black and his team are going to escort you back to Doha. Immediately.*'

'But sir . . .'

The Chief cut in. '*Make it count, or a lot of people are going to suffer.*'

Danny's mind was moving quickly as he tried to assimilate this information. Ahmed. Buckingham. The Caliph. Qatar. The spooks on the screen looked desperate. Yesterday they were trying to shaft Danny and his team. Today they were begging for his help again.

He leaned into the screen. 'One more thing,' he said.

'*Go ahead,*' said the Chief.

'You've been setting us up for a fall ever since we landed in Nigeria. If you think we're going to take a hit for your fuck-ups, or for his –' he indicated Buckingham '– think again.'

There was a moment's pause as a flicker of uncertainty crossed the Chief's face. '*Your codename is Operation Hellfire. Do your job, Black, and make sure it's a success,*' he said. Then the screen went blank.

Buckingham turned to Danny. He looked pale. Frightened. But he hadn't lost his arrogance. 'You've got ideas above your station, Black.' He looked over at Tony and Caitlin. 'You should think about how behaviour like that reflects on the rest of your unit. That was the Chief of SIS you just spoke to.'

'That was a man in a suit. He'll be replaced by another man in another suit before long.' Buckingham could play divide and rule all day long. It didn't matter to Danny.

They exchanged a long glare. 'You heard the man,' Buckingham said finally. 'Do your job. Get ready to leave.'

Danny was already standing up. 'Make contact with Hereford,' he said. 'We need a movement order.'

He walked across the ops room. Dr Phillips, the Porton Down guy, was standing in one corner, his face etched with tiredness and worry. Danny approached him. 'If there's a bio-strike in London, how long before the infection spreads to the rest of the country?' He was thinking of Clara, giving birth in a provincial hospital, which would very likely become a centre of infection if this thing spread out of London. But what could he do? Tell her to leave the country? She'd never do it. Not when she was about to give birth.

'Impossible to tell,' Phillips said. 'A few days. A week at most. But it's the inhabitants of London that will be in immediate danger.'

Danny narrowed his eyes, nodded, then walked straight to Tony, grabbed his arm and led him out of the ops room.

'What the fuck . . .'

'Just walk with me,' Danny told him.

A minute later they were on deck again, the immense noise of the sea and the grind of the ship's engines almost drowning out their conversation. 'Your missus is running the marathon in two days, right?'

Tony nodded.

'They'll know that. They'll be monitoring any communication

you make with her. You can't warn her directly. But she's going to be right in the middle of this thing if it all turns to shit.'

Tony gave him an impassive stare.

'I'll get in touch with Spud!' Danny shouted.

'Why would you want to talk to that limping fucker?'

Danny let it pass. 'He can get a message to Frances. Tell her not to go. The Firm are clutching at straws. If we don't get direct proof there's going to be an attack, they won't stop the race going ahead.'

As Danny spoke, he was aware of movement along the deck. Caitlin had appeared, about fifteen metres from their position. She watched them, her hair blowing in the wind, one eyebrow raised at their sudden secrecy.

'Nah,' Tony said, suddenly dead-eyed. 'You're okay. Leave it.'

Danny blinked at him in shock and disbelief. '*What?*' he breathed.

'You heard me, Black. I said leave it.' He glanced towards Caitlin, then walked purposefully off in her direction. The two of them headed back to the flight deck where, in the grey light of morning, Danny could see the stealth Black Hawk being wheeled back on to the LZ, a hubbub of Australian naval crew all around it, preparing the aircraft for take-off . . .

TWENTY-ONE

Sir Colin Seldon stared at the blank screen. Danny Black had just called him out, and he felt a strange mixture of irritation and embarrassment.

They had made the call out of the way of the main ops room, in Seldon's top-floor office overlooking the Thames. Dawn was creeping over the city, which was still illuminated by street lamps and office lights. A few boats shone as they meandered lazily up the Thames. Seldon pictured the streets filled with hundreds of thousands of people – both runners and spectators. What would it take? A handful of nutters among the runners to spray aerosols as they went? They could do it discreetly, without anyone even knowing it was happening . . .

He turned to Bixby, whose head was – as always – leaning listlessly against the cushioned pad, but who was eyeing his boss with an intensity that sometimes unnerved him.

'We're chasing shadows, sir,' Bixby said. 'The Qatari lead's too little too late. Danny Black's right. We should call off the marathon.'

'We don't *know* there's going to be an attack, Bixby. And if we call off the marathon, you and I are out of a job.'

'We *don't* call off the marathon, we find ourselves in the middle of the worst terrorist strike in history.'

The Chief bowed his head. Bixby noticed that his hand was trembling. 'Do we have a list of all the marathon runners?'

'Of course, sir.'

'I want them broken down by race. Start by getting our systems to cross-reference every runner of Qatari origin with any

241

individual already known to us. Once you've exhausted the Qataris, move on to the Saudis, then continue to widen the net. Anyone who comes up positive gets a knock on the door.'

'Racial profiling, sir?' It was clear from the tone of Bixby's voice that he didn't approve.

Seldon gave him a dangerous look. 'Don't even start, Bixby . . .'

'It's unreliable, sir. It's a time-suck and a drain on our resources . . .'

'Just shut up and do what I tell you, Bixby. And do it *now*.'

Bixby stared at his boss. Then, without another word, he manoeuvred his wheelchair backwards, before spinning it round and heading to the exit. But before he left, he stopped and turned the wheelchair back again.

'Sir, in the past twelve months we know of at least three hundred British nationals who have left the UK to fight in Syria. What if the person we're looking for isn't Qatari, or Saudi, or even Middle Eastern. What if he's British?'

The Chief flashed back a dangerous look. He was sweating badly. 'What if he *isn't*, Bixby?' he said. Then he looked towards the door, and Bixby knew it really was time to leave.

The rush-hour traffic around Birmingham was heavy, but Spud weaved expertly in and out of the lines of traffic on his motorbike as he headed in the direction of Dudley. It was a little after nine when he found himself in the car park of the same pub – the Hand and Flower – that he'd been in with Eleanor, facing the minicab office. Nothing would be less covert than standing there with his helmet on, so he removed it. His gamble was that nobody in the minicab office would notice him from this distance. And if al-Meghrani *did* see him, chances were that at a distance he wouldn't remember him from yesterday. Unlike Spud, he hadn't been highly trained in the art of observation.

Time check. 09.37. He stayed astride his bike and kept his attention focused firmly on the frontage of the minicab office. There were three cars parked outside: an old BMW and two Renaults. The same old tramp that he'd seen circling the block and getting increasingly arseholed was there again, a full bottle in his fist, his gait relatively steady. But there was no sign of al-Meghrani's white VW.

No problem. Spud was prepared to put in the hours.

His mind drifted to Frances, and the night before. He remembered the look in her eyes as she'd drunkenly told him about Tony. There was no doubt that she was scared of him. And he wondered if it was just a figment of his drunken imagination, but was there a patch of bruising under her left ribs? He wouldn't mind a chat with Tony about that one of these days. Spud wasn't in the business of righting wrongs, but he didn't have much time for a guy who knocked his missus around.

Or maybe he had just been seeing what he wanted to see, because he liked Frances and loathed Tony. And maybe he was doing the same thing here, waiting for al-Meghrani. He heard Eleanor's voice in his mind. *You have to understand that we can't afford to chase shadows. We have to make sure we see what's there, not what we want to be there. He's just a cabbie, going about his business.*

Spud swore under his breath. He'd let his mind wander. And now a white VW had just parked up in the rank outside the cab office. Al-Meghrani was getting out. Spud's attention snapped immediately on to his target. The driver walked towards the cab office. But he didn't go in. Instead, he walked past it, and entered the cafe immediately to its right. Spud watched fiercely. His target sat down in the front of the cafe, his face obscured by the 'L' of the window lettering advertising lasagne and chips.

Spud swallowed a moment of frustration. If he was here with a team, his next move would be straightforward: send one of them in to keep eyes on al-Meghrani – even get them to engage him in conversation, see what came of it – while the remainder of the unit kept their distance. But he didn't have a team. There was just him. Entering the cafe was a gamble. Close up, the target might recognise him. His chances of gathering some kind of intelligence, though, were much better if he could get close and listen to his conversations or phone calls. Maybe he could work out his movements, establish a time and place where he could properly corner him . . .

243

He decided to go for it.

Leaving his bike in the car park, and with his helmet under his arm, Spud crossed the road. Thirty seconds later, he was walking into the cafe. As the smell of fried food hit his senses, Spud knew this was a bad idea. The breakfast rush had finished. Aside from al-Meghrani, sitting by the window, there were only three other punters, and one of them was finishing up a plate of food and looked to be leaving any moment. On the far side of the cafe was a counter with a big tea urn and a balding man in a dirty apron checking his phone. It was very hard to melt into the background.

But Spud was committed now: to turn round and walk out would just bring more attention to himself. He grabbed a copy of the *Mirror* from a newspaper rack by the door, then took a seat at the table adjacent to al-Meghrani's, facing him. Distance between them, three metres. A Radio Two jingle played softly from some old speakers on the far wall. Spud placed his helmet on the table, made a cursory study of the greasy laminated menu, then placed his newspaper in front of him.

The headline caught his eye: *Missing Plane: 9/11 Style Attack Feared*.

He scanned the text underneath: a British Airways flight from Lagos had dropped off the radar somewhere to the north-west of Nigeria. He found his mind drifting to Danny and his team. He knew this was nothing to do with them – they were on a bog-standard bodyguarding gig – but the headline still made him feel uneasy. Something bad was going down ...

He purposefully turned to the sports pages to stop himself reading the story further, and to keep his mind on the job in hand. A picture of Mourinho looking petulant didn't appeal. Spud glanced over at the cab driver.

Al-Meghrani looked like he was in his own little world. His hands were on his knees under the table, and he was staring into the middle distance, seemingly unaware of anything around him. He hadn't shaved for a couple of days, and Spud noticed a few flecks of grey in his beard. There were dark rings around his eyes and his hair was dishevelled.

Spud turned back to the football reports. When the counter guy walked over he ordered a full English with tea. The drink arrived a minute later, and on the same tray was a plate of food for al-Meghrani. The counter guy set it rather unceremoniously on the table in front of him, then stomped back to his place behind the tea urn.

Spud glanced at the cab driver again. He was examining his plate of food – it looked like he'd gone for the vegetarian break-fast – as if he was checking each item was there. As Spud took a sip of his tea, al-Meghrani drew his hands from under the table for the first time. He was still wearing the same black gloves that he'd had on yesterday.

Al-Meghrani started pulling the fingertips of his right-hand glove, loosening each one carefully as he prepared to remove the whole glove. Just as he'd loosened the final finger, his head turned. He caught Spud looking at him.

Spud cursed inwardly and quickly flickered his gaze back to the newspaper in front of him. But he could feel the heat of the cab driver's glare, and in his peripheral vision could sense that he was pulling the loose glove firmly back on to his hand. At that moment, Spud's food arrived. As the counter guy dumped it in front of him, Spud managed to get another look over at al-Meghrani's table. He was wolfing his food down with his gloves still on. By the time the counter guy walked away, Spud's target had only eaten a few mouthfuls, but he was already pushing his plate away and casting a long, suspicious, sidelong glance at Spud. He scraped his chair back, dropped a ten-pound note on the table and hurried out of the cafe, his food barely eaten.

Spud's mind was racing. Something had freaked al-Meghrani out. What was it? Had he recognised Spud from yesterday? Or had he suddenly got shy about removing his gloves when he saw that Spud was watching him do it?

And anyway, Spud thought: who eats breakfast in a warm cafe with their gloves on?

And if the guy had nothing to hide, why would he suddenly leg it?

245

He grabbed his helmet and scraped back his own chair. He felt the eyes of the few other punters – and the counter guy – on him as he emulated al-Meghrani in leaving a tenner on the table before hurrying out of the cafe. On the pavement, he focused on the white VW. The cabbie had already climbed in and was revving the engine. No passenger. With a screech of his tyres he pulled out into the road. A Transit van had to hit its brakes to avoid colliding with the VW, which accelerated down the road.

Spud winced suddenly: a sharp pain down his abdomen. It took a few seconds to subside, by which time the VW had disappeared. He considered running over to his motorbike, trailing the bastard, who obviously had something to hide, no matter what Eleanor the spook thought. But he decided against it. Al-Meghrani was alert. He'd be keeping his eyes open, and there were few things harder than a single person trailing a target who suspected he was being followed.

No. Spud decided he'd have to think a bit smarter.

He took a few deep breaths to steady himself.

Then he walked along the pavement and into the cab office.

There were two drivers and a controller in here. They'd obviously seen al-Meghrani speed off, and were talking about him. 'Fucking weirdo,' one of the guys muttered in a Brummie accent.

'He's a good driver, innit?' the controller said. He looked up at Spud. 'Yes, mate?'

Spud put one hand to his chest. 'Do us a favour mate,' he said. 'Let me use your toilet, I'm bursting.' He nodded towards the closed wooden door behind the controller's little desk.

'Not for customers, mate,' the controller said.

Spud gave him a painful look. 'I'm going to fucking piss myself, mate,' he said. 'Do us a favour.'

The controller's radio burst into life. The voice of one of his drivers blared incoherently through the loudspeaker. He gave Spud an exasperated looked, then waved one hand towards the wooden door. 'Go on, go on,' he said.

Spud gave him an embarrassed nod, then hurried past him, opened the door and went through.

He'd calculated that there had to be another room back here. The guy out front was running a business, and that meant files and paperwork on all the guys working for him. He was right. At the end of the short corridor there was a door marked with the word 'Toilet' – Spud could smell it from here. But to his right was another door, slightly ajar, which led into a small room, three metres by three. A grey metal filing cabinet in one corner. Two chairs. A table with a rotary index card holder. A dusty water dispenser with an empty water barrel.

Spud strode over to the filing cabinet and tried each of the three drawers. All locked. He cursed silently, then turned to the table. The rotary index card holder was open at a card that had a name and address scrawled all over it: Alan Lack, 13 Danes Drive, Dudley. Spud put down his motorbike helmet and quickly flicked through the cards – they were alphabetical – until he reached the 'M's. There was a 'Masters' and a 'Monk', but no 'Meghrani'. He flicked quickly back to the As, and there he was: al-Meghrani, Kalifa. Spud yanked the index card out of the holder and stuffed it into his pocket.

'What the bloody hell you doing?'

He spun round. The cab controller was standing in the doorway, his face angry. Spud allowed an open smile to spread across his face. 'Mate!' he said. 'I got lost! You wouldn't want *me* driving one of your cabs, eh?'

The controller eyed him very suspiciously, then looked pointedly at the helmet on the table. Spud grabbed the helmet, then jutted out his chin and threw back his shoulders. He knew he looked imposing when he wanted to. The controller appeared to lose a little of his confidence. He stepped back from the doorway and glanced towards the front office with an expression that said only one thing: *Get out.*

Spud pushed past him, through the front office – where the lingering cab drivers stared hard at him – and out into the street. He waited for a break in the traffic, then ran across the road back to where his bike was waiting for him. Only then did he pull out the index card and examine it more closely. The cab driver's address was 27a, Jackson Road. He plugged it into his phone and a map of its location appeared. Distance: 3.7 miles.

He could be there in ten minutes. If this was an official operation, he wouldn't hesitate. But as he stood by his bike, staring at the scrawled handwriting on the index card, something made him hesitate. He was operating on his own. If he was caught breaking into the cab driver's house, or interviewing the shifty bastard, Hereford would throw the book at him. He was a weight round their neck that they'd love to get rid of.

Maybe he should call Eleanor, but would what he say? That he thought al-Meghrani was a bad guy because he ate breakfast with his gloves on? He knew how *that* conversation would go.

Spud wasn't the kind of guy who normally doubted himself. But he doubted himself now. It wasn't a feeling he liked.

Regiment ops officer Major Ray Hammond hurried into the Hereford ops room. His day had just got a hell of a lot busier. What was it with Danny Black? Whenever an op included him, things seemed to escalate.

There were already five guys in there, each of them talking urgently into telephones as they made speedy arrangements to get Black and his unit from a frigate in the eastern Atlantic over to the Arabian Peninsular. One of the guys put down his phone, strode up to the ops officer and handed him a piece of paper. Hammond quickly scanned it.

'This is their quickest route?' he said.

'Yes sir.'

'No military transports?'

'Not that we can get covertly into the Middle East.'

'OK. Get them on the line.'

Thirty seconds later, Hammond was wearing a headset and boom mike. An image direct from the frigate appeared on a screen in front of him. He recognised Danny Black's features. Black looked like shit. His face was drawn and dirty. Rings under his eyes. Several days' stubble. Tired? Bad luck. Get over it.

'The Australians are going to put you on the ground in Ghana.

We're avoiding the Nigerians for obvious reasons. From Ghana you're on a commercial flight to Bahrain. There's a one-hour stopover in Dubai. That puts you on the ground in Bahrain at approximately 23.30 hrs. You'll be transported to the UK military base there. We're diverting an eight-man SBS support team into Bahrain from southern Iraq. They should hit the ground at about the same time as you. We don't how this meeting with your tout is going to pan out, but they'll be there if you need them.'

'*Roger that.*' Black's voice sounded scratchy and distant.

'From the Bahrain base you'll insert into northern Qatar. You're going in under the radar. We don't want the Qataris aware of your presence.'

'*How do we get into Doha?*'

'We're still working that out. We'll have it sorted by the time you're on the ground.' Hammond paused. 'We've been hearing whispers about Ripley. Anything we can tell the family?'

'*Enemy fire,*' Black said.

'That's not true, is it?'

'*They don't want to know the truth.*' Black looked over his shoulder. '*I've got to go,*' he said. Without waiting for another word from his ops officer, the Regiment man disappeared from the screen.

Hammond stood up. 'I want a list of all our assets in Qatar within the hour,' he announced to the room in general. He turned to leave – he needed to update his boss – but right then another soldier entered. He looked a bit perplexed, and was holding a mobile phone.

'What is it?' Hammond demanded.

'Er . . . Spud Glover,' the soldier said.

Hammond blinked. 'What the fuck? I thought he was wiping the Firm's arse for them.'

'He says it's urgent, sir. Demanding to speak to you.'

Hammond sighed, then grabbed the phone and spoke as he walked out of the ops room. 'What is it, Spud?'

He was expecting one of Glover's sarky remarks. What he got was a moment's silence.

'Glover, are you there?'

'*Yes, boss.*' He sounded uncharacteristically unsure of himself.

'What the hell is it? I'm busy.'

'*I . . . I'm following down a lead, boss. This bloke in Birmingham, acting strangely. Firm don't seem that interested. Requesting permission to ask him a few questions.*'

Hammond stopped walking and pinched the bridge of his nose. 'Spud, what the hell are you talking about?'

'*It's just, there's this bloke . . .*'

'Where's your MI6 liaison?'

'*We parted company, boss. Didn't see eye to eye.*'

'Spud, we're doing our fucking best for you, but there's a limit to how much dead weight we can carry. Get your arse back to London and do what you're fucking told for once. That's an order.'

Without waiting for a reply, Hammond killed the line and handed the phone back to the owner, who had followed him up the corridor. 'If he calls again, I'm busy,' said Hammond. Which was true. He had two units to mobilise covertly into the Middle East, and waves of barely concealed panic emanating from Whitehall. Black and his team had a big job to do. They were exhausted, and a man down.

He just hoped they were up to it.

PART THREE

The Caliph

TWENTY-TWO

10.00 hrs

Danny, Tony and Caitlin had ditched their military kit. As they ran across the flight deck and ducked into the chopper, they carried no personal weapons, no ammo, no webbing, no blades. They had showered and changed into civvies provided by the Australians. If they'd been taking a BA flight across Africa, the Firm might have pulled some strings and they could have taken their gear with them. But the plane transporting them from Ghana into Dubai was operated by Emirates, which meant they needed to look entirely ordinary. Danny felt naked without his kit, but there was no other option.

The chopper lifted up from the flight deck the moment they were inside and the side door was shut. Flight time to Kotoka International Airport in the Ghanaian capital of Accra: thirty-five minutes. The ocean had settled, and the sun reflected dazzlingly off its surface. As Danny stared through the window of the chopper, watching the frigate disappear until it was a dot in the distance, and the shadow of the aircraft rippling over the water below, the events of the previous night felt strangely distant. In the middle of an op, there's no time for looking back. You can only look forward.

He glanced at his team-mates. Buckingham was asleep. Caitlin had taken her place next to Tony, and had her head resting on his shoulder. Tony himself was staring into the middle distance, expressionless. Danny couldn't stop thinking about the last conversation they'd had on deck. He tried to put to the back of his mind his distaste for Tony's refusal to warn his wife. He didn't have to like Tony. He just had to work with him. But he couldn't help thinking of Frances, and remembering the words of the Porton Down guy in Chikunda. *Forget 9/11. Explosions are yesterday's news.*

They suddenly saw land. Danny saw the grid-like outskirts of an African town. Accra. Even from the sky he could tell it was sprawling, dense and over-populated. Nose-to-tail traffic. Busy streets. Lines of palm trees and a dusty, sun-soaked haze covering everything. There would be slums on the outskirts and tired government buildings on the interior. Danny had never been here before, but he'd seen enough large African towns to feel like he knew it well enough.

Moments later, they were losing height. Danny saw the dull, grey tarmac of Kotoka International, with the bleak, utilitarian terminal building a couple of hundred metres away. They touched down on to a busy landing zone and spilled out of the chopper. A member of the ground staff was waiting for them in an old electric buggy. He ferried the team to the terminal building, where a uniformed immigration official made a brief study of their passports before waving them through.

The terminal concourse was crowded, with the usual collection of tawdry gift shops and tired-looking cafes. A member of the British consulate was waiting for them by the Emirates ticketing desk. Young guy, fresh-faced. Danny supposed that Ghana was pretty low on the ladder of diplomatic postings. He, Tony and Caitlin held back while Buckingham approached him and, in the course of a two-minute conversation, received a handful of tickets for their journey. The consular official glanced inquisitively over towards the military trio. He received nothing but grim faces in response, before nodding at Buckingham and disappearing into the crowd of the terminal. Buckingham handed out the travel documents – business class into Dubai, economy from Dubai into Bahrain. Departure time, 11.35.

At the check-in desk, a bored-looking airline employee looked Danny up and down. He clearly didn't get a lot of white guys at his counter. 'What is your reason for travel?' he asked in faltering English.

'Business,' Danny said.

'What business?'

The lie came automatically to Danny's lips. 'I work for an oil company. Mineral Explorations.'

The guy nodded slowly, as if he knew a great deal about this company and its business. Without another word, he printed out Danny's boarding card and handed it back.

By the time they were all checked in, their flight was being called. They walked to the gate, very obvious among the Africans and Arabs who made up the rest of the passengers. Buckingham fell in alongside Danny. He'd been mostly silent since they left the frigate. Danny could feel the anxiety emanating from him. Good. A few nerves might stop him fucking up. But they didn't stop that tone of superiority in his voice. 'Ahmed's a tricky character,' he said. 'You need to know how to handle him. I'll brief you further on the flight.'

'You'll keep your fucking mouth shut on the flight,' Danny murmured. 'We're under the radar. You don't say *anything* that an oil company employee wouldn't say. Got that?'

Buckingham gave him an evil look. 'You'd do well not to speak to me like that, old sport,' he said.

'You'd do well not to speak to me at all.'

They continued for a few paces in silence.

'I saw you looking at her,' Buckingham said. 'Probably for the best that she's getting shacked up with Tony, eh? Your record's hardly exemplary. I heard Clara ditched you. Not really a surprise, old sport. Girl like that needs a man who won't drag her down.'

Danny forced himself to look ahead and ignore the lava in his veins.

'I could bury you with a single word,' Buckingham said quietly. 'I could have your head on a plate.'

A poor choice of words, Danny thought, all things considered. He continued his walk towards the gate. This time the spook lagged a few paces behind.

A rickety old bus took them to the 737 that was waiting on the tarmac. On the aircraft they turned left, and at 11.35 exactly, they were thundering down the runway.

Tiredness overcame Danny. As he waited for sleep to take him, he watched the ground recede. There were no clouds, so within two minutes he had a vista over the African continent. It spread out beneath him, vast, unending. An uncomfortable thought wormed its way into Danny's brain. Somewhere down there – not in Africa maybe, nor even in the Middle East where they were heading – someone, perhaps just one person, was preparing for a spectacular. Forget about needles in haystacks. They could be looking for just a single person on the planet. In less than forty-eight hours, tens of thousands of potential bio-terror targets would congregate on London, and their only lead was a dodgy Qatari businessman mate of Buckingham's.

He closed his eyes. In his mind he saw a faceless terrorist preparing for an attack on London, knowing he was impossible to find. Danny shoved away the negative thoughts. There was no place for them. He needed to focus on finding his man.

And he needed to forget that it was a billion-to-one shot.

His name was James Bailey, but he preferred to be called by just his surname.

He had a shaved head, a sleek, thin nose and a protruding Adam's apple. He lived alone in a comfortable house – two bedrooms and a garage – on the south side of St Albans. He liked it here. The countryside was just a five-minute drive away, but he could get into London when he needed to, as he often did. At first glance, there was very little to distinguish his house from any other. In the front room where he now stood there was a slightly tatty three-piece suite, an Ikea rug on the floor and an Ikea coffee table in front of the electric fire, which had both bars on. An old, out-of-tune upright piano that the previous occupants of the house had left here, and which Bailey had never bothered to get rid of. A laptop sat on top of the piano. On the wall was a black and white picture of the Eiffel Tower, and next to the flat-screen Samsung TV was an ageing CD player, with a Cat Stevens CD box open on top of it.

There were two sets of unusual objects in the room. The first was the camera equipment. It was piled in one corner by the front door that led directly out on to the street. A steadicam rig was packed up in a set of flight cases. A couple of tripods were leaning up against them. On top, open, were two smaller cases – one of lenses, the other of gels. There was a light meter, and of course a camera – a Canon 7d DSLR. A sturdy, well-worn North Face jacket was draped next to it.

The second unusual object was the prayer mat. It was neatly rolled up and wrapped in a cotton drawstring bag to protect it from becoming unclean.

Bailey was preparing for his second prayer of the day. He had not taken any food or drink since dawn, but had carefully washed and dried his hands several times. He did so again now, before moving directly from his bathroom to the front room, where the thick curtains were still shut, the morning light peeping in around the edges. He carefully removed the prayer mat from its drawstring bag, and rolled it out on the ground, facing east. He knelt reverently, then bowed his head to the floor with his arms stretched out in front of him.

He prayed. He spoke the *takbir* in little more than a murmur, and his voice didn't get any louder as he performed the *rackat* and recited the Quran, before finishing with the *takbir* once more.

When his prayer was over, he rolled up the prayer mat again and replaced it in the cotton bag. Then he picked up his laptop, sat down in his favourite armchair, and opened up the computer.

The folder to which he navigated contained five quicktime files. He hovered the mouse over them, before selecting the third file on the list. He double-clicked and the video appeared in a window that filled half the screen. Too big. The image was massively pixellated. He reduced the window to the size of a matchbox – much better – then pressed 'play'.

A white room. Five masked men. A sixth man, Western – he didn't look much different from Bailey himself – kneeling down with his ankles and wrists trussed. The picture jumped to scenes of the same man talking about his family in a slurred voice, how much he loved them, missed them and was looking forward to seeing them again. Then back to the white room. One of the masked men started reciting something in Arabic – Bailey didn't know what it meant, but he liked hearing it anyway.

A pause. The masked man made a shout of *Allahu Akbar*, then he and his companion rushed towards the trussed man, forced him face down on to the ground and pinned him to the floor. The hostage was weirdly silent – drugged, Bailey assumed, to make him more compliant. One of the masked men had a short hand saw, with deep, jagged teeth. He went to work immediately on the back of their victim's neck.

Suddenly there were screams from the hostage, but they stopped as soon as the spine was sliced. Bailey counted the thrusts: one, two, three, four, five swipes. The blade was halfway through his neck before the twitching stopped. He had read somewhere that the brain of a decapitated man remains conscious for fifteen seconds while it burns off its remaining oxygen. He found himself counting to fifteen as the masked men completed their grisly work, before holding up the severed head by its hair for the camera, blood slicking from the body that still lay on the ground.

The video stopped. Bailey played it again. Of the five quick-times, this was the most graphic. He watched it repeatedly after prayers every day, to desensitise himself to what was to come. And as he watched it this morning, he felt his eyes wandering occasionally over to his own camera equipment, piled up in the corner of the room.

A knock on the door. Bailey started and quickly slammed down the lid of his laptop.

He kept very still, barely daring to breathe, staring over at the front door.

Who was it?

Silence.

A clattering sound. The person at the door was pushing something through the letterbox. A magazine. He saw the name 'Watchtower' on the front. Jehovah's Witnesses. He felt himself frown.

After five seconds, he heard footsteps walking away. A bead of anxious sweat was trickling down the side of his face. He stood up gingerly and laid the laptop on the coffee table. He stood for a moment in the front room, anxiously wondering how to fill his time. Then he moved through the house into the kitchen. There was a locked door at the far end that led into the garage. There was only one key to that door in existence. Bailey now removed it from his pocket, unlocked the door and stepped into the dark, chilly garage.

There was an old white van in here. It had been reversed in, and its nose was very close up against the garage door to make room for what was behind it. Two metallic canisters, each about a metre high and half a metre in diameter. They looked a bit like beer barrels, Bailey thought, but it would be a bad move to take a sip from their contents. On the side of the barrels was some Chinese lettering. He had no idea what it said, but it was identical on both.

Bailey stared at them for a good long while. Then he turned his back on the garage, returned to the kitchen and started to fix himself some coffee and a late breakfast. No bacon, of course, but eggs, toast and tomatoes.

It wouldn't be long now. James Bailey really needed to keep his strength up.

Midday

The pub in which Spud found himself was a bleak, spit-and-sawdust establishment. The kind of place a man goes to drink, not to socialise. There were no women among the few punters. Just old guys, their faces raddled and reddened from years of daytime drinking. Thrash metal played softly over the pub loudspeakers, and the only brightness inside the dim interior came from the flashing of a fruit machine in one corner. The floor was sticky to walk on, and the air smelled stale.

The barman had a shaved head and tattoos, and as Spud approached he looked at him like he was a piece of shit. Spud didn't care. He sat on a stool, plonked his bike helmet on the bar and pointed at the Carling tap. 'Pint,' he said.

The barman wordlessly poured the drink. Spud fished around in his pocket for a ten-pound note. As he passed it over to the surly barman, he noticed that his hand was trembling. He stared at it, trying – unsuccessfully – to control the shaking. Only when he noticed that the barman had grabbed the note from his grasp did he clench his fist and put it down out of sight. When the barman plonked his change back on the counter, Spud left it there. He'd be needing it in a minute.

He took hold of his pint. His trembling hand spilled a little as he brought it up to his lips and drank deeply.

Danny slept over Nigeria and Chad. A troubled sleep, filled with visions of plague-ridden bodies. He woke as the sun followed them east over the arid plains of Sudan. He stared out over that war-torn country, which just looked like featureless desert from this height. In Danny's line of work, there was always something safe about being in the air. Out of reach.

But then he thought about flight BA33489. The uncomfortable truth was this: nowhere was safe any more.

The sun turned blood-red as they saw the Red Sea, and the sky deepened in colour as they travelled over Saudi Arabia, with the burning torches of the oil fields glowing constantly below them. As the 737 began to lose height over the UAE, dusk was upon them. Danny caught glimpses of the impressive, metropolitan lights of Dubai glowing in the distance, a beacon of extreme wealth in the desert, the Burj Khalifa sprouting up, higher than any other building in the world, from its centre. The sight of this desert city made Danny's pulse race. He wasn't fooled by its glowing swimming pools and high-rise hotels, by its extravagance or its desperate attempt to look modern and Western. He knew that the money required to keep bastards like Isis and Boko Haram in business came directly from oil-rich cities like this. From the businessmen who paid lip service to the West in public, and funded its downfall in private. There were guerrillas and militants along this coast just as surely as there were in Chikunda. They just wore finer clothes, and got other people to do their killing for them.

Wheels down 21.05 Arabic Standard Time. Their connecting flight to Bahrain was already on the tarmac when they landed, and their one-hour window was soon eaten up at passport control. At 22.10 AST they were in the air again. But as they walked out on to the tarmac at Bahrain International Airport at 23.35 hrs, their short stint as ordinary civvies came to an end. A military vehicle was waiting for them by the steps. Ignoring the curious looks from the other passengers, Danny, Tony, Caitlin and Buckingham, accompanied by a young British army soldier with bad acne, got into the vehicle. They were out of the airport in a couple of minutes, and hurtling down a broad motorway.

'Mina Salman Port.' Buckingham broke the silence in the car with his maddeningly smug voice.

'What about it?' Tony said.

'It's where we're headed. The British government is setting up a permanent military base here. Protests from the bloody lefties, of course, but what they don't understand is . . .' His voice trailed off as he realised that Danny, Tony and Caitlin were looking out of their windows, not listening.

It took twenty minutes to reach the military base. The warm air smelled strongly of the sea, and Danny heard the distinctive sound of a ship's horn, though he couldn't yet see the water or the vessel itself. Their driver handed a plastic ID card to the uniformed guard at the gate, who waved them through a checkpoint in the three-metre-high wire boundary fence. They drove immediately to a large hangar, about five hundred metres from the boundary line. It stood on its own, fifty metres from any other building or vehicle – a sure sign that this was the area of the base reserved for SF operations. The green army guys would know to keep their distance unless they'd received a specific instruction to the contrary.

They alighted bang on midnight. Danny was instantly aware of the familiar bustle of a forward mounting base. A chopper flew overhead. In the distance, he saw the headlamps of a number of vehicles driving round the base. Piercingly bright floodlights illuminated a hotchpotch of hangars, Portakabins and signalling aerials. A second helicopter was sitting on an LZ thirty metres to the left of the hangar, a refuelling truck right next to it. Another three military trucks were parked up outside the hangar, the entrance to which was guarded by two green army guys in camo gear and carrying standard-issue L86s. As the team slammed their doors shut, another guy exited the hangar and strode directly up to them.

'Major Anderson,' he introduced himself.

Buckingham pushed his way to the front of the group. 'Hugo Buckingham.' He held out his hand. 'Bloody good to meet you.'

Anderson glanced at the outstretched hand. 'This way,' he said.

He led them into the hangar. It was fifty metres long, thirty metres wide. Halfway down, and to the left-hand side, was another grey Portakabin. Its windows were blacked out, and several wires crossed the hangar floor and led into the Portakabin – internet and secure comms connections. At the far end, eight men congregated around a TV screen holding polystyrene coffee cups.

'SBS?' Danny asked, nodding towards the unit.

Anderson nodded. 'They're on standby. I'll introduce you in a minute. First I'll run through your itinerary.' His voice was slightly drowned out by the scream of an aircraft taking off somewhere on the base. He led them up to the Portakabin and unlocked it with one of several keys on a small keychain. There were three more guys sitting inside, laptops in front of them, cans and boom mikes on their heads. The walls were covered in maps of the area, and there was a briefing table at one end. An A4-sized black and white photograph was lying loose on this table. Anderson handed it to Danny. It showed a man in his fifties, streaks of white hair at his temples, a strong jawline and a nose that had obviously been broken in a couple of places.

'His name's Jimmy Morgan. Ex-Regiment, currently chief training officer for the Qatari special forces. But he's also double-dipping for the UK government. He'll RV with you at your dropping-off area on the Qatari coast and get you into Doha.'

Clipped to the photograph was a separate sheet containing certain items of personal information relating to their man.

Danny committed them to memory as he asked, 'Does he know who we are?'

Anderson shook his head. 'He's just expecting four guys ...' He glanced at Caitlin. '... I mean, four personnel, at 02.30 hrs. His instructions are to transport you to an RV with ...' He checked some notes written on another piece of paper on the table, 'with Ahmed bin Ali al-Essa. London have confirmed that Al-Essa will be waiting for you in his offices in central Doha.'

Danny looked at the maps on the wall. 'Where's the drop-off point?' he asked.

Anderson approached a map that showed the Qatari coastline. He pointed to a patch of coast approximately eighty klicks north of Doha. 'This beach is an underpopulated area,' he said. 'The nearest road is about a kilometre away. We'll put you down there. You'll need to head directly west to find the road. Your man will be waiting for you there. He knows the score, he won't ask you any questions and he's expecting the four of you.' He handed Danny a piece of paper. 'Here are your ident instructions.'

Danny committed the few lines on the piece of paper to memory. 'We need to get kitted out,' he said.

Anderson nodded. 'Your timing's good. We get one supply plane a week from the UK. It arrived an hour ago. Hereford managed to get a couple of laycorn boxes on board.' He pointed to the corner of the Portakabin. There, piled up, were three scuffed, grey, heavy military storage boxes. 'I don't know what they've got you doing,' Anderson said, 'but they're pulling the fucking stops out, that's for sure.'

If Anderson was angling for information, he was going to be disappointed. Danny, Tony and Caitlin walked up to the laycorn boxes, separated them out and opened them up. They contained a mobile armoury. Pistols – three Smith & Wesson M&P body-guard handguns. Short machine guns – KH-9 close-quarter battle rifles, compact enough to carry under your jacket or in a small rucksack. Well suited for urban conflict, and since they were heading into the centre of Doha city, that suited them well. These weapons were not regular Regiment issue. The KH-9s were

Russian-made and Danny knew that their serial numbers would have been scratched out, making it practically impossible to link them back to the British army. This was non-attributable hardware. There were boxes of flashbangs and ammunition tucked into one of the laycorn boxes – nine mills for the handguns, 5.56s for the KH-9s. Radio packs with concealed earpieces and clothes – including tactical vests – in another. The same garb for Caitlin as for the men: jeans, white trainers and a selection of tracksuit tops – baggy enough to conceal a weapon, easy enough to unzip should you need to get at it. There were four sports bags and, incongruously, a couple of squash rackets.

They quickly changed into their jeans and tracksuit tops. Caitlin seemed to have no qualms about getting undressed in front of this roomful of men, but Danny noticed all their eyes wandering. Tony looked calmly appreciative. Buckingham couldn't stop his eyes bulging at the sight of Caitlin's curves as she strapped her handgun to her abdomen before covering herself up with her tracksuit. Once they were changed, Danny, Tony and Caitlin started packing ammunition under the flap at the bottom of the sports bags, followed by their radio packs and a flashbang each, before secreting their KH-9s and tactical vests on top and covering them with more loose clothing.

Buckingham watched the soldiers pack their kit with obvious impatience. His tracksuit top looked a bit oversized on him. 'Why the bloody hell have they sent us squash rackets?' he demanded.

Danny and Tony gave him a frosty look. Then they each took a racket and placed them head first into their bags, so just the handle was protruding. They held their bags over their shoulders. To look at them, Danny knew, you'd never guess that they weren't simply on the way to the gym. They'd look no different from any other Westerners in Doha.

'Well, what the hell am I going to put in *my* sports bag?' Buckingham said. Caitlin leaned into one of the laycorn boxes and pulled out a small box, which she lobbed across the Portakabin to Buckingham. He clearly panicked at the thought that she'd chucked some dangerous weaponry at him. He didn't so much try to catch the box as swat it away before it hit him. It burst open in mid-air, and three squash balls flew out across the Portakabin. Buckingham's face reddened, and it wasn't helped by the smirks of the military men in the Portakabin.

Danny chucked him a few loose pieces of clothing. 'Fill it with these.'

'I should take a weapon.'

'In your dreams,' Danny said. He looked over at Anderson. 'Is that our chopper waiting outside?'

Anderson nodded.

'Let's get it turning and burning,' Danny said. 'We need to move.'

TWENTY-THREE

Estimated flight time from the military base to the drop-off point on the Qatari coast: forty-five minutes. It was now 00.30. That put them on the ground at 01.15 hrs and gave them an hour and a quarter before their 02.30 RV time. As the chopper rose into the air, Danny saw the lights of a Royal Navy frigate docked in the port and, in the opposite direction, the yellow glow of a nearby town. The helicopter banked and headed towards the sea. It continued east in order to clear the northern tip of Qatar.

'Okay,' Danny said once they were airborne, 'what do we need to know about this Ahmed character?'

Danny had the impression that Buckingham was still sulking from his humiliation back in the SF hangar. He looked deeply uncomfortable in his baggy tracksuit top, and he wore a nervous frown. But he cleared his throat, clearly trying to sound authoritative.

'He's much like every super-wealthy Middle Eastern businessman,' he said.

'Well, that's very helpful,' Tony cut in, 'because we spend a lot of time hanging out with people like that.'

'Let me finish,' Buckingham said. He thought for a moment. 'I'd say he's very determined, used to giving orders and used to getting what he wants. But when I spoke to him about the Caliph, he was also very scared.' His frown grew deeper. 'Something bad must have happened for him to change his mind about informing on this character.'

'If someone had murdered *my* parents,' Caitlin said, 'he'd be picking his guts up off the floor.'

'Do you trust him?' Danny asked.

'I trust that he knows more about the Caliph than he was letting on to me. Or at the very least, that his driver did.'

'Fine,' said Tony. 'We hang him up by his bollocks and get him to talk.'

'You'll do nothing of the sort,' Buckingham said, in a schoolmasterly way. 'He's a valuable asset who—'

'Great,' Tony growled. 'So we just check our weapons at the door and have a nice chinwag over a cup of tea?'

'Leave him to me,' Danny said.

The unit fell into silence.

When the loadmaster announced that they were five minutes out, Danny, Tony and Caitlin unzipped their tracksuit tops and gave their handguns the once-over. Danny was aware of Buckingham eyeing the weapons nervously. But he said nothing as the chopper started losing height. 'When we land,' Danny told Buckingham, 'we'll secure the LZ before you get out.'

'I'm perfectly capable of—'

'Button it, Buckingham. When the loadie tells you to disembark, do what he says and hit the ground.'

Buckingham didn't have chance to respond. The chopper wobbled with a sudden turbulence. Seconds later the view from the windows was obscured by a sudden brown-out as a cloud of sand surrounded it.

'Go!' the loadie instructed, opening the side door.

Danny exited first, followed by Tony and Caitlin. With his handgun engaged, his chest tight with tension, he cleared the landing site by about twenty metres so that he emerged from the brown-out, then hit the ground face down. Behind him he was aware of the other two taking up positions five metres to his left and right, and also of the strange circular glow the rotors made as particles of sand sparked against them. He looked forward. They were on a deserted beach. Tufts of cactus-like greenery sprouted from the sand, and there were patches of rock here and there. A low moon hung in the sky, and it illuminated a long sand dune about a hundred metres away. No immediate sign of any potential threats, but Danny remained alert.

The chopper rose in the air. Danny glanced back. The brown-out was subsiding, and Buckingham was visible in what remained of the cloud, standing ten metres behind with his hands covering his eyes.

'Get down!' Danny hissed at him.

Buckingham didn't move. Within a second, Tony had got to his feet. He ran back to where the spook was still rubbing his eyes, and thumped him heavily to the ground.

The chopper disappeared quickly out to sea. The noise of its engines were gone within thirty seconds, leaving only the sound of the waves lapping gently on the beach.

The unit remained prostrate for five minutes. Danny carefully scanned the surrounding area for movement. There was none. 'Make for the dunes,' he said finally.

They stood up. Danny replaced his weapon under his tracksuit and started to jog towards the dunes, aware of the others following him a few metres behind. The moon cast shadows on the sand, and Danny knew they'd be visible to anybody watching. His civvy trainers slipped in the sand as he upped his pace, wanting to get to the cover of the dune as quickly as possible.

They reached it in about thirty seconds. It wasn't high – maybe ten metres. Danny left the others at the bottom, then scrambled up to the ridge. With his naked eye, he could see open, sandy terrain for another 250 metres or so, then the road, broad and straight, heading north–south. No cover. And no sign of any vehicles. He checked the time. 01.25 hrs. Sixty-five minutes till RV.

Danny raised one hand. The others joined him at the top of the ridge. They all lay on their front, quietly observing the deserted road.

There was no movement on the road until 02.07 hrs, when they saw the headlamps of a vehicle approaching from the south. It stopped directly to their twelve o'clock. The driver killed the headlamps and stayed behind the wheel.

'Aren't we going to—' Buckingham tried to say.

'Shut up and don't move,' Danny interrupted him.

They stayed in position for another twenty-three minutes. At

02.30 exactly, the driver of the car switched on his headlamps for fifteen seconds, then killed them again.

'Keep me covered,' Danny said.

Movement as Tony and Caitlin removed their weapons from their bags. Then, knowing they had his back, Danny pushed himself to his feet and walked over the brow of the ridge, carrying his own bag over his shoulder.

He walked purposefully, covering the 250 metres in two minutes. As he approached the car he saw that the window was wound down. The guy behind the wheel was looking towards him. 'Are you lost?' he asked when Danny was five metres away. 'Do you need help?'

'Can you tell me where the nearest bus stop is?' Danny replied.

'Okay, buddy,' said the driver, 'you're clear. Bring the others in.'

Danny turned back towards the ridge and raised one hand. Moments later, Tony, Caitlin and Buckingham were jogging towards him. 'Get in the back,' he told them as they approached a couple of minutes later. 'I'll take the passenger seat.'

The unit climbed into the car. Danny sat in the passenger seat with his sports bag on his lap. He turned to their driver. 'Go,' he said.

23.35 hrs GMT.

Spud had done everything he could to get arseholed. He'd lost count of the number of pints he'd downed in this rough Birmingham pub. But the deep drunkenness he craved hadn't arrived.

Perhaps it was the TV that had kept him semi-sober. His eyes had been fixed to it all day. The news wires had been buzzing with the story of flight BA33489, which had disappeared in West African airspace. Spud had to admit it was weird. There was no doubt in his mind that somebody knew more about it than they were letting on. Aircraft didn't just disappear like that. There were too many safeguards in place. He thought about Danny. He was in that part of the world. Did he have anything to do with it? Spud shook his head. That was the beer talking. Danny and the others were just bodyguarding some diplomat . . .

But then, around mid-afternoon, a new story started to break. Unconfirmed rumours that the British High Commissioner in Nigeria had been kidnapped, possibly by Boko Haram militants. Spud stared agog as a breathless reporter, standing outside the Foreign Office, announced that the government were neither confirming nor denying the rumours: a sure sign that someone, somewhere was shitting bricks. Spud found himself edging off his seat, wanting to *do* something, *go* somewhere. To be part of whatever the hell was going down in West Africa. But reality hit home as he realised he was in a shit-hole pub on the outskirts of Birmingham. And his ops officer's voice rang in his head. *We're doing our fucking best for you, but there's a limit to how much dead weight we can carry.*

The ops officer was right. What the hell did Spud think he could do? He should just accept that he was washed-up.

The frustration was almost too much to bear. He'd gone back to drinking to try and drown it out. But the booze wouldn't slow the cogs in his mind, and he found himself staring at the index card with al-Meghrani's address on it. He pulled out his phone and punched the postcode into Google Maps, which told him the address was twenty-five minutes away from his current position.

Get your arse back to London and do what you're fucking told for once. That's an order.

He'd put his phone away and got back to his drinking and TV-watching. Now the news channel was reporting from London, where the preparations for Sunday's marathon were under way. But he didn't get to watch the end of the report. The barman switched the channel, and the footie appeared. Spud ordered another pint.

Despite all the booze, Spud was just slightly shaky on his feet as the barman called time. As he staggered past the blinking fruit machines with his helmet under his arm, he almost wished one of the Friday-night drinkers would be stupid enough to pick a fight with him.

The cold night air hit him as he stepped outside. His bike was the only vehicle parked up in front of the pub, and he stared at it for a moment, knowing that he shouldn't really risk riding it.

'Fuck it,' he muttered. He turned, walked down the side of the pub and took a piss by the bins. Then he returned to his bike and turned the engine over.

The roads were fairly clear at this time of night. It didn't matter that he was swerving slightly, he told himself, or that every time he came to a red light he braked just a little bit too late. Each time a car beeped him, he waved a dismissive hand at them.

He'd been driving like this for a full ten minutes when he realised he was following precisely the route he'd brought up on his phone a few hours previously. The route to al-Meghrani's house seemed to be imprinted on his brain, and after another ten minutes of dangerous driving, he found himself turning into Jackson Road.

The street was even shabbier than Spud expected it to be. Music thumped from a house at the far end. An upturned supermarket trolley lay in the middle of the road. There were dog turds on the pavement where Spud parked up. He didn't like leaving his bike there, because he could see at least three beaten-up old cars with their wheels missing. He walked up and down the road, looking for al-Meghrani's white VW. No sign of it. Several of the houses had broken windowpanes. A few of them even looked occupied – squatters, Spud reckoned. He approached number 23. It was an ordinary terraced house divided into two maisonettes – 23a and 23b – each with their own front door. There was no sign of any lights on either the ground or the first floor. A small paved yard facing directly on to the pavement, with three wheelie bins stuffed full of rubbish.

Was al-Meghrani home? The absence of his vehicle didn't mean anything. He could have parked it in another street. In any case, what did Spud expect to find by breaking in to his house? And what if someone called the police? He'd be down the job centre before you could say RTU.

Spud suppressed a wave of nausea. Maybe he was drunker than he thought. Maybe he should get the hell out of here. Put his head down somewhere. Sleep it off.

He turned to walk away.

Then he stopped.

A little voice in his head was telling him to follow his instinct.

He looked around. The street was deserted. And really, who would notice another break-in in a dump like this?

Spud walked past the wheelie bins, aware that he was still slightly staggering. He approached the ground-floor window to the right of the front doors. It was a sash, with glazing bars dividing each half into six rectangles. No curtains. The interior latch was clearly visible behind the middle lower rectangle of the top pane. No sign of any window locks.

Spud looked around again to check he wasn't being observed. There was nobody watching. He laid his bike helmet on the ground, raised his right elbow and casually jabbed the window-pane. The glass shattered immediately, but only made the smallest tinkling sound. Spud put his hand through the hole, undid the latch and raised the lower sash. Seconds later he was inside. He closed the window behind him and looked around.

The room in which he found himself was very sparse. An old sofa. An occasional table. A set of dumbbells was propped up against one wall, and there was an unlit gas fire in the fireplace. Nothing else to see, but plenty to smell: the musty, unwashed stench of a single man's house. Spud found himself flexing his fists. If al-Meghrani was home, Spud would want to put him down quickly and efficiently before he recognised the face of his intruder. He walked across the room to the closed door on the other side.

He listened carefully.

Silence.

He opened it.

A corridor. Narrow. Dark. The front door to the left. Spud could just make out pizza delivery slips on the floor. Still didn't mean he was out. He could have just been walking over them.

He turned right, past a scummy bathroom, empty. He could see that there were two more rooms in the house: a kitchen at the end of the corridor, its door open, crockery overflowing in the sink. And what Spud had to assume was a bedroom, its door closed.

He silently approached the closed door and listened hard. Nothing.

He opened the door.

The smell was worse in here but it was obvious, at a glance, that the bedroom was unoccupied. The blankets on the double bed were stripped back and crumpled. There were clothes on the floor and a chest of drawers had all three drawers half-open. Spud checked behind the door as he entered, but he knew there was nobody there. This was the room of someone who had left in a hurry. He pulled out his phone and switched on the torch app. By its small, bright light, Spud made out more details: al-Meghrani's cab-driver's ID lying on top of a chest of drawers, an empty Burger King cola cup and fries wrapper. A bulky old CRT telly on a stand in the corner, and an electric fan next to it. Wire coat hangers on the floor. And at the foot of the bed, a pile of papers.

Spud sat on the edge of the bed, picked up the papers and started flicking through them.

There were gas bills and council tax demands, all of them overdue. A receipt for a pay-as-you-go phone. Nothing of any great interest, until he got further down the pile. Here there was a green paper wallet which bore the words: 'Your Prints Are Enclosed'. It contained photographs.

Spud examined them. The first was a picture of al-Meghrani. He was standing against a plain wall, naked from the waist up. He was quite ripped, which explained the dumbbells. Spud's eyes focused in on his hands. He wasn't wearing his gloves, but was clutching his fists by his side. In the second photo, however, he was holding them up, almost as though he was showing them off. Spud frowned. The photo wasn't great, but he could see that there was something wrong with those hands. It was like they were covered in some kind of rash. Or a scar.

He looked at the next photograph, and suddenly felt his heart rate increase.

This photograph was a close-up of al-Meghrani's hands. Palms upwards, fingers spread. The skin was covered in a network of cobweb-like scarring. Beneath the skin there were little black dots, like grains of ground pepper.

'Mother*fucker*,' Spud whispered to himself.

He knew what he was looking at. Shrapnel scarring. He'd seen it before, on the hands of a mate of his who'd had a bad experience with a dodgy old Russian fragmentation grenade. These were the telltale markings of someone who'd been playing around with poorly made gunpowder explosives.

The fourth and final picture showed the same hands palms down. The scarring was not so bad on this side, but it was still there. There was no doubt in Spud's mind: these were the hands of a man who had handled low-grade explosives, albeit inexpertly. No wonder he wanted to keep them covered.

Any beer-induced wooziness had disappeared. Spud's thinking was clear-cut, and he no longer doubted himself. He tucked the pictures back into their wallet and continued to shuffle through the papers. More bills. A begging letter from a charity that donated goats to families in Darfur.

And at the very bottom, two email printouts.

They were flight confirmations. The first: London Gatwick to Athens, Greece. Flight time: 23.58 hrs the following day, departing South Terminal on easyJet. The second: Athens to Ankara, Turkey.

He checked the name on the ticketing details. 'Mr K. al-Meghrani'.

Spud inhaled slowly. For a moment he was back in the MI6 building with Eleanor. *He's never owned a passport, Spud. He's never even left the UK.*

'Oh yeah?' he breathed. Passports could be faked. MI6 intelligence could be wrong. It wouldn't be the first time.

Spud folded up the flight confirmations and put them, along with the photographs, into his jacket pocket. Then he stood up and left the room. He exited the flat by the front door. A couple of teenagers were loitering on the other side of the road. They gave him a suspicious look. Maybe they knew al-Meghrani and they thought it was strange seeing Spud leave his house at this time of night. Maybe they'd clocked the broken window and were considering ransacking the place. It didn't matter to Spud either way. He knew from the state of the place that al-Meghrani wouldn't be back any time soon.

He hurried to his bike, got behind the wheel and evaluated his options.

Option one: call Eleanor, tell her what he'd discovered. Forget it. She'd already ticked al-Meghrani off her list. She'd probably look at the photographs, sigh heavily and tell Spud his suspect had eczema.

Option two: call Hereford. No way. They'd told him to get back in his box once already. They wouldn't hesitate to do it again.

Option three: head for Gatwick, kill the following day there and intercept al-Meghrani when he arrived to catch his flight. Do what he should have done the moment he saw his Claymore bag: make the fucker talk.

Decision made. He turned the engine over, set his sat nav for Gatwick, and pulled out of his parking space. In his rear-view mirror he saw the two teenagers approaching al-Meghrani's flat.

Help yourself, he thought. He won't be needing the place, by the time I've finished with him.

TWENTY-FOUR

05.00 hrs AST.

Dawn was arriving as the unit hit the outskirts of Doha, but the lights of the high-rise buildings were still burning, illuminating the sky with a neon fluorescence. As their guy drove along a broad, beach-side highway, streaks of salmon pink crept across the sky from the horizon. The sea itself was dotted with yachts, many of the size that only the oil-rich could afford. Even at this early hour, commercial helicopters were coming in to land on the top of brightly lit skyscrapers – an airborne reminder that this was a place where the super-wealthy came to work and to play.

'Your drop-off location is in the West Bay district,' Morgan told them. 'Poshest part of the whole fucking Gulf. Your guy must be quite the playboy.'

Danny nodded as their guy looked in the rear-view mirror. 'Don't take this the wrong way, love,' he said to Caitlin, 'but when girls looking like you rock up at the offices or apartments of men like him, they're normally charging by the hour – and making a fair whack out of the deal too.'

'Thanks for the heads-up,' Caitlin said, her voice frosty.

'I'm just saying people notice it, if you're trying to stay under the radar.'

'You train up Qatari SF?' Danny asked the driver, trying to change the subject.

'Uh-huh.'

'They good?'

'Not bad. No problem getting them the gear they need. You know . . . oil money.'

'They end up working for the West Bay playboys?'

Their guy shrugged. 'Some of them,' he said. 'But the truth is these Qatari guys can afford to recruit from the flashier end of the market. It's kind of a status symbol to have a couple of Seals in your security detail.'

'Even after Bin Laden?'

'Sure. Money talks louder than religion in Doha. For most people, at least.'

As the city around them grew more built-up, Danny felt increasingly uncomfortable. They could easily be walking into a trap. What if the Caliph – whoever he was – had already got to Al-Essa? What if he was forcing this rich Qatari oil merchant to reel Buckingham and his SF team in? Danny looked in the rear-view mirror at Tony and Caitlin. Their severe faces suggested they were having similar thoughts.

Their driver indicated left and headed down a slip road. Thirty seconds later they were driving through the centre of the metropolis, skyscrapers left and right, the streets perfectly clean and well-ordered. The way the neon reflected off the buildings, the pavements were shining. They drove for about a mile, until Morgan indicated again and pulled up outside an impressive building whose ground floor had a huge glass frontage and a marble-clad foyer.

'This is where we part company,' their guy said. He glanced towards the building. 'There's a service entrance round the other side of the building. Word to the wise – if there's no covering security round this place, I'm a fucking Chinaman. Take my advice and keep your eyes peeled.'

Danny turned to Tony. 'Take the service entrance,' he said. 'Caitlin, front entrance. Any suspicious activity, let me know. I'll go up with Buckingham. Work out whether this guy is on the level.'

'Now look here,' Buckingham cut in. 'Ahmed is *my* contact. I'll do the—'

'You say a word before I give you the go-ahead, I'll rip your fucking throat out.'

277

Buckingham fell silent. Danny noticed the sweat on his forehead. He was obviously as tense as the rest of them.

The unit alighted on the pavement in front of the foyer. There were no farewells. Once the doors of the vehicle were shut, it pulled out and became just another set of red lights on the increasingly busy main road. Danny looked around. There were only a handful of passers-by in the area, and no immediate sign of any surveillance on the building, but that didn't mean it wasn't there. There was a second skyscraper opposite, covered with mirrored glass which could conceal any number of observation posts. And there was enough traffic passing for at least one of the vehicles to be doing surveillance rounds of the building.

Danny slung his sports bag over his shoulder. 'Take your positions,' he said. 'Let's go.'

The foyer of the building was air-conditioned to perfection. There were seven or eight indoor palm trees, and a brightly lit interior fountain. In the centre was a concierge desk of burnished wood and shining brass. A man in full traditional robes sat behind it. There was nobody else apart from him. Danny strode up to the concierge, with Buckingham trotting behind him.

The concierge made no attempt to hide his disapproval of two men with tracksuits and sports bags approaching his desk. 'May I help you, sirs?' he asked, obviously assuming that they would speak English.

'Ahmed bin Ali al-Essa,' Danny said. 'He's expecting us.'

The concierge inclined his head, as if to say: I don't *think* so. But he made a call, spoke a few words in Arabic and then, with a small bow, led them to an elevator at the back of the foyer. Danny's earpiece crackled as he walked towards it. Tony's voice. '*In position.*'

Danny checked the foyer again before stepping into the elevator. Nobody appeared to be watching them. Once inside the lift, he and Buckingham stood silently. Danny unzipped his tracksuit top and felt for the handgun strapped to his body.

The lift stopped. The doors pinged, then slid apart.

The elevator opened up on to another marble-clad reception

room. To one side there was an enormous tank full of tropical fish. To the other, a door. It was open, but there was no sign of anyone.

'Stay behind me,' Danny said. He pulled his handgun and the two men stepped out of the lift into the lobby.

Buckingham's feet clattered across the marble floor. Danny's were much quieter. They approached the open door. Danny was tense. He was pretty sure nobody inside the building had been watching them, but he didn't know what to expect inside the penthouse apartment itself. He raised his weapon and crossed the threshold.

He wasn't prepared for what he saw.

It was a lavish apartment. A window on the far side looked out over the sea. There was expensive-looking art on the walls, and stylish items of furniture dotted around. Two more doors led off the room, at Danny's ten and two o'clock. A large coffee table in the centre with a mirrored surface and a pile of magazines on one side. And behind it, sitting on a sofa, there was a man.

The only image of Ahmed bin Ali al-Essa that he had seen had shown a neat, confident man with a well-trimmed goatee beard and full Arabic dress. Buckingham had spoken of a proud, deter-mined businessman, used to giving orders.

The man who sat on that sofa was anything but.

He wore a plain, white robe, but it was stained down the front. His face was gaunt, his beard scraggly and his hair unkempt. His eyes looked red and sore. He was the picture of a broken man. The sight of Danny's handgun didn't seem to worry him. He stared instead at Buckingham.

'You came, Mr Buckingham,' he whispered.

Buckingham was about to speak, but a deadly look from Danny silenced him. Danny himself stepped forward. 'Who else is here?' he demanded.

Ahmed looked at Danny as though for the first time. The gun still didn't seem to worry him. 'Nobody,' he said. 'It is just us.'

Danny spoke into his radio. 'Tony, Caitlin, what you got?'

Caitlin clocked in first. *Nothing, unless you count being eyed up by a few lecherous old Arabs.*

Tony: '*Kitchen staff. Nothing else.*'

Danny didn't like it. Like Morgan had said, the chances of this guy having no CP were a thousand to one.

He moved suddenly forward, past the mirrored-glass coffee table, up to the sofa. With one strong hand, he grabbed the front of Ahmed's robe and pulled him up from the sofa. Ahmed's limbs flopped weakly – he seemed to weigh almost nothing. Danny pressed his weapon hard into Ahmed's temple. 'Who have you got watching us?'

Ahmed closed his eyes. Danny felt his body start to shake.

'Nobody,' he whispered.

Danny made a dismissive hissing sound. He spun Ahmed round, then forced him to his knees so he was facing back towards where Buckingham was standing. With his handgun still pressed against the Arab's skull, Danny grabbed his left arm pulled it behind his back, forcing the joint up to breaking point. Another inch, he knew, and the bones would snap. Danny was aware of Buckingham taking a couple of steps back, his eyes bulging. The bulk of his attention was on Ahmed.

'Listen to me,' he said, his voice very quiet and very menacing. 'You might have all those twats in the Firm fooled, but I don't trust you any further than I could fucking throw you. If I don't get the answer I want, I'll break this arm and then start on the other. Trust me, five minutes and you'll be begging to give me information. So I'm going to ask you one more time: who have you got watching us?'

To add a final piece of emphasis, he squeezed the joint just a fraction of an inch harder. Ahmed whimpered.

'For God's sake,' Buckingham breathed. 'He's our only ...'

'You've got five seconds, Ahmed. Five ... four ...'

'Jesus, man,' Buckingham said. 'Look at him ...'

Danny stopped counting. He forced Ahmed's head forward so that he was bending over the mirrored coffee table. He looked at Ahmed's reflection. At first, his eyes were closed. But a second later, he opened them again. They were brimming with tears. Ahmed blinked. The tears dripped down his face. A couple of them splashed on to the coffee table. Ahmed's face was etched into an expression of complete despair.

'Please,' he whispered. 'Look . . .'

His reflection nodded towards the pile of magazines on the opposite side of the table. Lying on top, face down, were several sheets of photographic paper. Danny hadn't noticed them before.

'Look at them,' Ahmed breathed.

Danny hesitated for a second. Then he looked over at Buckingham. 'Spread them out on the table,' he said.

Buckingham's eyes tightened slightly at being told what to do. But he stepped over and picked up the images. He looked through them, and visibly paled. With trembling hands he laid them out on the table.

Even Danny, who had seen things most people could never conjure up in their worst nightmares, was sickened by what he saw. An old lady lying back, her rictus grin matched by the open wound on her throat. A man in the same position, his eyes and tongue gouged out. A fat man on the floor, lying in a pool of his own blood. And more blood on the walls scrawled into Arabic lettering.

'What does it say?' Danny demanded.

'You need to ask?' Ahmed said. Danny looked at his reflection again. His cheeks were wet. Danny tightened the arm another fraction, and Ahmed hissed in pain. 'You are looking at my mother and father,' he whispered. 'That is what he did to them. That is the Caliph's work.' More tears splashed on the mirrored surface of the coffee table, and Ahmed's body started to shake even more violently. Danny suspected that it was not just down to the pain he was inflicting. 'That is what he will do to *me*,' Ahmed continued, 'if he finds out I am speaking to *you*. And he *will* find out if I allow *anyone* else to know that we are speaking. He has eyes and ears everywhere. There is nobody else here because nobody would dare to cross the Caliph, and I do not dare to let *anybody* know that this is what I intend to do.'

Danny stared at his reflection again. His eyes were still welling with tears, his brow still creased with pain. But there was something else in his expression. A grim severity. The determination of a man bent on revenge. Danny could see the hate in his eyes. It told him more than any words.

Slowly, he released the tension on Ahmed's arm, and removed the gun from his head. He spoke into his radio. 'Tony, Caitlin, make your way up to the penthouse.'

'*Roger that.*'

Ahmed was still kneeling. He had buried his face in his hands, and his shoulders still shook. After a few seconds, though, he looked up again. He wiped his face with the sleeves of his grubby robe, then stood and addressed Buckingham. 'I thought it was only *my* people who could be so brutal.'

'You don't know the half of it, old sport,' Buckingham muttered.

'Sit down,' Danny interrupted them, 'and shut up.'

Ahmed looked over at Danny and bowed his head acquiescently. He clearly had no wish to pick an argument with the Regiment man.

'The situation is this,' Danny said. 'We think that the Caliph, whoever the hell he is, is orchestrating a bioweapon strike on the London Marathon. That's tomorrow morning. We've got twenty-four hours to find him, or someone who knows what he's got planned. The Firm played us your cryptic call to London. Whatever your big idea is, it had better be good, or a lot of people are going to be killed.'

It was as if Ahmed had suddenly forgotten what he'd undergone at Danny's hands in the past couple of minutes. He stared at him, shaking his head slightly in disbelief. 'Who would do such a thing?'

'A sick fucker,' said Tony. He and Caitlin had appeared at the door to the penthouse.

'So if you know how to find him,' Danny continued, 'tell us now.'

'Do we trust him?' Caitlin demanded as she walked into the apartment. At first she seemed oblivious to the faint look of disapproval she received from Ahmed. But then she turned to him. 'Don't worry, darling, they're only tits, they won't bite.'

'We trust him,' Danny said, 'as soon as we've heard his strategy for getting close to the Caliph.'

The unit were now standing round Ahmed in a semicircle. He seemed very small, hunched on the sofa in his plain white robe.

'So let's hear it,' Tony said.

Ahmed bowed his head, then stretched out one hand to indicate their lavish surroundings. 'I am a wealthy man,' he said. 'One of the very wealthiest. And I have learned something very important. Money opens doors. It buys you anything, except long life and happiness. Everybody has their price.' He looked at each of them in turn. 'Even the Caliph.'

He looked at each of them in turn.

'Go on,' Danny said.

'Terrorism costs money. A great deal of it. Each bullet fired, each man trained is an expense.' He gave a rueful smile that looked strange against his wet cheeks. 'You could say that it is a very poor business model: all expenditure, no income.'

He had a point. Danny remembered Ntoga, the corrupt Nigerian official, who'd received fifty grand from Boko Haram for help in kidnapping Target Red.

Ahmed stood up and walked to the wide windows at the back of the penthouse. He lifted his left arm and indicated a line of skyscrapers along the waterfront. 'Men like the Caliph have support in this part of the world, and not just because people fear him. There are rich businessmen in Qatar and Saudi Arabia who fund his activities – and the activities of people like him – to the tune of hundreds of millions of dollars. They see it as their responsibility as good Muslims, while they rely on the West for their more worldly needs.' He turned to look at them again. 'We businessmen like to hedge our bets. If we invest in one stock, we also invest in another equal and opposite stock. If one goes down, the other goes up and so we minimise our losses. Those Qatari and Saudi businessmen who donate money to the Caliph and his like, they are doing the same thing: a spiritual hedge fund to guarantee them entry into Paradise, if it turns out Allah takes a dim view of their worldly wealth.'

'Very poetic,' Danny said. 'Get to the point.'

'The point is this. I have heard rumours – and I must tell you that they are just rumours – that the Caliph is accustomed to accepting large financial donations from men like me. He is not independently wealthy, so how else could he operate? It is also true that I am able to make him a financial offer he cannot refuse. Excuse me for a moment.'

Ahmed left the room through the door at Danny's two o'clock. When he walked back in twenty seconds later, he was carrying a metal briefcase.

'What's that?' Danny said.

Ahmed put the briefcase down on the table. He clicked it open. Inside, neatly arranged, were piles of crisp, new American dollars.

'Five million,' Ahmed said.

Danny lowered his gun. So did the others. Something made Danny glance at Tony's face. The greed in his eyes was plain to see.

'I have another twenty cases waiting. A hundred million in all. I propose offering it to the Caliph, in return for my life.'

There was a silence in the room. It appeared that nobody could take their eyes off the money. Danny found it amazing, how little space five million could take up. It would be the easiest thing in the world to swipe it now, go off the grid and never have to worry about anything.

'It's all very well having the money,' Danny said. 'But the whole point is that we don't know how to contact the Caliph.'

'Yes we do,' Ahmed said quietly. He stared meaningfully at Buckingham.

For a moment Buckingham looked confused. Then realisation dawned on his face. 'Your driver,' he said. He clicked his fingers excitedly. 'The one you asked about the Caliph when we met in Riyadh. What was his name . . . Mustafa!' Buckingham turned to Danny. 'Mr Al-Essa asked his driver if he'd heard about the Caliph. He denied it, but he looked nervous, as if he knew something but was too afraid to say it.'

Ahmed nodded. 'Mustafa was the only person who knew we discussed the Caliph. I mentioned it to nobody else. I didn't dare.'

'You think your driver was the Caliph's man?' Danny asked.

'I doubt it. But it would only have taken Mustafa to mention our conversation to one person . . .'

'Where's Mustafa now?' Danny asked.

'He lives outside of Doha. I can have him here within a couple of hours.'

'Do you think he'll be happy to talk to us?'

Ahmed gave Danny a flat look. 'No,' he said. 'I do not think he will be at *all* happy to talk to you. He will be scared for his life and for that of his family. He will need . . .' – Ahmed bowed his head as if he did not like what he was about to say – '. . . persuasion.'

'Fine,' Tony said. 'Persuasion we can do.'

'He is an innocent man, my friend,' Ahmed said quietly.

'So are all the people who'll die in London if we don't get to the Caliph,' Danny said. 'Call him. Now.'

06.00 GMT.

Daniel Bixby felt like he hadn't slept in days. The glare from the lights in the subterranean offices of the MI6 building hurt his head, and the noise of his electric wheelchair grated as he moved it along the corridor to the office where he knew the Chief was waiting for him.

Bixby hoped he didn't look as bad as his boss, whose pale, drawn features looked out from the other side of his desk. His glasses had slipped a centimetre down the bridge of his nose. He looked like a man who was losing grip of the situation. 'Well?' he asked.

'There are no Qatari or Saudi nationals registered for the marathon,' Bixby said. 'We have two Yemeni men, three from Oman and five from the UAE. No women.'

'So that's ten suspects?'

'If that's what you want to call them, sir,' Bixby said mildly.

'You have addresses for them all?'

'Of course. We just need your go-ahead to deploy the appropriate resources. SCO19 are standing by.'

The Chief hesitated for a moment. 'You think there's a low chance that one of these Arabs is involved in the strikes, don't you?'

'Vanishingly small, sir. But I think there's a very *good* chance of fomenting anti-Western feeling if they and their families are woken up by masked officers brandishing MP5s.'

'Spare me the liberal claptrap, Bixby,' the Chief said irritably.

'Not to mention,' Bixby persisted, 'the lawsuits we'll open ourselves up to. Our legal people on the third floor are having kittens.'

'Alright, alright!' The Chief hesitated. 'What word from Black and Buckingham?'

'They've made contact with Al-Essa. Apart from that, nothing.'

'They're chasing shadows, aren't they?'

'Yes, sir,' said Bixby. 'But so are we.'

The Chief's eyes narrowed. He stared into the middle distance. Then he spoke.

'Make the raids,' he said.

The operations room in Hereford was buzzing, despite the early hour. A large screen on the wall showed a close-up of the Qatari coastline. On a second screen was a map of London. The marathon route was marked on it in red. Ops officer Ray Hammond was staring at the map when he heard his name. He turned round. One of his guys in camo gear was approaching, carrying a clipboard. 'We've had communication with Bravo Nine Delta, sir. They've made contact with Al-Essa.'

Hammond nodded. 'Support units?' he asked.

'Our eight-man SBS team is online in Bahrain. They can mobilise whenever they get the call. We have a sixteen-man team from B-squadron en route to the Gulf from Syria. They should be on the ground within the hour.'

'London?'

'Two eight-man CT units on standby, north of the river at the Artillery Garden. We have a standby squadron in camp ready to deploy tomorrow morning in time for the marathon, leaving Hereford at 05.00 hrs.'

Hammond looked round the ops room. Fifteen men sat at computer screens, plugged into headsets, ready to mobilise astonishing amounts of firepower both in London and the Middle East.

But there was a problem. All the firepower in the world is no good, if you don't know where to aim it.

It was still dark in St Albans. But the lights in one house were burning brightly.

Bailey had made himself a cup of tea, but it had grown cold as he sat in his front room waiting. He checked the time. Five minutes past seven. His associate was late.

He stood up and paced the room. His camera equipment was still piled up in the corner, next to the old piano. He lifted the piano lid and played a few random notes.

A knock on the door made him startle, even though he was expecting it.

He closed the piano lid, walked to the door and opened it.

A man about his own age stood on the threshold. He wore a charcoal-grey oversized beanie hat, and had a few days' ginger stubble on his face. A black puffa jacket on which he'd pinned a small enamel badge in the shape of a helicopter. Jeans. Trainers. Bailey nodded a curt greeting at him. 'McIntyre,' he said.

'Bailey.' McIntyre walked into the room and closed the door behind him.

'You're late,' Bailey said.

'I took precautions, in case somebody was following me.'

'*Who* was following you?'

'Nobody. They were just precautions.' He looked round the room and his eyes fell on the camera equipment. 'I shouldn't stay long. Let's get started.'

They each took a flight case and carried them through the ground floor of the flat to the kitchen. Bailey unlocked the door leading to the garage. McIntyre followed him in.

Nothing had changed since the previous day. The old white van still had its nose pressed against the garage door. The sealed metal canisters were still there. McIntyre's eyes lingered on them. 'Is that it?' he asked.

Bailey nodded.

'How did they get it here?' McIntyre's voice cracked slightly as he spoke.

'The Caliph has his networks,' Bailey said. 'I don't ask about things I don't need to know.'

At the name of the Caliph, both men fell silent for a moment.

'Let's load up,' Bailey said. 'It's what you're here for, after all. They're too heavy for one man.' He opened the back of the van. It was empty, and smelled faintly of petrol. 'Camera gear first,' Bailey said. He climbed into the van and piled his flight cases up against the front wall, before accepting the two McIntyre was holding and stacking them too.

It took another two trips for them to bring all the camera equipment out of the front room and stash it in the van. Only then did they turn their attention to the remaining items in the garage.

The canisters with the Chinese lettering were very heavy. Even with two of them lifting, it was a struggle to get them off the ground. As they shifted them carefully towards the van, Bailey noticed how McIntyre couldn't take his eyes off the seal. Beads of sweat had appeared on his forehead, and they were nothing to do with the heat or the exertion. McIntyre was obviously very scared of these canisters. Bailey didn't blame him, because he was scared too.

It took a great effort to lift the first canister into the back of the van. Just as they had manoeuvred it inside, it slipped from McIntyre's hands, and the base clattered noisily on the floor of the van. '*Shit!*' Bailey hissed, just managing to hold on to the rim and stop it toppling. McIntyre grabbed his side of the rim again to steady it, and the two men exchanged a glare. 'Slowly,' Bailey said.

They eased the canister carefully to the side of the van, where Bailey strapped it carefully in place using six roof-rack cords. Then they lifted the second canister into the van and secured it tightly, before jumping back down into the garage and locking the van's rear doors.

Bailey led his associate back into the kitchen and locked the garage door.

'All set?' Daniel asked.

'All set,' said Bailey. He shook his associate's hand. '*Allahu Akbar.*'

'*Allahu Akbar,*' Daniel said.

They moved back to the front room, where Bailey held the door open for his accomplice. 'You're sure you weren't followed?'

'I'm sure.'

'And you're okay to set up the machinery?'

'Don't talk to me like I'm an idiot. You take care of your bit, I'll take care of mine.'

'Until tomorrow, then,' Bailey said.

'Yeah,' McIntyre replied. 'Until tomorrow.'

TWENTY-FIVE

09.00 hrs, Arabic Standard Time.

Mustafa, Ahmed's driver, was scared.

'He will know something is wrong,' Ahmed said as they waited for him in the luxurious penthouse apartment. He had changed out of his stained white robe and washed his face. He now looked every inch the Arabic businessman. 'I have never invited him to come up here. He always waits for me in the car.'

Sure enough, when the knock came on the door of the room in which they were all standing, it was faint and hesitant.

Ahmed walked across the room and opened the door.

The man who stood there wore a *dishdash* and headdress. His face was slightly podgy, and he had a silvery moustache. He exchanged a few words in Arabic with Ahmed, who stepped back and ushered him in with a sweeping gesture of one hand. Mustafa was obviously deeply uncomfortable. His eyes darted around the room as he crossed the threshold. It was as if he couldn't decide whether to ogle the rich furnishings or acknowledge the four other occupants of this room. Buckingham was standing by the window, looking out. Danny, Tony and Caitlin stood in a line behind the sofa. Grim sentinels, their arms folded.

Ahmed closed the door. 'I have asked you up here, Mustafa,' he said, reverting to English, 'to answer a few questions. You do not mind, I hope?'

'Sir . . . I . . .' Mustafa stuttered.

Then he fell silent.

Buckingham had turned from looking out of the window. Mustafa clearly recognised his face. The last time he had seen

Buckingham, Danny knew, they had discussed the Caliph. So there was no doubt what *this* discussion was about.

Mustafa suddenly started to sweat. He turned to Ahmed. 'Sir . . . *please* . . . my family . . .'

'These gentleman – and lady – only want to ask you some questions, Mustafa. It is my wish that you answer them.'

'But sir . . .'

'That's enough talking,' Danny said. 'We haven't got time. Ahmed, you'd better leave the room. You won't like this.'

Ahmed swallowed nervously. He put one hand on Mustafa's shoulder. 'Tell them what they want to know, my friend,' he said quietly. Then he turned and left through the door that led into his bedroom.

Silence in the room. Danny stepped out from behind the sofa and strode purposefully up to Mustafa.

'Bathroom,' he said. 'Now.'

'What?' Mustafa demanded. 'Why?'

But Danny had already grabbed his arm and was dragging him across the room to the other door. Tony and Caitlin followed. Buckingham made to follow, but Danny pointed at him and said: 'You, stay where you are.' Buckingham's face was thunderous, but he obeyed.

The bathroom was large and well-appointed: a roll-top bath with gold-plated taps and shower attachment, a separate walk-in shower, twin sinks, a toilet, a bidet and two chairs. The walls and floor were covered with translucent, aquamarine glass tiles. When all four of them were inside, Danny locked the door. He turned. Mustafa was backing away from him towards the sinks. His lower lip was trembling.

Danny surged towards him, grabbed him by the throat, lifted him from the floor and slammed his body against the mirror behind the sinks. 'You want to know why we're in this room and not the other one?' he whispered.

Mustafa could do nothing but nod his head.

'Easier to clean up,' Danny said.

Mustafa's eyes bulged.

'Understand this,' Danny continued, his voice deathly quiet. 'There is *nothing* I won't do to make you talk.'

'I . . . I understand,' Mustafa said, his voice strangled and weak.

'I don't think you do,' Danny said. He let go of Mustafa's neck and quickly grabbed his right hand. Mustafa seemed to have some idea of what was coming, because he tried to clench his fingers. But too late. Danny had his fist around the chauffeur's little finger. He yanked it sideways. The bone cracked, snapping as easily as if it were a piece of raw chicken.

Mustafa inhaled sharply. Tears welled in his eyes. But Danny hadn't finished yet. He grabbed the chauffeur's fourth finger and snapped it with the same brutal ease.

Mustafa cried out, but Danny slammed one hand over his mouth to deaden the noise. He jabbed one thumb over his shoulder to indicate Tony. 'See him?' he asked.

The chauffeur nodded vigorously.

'He makes me look like a fucking schoolteacher. My advice is not to put me in a position where he has to take over. Understood?'

Mustafa was still nodding from the previous question.

'I'm going to ask you a simple question. You spoke to your boss about the Caliph. Then you told someone about the conversation. Who was it?'

Danny removed his hand from Mustafa's mouth. Mustafa sucked in another deep intake of breath and looked in horror at his two fingers jutting out at an unnatural angle from his hand. Then he looked at Danny. 'I . . . I told nobody,' he stuttered, before wincing again with the pain.

Danny gave him a level look. Then he turned his back on him. 'He's all yours,' he told Tony. Then he nodded at Caitlin, and the two of them left the room.

They stood with their backs to the closed door. Buckingham was a couple of metres from them, his handsome face drawn. 'What's going on in there?' he asked.

Danny didn't reply. The noises coming from the bathroom answered the question for him. They heard glass breaking, and the thump and clatter of a body being manhandled across the room.

Mustafa cried out several times. Then, after about a minute, there was silence.

Danny and Caitlin walked back into the bathroom. It was a mess. The mirror behind the sink was cracked at about the height of Mustafa's head. The wall and floor tiles were streaked with blood. On the floor, halfway between the door and the sinks, Mustafa was lying in a foetal position with Tony standing over him. His moustache and mouth were covered in blood, and just to his right a tooth lay on the floor, the bleeding root still attached.

'I'll ask you again,' Danny said. 'Who was it?'

Mustafa shivered on the floor. It took a moment for Danny to realise that he was shaking his head.

Danny exchanged a look with Tony. They had to be careful. Too much force would make Mustafa pass out, or worse. Right now, he was their only link to the Caliph. If they lost him, they lost everything.

Caitlin stepped forward. 'Put him in the tub,' she said.

'I can handle it,' Tony said aggressively, but Danny glanced towards the roll-top bath with its gold-plated taps. Then he nodded at Tony.

'Do it,' he said.

They bent down and picked a squirming Mustafa up under the arms and by the legs. Ten seconds later they had dumped him in the bath, with his head at the tap end. His face was still bleeding, and the edge of the bath was smeared red where his hands gripped it.

Caitlin grabbed a fresh flannel from the side of the sink, soaked it in tap water, then crammed it into Mustafa's bleeding mouth. He tried to cry out, but the sound was muffled and pathetic. Caitlin slipped her hand into the inside pocket of his jacket and withdrew his wallet. It took her just a few seconds to pull out an ID card and a picture of two small kids that the driver obviously carried everywhere with him. Very cute, a boy and a girl.

An image of Clara, pregnant, flashed across Danny's brain. He pushed it to one side. He couldn't think about that. He knew what was coming.

Caitlin held the pictures up in front of Mustafa's eyes. 'I'm going to torture you now,' she said bluntly. 'If I don't get what I want, I'm going to kill you, then I'm going to go after your family.' She waved the ID card. 'I know where you live.'

Mustafa's muffled squeaking instantly stopped. Danny and Tony exchanged an approving glance. Tony was obviously as impressed as Danny was.

'Put his head back,' Caitlin said, as she took the shower attachment in her hand. Danny forced the heel of his hand under Mustafa's chin, forcing his head back at an angle, while Caitlin turned the hot tap on and directed the flow through the shower attachment. Without hesitating, she sprayed the scalding water over Mustafa's upturned face.

The chauffeur's body arched suddenly. His arms and legs flailed and he tried to inhale. Bad move: there was a sucking sound as he drew more boiling water into his nostrils. The panicked flailing of his body increased – so much so that Tony had to lend his weight to keeping him as immobile as possible.

Ten seconds passed. Danny knew that ten seconds of drowning could feel like an hour. Caitlin moved the shower attachment so the scalding water was now soaking his abdomen. The blood on his face, which had been washed away, immediately started oozing again from his lips and nose. She pulled the flannel out of his mouth. He made a terrible retching sound, then vomited up a quantity of faintly pink water that he'd sucked in through his nose.

'Who was it?' Danny repeated.

Mustafa's eyes rolled. 'You don't understand,' he whispered, 'what the Caliph will do if . . .'

He didn't finish. Caitlin had shoved the flannel back in his mouth. She moved the shower attachment back to his face.

Twenty seconds this time. The flailing started strongly, but grew a good deal weaker. When Caitlin moved the shower attachment again, Danny momentarily worried that they'd gone too far. He pulled out the flannel and Mustafa made another retching sound. His eyes flickered open as he vomited water for a second time.

'Please . . .' he whispered. 'I'll talk . . . *please* . . .'

'You just need to give me a name,' Danny said. 'Then it stops.'

Mustafa closed his eyes. 'It was . . . it was my friend Rashed,' he whispered.

Caitlin immediately turned the water off. 'There,' she said. 'That wasn't so difficult, was it?'

Two minutes later they were back in the room. Ahmed, sitting on the sofa, stared at his soaked, bleeding chauffeur in horror. 'What did you do to him?' he asked, clearly aghast.

'Persuasion,' Tony said.

'What does Rashed have to do with the Caliph?' Danny demanded.

Mustafa hesitated and looked away, but then caught sight of Caitlin standing by the door. The sight of his tormentor made him shudder, and he looked resolutely back at Danny, as if that were a safer option, though his eyes did flicker nervously towards Ahmed.

'You may speak without fear of sanction from me,' Ahmed said.

'There are people who act as the Caliph's eyes and ears,' Mustafa said. 'We do not know who all of them are, but I have known for many months that Rashed is one of them. I thought . . .' He bowed his head. 'I thought that by mentioning your conversation with the British man to him, it would mean my family were safe.'

A silence fell on the room. Danny stepped towards the mirrored coffee table, where the photographs of Ahmed's parents were lying upside down. He turned them over and laid them out in front of Mustafa. 'Look at them,' he told the chauffeur.

For a moment, he thought Mustafa was going to vomit again as his eyes fell on the horrific scenes.

'That's the Caliph's work,' Danny said. 'It's what he did to your boss's family. Now listen to me carefully: it's the easiest thing in the world for me to arrange a large sum of money to land in your bank from an account linked to British intelligence. If you fail to do exactly what I tell you, I'll make sure Rashed knows you've been working for the West, informing on the Caliph. When *that* happens, *this* happens to your family. Understood?'

Mustafa closed his eyes and nodded.

'You're going to call Rashed now. You're going tell him that your boss is terrified, and that he wants to make a donation of a hundred million dollars to the Caliph's cause. That he wants to meet him and make his peace with him. Do you get that?'

Again, Mustafa nodded, but he looked sick with fear.

'Black,' Buckingham said. He was standing on the far side of the room, his hands behind his back and his lips tight. 'A word.'

Danny looked over at him. 'Not now,' he said.

'Fine.' Buckingham stepped forward. 'Then we'll discuss it in front of everyone. Let's ignore for the moment the fact that you're overstepping your authority. Do you *really* expect the Caliph to believe that this is anything other than a clumsy and obvious trap?'

Danny felt all eyes on him. And from the way Tony and Caitlin were looking at him, he could tell they agreed with the MI6 man.

He met Buckingham's stare full-on. 'No,' he said quietly. 'I don't.'

'Then why the bloody hell do you think this is a reasonable course of action?'

Danny looked at the others in turn. 'Here's what we know about the Caliph,' he said, his voice calm and measured. 'He's a fundamentalist. He's homicidal. He's probably psychotic. He's a control freak. People like that have vanity. They like to think that they've got the better of powerful men, like Ahmed. Plus, he won't want to miss out on a hundred million dollars. You can buy yourself a 9/11 with that kind of cash. Or worse.' He fixed Buckingham with a cool stare. 'Of *course* he'll suspect it's a trap,' he said. 'But a little part of him will be thinking: what if it's not? And that's what we need to exploit. Whoever he sends to the RV, I'll bet money that they'll know how to reach him. He might even come himself. We've two SF units on standby in Bahrain, one SBS, one SAS. Nobody's going to get past them. When the time comes, we'll have them in place. If the Caliph shows, we'll have the muscle to apprehend him. If he sends a lieutenant, we'll be one step closer to the main man. Anyone got a better idea?'

The only sound in the room was Mustafa's heavy breathing.

Outside it was almost completely light. Danny looked at his watch. 09.30 hrs. That made it 07.30 in London. In a little over twenty-four hours, the starting gun for the marathon would sound. Already, tens of thousands of people would be making their way into the capital. Danny and his unit had one throw of the dice. If this didn't work, the outcome would be too terrible to think about.

He looked at Mustafa. 'We're going to get in touch with London,' he said. 'I'm going to tell them what we know. Then you're going to make the call.'

The operations room in the basement of the MI6 building was suddenly ablaze with activity. At the centre of it all was Daniel Bixby, his head leaning as it always did against the padded head-rest of his wheelchair, but his tired eyes intense. The Chief stood next to him, chewing the nail on his right thumb. He said nothing. He'd lost control. Proceedings were up to Bixby now.

'GCHQ?' Bixby demanded.

'Online, sir,' one of his men shouted. 'They have a satellite trace on Mustafa's phone.'

'Are they ready to get a fix on Rashed's mobile?'

'Roger that, sir.'

'Translator?'

A pleasant-faced young man of Middle Eastern appearance sitting at a table five metres away raised his hand. He was wearing a set of headphones, though only one ear was covered, and had a notepad and pencil in front of him.

'Hereford?'

A voice crackled over a nearby loudspeaker. *'We're in contact with Bravo Nine Delta unit. They're standing by for your permission to go ahead.'*

'Everybody ready?' Bixby demanded. There was no suggestion to the contrary, so he gave the instruction. 'Make the call.'

'Make the call.'

Danny had his phone pressed to his ear, an open line to

Hereford HQ. He could hear the tension in Ray Hammond's voice, and could feel it in his own chest.

'Roger that.'

Mustafa's iPhone lay on the mirrored table. Mustafa himself was cradling his broken fingers, and fresh blood was still dripping from his mouth where Tony had ripped his tooth out. Danny had kept the photos of Ahmed's parents upturned to keep his mind focused, but in fact, all Mustafa's terrified attention was on the phone itself. 'Unlock it,' Danny told him. The chauffeur winced as he pressed his bloodied thumb to the start button. A wallpaper picture of Mustafa with two small children disappeared. 'Bring up Rashed's number, put it on loudspeaker, then dial,' Danny told him.

The chauffeur did as he was told. The sound of a dialling tone filled the room, then beeping tones of a number being dialled.

A pause.

Rashed's phone started to ring.

Three times.

A dry voice answered in Arabic. Mustafa licked his bloody lips, then spoke hesitantly.

'Rashed?'

The sound of the phone call filled the ops room at MI6. Three rings, then a distant voice.

'*Rashed?*'

Bixby's Arabic was good, but the translator spoke above the conversation, converting it into English in a flat, expressionless voice for the benefit of those, like the Chief, who couldn't understand it.

'*Who's this?*'

'*It's me. Mustafa.*'

'*I'm at work. What do you want?*'

'*I need to get a message to our friend.*'

'*What makes you think our friend would want a message from you?*'

There was a pause of ten seconds. Bixby and the Chief exchanged an anxious glance. The voice of Mustafa cleared its throat nervously before speaking again. But when the translator converted the conversation into English, he continued with his previous lack of expression.

'*Mr Al-Essa is scared. He won't leave his apartment.*'

'*That will teach him to have a loose tongue.*'

'*He wants to make our friend a peace offering. Rashed, it is a lot of money. I think the . . . I think our friend will be interested.*'

'*How much money?*'

'*A hundred . . . a hundred million.*'

There was another pause. Bixby swallowed nervously.

'*In return for what?*'

'*Mr Al-Essa's safety.*'

There was a barking, cynical laugh.

'*So you will contact him?*'

Bixby hissed quietly. Mustafa sounded too eager. Too jumpy. He sensed Rashed had picked up on it, because there was another long pause.

'*Maybe. Stay by your phone.*'

A click. The line when dead.

Instantly, Bixby raised his voice. 'Get on to GCHQ,' he announced. 'I want to know if they got a trace on Rashed's phone.'

A murmur of voices from the other side of the room. Then, out loud: 'That's a negative, sir. Rashed's line was fully encrypted. We can't locate it.'

Bixby swore. 'All we can do now is wait,' he told his boss.

Danny had a little Arabic, but not enough to have understood the conversation. He had to judge by the sound of Mustafa's voice whether the conversation was heading the way he wanted it. Rashed had sounded as hesitant as Mustafa. Hard to distinguish the tone of a different language, but Danny thought he sounded suspicious.

Now the conversation was over, Mustafa was profusely sweating.

'Well?' Danny demanded.

It was Buckingham who answered. 'I don't think Rashed bought it. He told Mustafa to wait by his phone, but he sounded very edgy.'

Ahmed stood up. He looked as though he had aged several years in the past hour. 'You will excuse me?' he said mildly. 'This meeting could take place at any time. I have arrangements to make.'

Danny shook his head. 'You're not leaving this apartment,' he said.

Ahmed nodded towards the door into his bedroom. Danny turned to Tony. 'Check there are no other exits through there,' he said.

Tony accompanied Ahmed into his bedroom, and returned thirty seconds later. 'It's secure,' he said.

Danny still had his phone to his ear, with its open line to Hereford. He heard Hammond's voice. '*Do you copy?*'

'Go ahead,' Danny said.

'*The B squadron team is on the ground in Bahrain.*'

'Roger that,' Danny said. 'Over and out.' He killed the phone, and found that everyone in the room was watching him.

'Support units are in place,' he said quietly. But his mind was elsewhere. This all felt like a game of chess. Danny had made his move. But it was up to the Caliph to make the next one, and Danny couldn't shake the uncomfortable sensation that he was about to be outplayed.

He suddenly strode over towards Ahmed's bedroom and burst in. Ahmed was semi-naked – boxer shorts and socks. He was surprisingly muscular, and seemed to be in the process of changing out of his robes and into Western clothes – a pair of jeans and a shirt were laid out on his enormous bed. On the far side of the room were several other suitcases, piled high, identical to the one that contained the money.

Ahmed's eyes flashed with irritation at the sudden intrusion, but he didn't say anything.

'You,' Danny told him. 'Get back in here. Any calls you want to make, you make them in front of me.'

Ahmed inclined his head mildly. 'Perhaps you will allow me to get dressed first,' he said.

'Quickly,' Danny told him, and he stood there impassively

while Ahmed put his clothes on. Then he marched him back out into the main room, where the others were waiting.

13.00 hrs GMT.
The first thing Spud had noticed, on his arrival at Gatwick, was the heightened security. There were armed police everywhere, and a high concentration of uniformed officers patrolling the busy concourse inside.

You didn't need to be a professional to spot that something was up. No doubt the general public thought this might be something to do with the flight that had gone down over West Africa. He kept registering people mentioning it in half-heard fragments of conversation. But Spud knew it was more than that. Security levels had been raised. Someone, somewhere was expecting something bad to happen here in the UK, not half a world away.

It made Spud's job harder. He was here to apprehend al-Megh-rani when – if – he showed. But al-Meghrani wouldn't be apprehended without making a scene.

The Costa Coffee at Gatwick South had tables set out on the concourse in front of the shop. Spud sat alone at one of them. From here he could see the queues of passengers lining up at the check-in desks, but he didn't yet know which one would be the desk for tonight's easyJet flight to Athens. The tabletop was full of empty sandwich packets and coffee cups. He fiddled aimlessly with the ticket the machine had spat out at him as he'd entered the car park to stow his bike. Yesterday's drinking, and Spud's sleepless night, was catching up with him. His head ached, and the wounds on his abdomen throbbed more than usual.

Worst of all, he was riddled with doubt.

He kept seeing in his mind the pictures of al-Meghrani's shrap-nel-scarred hands. Last night he'd been positive that was what they were. Now, with the benefit of daylight and sobriety, he wasn't so sure. Maybe he'd got the scars in some other way. Maybe the picture had been of somebody else's hands. And the flight details had been in al-Meghrani's name, but Spud knew he didn't

have a passport. Maybe there was another Mr K. al-Meghrani –
his brother, or something.

Maybe Spud was just wasting his fucking time. Maybe he
should stop trying to play cops and robbers, get his arse into to
London, apologise to Eleanor the spook and get on with the mess
that his life had become . . .

His phone rang. He checked the number. He didn't recognise
it, but answered anyway. 'Yeah?'

'It's me,' said a female voice he immediately recognised as
Frances.

Spud groaned inwardly. He'd hoped she was as uncomfortable
about their one-night stand as he was. Seemed not.

'Hi,' he said noncommittally.

'Where are you?' she said.

'Just . . . just at work,' Spud replied. 'You?'

'On my way to London,' Frances said. 'Big day. Got any tips?'

Yeah, Spud thought. *Don't sleep around again, because if that
psycho Tony finds out, you'll find yourself at the wrong end of a bad
accident.*

'Just keep going,' he said. 'Look, I'm . . . I'm kind of busy.'

'Right,' Frances said, her voice suddenly crestfallen. 'I was
thinking maybe we could meet up after the race. I've got a hotel
room – you could take care of my aches and pains.'

'Yeah . . . hello . . . it's not a very good connection,' Spud lied.
He killed the line, and when Frances tried again ten seconds later,
he sent it straight to voicemail.

He stared out on to the concourse. Hundreds of people
swarmed around the airport. He looked up at the departures
board. The Athens flight wasn't even listed yet. He got up from
the table, left the cafe and approached an information desk. A
smiling airport assistant asked how she could help.

'When does check-in open for the 23.58 flight to Athens?'
Spud asked.

The assistant checked her screen. 'Not until 8 p.m., sir,' she
smiled.

Spud nodded. He headed back to the cafe and bought more

black coffee. He didn't really want it, but it was the only way to pass the time.

The hours dragged. Nobody entered Ahmed's apartment, and nobody left. Danny wouldn't allow it.

Mustafa was suffering. He nursed his broken fingers constantly, and about lunchtime he suddenly stood up and ran to the bathroom, where he vomited copiously. He needed pain relief, but there was none in the apartment and the alternative was to call someone in or allow him to leave. Not an option. The Caliph had eyes in Ahmed's organisation. No information about their activities could leak from this apartment.

It was a waiting game, and it made Danny seethe with frustration.

At 18.00 precisely, Ahmed cleared his throat. 'Gentlemen.' It was the first time anybody had spoken for hours. His words earned him a harsh look from Caitlin. 'And *lady*,' he corrected himself. 'May I offer you some refreshment? I can call down to the concierge for food or ...'

Danny was on the point of telling him that he wasn't going to call *anyone*, when Mustafa's phone rang.

Everyone turned to look at it as it vibrated noisily on the mirrored table.

It had only rung once when Danny's own mobile vibrated. He answered quickly and was rewarded with Ray Hammond's voice all the way from Hereford. '*London's listening. Answer it.*'

Danny looked across the room. 'Answer the phone, Mustafa,' he said. 'Now.'

There was complete silence in the MI6 ops room. Daniel Bixby found he was holding his breath. He'd caught a couple of hours sleep around lunchtime and was bone-tired. But now, suddenly, he was as alert as he'd ever been.

An Arabic voice rang out from a speaker. As before, the young Middle Eastern translator did his work.

'*Hello.*'

'*Tell Mr al-Essa that our friend accepts his kind offer.*'

'*I will tell him that. He will be very relieved.*'

'*Tell him not to be. Our friend wishes to meet him face to face. And he wishes to meet you too.*'

Silence.

'*Where? When?*'

'*Tomorrow morning. Seven o'clock. 28.608174, 52.283936.*'

'*What . . . what are these numbers?*'

'*A grid reference, idiot.*'

Immediately, there was a fluster of activity in the ops room as several of Bixby's people keyed the coordinates into the computer. Bixby's eyes were drawn to a large flat-panel screen on the wall just beyond the bank of terminals. The image zoomed in quickly on a map of the Persian Gulf, and a red dot appeared in the middle of the ocean, approximately 150 miles off the coast of Qatar.

'That doesn't make any sense,' the Chief snapped. 'They can't rendezvous in the middle of the fucking ocean.'

'One moment, sir,' Bixby said mildly.

'*If you are late, or you arrive accompanied by anybody else, our friend wants you to know that it will end badly for you and your loved ones. Is that understood?*'

'*Yes.*' The translator failed to render the terrified stutter that was obvious to everybody listening to the conversation.

The line went dead.

'It's an oil platform, sir,' one of Bixby's people called out. 'An oil platform on the edge of Qatari national waters.'

'Does it have a name?'

'Yes sir. Qatar Drilling Rig 17.'

'Find out who owns it,' Bixby said. 'Now.'

'*It's an oil rig,*' Ray Hammond stated down the open line from Hereford. '*Qatar Drilling Rig 17.*'

'Qatar Drilling Rig 17,' Danny repeated out loud.

'*London's finding out who owns it now. Whoever it is, we'll put the screws on them, find out if they . . .*'

'Tell them not to waste their time,' Danny said. He was watching

Ahmed closely. At the name of the rig, the Qatari's face had changed into an expression of complete bewilderment. 'Wait out,' he said down the line, before addressing Ahmed. 'It's yours, isn't it?' he asked quietly.

Ahmed slowly nodded his head. His expression had turned from bewilderment to nausea. 'What kind of game is this man playing?' he whispered.

'A dangerous one,' Danny breathed. He looked at his watch. 18.05 hrs. Twelve hours fifty-five minutes until the Caliph's RV time. He spoke back into the phone. 'It's Al-Essa's rig,' he said. 'We need to mobilise. We don't have much time.'

TWENTY-SIX

'How many men are there on the rig?' Danny demanded of Ahmed.

The Qatari was clutching clumps of his own hair. His knuckles had turned white. Mustafa sat next to him, physically shaking.

'About two hundred,' Ahmed said.

Danny took a moment to process that. He knew enough about these floating cities to realise that they would be filled with a massive cross-section of individuals. Roughnecks, welders, rig operators, drillers, engineers, cooks, safety and medical personnel . . . The rig would be populated by foreign nationals from all over the world. There'd be a manifest listing everyone on board, and if they had the time, the intelligence services would want to dig deep and find out if anybody on the rig had a possible connection with the Caliph.

But there *was* no time. Their only option was to evacuate the rig. Clear it of all potential existing threats.

'We need to clear all personnel from the rig. How long will that take?'

Ahmed blinked at him. 'It's complicated. If I perform an immediate emergency evacuation, the Qatari emergency services will become involved. They will send a fleet of helicopters and will take perhaps two hours. But it will be common knowledge. The Qatari government will know what is happening.'

'What if you do it as a training exercise, without the involvement of the emergency services. How long will it take?

'I . . . I would need to summon my security staff.'

'No,' Danny said. 'I don't want anybody else in this room. You can make arrangements over the phone, but only with me listening.'

Ahmed nodded nervously. 'Very well,' he said. 'I will tell my security staff to initiate a training evacuation. We have a limited number of helicopters. It won't be quick. Perhaps ten to twelve hours. But we should keep *some* staff on the platform, to maintain the essential systems.'

Danny shook his head. 'Evacuate *all* personnel. Give the order now. I don't want anyone left on that rig. We can't risk an ambush.'

With a slightly stunned look on his face, Ahmed dialled a number on his phone.

'Hands-free,' Danny said.

Ahmed looked at him in surprise but pressed the keypad, and the sound of a ringtone came over the phone's speaker. An Arabic voice answered. Ahmed gave a few short instructions, then hung up. He nodded at Danny. 'It is under way,' he said.

Danny looked at Buckingham. 'Did he give the correct order?'

Buckingham nodded.

'How do we get ourselves out there?' Danny asked.

Ahmed looked momentarily flustered. 'I . . . I have a private helicopter. It can transport us.'

Danny gave that a second's thought. His preference would be to bring in one of the SF choppers from Bahrain, but that would mean alerting the Qatari administration, and the risk that the Caliph had eyes and ears there was too high.

'Where would they transport us from?'

Ahmed looked up and pointed to the ceiling. 'There is a helipad above us.'

'Get it on standby, but we don't leave until the rig is evacuated. And don't tell the flight crew that we're all going. I want them to think it's just you, Mustafa and the money.'

Ahmed blinked at him. 'Why?'

'The Caliph's infiltrated your organisation. From this point in, we trust absolutely nobody.'

'For God's sake, Black,' Buckingham said from the far side of the room. 'Tell me you're not actually thinking of *going* to this damn oil rig. It's suicide. You'll get us all killed. It's *obviously* a trap.'

'We're going to the rig,' Danny said flatly.

'Well, you can damn well count *me* out,' Buckingham said. '*You* might want to get yourself killed by some insane . . .'

He didn't finish his sentence. Danny had stridden over to him and grabbed him by the neck. '*Everybody* in this room goes to the rig,' he said. 'Including you.'

Buckingham had fiery hate in his eyes. 'Why?' he spat.

'Ahmed goes because the Caliph's expecting him and he might need to show his face before we can get close to the bastard. Mustafa goes because I don't trust him not to go singing to Rashed to save his own skin. And you go for two reasons: first, I need you to translate any Arabic that gets spoken. Second, because I don't trust you not to fuck something up when my back's turned. I saw my friend die of plague, and I'm not going to let the bastard responsible get away because you're an incompetent idiot and a coward. You're coming with us.'

Buckingham staggered back as Danny roughly released him. Danny's own phone rang, and he answered it to hear Ray Hammond on the line from Hereford. '*Update me.*'

Danny put the phone on to speaker so that Tony and Caitlin could listen in. 'We've given the order to evacuate the rig,' he said. 'It'll take approximately ten to twelve hours. I don't want us to approach until the last man's off the platform. Any of them could be in contact with the Caliph, and I don't want the bastard to know Ahmed and Mustafa have company. We're using Ahmed's chopper to get there, but we need to avoid any comms between ourselves in case the flight crew is compromised.'

'*Roger that. The oil platform is equidistant from the Qatari and Iranian coasts. But we expect your target to approach from the direction of Saudi Arabia to the north-west. That's where it's easiest for him to seek sanctuary if he needs to.*'

'What about other oil platforms in the area?'

'*There are two more rigs within a seven kilometre radius. They operate through UAE holding companies and we've managed to get our hands on the manifests. The analysts are examining them now, but we've pretty much discounted them as forward mounting positions for the Caliph or his proxy. Security's too tight on these platforms.*'

'You'd better be right,' Danny said.

Ray Hammond ignored that. '*At the RV time, you'll have a sixteen-man SAS team and eight SBS guys circling ten klicks to the north of the platform, out of sight.*'

'You'll be violating Qatari or Iranian airspace.'

'*Let us deal with that.*'

'Make sure they don't approach unless we give the order. If the Caliph or his proxy sees them, we'll lose our chance.'

'*Understood. GCHQ have established that there's a sat phone uplink on the rig. As soon as you get there, you're to establish an open line with Hereford HQ. In the meantime, we have active surveillance on the area. We're scanning a hundred-kilometre radius around the oil platform for any unexpected or suspicious radar splash. London have a contact in Iranian air traffic control, but we need to be aware that a seaborne approach will be much more difficult to pinpoint. If we get any sniff of the target approaching, we'll let you know what direction they're coming from and what their ETA is, as soon as you've established radio contact with us.*

'*And Black, listen very carefully: make sure your team understand that the Caliph is no use to us dead. If he knows about the strike on London, he could know about many other potential hits. We need his information, not his corpse.*'

'Roger that,' Danny said, with a nod at Tony and Caitlin.

'*And Black?*'

'Yes, boss.'

'*Be careful. This is all happening too quickly, and something about it stinks. If the little we know about the Caliph is true, he's no fool. We have to assume that he at least admits the possibility of a welcoming party, and he'll come prepared. There's a very good chance that this is going to go noisy.*'

'Roger that,' Danny said grimly. And silently, with an image fixed in his mind of Ripley rotting before his eyes, he said: *bring it on.*

'*One other thing, Black. When this is over, you and me are going to have a conversation about your mate Spud. I've got a nasty feeling he's turning nutcase on us.*'

Danny blinked. He hadn't thought about Spud for days, but

now wasn't the time to start worrying about him. He ignored the unpleasant sneer on Tony's face, muttered a final 'Roger that', and killed the line.

19.55 GMT.

With a belly full of coffee and a mood as foul as the clothes he was wearing, Spud stalked across the concourse of Gatwick North. Check-in for the Athens flight opened in five minutes. Two members of the airport staff, one male, one female, were busying themselves at the desk. Five metres to their right, an armed airport security guard stood, grimly scanning the crowds that swarmed around the concourse: a very visible presence.

Spud took up position by a long snake of luggage trolleys, about twenty-five metres from the desk itself. He looked up to see if he was being covered by airport CCTV. Sure enough, on the ceiling above him was an egg-shaped camera set-up. But they were dotted all over the concourse. It would be impossible to find a blind spot. There were two more armed security guards by entrances to the concourse at his nine o'clock and ten o'clock, distance about thirty-five metres. If they knew anything about their job, they'd notice someone standing and watching for several hours. Spud would have to use his basic fieldcraft skills to make sure he didn't look too suspicious. He'd bought a copy of *Esquire* magazine from a branch of WHSmith. And from a clothes shop, he'd bought three hats: a red baseball, a blue baseball and a black beanie. Now he loitered by the trolleys, the red baseball cap on his head, pretending to read the mag but in fact watching and waiting for the Athens-bound passengers to arrive at check-in.

There was a small surge of arrivals immediately the desk opened. A family: mum, dad, two excited kids. An old couple, with skin as tanned and leathery as their suitcases. A group of lads: tight T-shirts, ripped physiques, maybe on their way to a stag weekend.

But no al-Meghrani.

Within ten minutes, the queue had extended to five metres back from the desk. After half an hour, it was ten metres long. Spud's view was occasionally blocked by people walking across his line of sight, but he kept his attention properly focused on the queue every time he had a clear view.

Forty-five minutes passed. Spud bent down, ostensibly to tie his shoelace, but in reality to swap his red baseball cap for the black beanie. When he stood up again, he walked to a new position on the other side of the check-in queue, where he leaned against a departure-time board, out of sight of the two guards by the entrance.

By the time the check-in had been open for an hour, the queue was bustling and busy. Spud became aware that it must be raining heavily outside, because the newcomers had wet hair and clothes. Kids ran up and down the queue – one of them pointing excitedly at the armed guard by the check-in desk – and exasperated parents shouted at them to stand in line. Tannoy announcements echoed across the concourse, but Spud didn't hear what they said. He was in the zone, robotically picking out faces in the line and comparing them to his mental image of al-Meghrani. None of them matched.

His phone rang. He glanced at it and vaguely registered Frances's number before sending it straight to voicemail again. Then he turned his attention back to the queue.

It was growing shorter. He checked the time. 23.10 hrs. Check-in would close half an hour before the flight left. That meant al-Meghrani had only fifteen minutes. Why was there no sign of him?

The doubts doubled in Spud's mind. He felt slightly sick, and asked himself again what the hell he thought he was doing. Some bird with her tits half hanging out looked out at him from the *Esquire* magazine, and for some reason it made him irrationally angry. He felt like throwing it to the floor and stalking off, giving up on the whole thing, accepting that he was chasing shadows ...

He stopped, very still.

Forty metres across the concourse, walking from the entrance to the terminal towards the check-in desk and completely unobscured by passers-by, he saw a face he recognised.

Al-Meghrani didn't appear to be in a hurry. His shoulders were hunched and there was a frown on his brow. He was pulling a small suitcase on wheels behind him, and as he grew closer Spud saw that in his spare hand he was carrying a passport with a folded piece of paper inside it – presumably a copy of his e-ticket. His hands, as always, were gloved.

It took him thirty seconds to reach the back of the queue. Spud watched carefully as he put his passport and ticket into the pocket of his overcoat. He stood there with his arms folded, approximately ten people in front of him, waiting to reach the check-in.

Spud smiled grimly. His plan had been to pretend to be a security guard and usher his target away from the queue. But al-Meghrani had just given him a much better option.

Spud dropped the magazine into the basket holder at the back of one of the luggage trolleys. Then he advanced. With his head bowed, he joined the queue directly behind al-Meghrani.

He knew he didn't have much time. If the cab driver turned round and looked at him full-on, he'd recognise him from the cafe. So he didn't hesitate. Standing just a few centimetres behind al-Meghrani, he glanced round to make sure he wasn't observed, then quickly and surreptitiously slipped his hand into his target's overcoat pocket and deftly withdrew the passport. Within seconds he had it secreted in his own jacket, and was walking away, his heart thumping fast.

He took up position by a departure board twenty metres from the check-in desk. It took ten minutes for al-Meghrani to reach the front. Spud watched from a distance as he put his hand into his pocket, then hurriedly started to pat himself down.

Commotion at the check-in desk. Al-Meghrani was waving his hands around. A second assistant joined the one he was arguing with. But when al-Meghrani noticed an armed airport security guard approaching, he appeared instantly to back down. He grabbed his suitcase and tugged it furiously away from the check-in desk. Spud could see that he was muttering angrily to himself.

He followed his target at a distance of ten metres, knowing that without a passport his only option would be to leave the airport.

Sure enough, al-Meghrani stormed in the direction that the overhead signs indicated led to the car park. Spud stuck to him, along the travelator, to the car park pay-stations. Al-Meghrani paid for his ticket with cash. Spud paid for his with a card at the adjacent machine. He pulled the peak of his red baseball cap down over his face as he followed al-Meghrani into the nearby lift.

There were nine others in the lift. Spud watched his target press the button for level three. Then he stood with his head down, his baseball cap covering his eyes, as the doors opened and closed at levels one and two. By the time they reached level three, there were only four of them remaining in the lift. The others were obviously avoiding al-Meghrani, who was muttering under his breath like some crazy tramp.

The doors hissed open and the cab driver stepped outside. Spud was the only one who followed.

At this late hour, the car park was not busy. Spud clocked a couple of people on the western side, and heard the distant screech of a single vehicle's tyres as it left the level. Otherwise, nobody. The trundle wheels on al-Meghrani's suitcase echoed across the concrete as he stalked to the far side of the level, seemingly unaware that Spud was shadowing him, still at a distance of ten metres. When he finally arrived at the familiar white VW, which had empty spaces on either side, he fished his car keys from his pocket and used them to unlock the boot.

Spud quickly checked his surroundings. Nobody was observing him. He ran forward.

Al-Meghrani spun round at the sound of Spud's footsteps, but too late: he didn't stand a chance. Spud thumped him hard from behind in the side of his abdomen. He doubled over as the wind escaped his lungs, by which time Spud had already grabbed him by the back of the neck. With fierce, brutal efficiency, he forced al-Meghrani headfirst into the boot of the car, then grabbed his legs and stuffed him inside. The cab driver wriggled and flailed, but he was too winded to shout out. Seconds later, Spud had slammed the boot shut, locked it and pulled out the keys.

He grabbed the suitcase and moved round to the side of the

car, where he chucked the case into the back before taking the wheel and quickly starting the engine. The radio blared loudly, but it was distorted because they were undercover. Spud switched it off, and could now hear his hostage thumping frenziedly in the boot, and shouting. He knew he had to get out of earshot quickly. The VW's tyres screeched as he reversed from the parking spot and cut across a line of empty spaces towards the spiral ramp that led to the exit.

More thumping from the boot, but the car park wasn't busy and the ticket booths were unmanned. Spud used his own ticket to exit the car park. Within minutes he was pulling on to the M23.

It was pissing down with rain as he headed south – the wipers made almost no difference – but Spud was sweating so profusely he might as well have been out in it. The blue motorway sign for junction ten loomed up ahead, and he indicated left. As he listened to the tick-tock of the indicators, he realised the banging from the boot had stopped. He pulled off the motorway, the wipers still unable to keep up with the torrent of rain. The road ahead was a busy dual carriageway, red tail lights streaming off into the distance. Spud knew he needed to get away from the brightly lit tarmac, to take al-Meghrani somewhere deserted and covert where he could question him properly. When, after about three minutes, a road sign loomed towards him indicating a slip road a mile in the distance, he manoeuvred himself into the outside lane.

A minute later, they were curving off the main road. Spud didn't slow down for the roundabout up ahead, and ignored the angry horns as he muscled his way on to it, then off at the second exit. He felt his back tyres skidding slightly on the wet tarmac as they joined a much narrower road, hedges on either side that grew thicker after about 750 metres.

There were no vehicles up ahead. In the rear-view mirror, Spud saw a single set of headlamps at a distance of, he estimated, a hundred metres. Suddenly, twenty metres away, he saw a cutaway section in the grass verge for parking. There were no other vehicles there, so he slammed the brakes hard. They squealed in the wet, and Spud surged forward as the vehicle skidded through the rain. Spud skilfully kept control of the vehicle, steering into the skid and coming to a halt neatly in the verge.

He switched off the engine. The headlamps and the light on the dashboard faded. The car coming up behind them passed and disappeared.

Darkness.

Spud stepped outside into the rain. By the time he reached the boot, he was already soaked. He put the key in the lock, turned it and opened up.

He was ready for al-Meghrani's pathetic attempt. As the cab driver lashed out from the boot, Spud grabbed his wrists and yanked him out. In a matter of seconds he had pulled off his gloves. The skin of his prisoner's hands were just as he'd seen in the picture: peppered and shrapnel-scarred.

'Who are you?' al-Meghrani breathed, rain streaming down his terrified face. His Brummie accent wasn't quite so pronounced as it had been in the car with Eleanor. 'What do you want with me? I haven't done anything wrong.'

'Except carry a Claymore bag, fuck your hands up with dodgy explosives and . . .' Spud plunged one hand into his own jacket pocket and pulled out the passport. The cab driver feebly attempted to grab it back. For his trouble, he received a brutal thump in the pit of his stomach, which made him bend double, half-gasping, half-spluttering. Spud flicked through the passport until he reached the photo ID page. He checked the name: Khaled al-Meghrani. Not Khalifa. And the picture, though a very good likeness, was not a perfect one.

'Who is he?' Spud asked. 'Your brother?'

Al-Meghrani made no reply – he was too busy trying to suck in air – but it didn't really matter. Spud ripped the photo ID page out of the soggy passport to render it useless, then threw the remnants into the boot.

The cab driver struggled again and tried to escape. It was totally in vain. Spud simply grabbed a clump of al-Meghrani's sopping hair, then forcefully tugged his head towards him.

'Where were you headed, sunshine?' he breathed, his voice

315

almost drowned out by the pouring rain. 'Athens first, then Turkey, then on to Syria maybe? Let me tell you something. I've been the guest of the Syrian *mukhabarat*. They did things to me that would make you piss your pants just to hear about. I've had African warlords threaten to feed me to the fucking dogs. If you spend enough time with people like that, you pick up a thing or two. So here's the bad news, you piece of shit. I'm going to ask you some questions, and if you find yourself lying, it's going to fucking hurt. Understood?'

Al-Meghrani was taking short, shaky breaths. He nodded, almost imperceptibly. The rain hammered noisily on the roof of the vehicle.

'Good,' Spud said. 'We're getting somewhere. Question one: where did you fuck your hands up?'

The cab driver closed his eyes. 'Iraq,' he breathed. 'A training camp. There was a faulty grenade . . .'

Spud didn't let it show in his face, but the relief that washed over him was like a warm shower: he *hadn't* been making this shit up after all.

'Question two: where *were* you heading after Turkey?'

Al-Meghrani seemed more reluctant to answer this question. He tried to look away, but a firmer grip on his hair made him yelp the word: 'Syria!'

Spud nodded. 'Question three,' he said. He twisted the cab driver's head closer so they were just inches away from each other. 'What do you know about the Caliph?'

Whatever reaction Spud had expected, it wasn't this. Al-Meghrani's shaking became more violent. He whimpered, and with a sudden surge of energy started flailing around, trying to release himself from Spud's grip.

Spud didn't hesitate. With one great swipe of his free arm, he slammed al-Meghrani's solidly in the centre of the face. There was a brutal thud, accompanied by the cracking sound of a bone splintering. Al-Meghrani gasped in pain. When Spud lowered his fist, he saw that his nose was impressively broken, and blood was streaming down over his lips and dripping from his chin.

'Let's try that again,' Spud whispered. 'What do you know about the Caliph?'

'Nothing,' al-Meghrani whispered. But his pathetic denial was accompanied by a waft of urine. His companion had pissed himself with fright.

'You're scared of him?' Spud said.

Al-Meghrani looked at him with a pitiful expression. He nodded.

'Right now, my friend, you should be more scared of me.' And without warning, he slammed his fist against the cab driver's broken nose again. A yelp of pain filled the air, and when Spud looked at the bleeding face again, he saw streaks of tears on the blood-smeared cheeks. But both blood and tears were almost immediately washed away by the rain.

'Please,' al-Meghrani whispered. '*Please . . .*'

'Have you met him?'

Al-Meghrani nodded faintly.

'Where?'

'In . . . in Iraq. At the training camp.'

'So why's he so fucking scary.'

Al-Meghrani could barely speak. Over the noise of the rain, Spud only faintly caught certain words.

'*Beheadings . . .*'

'*Burnings . . .*'

'*Families killed . . . villages wiped out . . .*'

'*Crucifixions . . .*'

The cab driver buried his head in his hands. His shoulders shook. Spud released his grip on the man's hair. He'd broken him. Al-Meghrani's pretence was over.

Spud stepped backwards. He was cold and soaking wet. But there was a fire inside his gut that kept him warm. A car sped past, momentarily lighting them up, but it didn't stop. Spud looked at his shaking, bleeding hostage. He had a decision to make. Should he call Eleanor? Tell her what he'd discovered? Drag this bleeding, battered, wannabe jihadi into the MI6 building and wait for her to tell him exactly which procedures he'd failed to follow, and fit the target up with a medic and a decent lawyer?

Or should he head for Hereford, his home turf that no longer felt like home? Where Ray Hammond could tell him what a dead weight he was, and scoff at his attempt to keep in the game while the Regiment had bigger fish to fry?

He drew a deep breath. Neither choice appealed to him. But he couldn't stay here, stuck down a country lane, with a terror suspect who might just have a link to the guy the Firm were chasing . . .

Spud suddenly grabbed the cab driver by his neck again.

'What are you doing?' Al-Meghrani whimpered. 'What's going on?'

Spud didn't answer. He pushed the struggling cab driver back down into the boot cavity. Al-Meghrani shouted out in panic, and Spud winced as a shock of pain ran down his abdomen. But he kept the pressure on, and once more managed to bundle the cab driver and his scuffling, flailing limbs into the cavity and cram the boot shut with a dull clunk. Al-Meghrani's renewed, panicked shouts became muffled. He banged furiously but ineffectually against the inside of the boot. Spud ignored the noises, walked round to the passenger door, slammed it shut and then clambered back behind the wheel.

He was drenched and slightly out of breath. His wounds throbbed agonisingly and he had a bastard pain between the eyes. He was in a bad state to make a clear decision, but that was what he had to do.

He inhaled deeply, started the car, lit the headlamps and knocked the engine into first. With screeching tyres, he pulled a quick 180-degree turn over the wet tarmac. Then he accelerated hard down the country lane.

He'd made his choice. He was heading to Hereford.

TWENTY-SEVEN

04.00 hrs AST.

They had taken it in turns to sleep through the night, but now everyone, even Mustafa, was awake and alert. From the window of Ahmed's penthouse apartment, Danny saw the lights of a chopper approaching across the glowing Qatari skyline, its trajectory heading straight for them. It almost looked as if it was going to slam straight into the penthouse itself, but once it was fifty metres out it became clear that this was just an optical illusion. It was flying a good twenty metres higher than the building and disappeared overhead. Danny faintly heard the sound of its rotors beating on the roof above.

He turned to check out his crew. Like Danny himself, Tony and Caitlin had ditched their tracksuit tops and sports bags, and since there was now no need to hide the hardware they'd picked up in Bahrain, it was on full display. They wore T-shirts over which they'd donned their tactical vests. Their S&W handguns were tucked into the vests, and their KH-9 rifles were slung around their necks. They wore radio packs connected to their covert earphones, and their vests were packed with spare ammunition for their personal weapons, along with a flashbang each.

Mustafa and Ahmed couldn't keep their eyes off the hardware. Buckingham was scowling, like a petulant child. 'We should leave the fucking spook here,' Tony had already suggested. 'Cunt'll only get in the way.'

'He's staying where I can see him,' Danny said.

'You're fucking crazy. We should leave them all here – Buckingham, Mustafa, Ahmed.'

'I don't trust any of them. Until we've got the Caliph, they stay with us.'

Tony shrugged. 'You're the fucking boss,' he said bitterly. 'You can take the rap when they screw things up for us.'

Ahmed's phone rang. He didn't need to be told to put it on hands-free. Everyone in the room heard the conversation in Arabic, even though they didn't all understand it.

'The platform has been evacuated,' Ahmed said once the call was over. 'The last helicopter left two minutes ago.'

Danny shot Buckingham an enquiring look that said: is that what the conversation was about? Buckingham nodded. Danny took his own phone out and dialled through to Hereford. The call was answered immediately. 'This is Bravo Nine Delta,' Danny said. 'We're advancing to target.'

'*Roger that,*' came the reply. '*We'll expect you to contact us as soon as you're on the platform.*'

Danny killed the line. 'Move the cases of money,' he told Tony and Caitlin. As he spoke, he saw Ahmed's face twitch. 'What?'

'What if I lose it?' Ahmed asked quietly.

'What if a psychopath releases a bioweapon in the middle of London?' Danny countered. 'Anyway, it was your idea.'

It took five minutes for Danny's two companions to transport the flight cases of cash from Ahmed's bedroom. They carried them out of the main entrance to the apartment and up on to the helipad above. Once they were fully loaded, Danny gave a single grim-faced command and all six of them prepared to leave.

Caitlin and Tony led the way. Ahmed and Mustafa followed, their shoulders sloped, like men walking to their death. Then Buckingham and Danny. But as the other four disappeared through the apartment's main entrance, Buckingham held Danny back. Danny looked him up and down. The spook's hands were shaking. He was clearly terrified. 'Black,' he hissed. 'There is no *need* for me to come with you. I'm much better deployed here, as a conduit to—'

'You're coming,' Danny told him.

'Black, I swear to God, I know things about you that will put you in a military prison for the rest of your life, and that's if you're lucky. I know people in Langley who'd prefer you dead. One word from me and they'll—'

'You're coming.' Danny grabbed Buckingham's arm and pushed him towards the exit. Buckingham was sweating as he staggered out of the apartment, Danny stalking him close behind. They moved past the dedicated elevator towards the metal door at the far end of the corridor, which the others had left open. The noise of the chopper was louder here. On the other side of the door was a flight of steps that led up to the rooftop helipad. The warm wind was strong this high up, and not just because of the chopper's downdraught. All of Doha seemed to shine in the night beneath them, and seawards to the north and east, Danny could make out a busy coastline full of glowing vessels that became gradually less numerous as the distance from land increased.

Buckingham looked bilious – he clearly wasn't good with heights – so Danny grabbed him by the arm and ushered him roughly across the helipad. Danny recognised the chopper as a Sikorsky S-76: blue tail, red body, orange- and white-striped rotor blades. From the outside it looked like a standard offshore-transport aircraft. The chopper's side door was open, and the others were already inside. Danny pushed the spook aboard, then jumped in himself and closed the door.

'GO!' he shouted over the deafening noise of the rotors.

There were two flight crew, each of them wearing headsets. Danny noted with satisfaction that they seemed confused to be transporting anyone other than Ahmed. It took a word of instruction from their boss before the chopper rose from the helipad, buffeted slightly by the winds, and sped directly over the lower rooftops of the city towards the coast.

The interior of the Sikorsky was a lot more comfortable than any military transport Danny had ever been in. Twelve comfortable leather seats. A fridge with iced water. Ahmed was a man who liked to travel in style. But this morning he looked terrified. The dark rings around his eyes were more pronounced, and he kept glancing anxiously at the unit's personal weapons.

Estimated flight time, thirty-five minutes. Land became sea. A couple of minutes later they had passed the bulk of the vessels mooring in Doha, and all Danny could see through the window of the chopper was the reflection of a bright moon on still water. He estimated that they had an hour till sunrise. He didn't like not having a direct line into Hereford. He knew the head shed would have full surveillance on the area, but until they got on to the rig and opened up a secure line to them, it was useless to Danny and his team.

As the rotors spun rhythmically, Danny looked at his two unit colleagues. Unlike Ahmed, Mustafa and Buckingham, Tony and Caitlin's faces were pictures of calm. They sat next to each other, and Danny noticed how Caitlin's knee was pressed against Tony's. He felt like warning her not to get too close. Tony was a man who ripped off the Hereford armoury and flogged the spoils on to the sort of people who shouldn't be within a hundred metres of live ammo. A man who could call on a seedy underbelly of criminality to do his dirty work for him. A man who thought nothing of allowing his wife to head blindly into a terrorist atrocity. For one of the good guys, he had a bad way of looking at the world. Danny would have far preferred to have Spud or Ripley here, but he didn't have that option. He just had to get on with it.

In the distance – it was hard to judge how far, but maybe ten or fifteen klicks – Danny caught sight of a structure glowing in the sea. One of the many oil platforms that dotted the Persian Gulf. Even from this distance it looked vast: a floating city.

The pilot looked back over his shoulder and shouted something in Arabic. Both Ahmed and Buckingham turned to Danny. 'Five minutes,' they translated in unison.

Danny nodded. He checked over his weapons, and saw that Tony and Caitlin were doing the same. The chopper started to lose height. Danny craned his neck to look through the front window of the aircraft. His angle of vision was awkward, but he could just make out another structure, much closer this time.

You would never know from up here that Qatar Drilling Rig

17 was abandoned. The vast rectangle glowed brightly in the dark sea. An enormous scaffolding column protruded upwards from the centre of the platform, and Danny counted two vast orange and white cranes hanging outwards from the rig over the sea. The platform itself was surrounded by suicide nets, and it seemed from this angle to hover above the surface of the sea because its vast supporting legs were shrouded in darkness, although he could just make out white horses on the water's surface where the sea broke against them. He identified a circular LZ – green, with a yellow circular landing spot marked with a glowing 'H' – on the nearest edge of the platform, which the chopper now headed for.

Danny turned to his unit. 'Secure the LZ,' he said. 'The rest of you, stay on board till we give you the word.' He cocked his rifle. Tony and Caitlin did the same.

Thirty seconds later, the chopper touched down, its nose facing inward towards the platform, its tail pointing back out to sea. Danny, Tony and Caitlin exited quickly and congregated about the chopper's nose, Danny positioned centrally, Tony to his left, Caitlin to his right. Danny could hear the chopper's rotors start to slow, but the downdraught was still strong. He scanned the scene ahead of him. The platform was huge – about the size of two football pitches – and was covered with a network of scaffolding frames, metal staircases and storage containers. Twenty metres below the LZ, Danny could make out a line of RIB lifeboats, and a vast salt water pump to deal with the constant threat of fire on board the platform.

But no personnel. No movement.

The rotors fell silent. Now they could hear the water crashing against the footings of the oil rig far below, and the movement of a breeze from the north-west. And on the edge of his senses, a humming sound, no doubt emanating from the generator that had to be keeping the electric lights burning, and some of the sound coming from the lights themselves. But there were no voices. It was eerie, being on a structure that was clearly meant to house humans, and knowing that they were the only people on board.

Danny turned to Caitlin. 'Get the others,' he said. 'The pilots too. We can't trust anyone. We'll find a safe place to secure them first, then get on the line to Hereford. We need to know if they have any surveillance intel. Leave the money in the chopper for now.'

A minute later, Caitlin had herded Mustafa, Ahmed and the two pilots on to the LZ.

'Where's the bridge?' Danny shouted at Ahmed.

Ahmed pointed towards the centre of the rig. 'On the far side of that tall scaffolding tower,' he said. 'You see the rectangular structure painted green? Is that where we're going?'

Danny shook his head. 'Not you,' he said. 'It's the first place anybody will look. What about the accommodation quarters?'

'Around the northern leg!' Ahmed shouted. 'They're very cramped. If you want somewhere safe to put us, I suggest the medical room. It's between our current position and the centre of the platform. I think we could lock ourselves in there.'

Danny gave that a moment's thought. Ahmed's suggestion made sense. If things went noisy, if and when the Caliph showed his face, it would be good to have them in the vicinity of medical supplies. He nodded. 'Lead the way!' he shouted.

A metal staircase led from the LZ to the platform itself. Ahmed trotted towards it, Danny at his shoulder scanning the way ahead for unexpected movement. The others followed, with Tony and Caitlin taking up the rear. Their footsteps clattered as they descended the metal stairs. Once they were down on the platform, Ahmed kept looking back at them nervously, obviously checking they were still with him, as he led the small group through a network of storage containers, scaffolding rigs and engineering platforms whose purpose Danny could only guess. The surroundings were hyper-industrial and factory-like, like being in the heart of a complex, deserted, metal maze. There were fire extinguishers every fifteen feet, regular signage pointing to emergency exits and muster stations, and bright strip lighting that made the deck almost as bright as daytime.

After a couple of minutes, they reached what looked like a grey

Portakabin adjacent to the huge central scaffold that Danny had seen from the air. Three metal steps, painted a vibrant yellow, led up to the door. Ahmed was about to walk up them, when Danny pulled him back. He approached the door himself, his rifle engaged, and thrust the door open. He stepped inside, aiming towards the four corners of the room, before shouting: 'Clear. Get inside, everyone, now!'

It was a standard med room: a stretcher bed in one corner, sterile-looking cabinets along the walls, a poster detailing how to perform CPR, and a faint smell of antiseptic. Ahmed, Mustafa, Buckingham and the two pilots huddled automatically against the far wall while Tony and Caitlin kept watch outside. Danny looked round for a key. He found it within seconds, hanging on a hook by the door. Buckingham stepped forward to take the key, but Danny gave him a sharp look and closed his fingers around it.

'For God's *sake*, man,' Buckingham breathed.

Danny ignored him and looked at the others. 'I'm going to lock you in from the outside. We'll be back in ten minutes. Don't make any noise. When and if the Caliph and his people arrive, it's best they can't locate you. You'll be safe here.'

He didn't wait for any response, but left the med room and locked the door behind him. Tony gave him an enquiring look. 'They're scared,' Danny explained. 'I don't trust them not to split up if they get spooked, and I don't want to be searching this whole platform for them.'

'You don't trust the pilots?'

'Right now, I don't trust anyone.' He checked his watch. 04.45 hrs. Two hours and fifteen till the Caliph's RV time. 'Let's get to the control room, make contact with Hereford, then move back to the chopper and unload the money.'

'You think this fucker's really going to show?' Tony said. 'You really think he doesn't know we've just pitched up with all our weapons?'

Danny had no answer for that.

They moved stealthily, rifles engaged, in a leapfrog formation along the metal deck. Distance to the main scaffolding tower:

thirty metres. There were storage containers on either side, mostly blocking their view, but with narrow, shadowy corridors between them.

They'd covered fifteen metres. Danny had his back against one of the storage containers, covering Tony and Caitlin as they moved silently past. Something flickered on the edge of his vision, down one of the shadowy corridors.

'Movement,' he hissed.

Tony and Caitlin stopped stock-still. Tony set his weapon in the direction of the scaffolding tower. Caitlin set hers back towards the med room.

The platform wasn't deserted.

Danny aimed down the narrow corridor between the storage boxes.

His finger rested lightly on the trigger. His eyes narrowed.

There was a sudden flap of wings as a sea bird flew out of the corridor. Danny felt his body relaxing. He turned to the others and gave them a nod that meant: go.

They continued to leapfrog towards the scaffolding tower, which Danny now saw housed the immense drill at the centre of the platform, surrounded by clusters of huge, vertical metal pipes. He figured that ordinarily, this would be the noisiest, busiest part of the rig, but now it was deserted and quiet. The green walls of the control-room unit were just visible through the far side of the scaffolding. They needed to get there, open up a line to Hereford and then set up offensive positions for when the Caliph arrived. They edged clockwise round it, weapons still engaged. Once they were on its far side, they were just another fifteen metres from the bridge. They moved forward and approached.

The metal box that housed the control room was four times the size of the med unit, and the five metal steps leading up to it were three times as broad. A couple of metres to its right was a signalling aerial, pointing west at a steep azimuth. As before, Tony and Caitlin took up positions on either side of the door, while Danny engaged his rifle, knocked the door handle down and pushed it quietly open with his foot.

Silence. A quick check to the four corners of the control room told Danny the room was empty.

He scanned round the bridge. There was a bank of computer screens against the far wall. They showed a bewildering display of spreadsheets and technical diagrams. There was a water cooler against the left-hand wall, and a large, square table in the middle of the room. Some of the chairs round the table still had thick hi-vis jackets slung over the backs, and the table itself had a couple of white hard hats upturned on it. Danny continued to scan round, looking for the platform's radio equipment. He quickly located it against the right-hand wall.

'Shit,' he breathed. He activated his personal comms so that Tony and Caitlin could hear his voice. 'We've got a problem.'

The radio unit was about the same size as one of Ahmed's suitcases of money. It had a digital dashboard with a number of LEDs. All dead. The unit itself had been pulled away from the wall. Danny could see, even from this distance of ten metres, that the mess of multi-coloured wires had been roughly cut. He knew there was no point even trying to use it.

'The radio's down,' he said tersely into his comms unit. 'Someone's taken it out.'

'*The regular platform crew wouldn't have done that before they left,*' Tony said. '*We've got company.*'

Danny quickly turned and made to exit the control room, his KH-9 engaged. As he stepped through the door, he saw Tony and Caitlin down on one knee in the firing position, a ninety-degree angle between the trajectories of their two weapons.

There was no warning. Like the last groan of a dying man, the background hum of the electrical generator on the platform slurred and died. All the lights on the platform faded with it.

Danny hit the ground as his vision suddenly blackened. He heard Tony hiss: 'What the *hell's* going on?'

It was totally dark – Danny reckoned they had another twenty-five minutes until sunrise. He clenched his eyes closed to force his pupils to relax more quickly. When he opened his eyes, the oil platform looked totally different – an impenetrable jumble of dark shapes and shadows, lit only by the light of the moon.

He issued a sharp instruction: 'We need to get back to the others . . .'

But his words were cut short by an unmistakeable sound.

Gunfire.

Three shots.

They echoed across the rig, but there was no doubt from which direction they came.

'*The med room,*' Danny stated. '*Get there now!*'

They ran with weapons engaged, retracing their footsteps back towards – and past – the centre of the rig. With every step, Danny's eyes panned left and right, searching for threats, or even the faintest movement in the dark. There was none. But as they approached the med room, and from a distance of twenty metres, he could just make out that the door was swinging open.

'*Shit,*' he breathed. With his weapon fully engaged, he approached, aware that Tony and Caitlin had his back.

Five metres out from the open door of the med room he paused. He could make out no sign of forced entry on the door, which meant that whoever had opened it up had a key.

There could also *easily* be shooters still inside there.

And although there was no light inside the Portakabin or out, anyone inside would have the advantage, because if he approached, the moon would light Danny up, and the door opening would frame him.

He reached into his ops vest and pulled out his flashbang. He silently held it up to Tony and Caitlin to indicate what he had in mind. Caitlin got down in the firing position, pointing away from the med room and at an angle. Tony ran quietly to the far side of the steps, continued for five metres and did the same. Only when they were in place did Danny approach the steps. He knelt two metres from the bottom step and looked up through the open door.

Just blackness. No sound.

He pulled the pin from his grenade and quickly lobbed it into the med room.

Three seconds. Danny looked away just in time to stop his vision being compromised by the blinding white flash that emerged from the doorway. He was, of course, expecting the deafening bang. When it arrived, he hurried up the steps, weapon still engaged, and slipped through the doorway. He switched on his Surefire torch, trusting that any shooters in the med room would be too disorientated to fire on him if he made himself a target. He conducted a broad sweep of the room with his weapon.

No movement. No armed personnel.

But three bodies, slumped on the floor just by the stretcher bed.

With a sick feeling in his stomach, Danny approached swiftly. The Surefire shone brightly on the faces. Each man had been shot point-blank in the forehead. The entry wounds were cata-strophic. Each forehead had splintered open and spattered blood over the stretcher bed and the walls. It was as much from their clothes as their damaged features that Danny identified the bodies.

'Mustafa and the two pilots are down,' he said into his comms. Danny realised he hadn't even known the pilots' names.

There was no point wasting time on the dead. Danny spun round and continued his sweep of the med room. There was no sign of Ahmed or Buckingham.

He returned to the door frame and scuttled back down the stairs before hitting the ground in the same position as Tony and Caitlin.

'Some fucker was waiting for us,' he said tensely. 'They took out the radio comms and now they've got Ahmed and Buckingham.' He realised he was sweating profusely.

'How?' Caitlin demanded. 'The head shed's had the place under surveillance since we made contact with the Caliph. How did somebody get here before us?'

'I don't know,' Danny stated. 'Maybe they were already here.'

'What now?'

Tough call. There were just three of them on a large oil plat-form against an armed threat of unknown size.

'We stay together as a unit,' Tony said. 'That way we have a better chance of defending ourselves if we come under fire.'

'And no chance of finding Buckingham or Ahmed,' Danny said.

'Who gives a fuck about Buckingham?' Tony spat.

'Not me. But Ahmed's the only reason we're here. If we lose control of him, we've no chance of getting close to the Caliph.'

'For fuck's sake, Black, have you taken a knock to the head? Isn't it obvious we called him wrong? He's sprung a trap and I'll bet he's not within a hundred miles of this place.'

'I say we get back to the chopper,' Caitlin hissed. 'Use the air-craft's VHF to get a Mayday signal out . . .'

It was a good call. But even as Caitlin was making the suggestion . . .

'What the *fuck!*' Tony shouted.

A massive explosion had just ripped the skies from the direction of the chopper. They didn't have a direct line of sight, but they could see the top of a huge cloud of orange flame licking towards the sky, which glowed for a full ten seconds before the explosion subsided. A stench of acrid burning hit their senses.

Nobody needed to say it: someone had taken the chopper – and the money – out.

'What the *hell* do we do?' Tony hissed, an edge of panic in his voice. He and Caitlin were both looking at Danny. 'This was *your* fucking idea, Black. What now?'

Danny kept his breathing steady. Things had turned to shit, but losing your head wasn't going to help.

'We split up and find Ahmed,' he said tersely. 'Any enemy targets, we shoot to wound. We still need that information. We'll start on the west side of the platform and sweep east. Caitlin take the north end, Tony take the south, I'll take the middle. Keep in contact.'

They nodded. Then each of them melted into the darkness.

Hereford. 03.27 GMT.
The noise coming from the boot of Spud's car – a frenzied beating – had subsided halfway round the M25. Now, as Spud pulled up in front of the barrier at RAF Credenhill, there was total silence from the back.

The MoD policeman at the barrier walked up to Spud's open window. Spud didn't know his name, but they recognised each other. As the policeman leant down to Spud's height, he frowned. 'Fuck me, buddy, you okay? You look like shit.'

'You going to let me in,' Spud said, 'or are we going to shoot the shit for another ten minutes?'

The policeman shrugged, walked back to his post and opened the barrier. Spud pulled into camp, but immediately parked up outside the guard room next to the barrier. He killed the engine, walked round to the boot and, under the watchful eye of the MoD policeman, prepared himself for an onslaught – physical or verbal – from al-Meghrani.

It didn't come. He opened the boot on a broken man. His split nose was a mess. His face was smeared with dried blood. He stank of stale urine. But it was the look in his face that told Spud he'd get no trouble from this man. Spud had seen it before on the battlefield – the thousand-yard stare of a terrified, traumatised soldier.

'What the hell's going on?' the MoD guy demanded. Spud ignored him. Al-Meghrani's body was almost limp as he yanked him from the boot and dragged him into the guard room.

It was a bland room with a couple of desks, a TV blaring in one corner and a door that led to the camp's holding cells, which served to isolate anyone who caused trouble on site. Spud himself had even spent a few nights acting as duty sergeant in the guard room. It was a total pain in the arse and the short straw for anyone in camp. But he was relieved to see that tonight, the short straw had been drawn by Bob Pickford, a mate of his from A Squadron, sitting behind a desk with a bored look as he stared at the telly.

The bored look fell away as he saw Spud, and the state of his bruised, beaten companion. 'Spud, what the—'

'Do me a favour, Bob,' Spud interrupted. 'Put this cunt in the holding cell.'

Bob nodded, grabbed the glazed al-Meghrani by one arm and dragged him roughly through the door into the cell. When he returned a minute later, Spud said, 'Is he secure?'

'Roger that.'

Spud pointed in the direction of the main Regiment building. 'Who's in charge?' he said.

'Hammond. Something's going down, I don't know what.'

'Give me the phone, mucker, I need to speak to him.'

The look on Bob's face made it clear he didn't think this was a good idea, but he passed Spud the cordless handset. Spud consulted a sheet of numbers pinned to the wall. When he found Hammond's internal line, he dialled it.

Three rings.

Four.

'*Hammond.*' The ops officer's voice was taught and stressed.

'Boss, it's me. Spud.'

A momentary silence that spoke volumes.

'*Glover, I'm right in the middle of a* fucking . . .'

'Listen to me, boss. Just *listen* to me, okay? You need to come to the guard room. There's someone you have to see.'

'*Glover, I'm on my way to the ops room, and you're on your way out of camp. If I see you*—'

'It's about someone called the Caliph.'

Silence.

'Seriously, boss. Come by the guard room on your way to the ops office. It'll take one minute, then I'll be off your back.'

The phone clicked silent.

Spud's palms were sweating. He laid the handset on the table and felt Bob's eyes boring into him. He was grateful to his friend for not asking any questions. They stood there in silence. Spud didn't know if he'd persuaded Hammond to come, and wondered if he could somehow drag al-Meghrani directly over to the ops room. Impossible. Security was too high. They'd never let him in . . .

The door suddenly burst open. Hammond was there, dark rings around his eyes. He slammed the door shut behind him, but seemed almost too angry to speak. He had a thick manilla folder under his arms.

Spud turned to Bob. 'Give me the keys to the holding cell,' he said.

Bob handed them over.

'This way, boss,' Spud said.

The holding cell had a steel door with thick rivets. Spud opened it up and led Hammond inside. Al-Meghrani was crouching in the corner, hugging his knees.

'The Firm are putting all their resources into finding this geezer called the Caliph,' Spud said. '*They* won't listen to me, *you* won't listen to me, but I'm *telling* you: *this* guy has met him face to—'

There was a sudden flurry of movement from the corner of the cell. Al-Meghrani had pushed himself to his feet and hurled himself towards the two Regiment men in an attempt to get through the open cell door.

It was the act of an optimist, or an idiot.

He slammed hard into Hammond himself, who dropped his manilla folder but barely moved from the impact. Al-Meghrani staggered back as the contents of the folder scattered all over the floor.

Spud was about to speak again, to explain his investigations to Hammond, when something stopped him. The cab driver's expression had changed. The thousand-yard stare had morphed into something else.

Dread.

He was staring at one of the pieces of paper that had scattered from Hammond's folder. Spud looked to the floor. He saw photographs. One of them was of his mate Danny, and for a moment Spud thought he was staring at that. But it made no sense. Al-Meghrani didn't even *know* Danny . . .

'What is it?' he hissed. 'What have you seen?'

He suddenly realised that there was another photograph lying face up on the ground, just inches from the one of Danny. A Middle Eastern face. Reading upside down, Spud saw a name printed at the bottom of the photograph: Ahmed bin Ali al-Essa.

'What?' Spud said. And when his prisoner didn't reply, he pulled him to his feet and raised one fist as if he was about to crash it down on his hostage's already broken nose. 'Fucking *what?*'

Al-Meghrani flinched backwards. There was a deep silence in the cell. 'That's him,' al-Meghrani whispered. 'That's the Caliph.'

TWENTY-EIGHT

Hammond blinked.

'What did you say?' he breathed.

Al-Meghrani was in no state to repeat himself. His whole body was shaking. It didn't matter. Spud threw his prisoner back into the corner of the room as the Regiment ops officer turned to him. 'Follow me.'

Hammond ran back into the guard room, shouted at Bob to secure the prisoner again and burst out of the door. It was an effort for Spud to keep up with him as he sprinted towards the main Regiment building, along stark corridors and past surprised-looking Regiment guards as they headed deeper into the Kremlin – the centre of the camp where the ops room was situated.

The ops room itself was guarded by two armed Regiment guys. Hammond burst past them and into the room, Spud following close behind.

Whatever was going down, it was something big. There were fifteen personnel inside the ops room, all in camouflage gear, many of them wearing headsets and studying laptop screens. A larger screen on the far wall showed a map of the Persian Gulf, where a flashing triangle indicated a location halfway between the Qatari and Iranian coasts.

'Get the support units on to the oil platform!' Hammond bellowed. 'Black and the others are walking into a fucking ambush! Give the order! *NOW!*'

Danny's heart pumped two beats to every step.

He had reached the western side of the platform and had his

back against a storage container, facing out to sea. The perimeter of the platform – delineated by a solid yellow railing a head-height shorter than Danny himself – was a scant five metres from his position. The night sky was beginning to lighten, just faintly.

A quiet voice in his earpiece. Caitlin: '*In position.*'

'Tony?'

'*In position.*'

'Keep the lines open. Remember, the enemy might have NV. Check in every sixty seconds . . .'

He was about to order them to commence their sweep of the platform when something stopped him. Through the mesh perimeter fencing, he could just make out some dark shapes moving across the ocean towards the platform.

'Wait out,' he breathed.

He checked left and right. No movement in the darkness, so he moved closer to the perimeter and looked out to sea.

RIBs. Eight of them. They were approximately seventy-five metres out and had positioned themselves in a straight line, perhaps twenty metres apart from each other. From this distance, and in this light, Danny couldn't see how many personnel were in each boat. But he knew one thing for sure: they were in formation.

'Shit,' he breathed.

There was something else. More movement. But not in the water this time.

To Danny they were just shadows in the almost-night sky, but he knew what they were. Choppers. And only SF pilots were skilful enough to fly that low over the water, with their lights out. It had to be their air support units. It was impossible to judge distances with any accuracy, but he estimated they were five hundred metres out, perhaps a little more, but moving towards the platform at high speed.

Why the hell were they approaching? Danny hadn't requested air support.

His eyes flickered towards the RIBs in formation, and one word rang in his head: '*Ambush!*'

The RIBs knew the choppers were coming.

'No!' he hissed. '*No!*'

He wanted to *scream* at them. To get a message to their flight crew that they were flying straight into a trap. But he was impotent. He had no radio. No flares. No means of communication.

There was nothing he could do except watch the horror that unfolded.

The surface-to-air missiles that erupted from the RIBs glowed like tracer fire in the dark sky. There were eight. One from each boat. Danny didn't know what type they were, but they were heat-seeking and deadly accurate. They made a screaming sound as they cut through the air.

The SAS and SBS choppers didn't stand a chance.

It took no more than five seconds for the impact to occur. Danny saw it before he heard it: two colossal fireballs filled the sky as the choppers combusted instantly and exploded.

A second later, the sound hit his ears: two deep sonic booms that brought with them a sinister wave of heat. Like the after-effects of a crackling firework, there were several lesser explosions as the remaining missiles detonated among the fireballs, which hung, seemingly weightless, in the air, before fading to a dark, ugly cloud of debris that fell heavily towards the ocean.

The RIBs peeled away and started heading back towards the platform.

'Boss, we've lost contact.'

'What do you mean?' Hammond shouted.

'Comms are down with both aircraft. I can't get a fix on either of them. It's like they've disappeared.'

'What the *hell's* going on out there?' Hammond roared. 'Why haven't we heard from Black? Where are those *fucking* choppers?'

Nobody had an answer.

'Boss,' Spud said.

Hammond looked like he was about to rip Spud a new arsehole, but then he seemed to remember himself and his expression became slightly less dangerous. 'What?'

'Is Danny out there?'

'If he's still alive.'

'Boss, I owe him one. Don't make me sit this out.'

'Spud, Jesus, some fucker's about to release a bioweapon at the London Marathon. I haven't got time for—'

'Put me there,' Spud said.

Hammond blinked. 'What do you mean?'

'Boss, I'm not a fucking pencil-pusher. The Regiment's short of men. Put me in London.'

They locked gazes. Something passed between them. Finally Hammond gave a curt nod. 'Standby squadron is deploying to the capital by chopper in ten minutes. Join them.'

It was all Spud needed to hear. He turned his back on the ops room and left, as Hammond shouted to the room in general: 'Someone confirm GCHQ are monitoring all available frequencies!' And as he hurried down the corridor, the full impact of Hammond's words hit him.

A bioweapon at the marathon. He pulled out his phone and dialled Frances's number.

It rang out. No voicemail.

He cursed under his breath, then continued to run along the corridor.

You'll have a sixteen-man SAS team and eight SBS guys circling ten klicks to the north of the platform, out of sight, Hammond had said. Which meant twenty-four SF guys, plus flight crews, had just lost their lives.

Danny saw red. He raised his personal weapon, fully intending to open up on the eight RIBs that even now were speeding towards the platform.

Then he stopped.

Two pieces of a jigsaw had just clicked together in his mind.

And not just in Danny's. Tony's whispered, urgent voice came over his headset. '*The fuckers in those RIBs knew the choppers were coming!*'

'They knew more than that,' Danny breathed. 'They knew which direction they were coming from too.'

He made a quick mental calculation. Who had been party to that information except the three of them: Mustafa? He had a bullet in his head. Buckingham? Why would he want to scupper his own support units?

Which left Ahmed. Back at the apartment, Danny's conversations with the head shed had been on speakerphone so Tony and Caitlin could listen in. But that meant Ahmed also knew where the support units were coming from.

Danny's eyes narrowed.

His peripheral vision sensed movement on both sides.

He looked at his right arm. A red laser dot traced its way up his shoulder. He sensed it coming to rest on the side of his head.

Danny knew he had a fraction of a second to save himself. He hurled himself back from the edge of the rig, crashing heavily against the storage container behind him, which boomed and echoed like a drum. As he prepared to swing round and fire in the direction of the laser sight, he saw four more dots dancing on his chest.

This is it, he thought. I'm fucked.

He expected the shots to come any second.

They didn't.

Instead, a voice called from the darkness to his right. He recognised Ahmed immediately, but the voice of the Qatari businessman had a different edge to it. 'If you lower your weapon, I will instruct my men to hold their fire. If not . . .' He let the threat hang there.

'I'm compromised,' Danny breathed into his radio. As he lowered his weapon and let it hang by its sling, he waited for a response from Tony or Caitlin. There was none. He raised his arms into the air.

The red laser dots didn't falter from his chest. From both directions along the deck, figures approached out of the darkness. The shooters emerged first, two from either side, weapons engaged in a professional manner. Twenty metres in. Ten metres. Behind the shooters to the right, Danny saw Ahmed himself.

'Remove your weapons,' Ahmed said. 'Do it very slowly.'

The shooters were five metres out on either side. Black

clothes, black balaclavas, black M16s with laser sights. They stopped and kept their weapons trained on Danny. He gave himself a moment to calculate his probability of nailing them. Non-existent. Even if he managed to down two of them, their colleagues on the other side would shoot him in a split second. He had no choice. He slowly unclipped his weapon from its strap, then laid it on the floor.

'And the handgun,' Ahmed instructed. Danny removed his S&W from his ops waistcoat and laid that on the floor too. 'Remove your earpiece,' Ahmed told him. Danny obeyed, dropping it on the floor with his weapon. He glanced to his left, past the two shooters. Where the *hell* were the others? Had they been compromised? Or were they still operational? Danny had no way to tell.

He looked towards Ahmed. 'I guess I'm talking to the Caliph,' he said.

'I won't lie,' Ahmed said smoothly. 'I expected you to join the dots a little sooner.' He glanced towards the sky, where the two choppers had just been taken out.

'Those pictures of your parents,' Danny said. '*You* did that?'

Ahmed's blank expression didn't change. 'They were old,' he said, 'and more use to me dead than alive. I feared Mr Buckingham was getting a little close to the truth. Perhaps I mistook his abilities. You are probably wondering about your companions. Please don't imagine that they are in a position to help you. My men have them. You will be kept separate.' He addressed the guys holding Danny at gunpoint. 'Take him to the drillers' cabin,' he said. 'I will deal with him there.'

Two of the guys lowered their weapons and roughly grabbed Danny's arms. He didn't fight it. He knew that one squeeze of the remaining two M16s would drop him. As they dragged him past Ahmed, the two men exchanged a look. It was almost as though Danny was looking at a different person. Ahmed's eyes were dead and dark. There was no humanity in them. Not even any hatred. Just an empty pit.

The balaclava'd men dragged Danny through the dark,

industrial maze of the oil platform. He tried to quell the fear that was rising in his chest, and to keep his senses alert. Every thirty seconds or so, he saw movement at the edges of his vision, down dark external corridors or on the other side of distant scaffolding rigs. His captors must have seen them too, but it didn't seem to worry them, which was bad news: it meant the rig was crawling with the Caliph's men. Maybe they were the same guys who he'd just seen in the RIB – there would have been time by now for them to climb up the platform legs and board the platform. Maybe they'd been here, in hiding, all along.

They reached a large cabin on the southern side of the rig, about twenty-five metres in length and painted the same yellow as the railings round the platform. A sign on the door said 'Drillers' Cabin'. The door was unlocked. Danny felt himself being shoved inside. There were blackout blinds against the windows, so it was entirely dark. He staggered halfway across the dark cabin before hitting a long wooden table set in the middle. He spun round to look back at the door, and saw the red laser dots still dancing on his chest.

'*Black!*' A voice hissed from the darkness. Danny immediately recognised Buckingham, his tone dripping with fear. 'What the *hell's* happening . . . ?'

There was no chance to respond. The gunmen were on him again, dragging him to one end of the room. As his eyes grew accustomed to the darkness, he could just make Buckingham out. The spook was on his knees. His hands seemed to be bound behind his back, and tied to a metal post, approximately eight feet high, connecting the floor to the ceiling of the cabin. As one of the gunmen dragged Danny to an identical post, about six feet to the left of Buckingham's, another withdrew a torch and shone it directly in Buckingham's face. Danny saw pale skin and bloodshot eyes. Buckingham's handsome features were so drawn that he was hardly recognisable.

They forced Danny to his knees in the same position as Buckingham. Two laser spots were still on his chest as one of the masked men cable-tied his wrists and ankles together behind his back, then tied both to the spare post. Danny knew there was no point expending energy by struggling. If he put up a fight, they'd just shoot him. It was an uncomfortable stress position that forced him to stay kneeling with his arms tight behind his back.

Only when he was fully secure did the laser spots leave his body. The gunman extinguished his torch. Without another word, all four men left the cabin. Danny heard them locking the door.

'This is your fault,' Buckingham breathed. 'This is *your fucking fault*, Black. Everything you touch turns to shit, and now *I'm* going to . . .'

Danny zoned out. He was trying to peer through the gloom to get his bearings, his eyes still adjusting to the renewed darkness. There was a gap of about five metres between himself and the table. Beyond that, he couldn't see anything. He strained to tug his arms away from the post behind him, but it just made the cable ties dig sharply into his skin, and he knew that was a no-go.

He had no weapons and no comms. No means of defending himself, or raising the alarm.

The Caliph had played them like a fucking instrument.

He zoned back in to Buckingham's voice. 'How long until the SAS and SBS support units get here?'

'You heard that big bang five minutes ago? That was them taking a swim.' Scowling, Danny looked to his left. He could just see Buckingham's pale face.

'What?' Buckingham's voice had raised an octave. '*What?* You mean they're . . .'

'Not coming,' Danny said.

'But . . . but Hereford will know what's happened?'

'All they'll know is that they've lost contact.'

'So they'll send someone else?'

'Sure,' Danny said. 'It shouldn't take more than five or six hours.'

'*What? Oh, Jesus* . . .' Suddenly, and without warning, Danny heard retching.

'Listen to me,' he said over the noise. 'When they come back, be compliant. You saw what Ahmed's men did to his own parents. You know what he's capable of, so don't antagonise them. It's your best chance of survival.'

'What do *you* fucking well know, Black?' There was the sound of more retching, and then of the door being unlocked. A faint light as it opened. Several figures – probably six, maybe seven – filed into the room.

Three of them had torches, which they shone directly at the prisoners, dazzling Danny and removing whatever night vision he'd acquired. There was activity in the space between them and the table. For a full thirty seconds, Danny squinted into the light, trying to work out what the figures were doing. Only when they stepped back a couple of metres did he realise. His stomach turned to ice when he saw that they had erected a camera on a tripod between him and Buckingham, three metres out. He remembered something Tony had said the day they'd left for Nigeria. *Remember the good old days when the time to shit yourself was when someone shoved a gun in your face? Now you know you're in for a much worse time when they get their fucking iPhones out and press record . . .*

The figures melted away towards the back of the room, but they kept their torches shining towards Danny and Buckingham. Danny caught a whiff of urine, and he knew Buckingham had pissed himself. He didn't fully blame him.

Another figure entered the room. Danny knew from the slow walk and the shape of his silhouette that it was Ahmed. He positioned himself just in front of the camera. The torchlight from behind made his outline very pronounced, and cast a long, thin shadow towards them. Danny couldn't see his face.

'Listen to me! *Listen . . . Ahmed . . .*' It was Buckingham talking, and he had a quaver of total panic in his voice.

'You will call me Caliph,' Ahmed said.

Hesitation. Then . . . 'Please, Caliph . . . You don't *need* to kill me. The other three are special forces. Imagine the publicity you'll get, putting them in front of the camera. But you haven't *got* the other two. You've only got *him*. Let me go and you can use me to draw the other two out.'

Silence.

'For God's sake, man, I'm more use to you alive than dead ...'

His words degenerated into a kind of nervous gasping.

There was silence in the room. Danny had the impression that Ahmed was letting Buckingham dig himself a deeper hole. Buckingham clearly didn't realise this, because after a few seconds he continued on the same tack.

'Think of it,' he whispered. 'One of them's a girl. A *white* girl. You can give her to your men.' Danny glanced in disgust towards Buckingham, who gave him a sidelong look, licked his lips nervously, and then continued with a quiet intensity in his voice. 'I bet they haven't had a woman for weeks. They'll *thank* you for it.'

Silence.

Ahmed crouched down so that his head was on a level with Danny's and Buckingham's. He looked from one to the other. Danny could just about discern that he had a grim smile on his face.

'You are so weak,' he whispered.

He stood up again, and this time he spoke more clearly. 'For your information, we have secured the other two. Who knows, I *might* let my men do what they want to the woman, but that is not your concern. I understand you killed one of my most promising young executioners, Danny Black.'

Danny shook his head. 'No,' he said, trying to keep his voice level. 'It was the Chinese guy.'

Ahmed almost smiled. 'The Chinese,' he said. 'They'll do almost anything for oil. They have weaponised plague, smallpox and other weapons you've never even heard of. They don't even want payment for their troubles. Just think how it will benefit them when the caliphate has spread and the West no longer has access to our natural resources.'

He held something up in front of Danny's face: a small vial of clear liquid. Danny didn't need to ask what it was.

'In London,' Ahmed whispered, 'we are beheading your soldiers in the street. In France, we are executing them in their offices. After today, thanks to this, your people will look back on those times as the good old days.'

Danny kept quiet. Any attempt to antagonise this lunatic would be counter-productive. To his left, though, he could hear Buckingham shivering with terror.

'But I see no reason,' Ahmed said, 'to dispense with the old ways just yet.' He pocketed the vial of liquid, before walking back behind the camera. He raised one hand and clicked his fingers. The three men with torches moved forward, coming to a halt a metre behind the tripod and shining their beams at Danny and Buckingham so that they were quite brightly lit up. There was a shuffling sound behind the camera. Danny, squinting again in the light, could tell that Ahmed was wrapping a shamagh around his head.

When he returned to the front of the camera, he was carrying something that made Danny's skin turn clammy. It was a knife. The blade itself was a foot long, and Danny could see that it had jagged, serrated teeth. Someone switched on the camera. A little red light glowed.

Ahmed paced in front of the camera, his long shadow moving erratically in the unstable torchlight. Buckingham was retching again. Great, heaving sounds from the pit of his stomach. 'Ordinarily,' Ahmed said, 'we would sedate you. It makes things easier. But a British special forces soldier and a British intelligence office demand special treatment. You are not our usual quarry of aid workers and do-gooders. The only question is, who first?'

He looked from one to the other. Then he stepped towards Danny.

With his free hand, Ahmed grabbed a clump of Danny's hair, then rested the blade on the back of his neck. Danny could feel the individual teeth pricking his skin. The serrations were clearly razor-sharp, because although there was barely any pressure, he felt spots of blood oozing over his skin.

'You've learned,' Ahmed said, 'that people fear me. You have learned that they fear to speak the name of the Caliph. I am going to show you – and everyone who watches this tape – why.'

Danny closed his eyes. His body was starting to tremble, and he focused on stopping it. He wasn't going to give this bastard the satisfaction of letting the camera see just how scared he was, now, in the seconds before his death.

The blade didn't move. Ten seconds passed. He wasn't sure, but he thought that maybe Ahmed was laughing softly. Unwillingly, he opened his eyes. Nothing had changed. The torches were still shining towards them. The light of the camera was still on. Buckingham was still whimpering to his side. But as he stared straight ahead, Ahmed released his hair and lifted the blade. Danny felt a strange surge of relief.

Ahmed was walking towards Buckingham. Danny watched grimly as he stood on Buckingham's far side, grabbed his hair and laid the knife on his neck.

'The girl,' Buckingham whispered desperately in a strangled voice. 'Let me . . . let me get the *girl* for you . . .'

'Do you remember our excursion in Riyadh, Mr Buckingham?' Ahmed said. 'Do you remember how the crowd pushed you to the front so that the last person the prisoner saw would be an infidel, so that she would burn in the hellfire?'

Ahmed forced Buckingham's head to the side, so that he was looking directly at Danny. 'Look at the infidel, Mr Buckingham,' he said.

Then he started speaking in Arabic, a dull, monotone chanting that Danny couldn't understand. But it seemed to echo meaning-fully around the room.

'I can be of *use* to you . . .' Buckingham tried to say over the chanting. He was crying. His voice was broken. 'I *know* things . . . secrets . . . please . . . Caliph . . .'

Ahmed continued chanting above Buckingham's panicked sobs. Twenty seconds later, he stopped.

There was a pregnant silence, as if everybody in the room was holding his breath.

'*For pity's sake, Black!*' Buckingham suddenly screamed. '*DO SOMETHING!*'

But there was nothing Danny could do. He could tell that the Caliph had already made his decision.

He didn't want to watch, but somehow he had to.

It wasn't the first swipe that was the worst. That went with the grain of the hooked blade and sliced easily into the back of Buckingham's neck. Buckingham took a sharp intake of breath, and Danny sensed that the blade was so sharp he hadn't even felt the first cut yet.

The second swipe was a different matter. Ahmed pulled the hooks of the blade towards him. Danny could hear the resistance exerted by the tendons in the back of Buckingham's neck. Ahmed had to yank hard to pull the blade through the sinew. By the shaky torchlight, Danny could just make out lumps of internal flesh hanging from the exposed teeth.

Buckingham's scream was inhuman: a loud, high-pitched, gurgling wail. Danny heard blood dripping from his neck and spattering on to the floor. As Ahmed made the third slice, the wailing suddenly cut out, and was replaced by the sound of Buckingham's body going into spasm. Danny could only assume that the blade had cut into the spinal cord. Seconds later, the body slumped still.

It took another minute for the job to be done. Danny turned his head away, but couldn't avoid listening to the wet, coarse slapping sound as Ahmed hacked his way through the remainder of the neck. Only when he heard a heavy thudding sound did he know it was over.

There was a hushed, church-like silence in the room. Danny glanced to his left. Buckingham – what remained of him – was still kneeling, and the torchlight illuminated the brutal wound. His internal organs looked like they were trying to escape from his neck, and fresh blood was sopping from its remnants.

Ahmed bent down and retrieved the head from the floor, then held it up for the benefit of the cameras. Strings of flesh trailed down from the neck as he continued his Arabic chanting for another thirty seconds. Then he dropped the head again and turned to Danny, while one of his men switched off the camera.

'Please don't imagine, Danny Black, that anyone is coming to help you,' Ahmed said. 'I have enough people in the Qatari government to stop any rescue mission or armed response. We could stay here for days, and nobody would come. I will make you beg for your life before I kill you. A scared soldier makes better TV than a quiet one. I'll leave you with your friend. We'll see how calm you are when *your* time comes.'

TWENTY-NINE

07.30 GMT.

Dawn had already broken over the Thames as Bailey's white Transit van pulled up at the vehicle entrance to the London Heliport.

He had arrived at the Battersea area from St Albans a full hour ago, where he'd pulled up in a side street off Battersea Park and waited. He hadn't wanted to be late, but neither did he want to show up at the helipad too early. It would be suspicious if he and his accomplice took to the skies before sunrise, but now was the perfect time to make his way to the entrance of the heliport.

There was a security checkpoint at the vehicular entrance. Bailey approached it slowly. A uniformed security guard walked up to his window. Bailey wound it down and handed him his press accreditation pass. The guard studied it carefully. 'Lovely morning for it,' he said.

Bailey smiled. 'Better than last year, anyway. Pissed it down all day. Pilot had to land the helicopter halfway through the race. Poor visibility.'

'You won't have that trouble today, mate,' said the guard, handing back the press accreditation. 'You'll get a close-up of Mo Farah's lunchbox in weather like this.' The guard chortled at his joke. Bailey smiled politely. 'Straight ahead and to the right, Mr Bailey. My colleagues will direct you on to the helipad.'

The barrier opened. Bailey drove slowly forward. To his right was a long hangar, with several cars and vans parked outside. Bailey drove the length of it – a distance of maybe thirty metres. The helipad itself came into view. There were three landing pads: two of them set back from the riverbank, one on a T-shaped pier that reached out into the Thames. There was a helicopter on each of the pads, two white Agustas and a yellow and black Twin Squirrel light utility chopper out on the pier. Bailey found his eyes zoning in on the Twin Squirrel. There was a figure standing right by it. Bailey could just make out the features of his colleague, McIntyre.

Up ahead were two guys in yellow hi-vis jackets. They both carried a handheld beacon but neither of them waved Bailey on, so he braked and waited for one of them to approach.

'BBC?' the ground steward asked. Shaved head, thick neck, broad Cockney accent and a smell of tobacco.

Bailey nodded and handed his press card over again, but the ground steward waved it away. 'Your pilot's here already, guv. He says you got some camera equipment to load up?'

Bailey nodded.

'Okay, you can take the vehicle directly up to the heli. We've got ten minutes before we need to clear the pad of non-aerial vehicles. You have the all-clear from air-traffic control.'

Bailey wound up his window and slowly drove towards the Twin Squirrel. McIntyre stood calmly by the aircraft, but Bailey found himself examining the chopper carefully at a distance. His heart rate rose slightly when he saw a thin length of metal tucked along the side of the chopper's landing skids. He couldn't make out the individual spraying nozzles at this distance, but he knew they were there, and that a second aerial spraying attachment would be attached to the opposite side of the chopper. Nobody would notice these understated attachments if they weren't looking for them. Once they were airborne, and the blades of this industrial spraying system had hinged outwards at ninety degrees, the helicopter would look a lot more suspicious. But by then, it would be too late.

When he was ten metres out, Bailey did a full turn and reversed up to the helicopter. He killed the engine and climbed out onto the tarmac.

There was a chill in the air. The river, just metres away, seemed very still, and clearly reflected the dark purples of the early morning sky. As Bailey walked up to McIntyre, he was aware of the glowing yellow lights of the modern apartment blocks on the opposite side of the river, and of a flock of birds flying in a V formation over the water. Two commercial airliners were visible, following the flight path down into Heathrow. That, along with the ground steward's comment about the all-clear from air-traffic control, gave him confidence: there was no sign of any nervousness in the coordination of UK airspace. Which meant they weren't suspected.

Neither man spoke. They just nodded silently at each other.

Bailey opened the back of the Transit van. Daniel dealt with the side doors of the Twin Squirrel. Together, they hauled the flight cases of camera equipment from the back of the van and into the helicopter. Bailey clocked the motor and tubes of the industrial spraying system's machinery at the back of the chopper. They piled the flight cases in front of it, so it was hidden from anyone who happened to peer inside. And once that was done, they turned their attention to the two canisters that they had so carefully loaded up the previous morning, still strapped to the sides of the Transit.

'Don't let them tip this time,' Bailey said.

Protected by the Transit van from the view of the ground stewards, they manoeuvred the first canister out of the vehicle, across the three metres of tarmac that separated it from the chopper, and with difficulty hauled it up into the body of the chopper.

They turned back to get the second canister. Bailey's muscles burned as they left the chopper to retrieve it.

The ground steward suddenly appeared. He looked into the almost-empty Transit van, his handheld beacon illuminating the contents: a solitary canister, with Chinese lettering.

Bailey felt his muscles tensing up. He exchanged a sidelong glance with McIntyre, whose expression had suddenly turned dangerous.

The ground steward looked back at them. He was wearing a frown.

'Fucking Chinks,' he said in his broad Cockney. 'They get everywhere, don't they?'

Bailey smiled.

'What is it, Hoisin sauce?' He laughed loudly at his joke. 'Nah, seriously, camera stock?' He said it casually, as though showing off his knowledge, and clearly not realising how out of date it was.

Bailey nodded carefully.

'Here, I'll lend you a hand,' said the ground steward. 'I need to ask you to get the vehicle off the pad.'

'You're okay, mate,' Bailey said quietly. 'We're on top of it.'

The ground steward shrugged. 'Suit yourself, mate,' he said, and he strode off across the helipad while Bailey and McIntyre loaded up the second canister.

By the time they were done, Bailey was sweating. He closed up the back of the Transit and drove it over to the hangar area. He jogged back to the Twin Squirrel. McIntyre had quickly pulled a hazmat suit over his clothes and was already at the controls with the rotors spinning. Bailey opened the side door, jumped in and closed the door behind him.

The helicopter rose from the helipad almost immediately. Bailey saw that McIntyre had his headset on and was talking into the boom mike, though he couldn't hear what he was saying. As they rose over the river, and the London skyline came into view – its buildings glistening in the early morning sun – he started to unpack one of his boxes. He withdrew his own white hazmat suit, then two rebreathing masks. He would hand McIntyre's his when the time came.

He turned his attention to the aerial spraying machinery at the back of the chopper. It didn't look like much, and when they had first told him what he was to do, he hadn't believed it would have the desired effect. But then he had researched the subject. It was amazing what information you could find, if you just knew where to look. He had read about an American bioweapons simulation, where a harmless substance was sprayed into the atmosphere from a ship out at sea. The substance had reached far inland, in quantities that would have been devastating if it had been a lethal agent. The more he had read, the more he had become convinced that they were right: spraying a bioweapon from a chopper at a height of 150 feet above the crowds would have precisely the effect they required.

McIntyre looked back and shouted at him over the noise of the aircraft. 'They want some shots of The Mall!' he shouted. 'Then over the Cutty Sark towards Shooter's Hill to see everyone arriving for the race.'

Bailey nodded. He started to unpack his TV cameras, ready to begin filming the tens of thousands of people who even now were swarming towards the start line. As he put his equipment together, he ran through the morning's schedule in his head. Wheelchair race, 08.55 start. Paralympic race, 09.00 start. Main race, 10.00 start. But by 08.00, he knew, the crowds would already be enormous, and their TV producer would not yet have requested that they travel further along the race route. That would be the best time to attack.

'Remember to stay at five hundred feet until I give you the word. Then drop down to a hundred and fifty feet and swoop over the crowd.'

The helicopter banked. Bailey fitted his TV camera to its secure tripod, then opened the side door. Through the viewfinder, he focused in on Buckingham Palace and The Mall. The broad street had been shut off to traffic, but was already lined with spectators and guarded by a police presence that was, Bailey thought, larger than he expected. The union flag was flying over the palace itself.

Bailey allowed himself a grim smile as he wondered how long it would be before that flag was flying at half-mast.

Danny's muscles burned with pain. The stress position – forced on to his knees and with his arms stretched behind him and cable-tied to the post – had been agonising after thirty minutes. But now, after two or three hours had passed, it was torment. The cable ties that bound his hands together behind his back were digging harshly into his wrists – he could feel wet blood where they were digging into his flesh – and the skin on the back of his neck that had been punctured by Ahmed's knife was angry and sore.

Physical pain, however, he knew he could deal with.

Psychological suffering was by far his greater enemy. Buckingham's butchered body, limply slumped at a gruesome angle with its wrists still tied to the post, was a sickening warning of what was to come. He was grateful that the spook's head, which lay between them, was facing away from Danny. A freshly dead body has a unique smell – halfway between a butcher's shop and a public lavatory – and that horrific odour filled Danny's nostrils now. He tried to play tricks on his brain: to remind himself how much he hated Buckingham, and how loathsome he had been during his final moments. But it was no good. He couldn't take his mind off what was to come: he was as focused on the camera on its tripod as he was on the severed head by its body . . .

Think positive. What would Hereford do, having lost contact with them? Scramble another rescue team? But the nearest suitable SF unit could still be hours out. He hadn't been joking when he'd told Buckingham that . . .

The door opened. Daylight flooded in. Danny squinted towards it and realised his vision was blurred. He felt a surge of adrenaline.

Tony!

He was mistaken. The man that entered had a similar physique, but it wasn't Tony. He had black clothes and a balaclava. Even more ominously, he had a shoulder bag. Danny didn't want to know what was in it. But he found out soon enough.

The man walked up to the camera and switched it on. Without a word he put the shoulder bag on the ground. Then he stepped towards Danny and pulled a smartphone from his pocket. He swiped the screen, tapped it, and then held it front of Danny's face.

He saw shaky video footage of a dark room. He couldn't make out much detail, but he could see a figure lying on his front on the floor. Two black-clad men each had one of their feet pressed into his back, and had rifles pointed at the back of his head. The camera panned down to the prisoner's face. It was bruised and bloodied. The nose was broken, the eyes swollen. But Danny recognised it as Tony. Ahmed hadn't been lying.

The juddery, dark camera footage panned upwards again. It

swiped round the room. More figures: three clad in black, plus Caitlin. She was unarmed and her face was largely intact apart from a swelling around the right eye. One of the guys held her at gunpoint. The other two stepped forward. One of them grabbed her between the legs. When she struggled, the other one tore at her hair and, with his free hand, smashed her again against the bruised eye. As the camera panned away, Danny just caught sight of Caitlin being bent roughly over by her two attackers.

Danny's blood burned in his veins. *Don't show your anger,* he told himself. *They're just trying to fuck with your head. Stay calm . . . stay compliant . . .*

The camera moved back to Tony. It zoomed in on his face. It was still pressed against the floor, and the wound on his cheek had started to weep. But despite his fucked-up features, there was a look of deadly concentration in his eyes.

Tony was down, but he wasn't out. Danny clung to that one fact. He had nothing else. He ignored the voice in his head that told him Tony was unpredictable and crooked. That there was no love lost between them. That there was a chance, even if Tony *could* help Danny, that he *wouldn't* . . .

The video clip died. Danny's new companion put it back in his pocket. Then he pulled out a sturdy piece of wood from his shoulder bag, the same heft and length as a baseball bat.

Danny clenched his jaw and prepared himself for the beating he knew was coming.

The man stood a metre in front of him, raised the cudgel over his shoulder, and struck. It connected brutally with the pit of Danny's stomach. Danny coughed harshly as the wind rushed from his stomach, then desperately tried to force his winded lungs to inhale, while the man raised his cudgel again.

The second blow cracked against the right-hand side of his ribcage. He felt a couple of ribs go instantly. His instinct was to shout out in pain, but he couldn't because there was still no air in his lungs.

The man leaned down so their eyes were at the same level. He examined Danny's face carefully, almost like a doctor, holding his chin gently in his free hand. Danny wanted to spit in his face, but he forced himself to remain compliant. That was his only chance of survival.

The third blow was to the face. It came from the opposite direction and cracked against Danny's left cheekbone. He felt the bone itself splinter as a spray of blood and mucus showered from his nose. He was breathing again now, and gulped at the air in an effort to handle the pain. He told himself that maybe – just *maybe* – that third blow had been a fraction softer than the two that preceded it. He allowed himself to believe that this was a good thing: maybe his attacker had been told to ensure that Danny survived this beating.

But survived it for what? Danny glanced down at Buckingham's severed head as his tormentor circled him menacingly. He felt him wipe the bloody cudgel on the sleeve of Danny's right arm. The pain was unspeakable. He could tell that his face was a mess of shattered bone and splintered wood. His broken ribs sent white-hot shards of intense agony through his body. It drained all the strength from him, and it was all he could do to keep his head upright in at least a semblance of dignity.

He closed his eyes, and told himself that he *would* withstand whatever else this bastard threw at him. But then he sensed movement again. When he opened his eyes, he saw that his attacker had repositioned himself in front of Danny again, and just to his right. He was holding the broad side of the cudgel just inches from Danny's face.

Danny looked up. He could see a ferocious intensity in his attacker's eyes. The bastard's hands were trembling with a barely contained thrill as he prepared to slam the cudgel flat and square into the front of Danny's face.

Danny set his jaw. *Protect your eyes*, he told himself.

He closed them. Which meant he didn't fully see what happened next.

There was the sound of the door being kicked open. It was followed, almost instantly, by the harsh bark of a round being discharged from a rifle. Danny opened his eyes just in time to see his black-clad tormentor tumble towards him as his cudgel dropped to the ground. His body fell heavily against Danny's face, then slumped to the floor, by which time two figures were halfway towards him: Tony facing Danny's way, Caitlin aiming her weapon towards the door.

Tony Wiseman was in an even worse state than he had been on the smartphone screen. He looked like his nose had been broken in two places, his face was smeared with blood, and there was a chunk missing from the lobe of his left ear. He had to be in a lot of pain, but there was no sign of it. Whatever had happened, at least some of the Caliph's men had clearly come off even worse.

Tony and Caitlin were carrying AK-47s that they must have stolen from Ahmed's men. He saw that Tony also had a knife. Brandishing it, he moved behind Danny.

'What's this?' he drawled, his voice dry and gravelly. 'He been playing with you? Fifty fucking shades of grey?' With one clean cut, he slit the cable ties. Danny lurched forward, almost falling face-down on the ground as he dissolved into a fit of uncontrolled coughing. The very act of coughing was agony, and he knew he'd definitely broken a rib or two. But Tony grabbed the back of his shirt and held him up. 'Don't do a Spud on me now,' he said.

'Ahmed's the Caliph,' Danny breathed.

'Tell us something we don't know.'

Danny regained control of himself. He pushed himself uneasily to his feet, wincing with the pain in his ribcage, then grabbed the post to which he'd been tied while Tony kicked the severed head on to its back to see who it was. He snorted. 'Couldn't have happened to a nicer bloke,' he said, before kicking the head out of the way. He turned to Danny. 'Get moving, Black,' he said.

'Wait,' Danny breathed. 'What happened? How did you get free?'

'One of Ahmed's men wanted to break my arm, so he untied me. Bit of a mistake, that.'

'How many men did you put down?' Danny asked. They needed to pool their information, and fast.

'Eight,' Tony said.

'Make that nine,' Caitlin cut in, pointing at Danny's dead tormentor.

Danny felt weak with pain, but forced himself to stay sharp. 'They'll know you've escaped,' he stated. 'They'll be all over us like flies.'

'Maybe not,' Tony said. 'We questioned one of Ahmed's guys before we nailed him. He told us there are seven more men on the rig, plus Ahmed.' He pointed at the dead body. 'Make that six. They're all heading for the LZ, waiting for a chopper to arrive and get him to the Saudi coast.'

'He might have been lying,' Danny countered.

Tony gave him a look, and for a moment Danny no longer saw the slightly pissed-off soldier who didn't like taking orders from him, or even the dodgy crook with interests in organised crime. He saw an SAS soldier, professionalism and aggression written on his face. 'Trust me,' Tony said quietly, 'he was telling the truth.'

Danny nodded. His wooziness was subsiding, even if the pain on his face and abdomen wasn't. He looked over at Caitlin. Her face was also smeared in blood and mud. 'Did they hurt you?' he demanded.

'Not as much as I hurt them,' Caitlin said. He saw that she had a second AK strapped across her back. She brought it over her head and handed it to Danny. He strapped it on and cocked it.

'The chopper could arrive any time,' Danny said. 'We need to get to the LZ before it does.'

'Remember,' Tony said. 'We want Ahmed alive.'

'The radio's out,' Caitlin reminded them. 'We've got no way of contacting anyone, even if we do get this fucker and squeeze some intel out of him.'

'We'll cross that bridge when we come to it.' Danny knew he was slurring his words slightly. He told himself to snap back to fitness. 'Everyone ready?'

'Roger that,' Tony and Caitlin said in unison.

'Don't assume all six militants are with Ahmed. There could still be shooters out there and they might engage us.'

Time check: 09.35 hrs. That made it 07.35 in London. There would be crowds. The hit could happen at any moment. It could *already* have happened.

They pressed the butts of their weapons into their shoulders, and advanced towards the door.

THIRTY

There was a deep silence on the platform. It was as if even the sea was holding its breath.

They all understood you don't just pick up an enemy weapon and expect it to be your best friend. Before they moved towards the LZ, they had a call to make. These stolen AKs were un-zeroed firearms. Whoever Tony and Caitlin had taken them from hadn't had the benefit of laser sights – they just had the standard AK-47 iron sight – which meant Danny had no idea how the rounds would fall if he fired this weapon. There was only one way to find out, and that was to fire the weapons. To do that could give away their location, but it was a risk they were prepared to take for the sake of accuracy.

Outside the drillers' cabin and to the left, at a distance of twenty metres, there was a fire exit sign two metres from the ground, with a green arrow pointing to the right. While Tony and Caitlin covered him, Danny lined up his sights with the centre of the sign and took a shot. The sound echoed across the quiet platform, and he saw that the shot had landed a foot and a half to the right of his intended target zone. It meant he would need to aim left to ensure accuracy of fire.

'7.62 shorts,' Danny muttered dismissively. Enough to put a man on the ground, but not as hard-hitting as the NATO rounds he'd have chosen for himself.

It took another thirty seconds for Tony and Caitlin to get the measure of their weapons – two more shots that rang out over the platform, and two more very good reasons to get the hell away from their current position as quickly as possible.

'Ready?' Danny demanded as Caitlin lowered her rifle.

A short nod confirmed that she was.

This time, they didn't split up. Order of march: Tony, Danny, Caitlin.

The sun was bright and already hot. It cast clear, sharp shadows. They moved carefully, with their stolen weapons engaged, in a leapfrog formation, through the industrial maze of the oil rig. Every time they turned, their weapons turned with them. Danny pushed the pain in his ribs and on his face to the back of his mind. His every sense was on the highest alert. Every time he turned a corner, he half expected to see the telltale red dot on his chest. But this time his trigger finger would be ready.

Caitlin moved to the front of the line while Danny and Tony covered her. They encountered nobody. From the heart of the platform, Danny caught the occasional glimpse of the sea, calm and still with a clear blue sky above. A couple of commercial airliners high overhead, but no sign of any other aircraft – or indeed anything else – in the vicinity.

None of them wanted to discharge another round. Unsuppressed, the sound of these AK-47s would pinpoint their position very precisely to anybody hunting them. But there seemed to be no personnel remaining on the platform, unless they were lying *very* fucking low.

Danny moved to the front, Tony and Caitlin covering.

As they stealthily passed the med room where Mustafa and the two pilots had been murdered, Danny saw that the door was still open, and there were bloody footprints on the floor outside. He spent a couple of seconds examining them, trying to read the movement of any personnel who'd passed by recently. But the blood stains were dry. They moved inexorably onward, towards the LZ.

Tony moved front, Danny and Caitlin covering. He held up one hand, palm outwards. They came to a halt.

Tony was alongside a yellow storage container. He got down on one knee, then indicated that Danny and Caitlin should join him. Danny approached carefully, aware that Caitlin was covering them from the rear. He got down on one knee next to Tony.

They could see the LZ from here. Distance: thirty metres. It was raised about ten metres high off the platform, almost as though floating over it. No sign of the remnants of Ahmed's chopper that had exploded an hour previously. The ground between them and it was a jumble of low machinery and scaffolding, but essentially open: anyone on the LZ would see them approaching, and would have a clean shot at them. Sure enough, kneeling on the circular edge of it were three of Ahmed's men, dressed in black, weapons engaged and pointing outwards, each man about seven metres apart. They were facing into the sun, no doubt squinting, which explained why they hadn't noticed the unit.

'They're guarding the LZ,' Tony breathed.

'The only person they'd be guarding is Ahmed,' said Danny. 'He must be up there.'

'We can take them.'

Danny sniffed. They were using unfamiliar weapons, none of them zeroed in for their user. But they didn't have a choice. The only way to get to Ahmed was through his guards. They didn't appear to have seen the unit so far, but that would probably change if they tried to move any closer.

Danny signalled Caitlin to join them. They knelt in a row, a metre apart from each other, and aimed their rifles, upward at a thirty-degree angle towards the ten-metre-high raised platform that was the LZ, each of them sighting the black-clad figure that corresponded to their own position.

Danny breathed slowly. This was high-risk. If one of them missed their mark, they'd come under immediate gunfire. All three guys had to be taken out at the same instant. He focused in on his man, very aware that the beating he'd received had left him woozy, maybe slightly concussed. He couldn't let that affect him.

His finger rested lightly on the trigger. Very deliberately he edged his line of fire a couple of inches to the left.

'Aim for the body mass,' he breathed. And then a second later: 'Ready?'

'Ready,' Tony and Caitlin said in unison.

A five-second pause.

'Take the shot.'

The three rounds sounded like a single discharge. Danny kept his position for a second – long enough to see Tony and Caitlin's guys collapse instantly. His own was hit, but not fatally: a shoulder wound, maybe, but enough to make the bastard scream at the top of his head.

The unit fell back behind the protection of the storage container.

'You missed,' Tony growled.

'Thanks for pointing it out,' Danny said. 'We need to—'

'*Quiet!*' Caitlin hissed.

They fell silent. Caitlin had cocked her head, and Danny could tell why. There was a distant sound of a helicopter approaching.

'Ahmed's transport,' Danny breathed. 'We haven't got more than a minute. We need to advance to contact.'

'They know our position,' Caitlin said. 'We should advance from a different direction.'

'We haven't got time,' Danny overruled her. 'Give me cover.'

'Forget it, Black,' Tony said. 'You're not on the ball. I'm going.'

For the briefest moment, Danny felt his head spinning. A picture flashed across his eyes: Ripley, in a makeshift field hospital in Nigeria, rotting in front of his eyes. And he heard his mate's voice: *Find the fucker who did this to me, Danny . . . just find the fucker who did this.*

The fucker who did it was thirty metres away, about to get into a helicopter. He was Danny's. No one else's.

Danny's head cleared. 'You're staying there,' he said. And before anyone could argue any further: 'In three, two, one, *go!*'

Danny stepped out from the protection of the storage container.

He could still see his wounded target, writhing in agony on the edge of the raised LZ. And in the clear sky beyond, he could see a dot approaching: Ahmed's helicopter, arriving to ferry him to the safety of Saudi Arabia.

Gunfire behind him: two rounds in quick succession from Tony and Caitlin, a warning to any militants remaining on the LZ of what they could expect if they approached its edge. Danny sprinted forward, skirting round the machinery and the scaffolding units as he made the most direct approach possible towards the LZ. He closed the distance to twenty metres, then to fifteen. The closer he grew, the steeper the angle between him and the LZ, the higher he had to raise his weapon and the less he could see who was approaching the edge. It meant he was totally reliant on his unit colleagues . . .

Another two rounds. Fresh screams from above. Tony or Caitlin had hit at least one more enemy target. That meant he could expect two more guys on the LZ, plus Ahmed.

He surged forward. Ten metres. Five. His ribs were agony. He ignored it. The sound of the chopper was much louder now. It couldn't be more than thirty seconds out. He hit the metal staircase leading up to the LZ, before raising his head and his weapon up at an angle and wincing at a shock of pain from his broken ribs. He didn't allow it to hinder him. Three-quarters of the way up the steps there was a bundled, bleeding body – one of the original three guards they'd taken out.

Danny, hyper-aware that his head was about to rise above the level of the LZ, was going to need him.

He hurried up to the corpse, then steeled himself. With shattered ribs, this was going to hurt. He bent over and ripped off its balaclava so that, at a distance, the enemy wouldn't realise they were shooting one of their own. Then he took the strain and hauled the body up off the ground. His ribs cried out, but he shut off the pain, gritted his teeth and, holding the body by the scruff of the neck, took its full weight in his left hand.

It took massive effort and self-control to lift the corpse even higher so that just a few inches of its head rose above the edge of the LZ. Danny thought he could feel his own broken ribs moving inside him. Almost immediately three shots rang out from the far side of the LZ. Two of them flew over Danny's head, but one slammed straight into the skull of the corpse, sending a chunk of brain and bone flying over the steps.

Danny let the corpse's head drop out of sight below the edge of the LZ. The noise of the chopper was very loud now. It had to be on the point of touching down. Four more rounds flew over his head from Tony and Caitlin's position.

Danny raised the corpse's head again. No shots fell from the LZ. He took that as an opportunity to show himself.

He dropped the corpse, which clattered heavily on to the metal staircase. Weapon engaged once more, he thundered up the staircase, swinging round towards the LZ itself, his AK-47 directly following his line of fire. He took in the scene in a fraction of a second. A chopper had set itself down on the far side of the landing pad, twenty metres from Danny's position, its nose facing him directly. The sun reflected brightly off the cockpit glass, dazzling him. But even with his suddenly compromised vision, he could tell that the side door was open, and there was no sign of Ahmed – Danny assumed he had already climbed inside. He could, however, see two more men, both dressed in black with their back to him. They were a metre out from the right-hand side of the chopper, and were obviously about to board.

Danny's aim was true this time. They both collapsed as 7.62s slammed into them. Danny was already advancing as they crumpled to the ground. Distance to the chopper, fifteen metres. He still didn't have eyes on Ahmed, and the chopper was rising. He directed his fire towards the cockpit, squinting to protect his eyes from the reflective glare. Danny could see very little inside the chopper as he released a two-second burst of rounds. The cockpit glass shattered and fell away. Danny could tell that he'd hit the pilot even before he saw him slumped over the controls, by the way the chopper, already a metre in the air, started to wobble precariously. It rotated ninety degrees clockwise as it collapsed back down to the LZ, its left-hand landing skids settling awkwardly on the body of one of the guys Danny had taken out, and presenting him with the open doors of the helicopter.

He advanced.

The downdraught from the rotors, still spinning, was a barrier he had to force himself through. Ten metres out he could see movement in the interior. He fired a warning shot just to the left of the area of movement, fully aware that if it was Ahmed, he had to be taken alive.

Seven metres out. The chopper shifted twenty degrees

clockwise. Danny realised it was only a couple of metres from the edge of the LZ. With the rotors still spinning, there was a high chance of it toppling. He upped his pace and in two seconds was alongside the chopper. He breathed deeply, suddenly very aware of the sweat pouring down his grimy, bloody, broken face. Then, the butt of his AK-47 pressed deeply into his shoulder, his finger resting carefully on the trigger, he swung round and faced the entrance.

Ahmed was armed and ready. His back was pressed against the far side of the chopper, both arms were outstretched and he had a handgun pointing directly in Danny's direction.

But he wasn't fast enough.

Distance to target, two metres. It was barely necessary to adjust for the rifle's skew. Danny fired first, discharging a round accurately into Ahmed's left shoulder. He juddered hard against the back wall of the chopper, a flash of blood spraying across the interior. As he fell, Danny turned his body and his weapon towards the cockpit: there were two flight crew, both dead.

He jumped into the chopper, just as it shifted another few degrees clockwise. There was a frantic juddering as the skids below shifted off the corpse that was propping them up. Danny hurled himself towards Ahmed, who had dropped his handgun and was now gripping his wounded shoulder. He'd never seen such hate in a man's face before. But that was okay. It was mutual. He grabbed Ahmed's weapon from the floor of the chopper. Then, with his free hand, he punched Ahmed's wound as hard as he could, knowing that the pain would put him out of action completely for a few precious seconds. Ahmed gasped, and Danny took his chance to hurl himself towards the shattered cockpit. He hauled the slumped pilot off the cyclic. The chopper shifted again – a full thirty-five degrees this time, so now it was facing directly out to sea. Danny twisted the throttle closed. Instantly he heard the loud beating sound of the rotors above diminish.

He turned back to Ahmed, a dark frown creasing his face and a familiar sense of hot anger rising in his chest.

He surged forward, grabbed his captive from the floor of the chopper and threw him out on to the LZ. As Ahmed landed with a heavy thud, Danny saw that Tony and Caitlin were at the edge of the landing pad, down on their knees in the firing position, protecting their location in case they hadn't eliminated all the enemy on the rig.

Good thing too. It meant Danny could focus all his attention on the man who called himself the Caliph.

Ahmed was on his back, still clutching his wounded shoulder, his face a mixture of fire and pain. Danny collapsed down on to him, pressing one knee so heavily against his sternum that he started to cough and choke noisily.

'You *are* going to tell me,' he breathed, 'the name of the person or people who are about to release the bioweapon in London. You might reckon at the moment that you won't. But trust me, you *will*.'

Ahmed spat in his face.

'Here's what you're thinking,' Danny continued relentlessly. 'You're thinking I'm going to threaten to kill you. You're thinking I'm just like you, and that the worst I can do is put a bullet in your skull or cut your fucking head off. But you want to know the truth? That Caliph bullshit means nothing to me, and I'm a hundred times worse than you can possibly imagine.'

Ahmed's eyes narrowed. 'I'm not afraid of dying,' he spat.

Danny gave him a grim smile. 'Oh, I know that,' he said. 'I know you're looking forward to your seventy-two fucking virgins. That's why I'm not going to kill you. Not even when you *ask* me to do it, which you will. When I've finished with you, you'll be begging me to put you out of your misery, like the dog that you are. But I won't. Not until until I know *every single thing* about the attack.'

Ahmed's lip curled into a nauseatingly arrogant expression, almost as if he was daring Danny to follow through on his words.

'You're beginning to believe your own PR, Ahmed. You might be the Caliph to everyone else, but to me you're just some cunt I'm going to hurt.'

Ahmed hissed at him.

'Ready for this, you piece of shit?' Danny said.

The London crowds were swarming like ants. Bailey watched them through the viewfinder of his TV camera. The *Cutty Sark* was a dot in the distance. Bright sunlight reflected off the snaking Thames, turning the water silver. The green spaces of Shooter's Hill were crowded. The chopper hovered above them.

Bailey took his eye away from the viewfinder. He looked down at himself. He had changed into his hazmat suit, but the mask was by his side, ready to be worn when the time came.

He checked his watch. 07:40. The time was arriving. Just another twenty minutes.

Bailey examined the rest of his equipment. A rubber tube led from the industrial sprayer into one of the heavy vats of liquid. He didn't know how long it would take to expel the contents of the first canister. Five minutes? Maybe ten? He didn't even know if they would have the opportunity to engage the second canister, but it wouldn't really matter. One would be enough to deal with the ants below.

He realised his hand was shaking. Anxiety? Excitement? A bit of both. Hardly a surprise, he thought to himself, when you know you're about to buy yourself a ticket to Paradise.

Danny knew that the most painful places to shoot a man are not always the most obvious. And of the most painful, only a few were appropriate if you wanted your victim alive and conscious. The stomach would hurt very badly, but at point blank range it will probably kill, and certainly render your target unconscious within minutes. You wanted somewhere with a mass of bone, cartilage and nerve endings. The hip would be good if it weren't so close to major arteries. The elbow would be a prime candidate if there wasn't a risk of the victim struggling.

Much better was the knee. There was a reason the IRA and the Mafia used kneecapping as a method of punishment. It was as much pain as a person could tolerate without passing out or bleeding out.

Danny stood above Ahmed, the heel of one foot pinning him down by his belly, the barrel of his gun an inch away from his right knee.

He fired.

Ahmed's whole limb slammed flat against the LZ. His trouser leg suddenly took on a dark, wet stain, but the bleed wasn't too bad. Ahmed's scream, however, was: a hoarse, high-pitched howl that seemed to echo across the platform. Danny moved his heel from his victim's belly, then slammed it hard down on the wounded kneecap. The scream became so intense and raw that it was barely audible. Danny ground his heel into the wound, then he kneeled down again. 'Names,' he said.

Ahmed scrunched his eyes closed. He whispered something. Danny listened hard. It almost sounded as if he was chanting something. Some kind of prayer. Danny could barely make out the words. '*I will drive him into the Hellfire . . . it allows nothing to endure . . . it blackens the skins of men . . .*'

Fine.

He stood up and released a second round into the good knee, then slammed his heel down on that one.

It was as if Ahmed had screamed himself out. His body was shaking and he was gasping for breath.

'*Names,*' Danny said.

Ahmed gritted his teeth and shook his head.

Danny felt a moment of anxiety. He hadn't expected Ahmed to withstand this level of pain. Most people would have cracked by now.

'*What's happening?*' Tony shouted from the edge of the LZ. '*What have you got?*'

Rather than tell Tony he had nothing, Danny rolled the shaking, muttering Ahmed over on to his front. He raised his victim's right leg, then laid his rifle directly underneath the knee joint so that his foot and the lower part of his leg were pointing up at a slight angle. Then he stood and slammed his foot down on the lower leg. There was a cracking sound as the damaged knee pivoted back, and Ahmed howled silently. His arms flailed despite the shoulder wound, and Danny managed to discern a single word.

'*Stop!*'

Quickly, he knelt down by the side of Ahmed's head. 'There's only one way to make it stop,' he said. 'You know what you've got to do. Give me names.'

'I . . . I . . . don't know them . . .'

'Well that's a big fucking shame for you, sunshine, because I'm not going to stop until you give me something concrete.'

He stood up again.

'Wait. *Wait . . .*'

'I'm done with waiting, pal . . .'

He shifted the blood-soaked AK–47 so that it was under the left knee and prepared to repeat his last procedure.

Ahmed was chanting again in Arabic, but Danny could hear the note of desperation in his frail voice. He pressed his heel against the lower part of the left leg.

Ahmed inhaled noisily.

'Bay . . .'

'I can't hear you?' Danny shouted. He put pressure on Ahmed's lower leg.'

'*Bay . . .*'

'That means nothing.'

More pressure.

'*Bailey!*' Ahmed screamed, although the volume of the scream from his ravaged throat was little more than a whisper. '*His name is James Bailey!*'

THIRTY-ONE

Danny didn't hesitate. He looked over his shoulder at Tony. 'Get over here!' he shouted.

Tony ran towards them.

'Don't let the fucker move,' Danny told him.

'What did he give you?'

'Enough,' Danny said. 'Maybe.'

While Tony kept guard over the prisoner, Danny sprinted to the chopper. Its rotors were still now, its interior deadly silent. He climbed in and clambered over the bleeding bodies of the two flight crew. He scanned the flight deck controls – collective, throttle, cyclic – until he found the VHF radio. He turned it on and tuned the radio to transmit at 121.5 MHz – the international civil aviation distress frequency. He grabbed the mouthpiece of the radio and immediately started transmitting. 'This is Bravo Nine Zero. Hellfire suspect is James Bailey. Repeat, this it Bravo Nine Zero. Hellfire suspect is James Bailey.'

He knew that GCHQ would be monitoring the distress frequency. All he could do now was continue to broadcast the information, and hope that they could do something with it.

07.50 GMT

'We've got something!'

The strained, stressed voice of one of Bixby's men rang out across the ops room in the basement of the MI6 building. Bixby manoeuvred his wheelchair across the room, past the Chief, who seemed to have lost all semblance of control, and past a couple of

Porton Down reps there to advise them should the unthinkable happen, to where his guy was sitting in front of a laptop, his right hand pressed hard against his earpiece.

'What is it?' Bixby demanded.

'GCHQ have picked up a radio communication from between the Qatari and Iranian coast. They're patching it through.'

'Everyone quiet!' Bixby shouted. 'Let me hear.'

The hubbub in the room immediately died. Bixby's guy tapped a few buttons on his laptop. A hissing sound from speakers set around the ops centre filled the room.

It was nothing: just feedback and white noise.

'Wait out,' Bixby's guy said. 'There's someth—'

A male voice, very faint, almost drowned out by the radio crackle: '*Bravo Nine . . . suspect . . . repeat . . . Nine Zero . . .*'

The loudspeaker reverted to white noise.

Bixby felt a dead, dread weight in his limbs. 'Patch it through to Hereford,' he said quietly.

More tapping at the laptop, while the white noise filled the air.

Then, suddenly: '*This is Bravo Nine Zero . . . Hellfire suspect . . .*'

White noise.

Bixby cursed. He felt the eyes of everyone in the ops room boring into him. He glanced up at a screen on the wall. It showed aerial footage – a crowd of thousands congregating at the marathon's starting area.

For a full minute there was nothing.

'I think we've lost it,' Bixby's guy said weakly.

If Bixby could have shaken his head, he would have done. 'Keep the channel open,' he said.

And as soon as he had finished speaking, the loudspeaker burst into life again. The voice was suddenly very loud. Very clear. Bixby recognised it. Danny Black.

'*This is Bravo Nine Zero. Hellfire suspect is James Bailey. Repeat, this is Bravo Nine Zero. Hellfire suspect is James Bailey.*'

'*FIND OUT WHO HE IS!*' Bixby shouted. '*NOW!*'

The Regiment's Agusta Westland flew low over north-west London. Aside from the flight crew there were five men in the chopper: a four-man unit plucked from the standby squadron, plus Spud. They'd seemed surprised when Spud had presented himself to them – it was no secret that he had been out of the game for a while – but respectful. Spud was the senior guy, and the younger Regiment soldiers had automatically deferred to him.

He sat a little bit apart from them, his body armour pressing painfully against his scarred abdomen, his Kevlar helmet and earpiece strangely uncomfortable as he hadn't worn them for so long. Even the assault rifle slung across his chest felt weird. They were each plugged into the helicopter's comms system, but neither the pilot nor Hereford had spoken for twenty minutes. There was nothing to say. They were on high alert, but they didn't know what for. They simply needed to be ready to respond when the time came.

Spud looked through the window. In the distance, shimmering in the early morning sunlight, he could make out the London Eye and Big Ben. In his mind, he pictured the massive crowds that would soon be snaking through London. He thought of Frances. He didn't know what he'd be able to do in the event of an attack. But he'd rather be here, in the thick of things, than sitting behind a desk at a safe distance while his mates were putting their arses on the line . . .

07.56 GMT

A voice rang out across the MI6 ops room. 'We have a James Bailey, a freelance cameraman, working for the BBC.'

'What do we know about him?' Bixby demanded. 'Is he a person of interest?'

'Negative, sir. British Caucasian, no criminal record, not previously known to any of the security agencies.'

'*Shit!*' Bixby hissed. A single name, barely heard over a crackly radio line from thousands of miles away, was hardly proof of terrorist intent. 'Where is he now?'

'We're on the line to the BBC control room. Give me thirty seconds ...'

'We haven't *got* thirty seconds. WHERE IS HE?'

There was short pause. And then, a slightly sick-sounding voice. 'Shooter's Hill, sir. He's in the air. He's over the start line.'

'Who's his pilot?'

'An Alan McIntyre. We've got nothing on him either.'

'Instruct the control centre to ground them. Monitor their response.'

The hubbub in the room grew louder. On one of the large screens on the far wall, a flashing red dot appeared on a map of London, south of the river, over a patch of green where Bixby knew the marathon crowds were congregating.

Twenty seconds passed.

'Sir,' came a voice. 'The BBC ops room are failing to make contact.'

Bixby blinked.

'They can't get hold of them sir. They can't establish comms with the chopper. What the hell do we do?'

'Is Hereford online?' Bixby demanded.

A voice came over the loudspeaker. '*Roger that.*'

'Options?' Bixby demanded.

A momentary pause.

'*We have one chopper coming in from Hereford. We have another two taking off from the Artillery Garden. They can force the target to move over the river. That gives us options, but you need to understand that we risk forcing their hand. As soon as they see three choppers coming their way, it might force them to release the bioweapon, or even crash land.*'

Bixby's eyes flickered towards the Chief. He was clutching his hair, unable to speak and seemingly incapable of making the call.

Bixby breathed deeply. 'Can you neutralise this threat without civilian casualties?'

The reply, when it came, was tinged with contempt. '*You bring the Regiment in if you want to fight violence with violence. It's your call.*'

Bixby closed his eyes. He breathed deeply.

'Do it,' he said. 'Do it now.'

From his vantage point above the start line, Bailey looked down on the crowds. It was a sea of people. Thousands of them, like herded sheep, just waiting to be infected.

He heard McIntyre's voice. It had an edge of panic. 'The control room want to ground us. Someone suspects something!'

Bailey turned away from his TV camera to look at the pilot. The time had come.

'What's our altitude?' he shouted.

'Five hundred feet.'

'Engage the spraying arms.'

McIntyre nodded. He flicked a lever on the flight deck. There was a grinding sound from beneath the helicopter. Through the open side door, Bailey saw one of the arms move open so that it was pointing out ninety degrees from the side of the aircraft. He checked the spraying motor inside the chopper, and the rubber tube that led to it from the canister. All was well.

'Put your rebreather on!' he shouted.

McIntyre clumsily pulled the rebreathing hood over his head with one hand. Bailey did the same. He reached out and clutched the red lever that would engage the spraying system. Then he looked over to his pilot again.

'Get down to one hundred and fifty feet. Do it! *Go!*'

Bailey's stomach lurched as they immediately lost altitude. He clutched the side of the chopper with his free hand as he felt the helicopter bank sharply, its nose dipping. The crowd came momentarily into view through the open side door, then disappeared as the chopper straightened up again.

'*We've got a problem!*' McIntyre shouted. His voice was very muffled, but Bailey could hear a high-pitched tone to it. '*We've got two helicopters on our tail, coming from the south! They're going to crash into us!*'

'No they're not!' Bailey shouted. And when he realised his voice was too muffled, he ripped off his rebreather. 'No they're not! They won't hit us, especially when we're over these crowds. What's our height?'

'Two hundred and seventy-five feet.'

'That's too high to spray – it won't be as effective! Get lower! A hundred and fifty feet! *Get to a hundred and fifty feet!*'

His hand left the lever. He looked through the windows. Sure enough, two hulking helicopters were on their tail. They were no more than twenty-five metres distant, and they were moving towards them: slowly, but implacably.

'*LOWER!*' Bailey screamed again.

But as he shouted, something else caught his eye. It was a third helicopter, speeding towards them from the direction of the river. Distance: a hundred metres, but rapidly closing. Bailey had the uncanny sensation that the helicopter's nose was heading straight for him.

McIntyre was edging the chopper north, away from the two choppers closing in on them. He was panicking. Bailey felt his blood burn. *He was going to mess the whole thing up!*

'*THEY WON'T HIT US!*' he screamed. '*THEY WON'T HIT US ABOVE THESE CROWDS. GET LOWER!*'

But even as he gave this final instruction, the third helicopter drew up alongside them. As it hovered thirty metres from their Twin Squirrel, it rotated ninety degrees so that its nose was pointing in the same direction.

Bailey's hot blood ran cold. He saw, quite clearly, a figure leaning at the open side door of this third helicopter. He wore a helmet and boom mike. Black body armour. And he had his eyes lined up with the sights of his rifle, pointing directly towards Bailey, ready to take a shot.

Bailey had no choice. They were still higher than 150 feet, but this was his last chance.

'*MOVE LOWER! MOVE LOWER!*' he screamed.

Then he stretched out to grab the lever that would engage the bioweapon.

The others hadn't been fast enough.

When the order had come in over their headset that one of them was to prepare to take a shot at the target chopper, Spud's companions had heard just that: an instruction.

376

Spud had heard far more. He'd heard Tony Wiseman: *Could be worse. Could be a bleedin' desk jockey, hey, Spud?* He'd heard Eleanor the spook: *Your army days are over, Spud. The sooner you come to terms with that, the better.* He'd heard Ray Hammond: *We're doing our fucking best for you, but there's a limit to how much dead weight we can carry . . .*

Before any of the others could move, he'd installed himself at the open side door of the chopper, one knee down in the firing position, weapon cocked and switched to semi-automatic, butt pressed into his shoulder, one eye closed, the other looking directly down the sights.

As the Agusta rotated ninety degrees, the camera chopper came into sight. Spud immediately recognised it as a Twin Squirrel. Distance thirty metres, but through the sight of the weapon it looked right next door. The thunder of the two choppers, 275 feet above the ground, roared in his ears, and a strong backdraught blasted towards him.

Spud kept firm. His crosshairs panned across the interior. He immediately settled on the coarse, blurry image of the figure of a man. He was wearing a white all-in-one.

'Target in sight,' Spud spoke into his microphone, even as the vibrations of the Agusta knocked his sights off-target. The crosshairs settled on a tall canister. Spud thought he could make out Chinese lettering on the side.

He yanked the sights back to target, but the Twin Squirrel was moving too, and a second later he had to re-aim again. 'He's wearing a hazmat suit. No mask. I can see a TV camera and two canisters. Possibly Chinese lettering.'

A voice in his ear. '*Can you take the shot without downing the chopper?*'

From one moving, vibrating platform to another? It would be the most difficult shot he'd ever taken. If a round went loose and hit the body of the Twin Squirrel, there was a very real possibility it would plummet to the ground, where it would take out hundreds, maybe thousands of people.

'Yes,' he said.

377

'*Wait for the order.*'

The crosshairs juddered to the left. Spud realigned. He could see the target screaming at his pilot.

And he could see him stretching out his hand to grab something.

Spud knew he couldn't wait even for a fraction of a second. The target's head was in his sights. He might not get another chance. He couldn't wait for the order.

He fired.

He knew, the very second that his round left the barrel, that he'd missed his target.

Bailey's fingertips were just brushing against the lever that would switch on the spraying system, when the round shot through the open side door of the Twin Squirrel. He felt the rush of air as it whizzed inches from his head. The proximity of the bullet made his whole body lurch. He threw himself back, and shouted in pain as his shoulder banged hard against the floor of the chopper. The round slammed into the far window of the helicopter, shattering it.

Bailey's face creased with frustration. He knew he couldn't rely on McIntyre any more. His pilot had lost his nerve. He *had* to get to that lever now.

He lurched forward again, towards the mechanism, his arm stretched out.

The Agusta juddered. It meant Spud didn't see the moment the round smashed into the far window of the Twin Squirrel.

Commotion behind him. Guys shouting. Urgent, panicked questions and reprimands in his earpiece.

And a voice in his head. *There's a limit to how much dead weight we can carry . . .*

Spud zoned it all out.

Spud knew that his target had been surprised by the loose round. That wouldn't happen a second time.

He realigned his sights.

The target was thrusting himself to his feet again. Reaching out once more for the mechanism at the back of the chopper.

Spud's crosshairs centred on the target's head.

He fired.

This time, there was no mistake.

Spud clearly saw the moment of impact. A flash of red as the round slammed straight into the target's skull, and his body slumped heavily to the floor.

'Target down,' Spud said tersely into his boom mike. He realised he was soaked with nervous sweat. His abdomen suddenly ripped with pain, but he ignored it and kept his eye to the sight. He panned round so that he had the pilot hazily in his sights through the cockpit glass. The guy was looking over his shoulder, shouting something, his face etched with panic. He was losing control of the Twin Squirrel, which shook and wobbled alarmingly.

The pilot looked forward again. Spud lowered his weapon. For the past thirty seconds he had zoned out the thunder and the wind. Now it hit him again with full force. He looked down. Two hundred and seventy-five feet below them he saw the swarm of marathon runners. He could see that they were trying to vacate that patch of park directly below the four low-flying choppers, but they were too many and too crushed. There was a small, open patch of green, like an impact crater. Spud couldn't hear the screams of the crowd above the thunder of the choppers, but he knew they were there.

'I have the pilot in my sights,' Spud shouted. 'He's panicking.'

'*Hold your fire!*' instructed the voice in his ear. '*HOLD YOUR FIRE!*'

Major Ray Hammond's voice rang across the MI6 ops room. '*We have one target down. The pilot's still in control of the aircraft. We think we can force him over the river.*'

'What then?' Bixby said.

'*Evacuate Battersea helipad. We'll force him along the river and try to ground him down there.*'

'What if he doesn't play ball?'

'*Then we'll take him out of the sky. He'll hit the river.*'

Bixby wheeled his chair round to face his Porton Down adviser. 'Implications.'

'Unpredictable. But if the bioweapon leaks into the Thames, it will probably become sufficiently dilute ...'

'Clear Battersea helipad,' Bixby instructed. 'Let's get this bastard to land.'

Spud watched as the two choppers behind the Twin Squirrel edged forward, closing the gap between them and the enemy chopper to fifteen metres.

It was a high-risk strategy. An unexpected surge of wind would mean disaster. Not to mention that there was a good chance, in a moment of panic or martyrdom, that the pilot would just let the chopper fall. The Agusta edged a further ten metres away from it, but the Twin Squirrel, bullied into motion by the two choppers following, headed north, towards the river.

Spud didn't move from his kneeling-down firing position. Thunder in his ears and wind in his face. From the corner of his eye he could see Canary Wharf in the distance, but he kept his attention on the chopper. The Agusta stayed alongside the Twin Squirrel as it edged north, metre by metre.

'*We're getting him over the river,*' the voice in Spud's earpiece stated. '*They're clearing the water now.*'

A smart move. Bully the fucker to a safer location, and if he fails to comply ...

It took a good ninety seconds to move clear of the marathon crowds below. They hovered over a road, and then a grid of residential housing.

Distance to the river, fifty metres.

Spud raised his weapon again. He panned his sights towards the pilot. The guy was clearly a mess. He kept looking over his shoulder, then forward again. Back, then forward. His eyes were pictures of fear and alarm.

A voice crackled in Spud's earpiece. '*On my order, down the aircraft. Rounds to the engine and transmission. If necessary, hit the rotor* mast. *Do not hit the tail rotor or boom, and do not take out the pilot. If he loses control, the chopper could hit land.*'

'Roger that,' Spud stated.

'*Do not lay down fire until you have the order. Repeat, do not lay down fire until you have the order. There's still a chance we can land him safely.*'

They continued to move over the water. Spud flicked the safety catch of his weapon to fully automatic, and kept his sights on the area to the left of the tail boom where the engine and transmission was kept. They were ten metres from the southern shore.

Twenty metres. A flash of reflected sunlight glinted off the water, momentarily blinding Spud. But he kept his aim true.

Fifty metres.

A hundred metres from both shores. They were bang in the centre of the river.

The two choppers following the Twin Squirrels eased back about twenty metres. They started to circle round to the far, eastern side of the chopper. The Agusta changed position too, edging round to the south so that it could fly alongside the Twin Squirrel as they bullied it west along the river. As the chopper moved, the Shard, glinting in the sun, flashed across Spud's sights. He could see the low, broad dome of the O2, then the higher one of St Paul's cathedral in the distance, and the BT tower off to the north. As the chopper continued to turn, he could see the river snaking away, and the familiar sight of Tower Bridge, and London Bridge beyond.

He refocused on the engine and transmission area of the enemy aircraft.

And even as he did that, everything changed.

The Twin Squirrel suddenly gained height. Spud tracked it with his rifle, but as he did so, the enemy chopper twisted 180 degrees in the air so that it was facing back towards Greenwich Park where the marathon runners had congregated. It was fifty feet higher than the Agusta and the two Regiment choppers following it, and its nose was down.

Spud heard a voice behind him. '*The fucker's going to crash land . . .*'

And in his earpiece: '*TAKE THE SHOT! TAKE THE SHOT!*'

He realigned his rifle once more, tracking the crosshairs directly over the Twin Squirrel's engine and transmission.

'*TAKE THE SHOT!*'

He fired.

A full burst from Spud's rifle ripped into the metal body of the Twin Squirrel.

Everything seemed to slow down.

Through his sights, Spud saw scraps of shrapnel splintering away from the chopper. His rifle clicked empty, but now there was a different sound: an alarming, high-pitched clunking, grinding noise from the enemy chopper.

Spud lowered his rifle in time to see, from below, its rotors sputtering and slowing.

The Twin Squirrel twisted in the air.

A lurch from the Agusta as it surged forward thirty metres to a safer patch of airspace. But as it moved, it shuddered from a rush of displaced air as the Twin Squirrel dropped, like a stone, towards the water. It thundered past the Agusta with a terminal screaming sound.

Five seconds later, it smashed into the water below.

Spud sucked in lungfuls of much-needed air. He hurled himself forward to the cockpit of the Agusta, even as a barrage of urgent shouting filled his ears. '*The bird is down! Repeat, the bird is down! Seal the area! Seal the area!*'

But these were instructions for someone other than Spud. Through the windows of the Agusta, he zoned in on the impact site two hundred feet below. There was no sign of the chopper. It had either broken up, or sunk. Peeling in, from both directions along the river, were the white trails of RIBs speeding towards the impact site. Spud could just about make out their occupants in white hazmat suits.

He winced. The pain in his abdomen was worse than ever. Guys were talking to him, but he barely heard them. His mind was elsewhere as it churned over the whirlwind of the past few days.

Al-Meghrani.

The Caliph.

And Danny. What the hell was happening with Danny?

The threat to London might have been neutralised, but somewhere, thousands of miles from here, his mate was in the shit. Spud realised he didn't even know if Danny was dead or alive.

THIRTY-TWO

Danny Black stared at the VHF receiver. A message was coming through, distorted and indistinct, but he could just make it out.

'*Bravo Nine Zero, this is Alpha. Your message has been received and acted upon. Wait out in current location for pick-up. Ensure the safety of your source, repeat, ensure the safety of your source.*'

Danny waited for the cascade of relief to wash over him. It didn't.

He breathed deeply, then turned to look out of the stationary chopper, across the landing pad to where Tony had Ahmed at gunpoint. Tony, his face beaten, swollen and dirty, was standing two metres from the man who called himself the Caliph, rifle aimed directly at his head. On the far side of the LZ, Caitlin was down on one knee in the firing position, aiming towards the platform itself, her back to Danny and Tony.

A strange sensation fell over Danny's body as he exited the chopper and walked towards their captive. It was like hatred, only deeper and more piercing. As he closed the gap between them, he tried to identify its source. Was it the moment he had witnessed Ahmed executing Hugo Buckingham in the most brutal way imaginable? Buckingham had it coming to him, but nobody deserved that, not even him. But no. It wasn't that which filled Danny with such loathing.

Was it the images he'd seen of Ahmed's parents? The sheer revulsion that a man could do that to anyone, let alone his own mother and father?

No. It wasn't that.

It wasn't even a plane full of infected innocents. Or two

choppers full of SF soldiers, downed in the Persian Gulf. Or a cynical, loathsome attack on London.

It was Ripley. Bravely dying. Rotting before his very eyes. Begging Danny to avenge him. He put one hand in his pocket and felt Ripley's dog tag and wedding ring.

Ensure the safety of your source, repeat, ensure the safety of your source.

He was standing over Ahmed now. There were pools of blood around his knees, and a face creased with pain. But he was still conscious.

'Your missus is safe,' Danny told Tony. His tone of voice expressed everything he felt about Tony. He glanced towards Caitlin. 'Maybe you should go and tell your girlfriend the good news. Hereford are sending a pick-up.'

'You should be thanking me, Black. I saved your arse back there. You should remember that, next time I want a favour.'

'I don't owe you any favours, Tony.'

Tony sneered. 'We'll see about that,' he breathed. He lowered his gun. 'All yours, Danny. Fuck him up good and proper. It's all he deserves.'

But Danny wasn't stupid. He knew Tony's game: if he nailed the Caliph, Danny would have to rely on Tony's good word that he'd had no other option. 'You've got it all wrong,' he said. 'I want him alive. A round in the head's too good for him. Let the bastard suffer.' It wasn't true, but it would get Tony off his back.

Tony stared at him, then glanced towards Caitlin. The lure of the female member of their group was too great. He shrugged, walked around Ahmed and headed off across the landing pad to join her.

Danny stood over his enemy and aimed the rifle at his head. The sun was hot on the back of his neck, and he cast a distinct shadow over Ahmed's prostrate body. Ahmed's breathing was very heavy, and for a full thirty seconds they remained like that: Ahmed's eyes rolling and his body shaking.

'I'm almost looking forward to it,' Danny breathed. 'The famous Caliph, cuffed and locked up. The picture might even go viral, like those videos your mate Jihadi Jim made.'

Through his pain, Ahmed grinned at him. 'You're just like the dog I executed,' Ahmed whispered. 'Weak.'

Danny didn't reply. He didn't move.

'You want to kill me,' Ahmed repeated, 'but you're too weak to do it.'

Danny felt his blood rising again. Deep down, he knew Ahmed was right. Despite what he'd told Tony, he *did* want to kill him. He wanted nothing more . . .

Ensure the safety of your source, repeat, ensure the safety of your source.

He lowered his gun, and met the Caliph's gaze, full on.

'Your attack on London has failed, you piece of shit. *You've* failed.'

Ahmed grinned again. A sinister grin, that told Danny maybe he was missing something.

It happened so quickly.

Ahmed suddenly raised his left arm. For a fraction of a second, Danny didn't understand why. Then he saw it. Clutched in his hand was the small glass vial of clear liquid that he had waved in front of Danny's face back in the drillers' cabin.

It would take nothing for Ahmed to smash that vial on the floor of the helipad. Danny knew, instinctively, that this was what he intended to do.

'*NO!*' he roared.

And before Ahmed could release the vial, he raised his weapon again and fired three rounds. They thudded hard into the Caliph's chest. His whole body juddered with each impact. His raised arm slammed back down on the helipad floor, and the glass vial rolled harmlessly out of Ahmed's hand.

'*What the fuck?*' Tony's voice exploded from across the LZ. He came running towards Danny who, having lowered his weapon, was stepping back from his target, his eyes fixed on the catastrophic, fatal wound he had just inflicted to the man's chest.

The vial had come to rest two metres from Ahmed's body. Tony stopped just next to it, then bent down to pick it up.

'He was going to smash it,' Danny said. There was a stressed edge to his voice. 'He was going to infect us.'

Tony held the vial between two fingers, then lifted it up to the sunlight. His lip curled at Danny, then he jogged over to the edge of the LZ. He hesitated for a moment, then hurled the vial over the side of the platform, far out to sea.

He walked slowly back to Danny, a superior look on his face.

'Our little secret,' he said. He looked down at the Caliph's dead body, then kicked it nonchalantly. 'Course, I'll *definitely* tell them you couldn't have done anything else. And I'm sure you'll repay the favour, one of these days.'

The surge of anger rose in Danny's chest again. He raised his rifle, and this time pointed it straight at Tony. His companion simply jutted out his chin. 'Even you're not that stupid,' he said.

Neither man moved. Danny was aware of blood seeping from the Caliph's body, but he kept his eyes firmly on Tony.

Then, slowly, he lowered his weapon.

'Attaboy, Danny Black,' Tony said.

With a bleak smile, he turned his back on Danny, and walked back towards Caitlin. She was waiting and watching at the edge of the LZ, her face bruised and beaten. When Tony put an arm round her waist she didn't object. They stared back towards him, a team of two from which Danny was obviously excluded.

Danny's hands were shaking, his body aching, his mind spinning. He looked out across the Persian Gulf, squinting in the sunlight, waiting for their pick-up to come.

Three thousand miles to the west, an aircraft lay in the rough sand of the African desert.

Its seats were full of corpses. Cabin crew lay dead in the aisle. Their skin was covered in welts and patches of black. Insects swarmed around the cabin, crawling and feeding off the dead human flesh. The interior of the aircraft stank: a revolting mixture of flesh rotting in the oven-like heat of the desert, and petrol. The bodies – the whole interior of the aircraft – were soused in fuel.

There were two Chinook helicopters on the ground two hundred metres to the west. A white field-hospital tent had been erected between them, and thirty men in hazmat suits had congregated outside it. They were looking towards the plane.

Empty fuel canisters were stacked close to the fuselage of the aircraft. Snaking out from them was a length of wire. It trailed a hundred metres from the plane, and ended with a small, remote-control detonator. One of the white-suited men held a black box in his hand. He flicked a switch.

There was a loud crack. It was instantly followed by an enormous surging sound as the fuel ignited. In the bright desert daylight the flames were barely visible, but the heat certainly reached the guys in hazmat suits, and they edged backwards from it as they watched the fuselage turning from silver to black.

Inside the cabin, a furnace raged. Hair and clothes blazed. Blackened skin peeled and blistered from the bodies. Tissue smouldered and revealed the bone beneath, which soon withered and crumbled as the corpses burned into nothingness.

Several small explosions blasted from different parts of the plane. It collapsed noisily, dropping down on to one wing.

The guys in hazmat suits turned away. They'd seen enough. They wanted to disinfect themselves and get the hell out of there. They knew that when they got back home, everybody would be talking about the missing flight, and they knew that they were obliged never to mention to anyone what they had seen in this desolate patch of desert.

But that was okay. There are some things you never want to talk about. The grisly fate of these unfortunate passengers was one.

In a private room at the maternity ward of Salisbury District Hospital, a woman was in the early stages of labour. On the wall was a TV. It was on, but the sound was down. The rolling news channel showed images of helicopters against the London skyline, and of panicked crowds dressed in running gear. But the pregnant woman wasn't watching. She was leaning over the edge of her bed, holding a mask for gas and air to her face.

A midwife entered. She checked the notes at the end the

hospital bed. 'Everything all right, Clara my love?' she asked, once she'd checked the woman's name. 'No birthing partner?'

The woman shook her head, and the midwife's lips thinned slightly in disapproval. It was quite clear what she thought about absent fathers. 'Well, never mind,' she said. 'Let's turn this television off, shall we? I don't know – first that missing plane, then helicopters falling out of the sky in London. You'd think they'd be able to stop these things from happening, wouldn't you? Anyway, I don't think we really want to be reminded of all these terrible things at a time like this . . .'

The woman didn't reply as the midwife switched off the TV. She just breathed in another lungful of gas and air, and winced at the pain of another contraction.

In the heart of Heilongjang Province in the People's Republic of China, close to the Russian border, the sun was setting over a high-security facility. Like the burning plane in the African desert, its very existence was an official secret.

It was surrounded by a ten-metre-high perimeter fence, and no unauthorised vehicles would get within five miles of the bleak, utilitarian concrete buildings at its centre. It comprised three laboratories, one storage warehouse and a security unit where closed camera TV screens kept 24/7 surveillance on every part of the facility.

In Laboratory 1 was a lone Chinese scientist. He was clad head to foot in white protective gear, and his breathing was heavy through his mask. He leaned down over a worktop and picked up a test tube holder containing five tubes, carefully sealed.

He walked, rather gingerly, to the other side of the sterile lab. Here there was a refrigerator, slightly taller than him, with a glass door. Inside were rack upon rack of test tube holders, just like the one he was carrying. They were divided into four shelves. On the top shelf was some Chinese lettering. Its translation was a single word: 'Smallpox'.

Each shelf below that had a different label. 'Anthrax'. 'Cholera'. 'Ebola'. 'Viral Equine Encephalitis'. 'Pneumonic Tularemia'.

And on the bottom shelf: 'Plague'.

He opened the fridge, knelt down, and carefully slid the test tube holder on to the bottom shelf. Then he closed the fridge and stepped back to look at it.

He wasn't a rich man, but he knew wealth when he saw it. The contents of that fridge – and of the nearby storage facility – were valuable products. There would always be a buyer for them, somewhere in the world.

He turned his back on the fridge and left the laboratory. He was tired. He wanted to disinfect himself, change back into his normal clothes, then go home and spend the evening with his family.

AUTHOR'S NOTE

The following biological toxins are known by the security services to have been weaponised:

Smallpox
Anthrax
Plague
Pneumonic Tularemia
Viral Equine Encephalitis
Botulinum
Ricin
T-2 Mycatoxin

It is not known how many terrorist organisations are in possession of these weapons.

You have to **survive it**
To **write it**

NEVER MISS OUT AGAIN
ON ALL THE LATEST NEWS FROM

CHRIS
RYAN

**Be the first to find out
about new releases**

**Find out about events with
Chris near you**

Exclusive competitions

And much, much more...

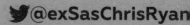